the
Last Tear Drop

L. LEE PARMETER

TATE PUBLISHING, LLC

ISBN: 1-9332906-7-6

DEDICATION

This book is dedicated to all the vagabonds who were waiting for the East Bound and never returned to their loved ones.

Acknowledgements

Without the help and inspiration of my cousin CJ Whitten, this book would have never been written.

If Robert Vaughan, the author, hadn't given me the reason to write, this book would have never been written.

If the old Marine, Richard Tate hadn't taken the time to acknowledge that another old Marine could write, I would never have been a published author. For this I have the deepest gratitude and thanks.

FOREWORD

The Last Tear Drop is an epic full bodied novel that brings to life one of the most difficult and stirring times in America, the Great Depression.

Lee is a skillful storyteller that weaves the long forgotten tales of Irish mule traders, hobos and gypsy's into the vagabond lifestyle of the main characters. He captures the parlance of the era and weaves an integrating and adventuresome tale that is historically accurate with a touch of writers' poetic license to make it a difficult book to put down.

The Last Tear Drop is one of the most significant books I have ever read. The story captures the true tone and tint of a forgotten time in our history.

Robert Vaughan, Author

Editors note:

Robert Vaughan, one of America's most prolific novelists, has written over 250 books, including The Valkyrie Mandate, which was nominated for the Pulitzer Prize, and Andersonville, which was made into the popular TNT Television mini-series. A member of the Writers Hall of Fame and a Spur Award winner, he is also a decorated veteran of the Vietnam War, and a much sought-after public speaker.

PROLOGUE

The traditional values of the average American were changed forever with the sights and sounds of the "Roaring Twenties." This turbulent period was symbolized by the awakening of the Jazz Age. It was the dawn of the "flapper girl." Women saw themselves in the new-fangled roll of the latest social order. It was a positive sign of the times.

American families were buying automobiles, household appliances and speculating in the stock market. Credit was the new medium to purchase many of the manufactured goods. The demand on the credit system caused a huge increase in the mechanization of manufacturing.

This in turn caused businesses to make huge profits. The American way of life was in balance and people were happy and content. Prohibition was in full swing from 1920 until 1933. Bathtub gin and "Speak Easies" were in style. Americans were content with their complacent lifestyle.

Black Tuesday, October 29, 1929 shattered the American way of life. The stock market crashed, triggering the Great Depression. It was the worst economic collapse in the history of the modern industrial world. It spread across the United States like wild fire. Banks failed. People lost their life savings, jobs, homes and their way of life. More than 15 million people were out of work.

The stage is set for two star-crossed lovers, Lyle and Marie, trying to make order out of the chaos of Depression life. They would embark on an adventure that would last them a lifetime. Marie "the flapper girl" and Lyle "the vagabond traveler" would explore the southern United States in search of their fortune. This is the beginning of their escapades into the world of campers, poverty and vagabonds.

A variety of characters interweave the story. They are the fundamental element of the traveler's world. The people vary from engineers to crooks to professional people from all occupations. They were real people doing real things as they enter and leave the pages of the story. They paint an authentic picture of where "the rubber meets the road" and the camaraderie they felt for each other.

Lyle was born in the last quarter of the 19th century in the rural logging countryside of Michigan. His father Leon was an enterprising sort, who spent some of his time running a logging business and a lot of his time chasing women. Lyle watched and listened well. He wanted to be like Leon, but didn't have a charismatic personality to make it in the fast business world. Lyle liked to live "high-profile" but didn't want to put forth the effort to make things happen.

Lyle was working for a large construction company as a concrete foreman in 1915. He was well liked and trusted by the owners. Leon urged him to borrow money from the company so they could buy speculative timber. Lyle borrowed a large sum of money with a promise to pay it back with a percentage of the profits as interest. They were quite successful in buying and selling large tracts of timber. The only problem was Leon and his brothers didn't pay the money back. Lyle was left holding "the bag" for a large amount of money. He was very tired of his restrictive life style and wanted out. One night, he went to Leon's home and "borrowed" his new Franklin automobile. He left for parts unknown leaving his wife Anna and daughter Ruth to get along by themselves.

It was 1916 and the time was right to head west. He had failed his military physical by eating small quantities of soap over a period of several days so his blood pressure would be elevated. With several hundred dollars in "appropriated funds" and his passport, he left for El Paso, Texas where he met with some representatives of Pancho Villa to join the Mexican revolution.

He left the next day in Leon's Franklin for Hidalgo de Perral, Mexico. He did as instructed and checked into the only hotel and waited. A band of rough looking soldiers came into town and met with him. They took Leon's Franklin and most of his money. They left him sitting in the hotel feeling rejected and angry. All they wanted was his car for Pancho Villa.

As the story goes, he stayed for a few months and earned the nickname "El Simpatico." It meant the nice quiet one. Everyone in town liked the "gringo" because he would buy them food and drink.

Lyle was sweet on a beautiful Mexican girl who lived on a large ranch outside of town. He secretly visited her as often as he could. One thing led to another and the owner of the ranch escorted Lyle to the

American border after several months of secretly visiting Juanita. He was asked never to come back to Mexico or see Juanita again.

We leave Lyle in El Paso, looking at a slow moving east bound freight train. He looked at the clear blue sky and then at the train. He walked down the overpass wondering where his next stop would be.

Marie was born in Askhabad, Turkestan in the early part of the 20th century. Turkestan was a Russian province on the Iranian border. Her father's name was Andrei and he worked as a clerk on the Trans-Siberian Railroad.

1918 was the beginning of a turbulent revolution in Czarist Russia. Andrei was stationed in Siberia where they felt little effect of the violent times. He made a conscious choice not to join the communist party. This made him a White Russian and an enemy of the communist state. He disappeared into the chaos of the turbulent time in 1926 and lost his family forever.

With the coming of spring, Marie and a girl friend began the long journey from Siberia to China. They had no official papers and had to hide from the communist soldiers. White Russians were placed in a Gulag when they were captured trying to leave Mother Russia. After a journey of many weeks, they made their way to Harbin, China. Marie and her girl friend bought a stolen or forged Nansen passport. It was never clear where the passport originated.

They used their new Nansen passport to travel in China. Nansen passports were issued to White Russians who were political exiles from revolutionary Russia. Marie became the woman on the passport. Her name became Stanislava or "Stan" because of the name on the passport.

They traveled by rail to Chefo, China where there was an American Naval Base. She met Howard Post while working at a local nightclub. They married and eventually made their way to Indiana where they started to raise Howard Charles and James Lewis. Local political influence and family turmoil forced Marie from Howard and her children.

Marie started using her real name in the early 30's when she tried to put aside the hurt and anger she suffered from her state of affairs. She went to work at a local restaurant to support herself. She had no idea what to do or where to go in the middle of the Depression. Her knowledge of English was limited to simple work a day things. She walked out after her shift was over and looked at the blue sky. She wished someone would take her away from this unpleasant life.

Lyle met Marie at the restaurant in South Bend, Indiana. After a whirlwind courtship, he convinced Marie to join him and travel the country. He would take her away and they would see the world together. It was late 1932 as Marie and Lyle joined hands, looked up at the blue sky and walked into the unknown world of the vagabonds' "open road" in Lyle's homemade tear drop trailer. This story follows them through a world of adventure, just a few steps ahead of the law.

CHAPTER ONE

The Camp

Summer, Kentucky Campground

The mirror was dirty, crooked and cracked on one side. It was part of an old small dresser, long ago discarded by some weary camper. The mirror hung loosely from a rusty nail on an empty wall. The small homemade tear drop trailer had part of one open wall with enough room to hang a mirror.

"It need's a new frame and backing to make it respectable," said Marie.

Lyle ignored her, as usual. The small, stained wooden shelf under the mirror held his personal items for shaving and dressing. Three ties were hanging on nails under the shelf. He changed them often as they were worn and thread bare. There was a light in place but he never got around to finish wiring the tear drop for electricity. A small, old, stained bulb protruded from a dingy yellowed socket with a yellowed cord hanging below. Marie had pulled on the cord many times in hope of seeing the dim glow of the light bulb, but it remained dark and grimy.

The trailer floor was bare plywood polished by the footsteps of feet across the floor. Marie found an old discarded throw rug and placed it by the door. She tried her best to keep things clean, but it was a loosing battle because of bare wood and Lyle dragging in dirt. He refused or ignored to clean his feet before he came in the trailer.

Tear drop trailers are exactly what the name implies. They are shaped like a teardrop with the rounded end in the front. They are usually small, light and easily made. Most were built with a hatch that opened across the back so it could be used as a kitchen with the hatch propped opened to provide shelter. It was a cheap way to travel for those who had the skills to build them. They were easy to maintain as the axles and tires were automotive, and the wood required some paint. Each was unique in design, but all had the same distinctive shape.

Times were difficult after the banks closed. Thousands of people took to the road and became travelers looking for work or to escape their former lives that were ruined by the Great Depression. Some went by choice and some by circumstance. Many never made it "on the road" and returned home to face the reality of their lives.

An area behind and below the hill of The Camp was called the "dumping place." It was a collection of broken lives and discards of all kinds, free for the taking. The front part of the dump contained mostly household and usable items. The back part was used for refuse. An old discarded tear drop destroyed by a careless fire marked the entrance.

Some less fortunate travelers barely had transportation in the form of some sort of car or truck that would run, more or less. Most of them didn't resemble a vehicle unless you looked very close to see it had tires and a steering wheel. They were stacked with all sorts of household items—cans of water, bedding and children riding in every available space. One had a cook stove strapped to a platform built on the old rear trunk rack. A woman was trying to get a fire started to fix their meager meal.

Some of the trailers were crude, homemade affairs mounted on a vehicle axle. A hitch was fashioned so it could be towed behind a car or truck. The shape varied from a box to a teardrop. The tear drop was a favorite because it was easy to make and light enough to tow behind an old car.

The more fortunate campers had a trailer of some sort. Most of the trailers were tear drops. Some had built as what resembled a living area in old enclosed truck. Others built what looked like a covered wagon on rubber wheels. It was a collection of every conceivable contraption one could call home and still be able to travel and live at least one step above the ground with some shelter from the weather.

Regardless of where you traveled or in what state you were, the camping area was always known as "The Camp." Individual camping spaces were called "my camp." All campers shared a "word of mouth" campground directory. When a new camper pulled in they were greeted with all the local news and they in turn passed along what information they had about their travels. It was a way of life to share information with each other. If one camper had some extra food items, he would trade them for what he needed. If one camper was destitute, campers of all walks of life pitched in and helped so they could make it to the next campground.

"Hey Camper! Where do you hail from?" was a common greeting as life on the road was a large brotherhood of travelers.

Some families followed the money trail from Florida up and down the east coast. Some campers ventured in to the inland states. The news of "work" would filter into the camp and by morning, many of the campers would be gone. The first to go were the campers who had transportation and little else. They depended on any kind of work to feed their families. Picking fruits and vegetables were a favorite because they paid every day by how much you picked. During the "picking" season, they would venture north to pick raspberries or work the cranberry bogs. Some went south to pick oranges. Picking cotton was reserved for locals.

Seasoned travelers had their special places in the campsite. They would dig small-sloped holes for the trailer wheels to fit. The holes would lower the profile of the trailer so wind wouldn't upset it as easily. This camp had many such holes and some had names. Lyle called his holes, "my place."

Some of the campgrounds were government controlled and had hot and cold running water, doctors and places for the uncounted number of children to play. Government control was too tight for people who ran small business operations. They required the travelers to fill out an accounting card with a lot of personal information. Many of the travelers weren't willing to do that. The camp was intended to be used by migrant families, which followed the crops. For some reason or the other, the Federal Government tracked these families.

People with trailers were not allowed to stay, except on the outside. They were asked to leave after they used the facilities for a few days. The campground Lyle and Marie choose was not government controlled. It was in a nice rural area outside of Hootentown, near Lexington, Kentucky. It was meagerly supplemented by the state of Kentucky. The cost for camping was 25¢ a night, and this included the use of the communal bathhouse, but no electricity. There were outside water faucets installed throughout the camp. It was one of the cleaner southern campgrounds. The rules were simple and everyone followed them–no loud noise, trash or fighting. There was no limit to how long you could stay.

There were many campgrounds throughout the southern route. Some were behind gas stations or in a farmer's field. Some were in forestland while others were in open woods. Camps were known and information was shared because of the travelers' brotherhood. Some areas and towns didn't allow campers and most everyone knew about them.

Many eligible men joined the CCC (civilian conservation corps) to provide an income for their family. The government gave five dollars per month to each worker and sent the rest to their families. It was hard, difficult work but "four squares and a flop" were included. The fourth square was a mid-morning snack. It usually consisted of coffee and a cold biscuit with ham or bacon. Work began before daylight and the men needed the energy to work their twelve-hour shifts. The CCC work had its rewards by seeing construction of National Parks and many camping areas.

Travelers tended to stay away from National Parks because there were too many rules. They were supposed to be showplaces and the government didn't want the public to see the itinerant vagabonds who traveled the roads trying to make a living for themselves and their families. They were considered an embarrassment to the government and needed to be in the shadows of the paying visitors. Most of the National and State Park visitors were for "well to do" gentry.

It was natural that campers had a variety of skills because of the many walks of life they left for the traveling world. They bartered and traded skills due to the lack of available cash. Lyle was an excellent carpenter and often did small jobs in exchange for food or something he needed. The jobs were usually small and he gave all kinds of advice instead of doing any work.

"Pope the Key Man" lived in his old green Hudson car along with thousands of keys that sounded like the tinkling of small bells.

Most of the campers knew Garland Pope. He traveled the southern circuit following the need for his trade. He was a federally licensed key maker and everyone trusted him. You couldn't see through the nicotine stained the windows of his old car, with the exception of the windshield. They were a dark yellow brown.

The campers were happy to see Pope, as he was called. He brought news from other camps and the world situation. People would gather and listen to his tales as he drank hot tea from an ancient stained cup. His accent was vaguely European. With the passing of time, his native country changed from Hungary to Poland to France. He was a warm and charming person who had many friends. On occasions he acted as a "Judge" to settle disputes and do minor legal work.

Lyle enjoyed looking for bargains and useable "junk." Some WW1 veterans in the camp were selling army surplus. He bought a mattress for the trailer to replace the blankets that served as a bed pad. The axle and rims were from the front of an old Dodge truck with good leaf springs. The inside of the trailer was about five feet wide and eight feet long. The front was the bed and the driver's side held a small cabinet area. The outside rear of the trailer was never was finished. The back area had a hinge so it could be opened and propped with a support pole. The initial plan was to construct a kitchen area with an icebox, but it was never finished. The roof area was less than six feet and had a push-up vent in the middle. The rear passenger side had a walled closet with an old curtain as a door. The bottom held the "thunder mug" covered by an old piece of discarded plywood cut to fit. Marie hated the idea of this kind of inside plumbing, but she had no choice.

Lyle didn't trust the hobos in the "hobo jungle." He didn't venture far from his camp because he was afraid of any interaction with the "Knights of the Road." There was an earlier incident with Lyle and a hobo and the "word" got around. Lyle was a timid man who was always looking over his shoulder for someone or something.

The lower back part of the camp was near a railroad where the hobos had their jungle. A small creek ran through a wooded area. This provided some shelter and security for the hobos.

Occupants would vary in size from a few to over fifty depending on the "touch" of the town. When the wind was right you could smell their Mulligan stew. Making the stew was a true hobo art form. The ingredients were any kind of meat and vegetables the hobos could find in the local area, cooked in a community pot.

A complex "touch code" marked local houses. The word "touch" meant how much the people would give. The code consisted of vertical and horizontal lines. The more lines in the horizontal meant they were good for food. The vertical lines meant clothing. An upside down cross meant to stay away. If a box was drawn, then you were welcome inside for whatever reason. The "touch marks" were made on the bottom of a post or fence out of view of the front door. There were other code alignments for everything one could imagine. The "Knights of the Road" had a very strict code of honor. There was no dishonesty, thievery or cheating. The King or leader would deal severely with any infractions of their strict code of honor. If someone stole anything, they were banished from the clan forever. "Honest panhandling" was their way or the highway.

The hobo lifestyle developed in the years after the Civil War. Soldiers couldn't find work so they left their families and "hit the road" looking for work. More often than not, they found field work. The word hobo derived from "hoe boy," describing the men who worked in the fields with a hoe. They were not homeless as most thought. A vast majority had families and homes. Some would stay on the road and some would return to their former lives. Those who stayed would be "waiting for the East Bound." In hobo parlance, until he dies.

The hobos were sometimes called "bindle stiffs" because the round bundle they carried on a stick was a bindle. A stiff is someone who rode the brake rods under trains. The bindle contained all their worldly possessions. The name stuck until the Second World War when the life of the old style hobo started to die.

The names of "Steamboat Rob," "Tall Knife Jake," "Cookie Sam" and "Doc White" died with their way of life. "Dapper Dan" was still thinking about the ways of the road.

Robert W. Service, a Scottish poet and writer, admired the Hobo and put his thoughts in to a poem called "Bindle Stiff." One verse catches the mood of the times.

Bindle Stiff

And as I tramped the railroad track
I owned a single shirt;
Like canny Scot, I bought it black
So's not to show the dirt;
A handkerchief held all my gear,
My razor and my comb;
I was a freckless lad, I fear,
With all the world for home.

Brake rods are steel rods secured under a car to operate the brakes from a remote location. There are between two and four rods, depending on the type of railroad car. They run the length of the car so both front and rear brakes can be applied together. The "stiffs" would fashion a flat board so it fit over the rods. It was very dangerous, but the easiest position to get away from the "bulls" (police) in the freight yards. When they fell off the rods, they became stiffs because no one survived the rolling wheels. Not all hobos "rode the rods," but the name stuck.

Lyle was trying to comb his hair so every piece was in place before he donned his hat that he liked to call his Fedora. The broken mirror didn't help nor did the poor light. His eyes had been bad since he was a child and required glasses for everything. The correct position of every hair was important for the proper dress of a twentieth century "Dapper Dan." He donned his yellow and gold vest and adjusted it with the precision of an engineer. His days as a hobo were over but he was still a vagabond and wonderer at heart.

His watch and fob was a very important component of dress. A fob is a short chain with a medallion or ornament, attached to a watch and worn hanging from a vest pocket. He traded a box of self-sticking bandages and a few dollars for the watch and fob. The young man who needed money said, "It used to belong to my father." The white curved tooth on the end of the chain yellowed with age, but the old Hamilton kept perfect time. When he talked or played checkers he was in the habit of taking the watch out and setting it next to him. He wished he knew what kind of tooth it was to help with his stories at the trading post. He was proud of his trading ability and liked to show off.

He learned the special knack of buying and selling old scrap gold and silver from Pug Andrews. Pug was a jeweler by trade and, like so many, he lost his business when the banks crashed in '29. The lung damage he suffered during the Great War from mustard gas caused him a lot of pain. He was selling all his prized possessions so he could make his way to his home in the Shenandoah. All who knew him felt a keen sense of loss and sadness as he headed home to live out the rest of his shortened life.

Lyle bought the scales, acid kit and weights from him over a year ago. With Pug's tutoring, Lyle made a good living in this part of the country by buying and selling old scrap gold and silver. The small carrying case was made of old wooden cigar boxes and finished with black leather from an old purse he found in the camp dump. The acid bottle was in one end surrounded by paraffin. The acid detected the presence of copper or brass in gold jewelry. You scribed jewelry on a small piece of slate, called a scratch. A drop of hydrochloric acid dropped on the mark would turn green if it was less than 10 karats (42%) gold. 10 karat was the smallest amount of gold which could carry the karat designation. Pure gold was 24 karats fine.

Pug taught him the Troy system of weights and measures. A pound of gold or silver was 12 troy ounces instead of 16 ounces in the Avoirdupois (common use) system. The smallest troy unit of measure was a pennyweight. A copper penny weighed two-pennyweight. Pug taught him the trick of using a penny instead of the pennyweight. He could buy twice as much gold or silver for the same price by substituting a copper penny for the troy pennyweight. The flim flam worked perfectly in most cases.

Lyle told people he was an engineer and earned his diploma through ICS (International Correspondence School). In truth, he finished the sixth grade before he ran away from home. It was the first of many times he ran away. He and his father, Leon, didn't get along very well and his new wife Carrie didn't help matters. He could not speak or ask of his birth mother, Estella.

He despised the idea of physical work, so he picked the title of "Engineer" to impress people. He read a lot and knew the right "catch phrases" to make his title look impressive.

He had artistic skills but rarely finished anything he started. The old mirror was still hanging with a piece of rusty wire, as it had for the past year. He had to stoop to see, even though he was only five feet, seven inches. Buying old scrap gold and silver fit Lyle's vagabond character to a tee.

The last and final touch to dressing was his moustache. He had a special tin of wax that he applied to make the thin gray line look stronger. A perfect thin gray line suited his ego. Lyle didn't like the idea of being born in 1886 and tried his best to look younger.

One day he found a bottle of "Color Back" hair dye on one of his many forays to the dump. He dyed his hair with a lot of enthusiasm. He couldn't see how to dye the back. As a result, his hair turned very black in the front and remained gray in the back. It took him several days to get the color back to gray. This didn't help his ego.

The rear of the tear drop opened like a large trunk the width of the trailer. It could be opened and propped with sawed off tent poles for protection against the elements. There was a flat area for the stove and a small workspace. Someday Lyle would finish the area. They had a small, portable wooden icebox to store perishable items. Lyle didn't like to spend money for ice.

Marie was trying to light the old green Coleman stove so she could fix some breakfast. It needed to be cleaned and repaired on a daily basis. The new Amoco white gas helped the stove burn a lot better than Naphtha and was a lot cheaper. The fuel regulator was worn out long ago and needed constant attention. She carefully filtered the gas through a piece of chamois skin to keep debris out of the internal working of the stove. She kept her tools, sand paper and spare parts in an old tin can.

Biscuits were usually fixed the evening before. They were covered with a bright red cloth so they would "rise" for the morning meal. The tiny tin oven came with a bluish isinglass window so she could see that her baked goods were done properly. Marie liked any little convenience to make her life easier. The Coleman oven was difficult to regulate. The right burner worked better than the left burner. It was the only new item she had and it was a prized possession. Marie could set it on one burner of the gas stove and bake cakes and biscuits like Lyle wanted.

Marie loved to cook and made the very best food she could with the small supply she had. Lyle was so particular that sometimes he would dump the food out if he didn't like it. If Lyle was happy, Marie's world was at ease.

The sweltering August heat was taking its toll on Marie. It seemed like she had been with child forever and the heat of the stove wasn't helping her feeling of nausea. She leaned in the trailer and asked Lyle for a clean dishcloth.

" I am getting ready, get it yourself."

Painfully, she pulled herself up and went into the trailer to get the items she needed.

She knew why he was angry again. She had bought some Bugler tobacco and rolled their cigarettes last evening. She used their old Bugler Cigarette roller. The trick was to get the exact amount of tobacco in the rolling pouch. It had to be spread evenly on the paper so the "draw" wouldn't be too easy or too hard. Marie had packed the rolls so the cigarettes were very difficult to smoke. Both liked to smoke and each used more than forty each day. When times were good, they had store bought "coffin nails." They favored Sweet Picayunes.

He was irritated again because they were too "hard" to smoke. Marie liked the tightly packed cigarettes because they were like the kind she used in China when she first started to smoke.

Lyle had a good week and Marie was able to buy some things she needed for meals. Marie would shop every day so the food was fresh. She had enough flour, salt and lard to fix a decent meal. Early this morning she put her waist long black hair in a tight bun. She walked slowly to El Mercado, the camp store, to purchase some eggs and slab bacon. Her stomach was huge and she had to waddle her five-foot frame very carefully to avoid the ruts in the dirt path. Thank goodness there was shade because she hated the heat.

She dreamily thought of August in her youth, when the family would go out on the steppes of the Russian Tundra to pick wild berries for Sunday dinner. August in Siberia was cold with heavy frost until late morning. She knew she would never see Mother Russia again, but she was proud of her heritage. Whatever was in her belly could kick like a mule. This was her third child and all had been boys. Howard Charles was born in 1928 and James Lewis was born in 1929. She missed them a lot, especially when Lyle wouldn't let her visit. She thought out loud, "Some day, some day." Little did she know, but a distant war would take Howard from her.

Carlos, the storeowner, and his wife Juanita were friendly people. They came from Mexico after the Mexican revolution and opened a small country store that catered to travelers and campers. It was complete with a pickle barrel and a potbelly stove. In one corner, Carlos had set up a checkerboard for the hombres (men) to play. He liked the game and was quite good at it.

Juanita patted Marie's tummy and said "bambino grande!" which meant "Big baby boy." Marie agreed it was going to be a big boy. Howard and James, her two other children, were small compared to the new baby. She made her purchases and looked at a red dress on the corner rack. It was so beautiful and expensive. Seven dollars was a lot for a dress. Lyle disliked red. He wouldn't let her wear it anyway. The only red item she had was the cover for rising biscuits. She thanked Carlos and Juanita and went down the dusty path. The way back was down hill and a little easier to walk. She wished the baby would stop kicking. "I think he wants out, and soon," she thought. She gave Lyle the receipt and he noted the entry in his "diaries." It was his way and she dutifully complied.

He kept every penny earned and spent in a dairy. He detailed all the sales and expenses on a daily basis as well as their travels and stories of the local area. Marie kept the money in an old tobacco sack attached to the center of her brassiere. What she didn't know was Lyle wrote things in Spanish that he kept from her. Mostly he wrote about extra money he had hidden. His spoken Spanish wasn't very good but he wrote well. This confused Marie because she had no secrets from him.

There was some attraction between Lyle and Mexico. He liked the Mexican way of life and the food. Because of a sensitive stomach, he couldn't eat spicy food, but he liked the flavor of tortillas. Marie heard Lyle say so many times.

"I want to go back to Old Mexico and visit my friends. In Mexico I was called Simpatico."

He liked his eggs perfectly done with the whites a little hard and the yellow glazed with bacon grease. He had the choice of the best food because he was the provider and needed his energy to make a living. He had a number of aliments that could be "called up" at the drop of a hat. His heart condition was at the top of the list. He had been dying since he was twenty-five because a doctor told him of a problem with his aortic valves. He was told that he shouldn't work at any strenuous job. He stressed his bad eyes because they were injured "on the job" and they hurt him to look at anything to long, especially if it required work. The kind of work Lyle was doing wasn't really called work, but it brought in enough money to keep the 28 Pontiac running and the homemade tear drop livable.

The summer before, Lyle and several of his acquaintances devised a scheme to make a bandage that would stick to a person without tape. They didn't put it into practice until this summer.

The idea was to dip a bandage in a solution of water glass and dextrose that would dry "sticky" on the bandage. "Water glass" was actually sodium silicate, which was used to fire proof clothing in the army. It worked very well to help the bandages stick to skin, and made a good lap over so you didn't have to tape the bandage.

The dextrose, water glass and bandages were WW1 surplus that he bought from the veterans who lived in the camp. The solution worked well except when it was exposed to the sun for a few hours, at which point it would turn brown and fall off. They set up shop in the woods behind the camp. Marie devised a simple way to unroll the "sanitary bandages" from their blue packing paper, dip them in solution, and repack them in the same box so they looked original. Of course, they remained "sanitary" throughout the entire procedure, even when they were hung to dry in the shade and an occasion bird would call.

They made several hundred rolls of bandages and repacked them like new. Marie and Betty, George's wife, wrapped and packed until their hands looked like pickled onions from the dextrose and water glass. They wasted only a few bandages to learn how to make them perfect. They would unwrap the blue paper, unroll the bandage, dip it in the solution and hang them to dry. Repacked, the result was a neat box of bandages, labeled "Sterile," with the ability to stick without tape.

George Planter, the out of work chemist from Idaho, and Lyle left in the old 28 Pontiac for the back towns of southern Ohio. It was George's formula and idea to make the bandages, as he was a brilliant chemist but needed someone like Lyle to market his ideas and make a little money. They did their best in Zanesville, Ohio the home of Hull Pottery. They worked the farms around Moxahalla, Darlington and Buckeye. They sold most of the bandages in six days and were on the way home with over $200.00 between them.

On the way back, they stopped in Zanesville, Ohio to visit the Hull Pottery Works. Hull Pottery sold seconds for ten cents apiece. The seconds had small color differences and imperfections. They could resell the lovely pieces of Hull Art Pottery for at least 50¢ or more.

They went to the sales office and the first person they met was the wife of a farmer who had bought ten rolls of the bandages the week before. The lady was very upset and immediately called the police. Lyle and George just cleared the yard when the police arrived at the Hull Pottery plant. They drove straight through to Moundsville, West Virginia and stayed in a familiar campsite. They met some old friends and sat around a bonfire telling stories until the wee hours about the bandages and the narrow escape with the police.

"Did you see the lady in the Hull Pottery office?" Lyle asked. "She still had one of the bandages on her leg and it looked like it had been dipped in a sheep tank!"

The stories went on for hours until they all finally went to sleep around the bonfire to the Irish tunes of a harmonica, played by a young red headed Irish Lad. Most of the stories stretched the truth. The first story teller usually told the biggest lie which left little room for the second liar to tell his whopper.

Marie had finished cooking breakfast with his favorite corn meal mush and eggs. They ate in silence and she absorbed the stress of Lyle's trap. What was she doing there? She had a good job at the Millside Diner in South Bend, Indiana. She was recovering from her turmoil with the Post family and the staged divorce. The Post family didn't want any foreigners in their community or family. They staged an adulteress affair with a paid informant. This, coupled with a "crooked" lawyer, caused her to lose her children and everything she owned except her prized leather suitcase and its secret contents.

She had carried her suitcase all the way from Chefo, China. She bought it with her earnings before she married Howard Post. She was glad she left the political conflicts of Mother Russia, but she was not at ease with her present situation.

Lyle had come into the diner and sweet-talked her into a date. They went to see "The Jazz Singer," with Al Jolson, which was the first "talkie" movie. They ate hot popcorn from the new popcorn machine in the lobby. The popcorn was good but the salt burned her chapped lips. She licked her lips when she was nervous. Marie was nervous and afraid because she was strangely attracted to this small, thin man.

Her old memories faded as she snapped back to reality. She didn't want to get involved with another man so soon but here she was, pregnant and living with a man who wasn't her husband. She was a strong woman and made the very best of the situation, but she wished she hadn't ever met Lyle. She knew in her heart that it was too late for her, but not for the baby she carried.

Marie was well educated by Russian standards. Many women, including her mother, grew up illiterate. The Russian School system was 10 years for girls and 11 years for boys. Male students studied math and science in the 11th year. Girls studied office work in the 10th year. Marie completed 10 years of school in 1924, which by American standards was the equivalent of two years of college.

She looked intently at the sky and thought about the "old country" with a regretful, sad face. This expression followed her for the rest of her life, carved deeply into her face by countless heartaches.

CHAPTER TWO

The Fob

Late summer, Kentucky Campground

Lyle finally went to sleep when the singing and clamber in the hobo jungle quieted down. He could still hear the quiet sounds of voices singing in harmony and it helped him pass into the half world of fitful sleep.

He was nervous about the gold he had bought a couple of days ago from Chicago Pete. Pete was a well-liked hobo by all members of the jungle. He had a quiet, likable personality but he didn't fit the mold of the average knight of the road.

Lyle examined and tested some gold he had to sell. He told him it was 14 karat gold but it was actually 18 karat gold. Lyle should have known better, but he tried the old scam of using a copper penny instead of a pennyweight so he could buy twice as much gold for ½ the price. Pete very quietly made him reweigh the gold with the correct gold weights so he wouldn't be cheated. He also told Lyle to look at the back of the broach. It was plainly stamped 18K, not 14K. It was the last piece of jewelry his wife had before he went "on the road" and he needed the money to get home. Lyle tried to talk his way out of the lies but Pete cut him short.

"Lyle, don't you ever try and cheat any of the boys in the jungle. If I hear of any more of your 'tricks,' I will tell them all and your name will be mud all over the south!"

He knew exactly what mud meant. He was the doctor who treated John Wilkes Booth's broken leg after he killed President Lincoln. From that day forward, the name mud was a stigma that no one wanted to wear. Actually, his name was Mudd, but was changed to mud over the years to accentuate something dirty.

"Ok Pete, I'll give you a good price for the piece if you keep quiet about our talk."

"I'll be quiet this time but if I ever hear of you trying to cheat anybody, you will have me to deal with."

Pete needed the money and didn't hesitate when Lyle paid him.

"I'll see you in better times." Pete said.

Lyle paid him a lot more than the broach was worth and went back to the trailer and got into bed as fast as he could. Marie was sound asleep and he was very careful not to wake her.

Lyle now understood what Pete meant by "better times" and it made him a little uneasy. He had enough uncertainties in his life without the additional worry of the hobo jungle. Lyle thought long and hard about doing any more business with the hobos.

Their money supply was getting low. Lyle decided he was going to work the Lexington, Kentucky hospital area for old scrap silver and gold. There were a lot of doctors and dentists around the Good Samaritan Hospital. He usually had good luck buying old dentures and gold teeth.

Lyle was careful not to disturb Marie because he didn't want to be bothered with her complaints. He took the mirror off the rusty nail and placed it on another nail by the edge of the closet so he could see to get dressed. He very carefully replaced it so Marie wouldn't complain about making a mess. She was easily irritated these days. He wanted to look as good as he could for his trip today. He was in a hurry because he didn't want to miss the breakfast that Juanita or Carlos prepared. He wanted to speak to Juanita alone, but he never got the chance.

Carlos and Juanita left Mexico in the winter of 1918 to escape the Mexican revolution and the effects of the Great War in Europe. People both Mexican and foreign who were in business and owned property bore the brunt of the revolution.

Mexico had been under foreign rule for years. The rulers had appropriated most of the accumulated wealth of the country. From the beginning of the Mexican revolution, through the Great World War and the American Depression, the world was in economic, political and cultural turmoil on a scale unprecedented in recorded history.

The world was caught up in this madness, with Carlos and Juanita rooted in the tidal wave of destiny. They were faced with a wilderness of decisions; none would be easy or pleasant.

Juanita went to school in Barcelona, Spain to learn fine arts and study music. She reluctantly went upon the insistence of her father, who wanted her to bring back some of the culture of the old country.

Her father and mother mysteriously disappeared while she was in Spain. The revolution on both sides removed influential people to have better control of the people and country. No one ever found any evidence of his or her demise.

Don Alvero Obregon, her distant cousin, insisted she come live at his hacienda. Juanita loved the rolling hills and splendor of the estate. She reluctantly accepted because she had no other place to go. The provisional government had taken her home, past life and many of her possessions. Like most Mexican families, they were very close. She brought back the timeless culture of Spain to adorn the hacienda with art and music. She loved Mexico and all the wonderful things it offered. Mexican life for those of means and culture was delightful. She loved her early morning horse rides. The gentle wind on her face soothed her fiery inner passions.

All countries needed great leaders and Juanita was a born leader. Her tenacity and foresight had brought them the point of an irreversible decision to leave the country. She had a small boy child. She named him Juan Carlos, even though Carlos wasn't the father.

She often thought of the Gringo who had romanced her into a relationship and left when she was with child. She remembered the small, thin man with the little moustache. She didn't hate him but she wished he had stayed and taken responsibility for his son. She had no idea that he was forced to leave Mexico long ago. Carlos had taken her in and loved the child like it was his own. The turbulent times were not appropriate to place a child in harms way. The journey would be long and dangerous and they had to go alone. Juanita regretted leaving the child in the care of the family, but she had to leave the country.

Carlos was a Marron, which was an authentic "peon" name.

Peons were the working class people who tended flocks and fields and did servant work. The name went back many years and mixed with native Indian. It became an honored name in the Mexican working class. The name meant "brown," and his complexion was the essence of his name. Somehow the name was changed to Moreno. It was never clear if they were married, but they went by the Moreno name. It was probably easier to get forged papers with Moreno than Marron because it was a very common name.

Don Obregon had planned well and smuggled silver pesos to a U.S. bank for many years. Because it was "hard currency," it was easily converted to dollars. He graciously made some of these funds available to Juanita and Carlos.

They opened "El Mercado," Spanish for "The Market," in a small Kentucky town. They used the savings they had from selling their belongings and horses. With the money Don Obregon had provided, they settled in their new roll and became a stable part of the community.

Carlos was a good butcher and soon had a thriving local business. Juanita was an excellent cook. You could smell the fragrance of tortillas and chili cooking on the stone topped stove. It was a nice feeling to stop and have a taco or bowl of chili with the Moreno's. Only the brave would try the chili, with Carlo's special green picanti sauce. Pancho Villa's actions and the government response had forced many Mexican families across the border. They brought with them their homemade recipes and cures for common illnesses. Many people believed that chili, properly prepared, was a natural cure all. The hotter it was, the better Carlos liked it. It tasted so good you couldn't stop eating it and many paid the next day with the pain and discomfort it brought. Some called it "Pancho Villa's Revenge."

El Mercado was built with the store in the front. The Mexican custom was to have their living quarters in the rear and Lyle knew that.

Lyle wanted to talk to Juanita without Carlos around. He walked to the back of the house and saw Juanita standing at the door, next to the patio. He watched her sweep the floor and pick up the dirt and leaves with an old iron dustpan.

She was finished sweeping when she looked up and saw Lyle. It gave her a start.

"Simpatico! You know it is wrong for you to be here! This is now my new life and I care for Carlos."

Lyle looked around at their very private living area, which was decorated with Mexican furniture and tapestries. The bed was a large four-poster, built high off the ground. This was their home away from home where they could remember the "old ways." Lyle loved Mexican culture and Juanita had brought it with her.

"I should have never left Mexico because I liked the way the people lived. I especially liked you." Lyle said.

"Yes, I know," said Juanita "but it is over forever. Marie is with child and you have to take care of her. I want you to leave and never return to my home. You may come to the store but never to my private home."

Lyle looked very dejected as he turned and started to leave.

"We have some food you like in El Mercado and I will serve you in the store." Juanita said. Juanita looked at Lyle with a sad face and a slight tear in her eye. They both wanted to take each other in their arms, but it would never be. She turned around and went through the door to the store.

Lyle went outside and stared at the ground for a long time. He knew the "Simpatico" part of his life was gone forever. He placed his hands behind his back and went around to the front and asked what they had for breakfast. Lyle's heart was beating very fast. He knew he shouldn't have gone to her bedroom but he wanted to talk to her. He was afraid to ask about the "little one" in Mexico.

Juanita wanted to tell him about "Little Juan Carlos," but she too was afraid and ashamed to say anything. It was a lonely, sad day for both Lyle and Juanita.

Juanita's cooking was a favorite of Lyle's. He would eat with them when he had extra money to spend. He was very hungry after the chance meeting this morning and was glad Juanita made him a good breakfast with strong Mexican café con Leche. Mexican coffee is made with hot milk instead of water and Lyle liked the flavor. He kept a little extra cash in his left watch pocket and usually ate with his left hand.

Lyle finished his breakfast and paid Carlos. He asked for a little help to push the old Pontiac to get it started. He left for Lexington with a good feeling that he would make some money that day. He thought a lot about Juanita and decided to put her out of his mind.

"Maybe some day I will return to Mexico and see if I can find my old friends if they are still there," he thought.

He had no remorse for the baby he left behind or for the sad feeling in Juanita's heart.

The Mexicans were superstitious of left-handed people. Lyle was born left-handed. His father, Leon, made him use his right hand, as was the custom in the old ways. When he started school, they tied his left hand behind his back and make him write with his right hand. It was a cruel and ineffective way to change the use of hands. He could now use either hand to do most tasks, including writing. He liked to show off writing with either hand. Lyle needed regular ego boosts and this was one of many. It gave him a feeling of power and control to hide money from Marie and keep things from her. After all, he wasn't married to her and felt no real obligation.

He liked to have a little money available when he wanted or needed it. Marie usually kept first-rate account of the money, but she was so tired with all the work and being pregnant that she didn't keep up with the cash balance as she should have, and this gave Lyle an edge on keeping things from her. She felt so bad she didn't really care, but wondered how he was making money. They had been there over two months and he worked very little. His phrase "I loafed today" appeared on many pages of his diaries.

Carlos was very patient with Lyle as he stumbled through his interpretation of Spanish grammar. Some people have an "ear" for languages. Strangely, if someone had musical talent, his or her language skills seemed to be better. Lyle couldn't carry a tune in a water bucket. He would listen very carefully as Carlos slowly pronounced a word. He tried his best to imitate the word, but the transition from ear to speech was lost in a cloud of confusion. Carlos had a lot of patience with Lyle and he slowly taught Lyle to speak a little understandable Spanish. He still couldn't understand it when spoken in a normal tone. He could get the meaning if one spoke very slowly. His mind would catch about every fourth word and it resulted in a puzzled translation. One must be able to think in a language to speak it clearly. Lyle couldn't learn to think in Spanish. His thoughts were only in English.

Juanita enjoyed visiting Marie because she liked her and they got along well. Both were foreigners in an unfamiliar land. They both had long black hair and they would frequently comb each other's. They would talk about their countries, although Marie didn't understand Mexico or the Mexican culture. She would listen for hours as Juanita told her of better times.

Marie was having problems with the heat and she wanted to lie down and rest. The toilet was a long way up the dirt path. Lyle wouldn't let her use the thunder mug during the day because he didn't want it emptied in the daytime.

Lyle made Marie wash some of his underwear and socks late that afternoon to keep her away from Juanita. Some days nothing was said about her talking to Juanita, but today was worse than usual. He didn't like to see Juanita and Marie together. He would ask what they talked about and seemed nervous when they were together. Marie really didn't care what Lyle thought. She was too uncomfortable with her pregnancy and the wretched heat.

Lyle had at least a dozen pairs of socks and as many underwear. Marie had two pairs of old cotton panties that were stretched out of shape and Lyle wouldn't but her buy any new ones.

Marie knew Lyle wouldn't let her wear hose because he said it made her look cheap. She liked to dress in hose but it was too hot, so she didn't challenge his authority. It was the hottest August in history.

It was dusk when Lyle came back to his camp. He was happy because he had bought some gold from a passing traveler. He would send it to Fishlows in Baltimore on Monday so he could get a check by the following Monday.

Fishlows dealt in old scrap silver and gold and were as honest as any he had found. Sometimes they would grade the gold a little better, but more often it was a little less. Lyle fudged the gold amount to make up for their in house grading. He had to grade the gold, which meant remove all the non-gold metal and check the karat amount. He had spent about $8.00 and had almost $30.00 worth of gold in addition to about

$20.00 of scrap gold teeth he bought from an old dentist for $3.00. Fishlows would send the money back the day they received the goods. Usually the address was "general delivery" at the nearest town. They had been there two months, so Lyle rented a post office box. He liked that idea so he could visit the local town without Marie tagging along.

Marie radiated a serene beauty enjoyed by women who are with child as they take on an air of creation known only to expectant mothers. She had two small blemishes on her right cheek. They resembled flat smallpox scars. They were actually the sign of a rare disease known to those in Turkistan, her birthplace. The right thumbnail was flat from birth. This was a genetic trait passed down for generations. Lyle thought these imperfections were ugly. The marks were actually a badge of her heritage. People in Russia recognized the marks with respect and courtesy. Lyle was ashamed of the way she looked both from the scars and the fact that she was pregnant.

Nothing seemed to bother or distract him from his amorous approaches. Shortly after sunset was his favorite time. He could take care of his "business" and go talk with the boys before it was too late at night. He liked to be in bed before nine. Today his approach was subtle, as he brought Marie some food from Juanita's kitchen. As she ate, he tried to sweet-talk her into something she didn't want to do. She hurt so bad and had no interest in anything except trying to get herself comfortable in the tear drop's small bed. She usually gave in to his insatiable appetite, but tonight she totally rejected his advances. He became very annoyed. He was seldom violent because Marie was much stronger than he, even in her present condition. More than once she had proven her strength when he was trying to be forceful.

Marie curled into the best fetal position she could manage and faced the wall away from Lyle. It was hot with little movement of air. He slammed the screen door and left for the store. She arose and opened the roof vent to let a little breeze into the hot, damp trailer. She thought of the cool starry evenings at home as she drifted into a restless sleep.

Her dreams were agitated ramblings about her home in Siberia. It would be so cold that spittle would freeze before it hit the ground. The schools were neighborhood units designed to house ten to fifteen pupils for days on end. The artic temperatures would often dip to minus sixty degrees Fahrenheit.

Marie's school was located at the edge of a small village and was well built with a large Dutch oven in the rear of the main classroom. The walls were at least 2 feet thick with a very dense sod roof that kept out the chilling cold. The Dutch oven covered one corner of the room and was large enough for at least 10 people to sleep on the top. It served the purpose of food preparation and provided a very warm place to sleep.

Vladimir was her favorite teacher. The grade levels varied from the 3rd grade to high school and he was skilled in all areas of studies. Her dreams were a mixture of sleeping and eating with Vlad. She had an extraordinary teenage crush on him. In the evening after studies, he would teach Russian folk dances. Most were ethnic and used in the rural areas on special occasions. She was jealous of Nadia trying to dance with him.

Sometimes he would tell mysterious stories about the snow creature from the Ural Mountains. All the children would huddle closely as he wove his tales of how the creature would sneak into a village and steal food. His voice would rise in tenor with a low growl as he told of children being stolen and taken to the mountain caves. As he told the story, he would act like the creature with outstretched clawed hands. The children would squeal as they grasped each other in delight or fear. He was a delightful teacher and put his all into passing on his endless knowledge to the students.

Marie felt the shudder of the Siberian wind as it howled around the schoolhouse. The temperature was below the minus sixty-degree mark and they would be there another day or so. It was an agreement that the children stay at school instead of risking the winter cold. The top hearth of the Dutch oven was like a warm blanket of security and she tried to get deeper into her warmth.

She awoke in a fright as Lyle slipped into bed and immediately started to snore. He smelled of cigarette smoke and rancid sweat. He rarely had a complete bath. He would wash the parts people could see and use powder to cover the rest. She hated to be awakened from a nice dream; she could never find the link between the dream world and the hot, humid little tear drop trailer. She wanted to dream some more but she just lay there in a dismal frame of mind.

Late that afternoon Lyle came back from Lexington with a smile on his face. He had done very well and they would have more gold to send to Baltimore. She knew she would have to clean the old teeth and dentures to extract the gold and silver. She hated the task as much as she hated the upper false teeth Lyle wore. The denture was clay red with 3 gold teeth. He would soak them in a glass with soda every night. Lyle had asked her to clean them but she refused. Marie thought that was the reason she had to "prepare" the gold and silver teeth for shipment.

The afternoon siesta was over in El Mercado as Lyle quietly walked in the front and saw Carlos seated at the checkerboard.

"Lyle, do you want to play checkers?" Carlos asked.

They settled in to play checkers in the corner of the El Mercado. Lyle read a checker book and numbered the checkerboard. It didn't help because he never won a game from Carlos. The old board was a painted piece of plywood with bottle caps for pieces. The black men were upside down and the red men were right side up. Several campers would join in the game to pass the long summer days. Lyle was by far the best player with the exception of Carlos. When Lyle started to play, he would take out his watch and fob and lay it on the table to time his play. The timing never worked because Carlos would always outplay him.

Juanita provided some delicious Mexican corn chips with a special salsa. The chips were tortillas that had been deep-fried with a little jalapeno oil for flavor.

Marie knew Lyle had a passport somewhere in his "valuables." These were possessions he kept hidden from everyone.

He told Marie on several occasions, "Those are my valuables, don't ever touch them."

Lyle was a collector. He had bits and pieces of family items and a lot of old pictures. He had two prized old watches. One was a very old chain drive watch with a hunting case. It belonged to his Grandfather Freeman. His father, Leon, gave him a railroad watch. He would often wear it because it worked. The fob was not as nice as the Hamilton he carried. He liked to finger the tooth.

Along with the watches, there were several little boxes and a lot of papers in a wooden box under the bed. It sat next to the leather suit-case that held Marie's memories. Lyle was busy being angry because he couldn't win playing checkers with Carlos. She had a little time to look through the forbidden collection. She was afraid, yet she wanted to know a lot more about Lyle than he was willing to tell, especially about Mexico.

She reached her hand under the bed and touched the box and jerked it back like it was very hot. She was trembling with fear and excitement as she did the unthinkable. Very carefully, she pulled out the box. With a quick glance up the path toward the store, she untied the small camping rope and opened it.

Carefully positioned on the top was his passport. It was perfectly centered between the corners. There were three small pieces of twine over two edges with one crossed over the passport logo. Marie carefully removed the twine so she could replace it exactly where Lyle had placed it. It was his way of detecting if someone had bothered his things.

Her hands were trembling as she opened it and saw Lyle of 1915 staring back at her. She quickly closed it because she thought he would see her through the picture. Nervously, she opened it again and avoided his intense stare. In the dim light of a single candle, she read that it was issued in 1915 and there was a Mexican entry for 1915 and 1916. There were two principal cities he visited: Monterrey and Ciudad Camargo. He made several side trips to Vera Cruz and Campeche. The back of the passport held a faded picture of a small child with an old gray haired Mexican gentleman and some old paper Pesos. She had no idea what it meant, but on the back she could make out the faded pencil writing spelling the name, "Juan Carlos."

Marie carefully replaced all of the items just like Lyle had left them quickly put the items back in the box and pushed it back under the bed.

She touched her leather valise as she placed the box in the exact position. It struck a pain in her heart as the memories of the past flooded out of the old leather valise. It seemed like her hand was in the past and yet her body was in the candle light of the little tear drop trailer. The reality of her present life made her feel cold inside, yet her hand felt warm on the cool leather.

She had some very personal things in the valise. The green silk kimono and Chinese shoes were presents from Howard, her first husband. Although they had been divorced since 1931, she still had a special feeling in her heart for these things and the children she had bore him. Many of her things she had purchased from the money she made as a taxi dancer. Each item had a story and Marie remembered each one with photographic clarity.

Cheefo, China was a port of call for the American Navy. The "China Sailors" were free to set up households and become a part of the local scene. In the old Navy, it was "Once a China sailor, always a China sailor." Marie worked as a taxi dancer in a nightclub owned by White Russians. She would dance with sailors for ten cents a dance. With a little imagination, she could get a lot of tickets from the sailors. On good days, she made at least $5.00 American. She liked the social life but didn't like to "dance" with all of the sailors, many who were over taxed with alcohol. There was an occasional confrontation with one of the women the sailors were living with. This was always an uncomfortable situation, but she endured the life with a positive attitude that some day she would leave the place. She liked the Chinese and their ancient society. The areas that were frequented by sailors were isolated from the ancient traditions.

Marie liked to live in the ethnic Chinese district because it reminded her of Mother Russia. The residents upheld the old traditions and ways that were slowly giving way to western ways. Marie befriended a young Chinese girl that was completely absorbed in the old way. They would take tea together and discuss their cultures. Fan Ying, which meant "breath of flowers," couldn't walk without help because she had her feet bound since she was a small child. The ancient art of foot binding caused the feet to remain the size they were as an infant. The reason for women binding their feet went deeper than fashion and reflected the role of women in Chinese society. It was necessary in China for a woman to have bound feet in order to achieve a good life and have endless beauty. Marie thought she would complain, but they continued to share their stories in their limited English accented by Russian and Chinese without an explanation or complaint.

Howard was stationed on a destroyer anchored in Cheefo harbor about a mile off shore. At night and on weekends, the sailors would put lights on a small flat barge anchored alongside the ship. They had a jukebox and they would serve cokes to their guests. Several of the young ladies would swim out to the ship and dance with the sailors. Marie liked to swim and joined the crowd one Sunday afternoon. Howard and Marie danced the afternoon away. They fell instantly in love and he would spend hours of his off duty time with her.

The bubble of old memories collapsed as she heard Lyle returning from his second night of "checkers" at the store. She quickly put her suitcase under the bed. Lyle had threatened many times to throw it away. Before she closed the suitcase, she felt the warmth of the silk gown and remembered the first time she wore it. It seemed like an eternity.

Lyle was pacing up and down on the fourth floor of the Good Samaritan Hospital in Lexington. The maternity waiting room was empty on this Thursday night. It was a little past midnight and he wanted to be in bed. Why couldn't Marie start labor in the daytime? His daughter Ruth was born during the day. He had taken a few hours off from his job in Detroit to see Anna and Ruth after she was born. He hated the smell of antiseptic and the hustle and bustle of something he didn't understand. He smoked and smoked until he was a little dizzy from the strong "store bought" smokes. Marie hadn't taken the time to roll some Buglers and he had to buy cigarettes.

He looked at his watch and fob and placed it on the table next to him. He picked it up and put it on the windowsill as he looked out at the lights of Lexington. He really liked the watch and fob since he had traded for it a couple of months ago. The lights reminded him of working in Montgomery, Alabama shortly after he left Anna and Ruth. He helped install the first gaslights in the city. It was hard work and he didn't enjoy it very much. The pay was low and the hours long, but he liked the nightlife of Montgomery, especially the Cloverdale district. He heard a lot about Mexico from some of the veterans of the Mexican war. He left as soon as he could get his passport in order. He felt like he was floating in a cloud as his mind drifted from the smell of a hospital to happy times in his life.

The Mexican people liked Lyle because he was quiet and easy going. He could live very cheaply and he liked the long afternoon siestas. The stores would close from 1:00 pm in the afternoon until 4:30 pm. This was siesta time and everyone would take his or her afternoon siesta. They then reopened their stores and would close after 10:00 pm. It was a good system to get people out of the heat of the day and allow the body to be in rhythm and contented with the lazy and laid back ways of Mexico. Lyle loved it because no one questioned his loafing days as his wife did. This gave Lyle plenty of chance to seek his pleasures with the very friendly local women. They all liked "El Gringo Simpatico." He longed for those wonderful, loving days again. He wished he had stayed in Mexico.

A man in doctor's dress broke his daydream. Lyle was supposed to sign the admission papers and provide a cash deposit for the hospital. Marie was in the pre-delivery room and in extreme pain. The hospital needed permission to give anesthetic so the pain would be bearable. The doctor's choice was "twilight sleep." Lyle only knew it cost extra and wouldn't approve it. The doctor tried to explain how painful it would be but Lyle wouldn't hear any of it.

As dawn approached, he could hear Marie scream with the pain of childbirth. He was callous to the noise and was unhappy that she had gotten pregnant and less than willing to sit there and wait for the babe to be born.

The doctor came back into the waiting room.

"I am going to administer the drug whether you like it or not. I won't charge you for the use of the anesthetic," the doctor said.

Lyle reluctantly gave his approval and finished filling out the papers. He returned them to the nurse and she quickly left. A short time later, the cries died out. Lyle was exhausted and sat down in a chair for a little nap. It only seemed like minutes when a nurse awakened him and asked if he wanted to see his new, twelve-pound, healthy son. He jumped up and followed the nurse down the hall. The early morning sun was beginning to fill the room.

The watch and fob remained on the windowsill and sparkled in the August, Kentucky sunrise. The tick, tick of the Hamilton was the only noise in the room. The fob hung lazily over the side of the window ledge. An old janitor happened by to clean the waiting room. It smelled of stale smoke and cigarettes. He saw the watch from across the room. He stared and couldn't believe his eyes. Was it true or were his eyes playing tricks on him? He hurried to the window and tenderly picked up the watch and fob. He examined it carefully and realized it was the watch that was given to him by his Brother Elks for 50 years of membership in the lodge. He thought it was gone forever after his son had stolen most of his valuables and left for the army. Inside was a small inscription: "To Jude Wade for your 50 years of faithful service." He listened to the rhythmic tick of the movement and put it in his watch pocket. It fit perfectly because the pocket was worn to fit and the watch felt happy and secure with someone who loved and cared. He held the elks tooth fob between his fingers and thanked God he had found his watch at last.

He would wonder now and then how watch how the watch ended up on the windowsill. Today, August 9th, 1934 was his last day of work. Monday he would begin his long awaited retirement. Since his wife died and his son had robbed him and left home, he had little left except memories. Finding the watch had made him a very happy man. He stared to whistle as he worked his rounds. He hadn't felt that special, warm inner glow for years. He checked the fob and watch again to make sure it wasn't a dream and walked out of the waiting room forever.

CHAPTER THREE

The Trail

Early fall, Southern Kentucky

Much-needed rain pelted the little tear drop trailer and cooled the sweltering countryside. The raindrops were a mixture of mud and water. The path to the bathrooms was a muddy river of rocks and dead leaves. This was the first time it rained in over a month and dust had collected on the tree leaves. The long spell of very dry weather mixed with the rain made it seem like it was raining mud.

You could hear the tear drop creak like an old dry boat when the joints expanded from moisture. The top of the tear drop was made of quarter inch plywood and covered in muslin cloth. Lyle painted the top with inside aluminum paint and finished the interior with forty pound cut shellac. The top paint would run and streak after any rain and leave sparkling bits of silver residue on the ground. The dry weather caused several leaks that needed to be repaired before it could be moved on the trail to the next camp.

Wind blew bits of moisture and mud in the roof vent as the trailer rocked gently to the cadence of the storm. The inside door hook was broken and, as usual, Lyle didn't fix it. The door was well made but still rattled with each flurry of wind and was only held from the wind by a small door handle.

Marie could see the faint glow of daylight through the window over her head. The rustle of leaves from the Catawba tree made an eerie sound. The tree provided good shade in the morning but only partial afternoon shade. Now Marie was afraid it would fall on the tiny trailer. The rain started to fall in sheets. A strong gust of wind shook the tear drop. She could hear the roll of distant thunder like far-away drums all beating at the same time without cadence. There was no insulation on the walls or teardrop shaped roof. The rain sounded like it was hitting her head.

She covered her head and the babe and tried to think about anything but the rain and wind. In her half sleep, Marie thought of the little cabin her father had in Siberia. She could picture him like he was ready to speak in his bass voice.

Andrea was a large man, well over six feet, with a jet-black handle bar moustache. His hands were large for his frame because of the hard farm work he did as a child. He had jet-black hair and a beautiful full moustache.

He married Anna Metaev, the daughter of a silk merchant who worked with her father. His earlier work, as a trader in Ashkhabad, Turkistan, required Andrea to speak several languages. He spoke Farsi like a native. A slight Arabic accent could be detected in his Russian. Much of the trading was done with Iran, a short thirty miles from Ashkhabad on the old silk route to China. Andrea had a beautiful bass voice and enjoyed singing old ballads as he worked or amused himself. He liked to play the Balalaika and sing to its very old three-string pitch.

Marie and her father would travel all day from Russia in their four-wheeled wooden sleigh to the gentle slopes of the Barguizen Mountains. During the winter, the wheels were folded and the sleigh became an ice surrey. Andrea made an attractive ornate top with decorative fringes and little bells that jingled. There were fitted canvas curtains in case of blustery weather. In Siberia, one could never trust the weather because it would change so rapidly. There was a large bearskin rug to cover your lap while the horse pranced on his well-known route.

Boris, the horse, was happier when his harness was trimmed with little bells that tinkled to his rhythmic gait. Boris had been with the family a long time and was always happy to pull the sleigh and strike his familiar trot. He was named after an unpleasant co-worker whose face favored the horse.

Marie loved the old horse and would give him sugar lumps when they stopped to rest. She saved an apple for the end of the journey and Boris knew it. It was evident he loved Marie because he would make happy horse sounds when she scratched his muzzle and fed him the apple.

Irkutsk is about thirty miles northeast of Lake Baikal. Beautiful pine and hardwood forests are carpeted with a rich bed of grass, flowers and lichen. Forests surround most of the lake. Gentle rolling hills and steep mountains complement the landscape to make it one of the prettiest places in all of the Russias. Andrea was assigned to the local Trans-Siberian railroad station in Irkutsk. He was glad to leave the arid desert country of Ashkhabad, where Marie was born. Marie's mother Anna was born in Penza, but they never went back to visit because of the Russian political climate.

The political exiles built small, decorated wooden cottages with sculptured decorations outside to set them apart from the other houses. Marie's family lived in one of these houses, not far from the railroad station and the central market.

Gold was discovered in the hills surrounding Lake Baikal in the middle of the eighteenth century. Many small claims were established with cabins and lean-tos built on the diggings. The gold was limited and the gold strike ended almost as soon as it started. Andrea bought a small plot of land with an old miners cabin from a family in the village of Listuyanka, near the Angara River.

Marie thought she was standing on the edge of the world when she gazed over the pristine forest and lake. She thought of early spring in May and June. Plentiful rain fed the lush forests and exceptional wildflowers grew everywhere. The warm seasons were so short that the flora and fauna took full advantage of beautiful days to display their myriad of colors, sizes and shapes.

Andrea would unhitch Boris and let him graze on the tender new grass after the trip from Irkutsk. It was said that there were no roads in Siberia, only directions and time. Andrea knew that feeling very well. When they visited his cabin, time wasn't important.

Marie was excited after the trip and would run to play in the woods. The little cabin was no more than a one room lean-to which was used by the miners of the late eighteen hundreds to dig a little gold from the semi-open pits and shallow mines. It still had some of the decorative lace curtains so common in those days.

Several times a year they made the trip so Andrea could pursue his hobby of "gold mining" and Marie could enjoy the beauty of nature. He found very little but took great pleasure in showing off the fine gold from the mine to his friends at the train station.

The mountains touched the edge of Lake Baikal, "The Blue Eye Of Siberia." The name was derived from the azure blue color of the water. It was the largest fresh water lake in the world and one of the deepest.

Marie's bed had an ancient wooden frame and a mattress stuffed with silver lichen from the forest. It was warm and comfortable sitting close to the old stove on the north wall. She would go to sleep listening to the gentle rain on the rough wooden siding.

For a moment, in her half sleep, she thought she was back in the comfort of the old cabin, covered with a warm afghan. She awoke with a start and listened to the rain as she tried to gather her senses after dreaming so vividly about the old country.

"The babe," as Lyle called Leone, was sound asleep between them. This was his seventh day at "home" and Marie was still very tired from the fifteen hour ordeal of birth. Seven days in the hospital provided some rest but Lyle wouldn't help with anything.

Marie would get up early every morning and wash the diapers before he awoke. There was an old clothesline tied between the Catawba tree and the back fence. She used it to dry Leone's diapers. She tried hard to have his meals fixed but she was so very tired. One day she baked biscuits and cooked a small roast Juanita brought to the trailer.

They kept ice in the old wooden icebox in the back of the trailer so Leone's milk wouldn't spoil. Marie would have to lift the heavy rear opening and secure it with an old pole to get the food ready for the meal. This morning she didn't feel like getting up because she had been awake most of the night keeping the baby quiet so Lyle could sleep.

Her incision was starting to hurt and she needed to see a doctor. It was impossible because Lyle hadn't paid the balance of the bill for the doctor or hospital. Lyle said he would take her to a druggist if it got too bad.

Leone was a large 12-pound baby at birth. Lyle didn't like to call him Leone because he didn't want him to have the family name. Leon was his father's name and he didn't want it used.

"He is half Russian and should not be called by an old American family name." Lyle said.

"I named him in honor of your father because I like and respect him." Marie said.

She thought it would please Lyle, but of course, it didn't.

She could barely see the birth certificate when the nurse brought it in for her to complete, but she saw Lyle wasn't listed as the father. Lyle hadn't put his name as the father because he didn't want the responsibility of caring for a wife and child. He changed his mind because of the strong objections of Marie and the doctor. He quibbled about the name but the doctor was very firm. In Kentucky, it was the mother's choice to name the child.

She gave him Lyle's last name even though they weren't married so Leone wouldn't have to grow up without a last name. Little did she know but Lyle sweet-talked the nurse into a different first name. Leone wouldn't know what it was for many years to come.

Lyle awoke with a start, as a clap of thunder caused by distant lightning echoed through the countryside. He was deathly afraid of wind and rain. Lyle and his father were caught in a tornado when he was a child in Cresse, Michigan. His father, Leon, had led his family to a shallow ditch behind the outhouse just in time to watch the roof leave the house and scatter over the neighborhood. His Brother Earl was so frightened that he didn't recover for many months. He was older than Lyle by a few years but smaller in size. He worshiped Lyle and followed him everywhere. Earl was slow in speaking and didn't do well in school. In a few years, he would have to go to the special school in Lansing. Little did he know that his future would end while he was trying to act like Lyle, catching a ride on the East Bound train.

Lyle was covered with mud and debris from the storm and by the terrible force of the tornado. Lyle would never forget the helpless feeling he had when the wind tried to pick him up. Every time the wind made a noise, he would shudder at the memories of the terrible storm and its aftermath.

He told Marie to get up and fix him something to eat. She wasn't able to do anything except feed Leone and change his clothes. Lyle became angry, got up and started to get dressed.

"I'll go to Carlos and Juanita, they will feed me even if you don't," said Lyle.

"Yes they will feed you, if you pay for it. We have enough expense with the new baby," Marie said.

He dressed in his usual manner, with vest and slick stripped pants. He was angry because he had "lost" his watch and fob to some ignorant janitor in the hospital. He had to use the one his father gave him with the small gold knife as the fob. It was a beautiful old railroad watch, except he had to wind it with a key instead of the stem.

"I'll get another watch with a nice tooth, just wait and see," Lyle mumbled to himself.

He straightened the mirror and slicked his hair to his liking. He added wax, trimmed his little moustache and left in a sulk. He slammed the little door and left. A shower of water drops misted over Marie and Leone from the moisture on the ceiling.

El Mercado opened early to catch the morning traffic and road weary campers. They served huevos rancheros (ranch style eggs), a favorite of Lyle's.

Marie didn't like Mexican food, partially because Lyle liked it and partially because she didn't like the spicy flavor. In the old country, Currie was the main spice with salt the most popular. Most of the meat was lamb, which Lyle wouldn't eat. She thought about the next meal but was too tired to plan, let alone cook. She never understood why Lyle was so dominant and selfish. She tried her very best taking care of both a baby and Lyle. But Lyle was a full time job by himself.

Marie rested on the little bed with her new son sleeping at her side.

"Lyle or no one else is going to harm this baby!" Marie said out loud.

Before she left the hospital, she looked at every part, including the fingers and toes, to make sure he was complete. So many babies were deformed in the old country. He was wrapped in a pink outfit because it was all she had.

The inside of the tear drop was painted with several coats of shellac, which was badly stained with layers of nicotine. She gazed at the ceiling and watched tiny beads of humidity form. They looked like golden drops of paint as they picked up the nicotine residue. She asked Lyle not to smoke inside because of Leone.

"He better get used to it, he has a long way to go under my roof," Lyle said, laughing.

Lyle's reflection in the mirror still lingered in her mind's eye, as she watched tiny golden rivers of moisture run down the mirror to the little shelf. The tinted drops caused a repulsive, distorted image of Lyle in the mirror. It made make Lyle look so strange, like someone she didn't know, and it frightened her. The old mirror seemed to attract water like a magnet as she fell into a deep sleep, wondering if the gold from Andre's mine looked like this when it was wet.

Marie awoke and the rain had stopped. She opened the door and looked outside. She saw Lyle get some tools out of the car. Lyle began scraping the outside of the trailer in preparation for painting. She knew they wouldn't be here very long because he was fixing the leaks in preparation for the next trail and camp.

He had plans to go to Tennessee. He wanted to meet a man that was developing an oil additive to stop vehicle engines from knocking and burning oil. From the way he talked about him he was an old acquaintance, but she didn't know his name. She knew it was another scheme in the making. They still had some bandages from the last one. It seemed that Lyle lived from one scheme to another. He did anything to make easy money without working hard.

The old 28 Pontiac used a lot of oil. Besides, he might be able to get a new line to make some money. He heard about an oil additive from Pug Andrews but had never seen it. Lyle scraped, patched and painted so the roof would weather another storm. He was very good at what he did, if and when he did it. Marie could never understand why he didn't use waterproof paint except it was twice as expensive.

She got up to change and feed Leone. He was having problems with his stomach digesting milk. She had mixed a solution of Carnation milk, water and sugar to see if he could hold it in his stomach. Leone would drink it hungrily and then tried to throw it up. She tried to talk to

Lyle about it but he said it was in her mind and there was nothing wrong with the babe.

"Stop bothering me and clean up the trailer."

Marie bit her tongue and tried to make up the little bed. When Lyle left, she would talk to Juanita about her stitches and Leone's problem drinking milk. Maybe she would have some ideas that would help her because Lyle would do nothing. When he had his mind made up, come hell or high water, he was going to do it.

Lyle filled two old, tin water containers he carried on the running board for the car's radiator. He finished loading his tools and some clothes in the back. He usually took out the rear seat so he could use it as a trunk. The outside rear trunk had to be removed so he could tow a trailer. He raised the hood and checked the oil; it was empty. He had some used oil he kept for an emergency. He put three quarts in the old engine. The battery was quite often dead, so he put the crank in the slot and turned the engine. It coughed to life with a cloud of blue smoke surrounding the back of the car. The engine finally settled down and started to run the best it could. Lyle put water in the radiator, closed the hood and put the crank away. After washing his hands and combing his hair, he left the camp without saying a word to Marie. He was on a mission and nothing could stop him. He did bring in money and Marie rarely asked where he made it. He took some cash with him so he was probably going to buy something to make money.

Marie managed to get up and tend to Leone and put on some clothes. She went to the bathroom, avoiding the muddy path. She bathed Leone, changed his diaper and laid him on an old but clean blanket. Marie washed and straightened her hair and put it in a large bun. She then started back up the path to see Juanita. She was glad Lyle wasn't there to tell her how to tend to the baby. He was always trying to tell her how to do things. Sometimes he was correct but this time she was right. Marie had given birth to two children before this one. One thing she knew very well was how to take care of babies. Leone was hungry, but he couldn't keep much in his stomach.

She found Juanita happily making tortillas in the small kitchen in the back of the house. She was always happy to see Marie. Juanita took the baby and rocked it gently in her arms. She loved children and always talked about how she would love to have one. On more than one occasion, she almost told Marie about the "little one" in Mexico, but thought better of it. She saw Marie was tired and worried.

"Juanita I am worried about the baby. He likes cow's milk but it doesn't like him."

Juanita called Carlos, who listened to the story.

"Ah yes, Senora Marie, I think I know what the problem is," Carlos said in broken English.

He left for the front of the store and brought back a bottle of milk.

"I think this is a better kind of milk for the little bambino," he said.

Juanita heated the special milk, filled Leone's bottle and fed him. Leone drank like he was starved, burped once and went sound asleep. Marie couldn't believe it. Leone was sleeping with no problems.

"Carlos, what kind of milk is it?" Marie asked.

"It was from Consuela, our pet goat. Leche de Cabra is the best thing for a baby that cannot drink cow's milk. Maybe in a few years he will grow out of it, but for now we have plenty of milk for the bambina," Carlos explained.

"Is the milk very expensive?" asked Marie.

Juanita said that it was not more expensive to her because she was their friend and could have it for nothing.

"It is several times more expensive than cow's milk, but we have plenty," Carlos added.

All Lyle would let her buy was canned Carnation milk. She was worried about how she was going to get milk with no money.

She had a long talk with Juanita about her problems.

"I think I have an answer. Come with me."

With Leone in her arms, they walked to the back part of the camp where "The Basket Weaver" lived. After the old camper's wife died, he lived alone in the untidy heap of a tarpaper shack and an old tear drop. He had a little awning with a small faded sign that read, "Home Made artifacts for sale." He had that timeless bronzed look from too many days in the sun and too little time to do the things he wanted.

His name was Harold Fletcher and he was a veteran of the Spanish American War and would often talk about the charge up San Juan Hill. He had received a powder flash burn in the face. His face was scared black and blue with only one good eye to make his trinkets. His Spanish was very good and he and Juanita got along very well.

Harold liked fresh tortillas and Juanita brought him enough for a mid-morning snack. He was sincerely grateful for anything she did to help. She spoke to him about Marie's problem. She needed to make some money to buy things for the baby. He said he would help if Marie would be willing to learn an ancient Indian art.

Marie readily agreed because she didn't want to be so dependent on Lyle. Juanita agreed to watch Leone as Marie learned the new trade. She listened intently as Harold told her how and why Indians made useful things out of pine straw.

He gave her a small basket and asked her to fill it with good dried pine straw. Soon, Marie had a basketful because they were so plentiful. Harold made her place each straw on a flat board and taught her how to examine the straws. He told her to discard the broken ones and place the others in a line. He then showed her a beautiful little whiskbroom made from pine straws.

"Marie, I am going to teach you how to make brooms, brushes and knick-knacks out of pine straw. The material costs nothing and the roll of wire is free. You can make hundreds of brooms with the wire," Harold said.

He continued his instructions throughout the day. By the end of the day, Marie had made six whiskbrooms and several little brushes. He gave her an old pair of Western Auto pliers to bend and cut the wire.

Marie was so proud of herself that she almost ran to show Juanita what she had made. Juanita bought three of the whiskbrooms and said Marie could set up a little place in the store and sell them when Lyle was away. It was Marie's answer to her prayers. At last, she had a way! She had many plans hidden deep in her mind. She could get all the little things she needed for herself and the baby without Lyle's help.

Lyle planned to be gone for several days and Marie worked very hard at making her pine straw brooms and knick-knacks. By the end of the third day, she had made $22.50. Now she could pay for the things Leone needed. If Lyle didn't come back by tomorrow, she would ask

Juanita to take her into town so she could buy some baby clothes for Leone.

She was tired of him wearing "hand me down" pink outfits. The couple across the dirt road had a girl and gave Marie several girl outfits and a lot of diapers. Lyle hadn't bought "the babe" anything, and she was glad to have any clothes for the baby. When she came home from the hospital, Juanita had given her a package with baby soap, oil and powder.

She was happy with her new found skills and ability to make her own money. She had to hide the money so Lyle wouldn't take it away. Marie carefully pinned the little roll of money into her bra and felt good about it. Thanks to Juanita and her newfound friend Harold, she had a little financial security. She spent 10¢ on a soft drink and some soda crackers from the barrel. She liked soda crackers because of the salt. There was nothing like crackers and soft drinks in Russia. Her first taste of a soft drink was when she got to China and an American sailor bought her a coke.

She put a little change in her pocket so she could buy something tomorrow. Before Harold and Juanita helped her, she had no money of her own. It felt good to feel 2 silver quarters in her pocket. It gave her some confidence she badly needed.

Harold asked her to come back when she had time and he would teach her how to make baskets. She hoped she would have time but she had to sneak away when Lyle wasn't home. She had never worked with her hands, except a short while as a waitress, and she loved the feeling of making something that was her original idea.

In Russia, her mother taught her how to sew and make things for the house. She was out of practice because she never had time to do anything except take care of Lyle and Leone. She went to the trailer and carefully stored the items she made with her personal stuff. She was physically tired but emotionally very pleased with herself. It was the first time since she had come to America that she was able to think for herself and it felt good.

She bathed Leone and fed him some goat's milk and they both went to sleep. She slept all night without Lyle bothering her or Leone waking with a hungry cry. She was so glad that she had the goat's milk.

It was like Leone was a different child. He was happy and bubbly like she hoped he would be when she was carrying him through difficult times.

She awoke early the next morning and her hands felt like two large numb things stuck on the ends of her arms. They hurt so bad she could cry, but it would be a happy cry. At long last, she was ready to go out in the world and do something worthwhile.

She got Leone ready and took him to be with Juanita and went to Harold's for some more practice. Harold gave her some udder cream and menthol cream to rub on her hands and they got better as the day progressed. During the last several days, he had been making some very special pattern molds to make baskets. The molds were carefully carved pieces of wood matching the lower and upper pattern of a basket. He used some seasoned willow and started to weave a beautiful basket around the molds. Harold was a practiced, patient teacher.

He showed her how to alter the weave and stagger the design to make each basket look different. She had strong hands with a good design imagination. Very soon, she was weaving the willow around the delicate moulds with precision. Harold complimented her on the wonderful job she was doing. An experienced basket weaver with good material could make six or seven baskets a day. Marie finished two by the end of the day. The following day, she would return and learn how to cut and cure the willow. She was so proud of herself she started to sing an old Russian folk song. Harold knew the tune and joined in. They both had a good laugh. He gave her the pattern molds and asked her to come back the next day and he would teach her more basket patterns.

Marie was very happy as she walked back to the little tear drop trailer, with Leone on her hip and the molds and baskets in her free hand. She had just reached the trailer when she heard the old Pontiac coming down the rough dirt road. It would be "hell to pay" when she told him about the baskets. She would not tell him about the brooms or the money she had hidden. She sat the baskets on the picnic table by the trailer and waited for him to get out of the car.

He bounced out of the car with a wide, happy smile on his face and chucked her under the chin, which she hated. She felt like he was petting a dog. He was very happy because he had "struck" a good deal with a farmer in Ford, Kentucky. He saw the baskets and asked Marie about them. She told him a short story about Harold and the baskets. He knew Harold from trips to the store and he liked him. To her surprise and bewilderment, he liked the idea.

"Now you can help with the expenses and it won't be so hard on me," he said.

She felt the money tucked away safely in her bra. It was still there. She knew Leone would always have his goat's milk to help him grow and build strong bones. She was so busy with all the things happening, she had forgotten about her pain. She asked Lyle to take her to a doctor and see about them. She told him about the terrible discomfort she was having with her stitches.

"Get in the car and I'll take you to a doctor," Lyle said.

Surprise of all surprises, he must have done well to be so nice.

She got in the old Pontiac with some difficulty and held Leone in her lap. Lyle jerked the clutch and got the old Pontiac going. They turned onto old highway 27 and headed toward Nicholasville. They stopped at the Rexall drug store in the center of the town and Lyle went in to see the druggist.

An old druggist in a soiled white smock came to the car and helped Marie out and into the "doctors office" in the back room.

Lyle sat at the lunch counter and ordered chocolate malt, one of his favorites. He thought he heard Marie's voice but ignored it and continued drinking his malt. He liked to talk and struck up a conversation with some men about President Roosevelt and the "New Deal." You could hear the same conversations all over the nation. The working class of people had little faith in the government since the banks had failed in '29. It was a typical conversation, except Lyle was trying to be the expert and show off in front of the men. The conversation went on and on until the druggist helped Marie to a seat.

The druggist held up an open hand with fingers outstretched, indicating five dollars. Lyle opened his little snap wallet and grudgingly gave him five dollars. The druggist told Lyle to buy some Vaseline with carbolic acid to help with possible infection and aspirin for the pain.

"Your wife should have been here sooner; the stitches needed to come out several days ago," the druggist said.

Lyle didn't like him at all because he was trying to make him look bad in front of the people at the lunch counter.

"We'll talk about this later," Lyle said to Marie in a hateful tone.

"Well, Marie, are you happy with your stitches out?" Lyle asked.

"It hurt a lot and the table was not very clean. The baby was very hard to handle and the druggist had to put him in a little basket so he wouldn't be in the way."

She wanted to rest, but Lyle insisted she have something to eat. He continued to talk with great gusto about how he would solve the economic problems of America if HE were president. He did this so the people would forget how the druggist had embarrassed him. He didn't like to be embarrassed and lose face for any reason. Lyle loved only himself and his ego was the most important thing in his life.

She ordered a bacon, lettuce and tomato sandwich with a fountain coke. She rarely had a chance to eat out, so she got what she wanted. She loved fountain coke in a frosted glass and the crisp taste of bacon with lettuce and tomato on toast. She had no way to make toast except to fry the bread, and that didn't taste anything like store-made toast. But all this, together with mayonnaise, was the best food she had tasted in a long time.

Lyle never took her out. He always went by himself while she was pregnant.

"You and your fat belly make me feel uncomfortable," he said.

She didn't worry about anything as she balanced Leone in one arm and happily ate with the other hand.

"He wouldn't even watch Leone when I went back to the office," she thought to herself as she ate her food.

As a matter of fact, Lyle had never held him. She wondered why he wouldn't hold such a pretty little blond haired baby.

"It would be hell to pay later," she thought as she ate every crumb of the sandwich, slurped the coke in the bottom of the glass and then crunched some of the ice in her mouth.

Lyle paid the bill for the lunch and reluctantly bought the items recommended by the druggist. He didn't want to lose face in front of his "audience." He tipped his hat and they left the store. Lyle went ahead and was already in the car as Marie struggled with the baby and the heavy car door. Fortunately, the battery was charged enough to start it and they left in a cloud of blue smoke. All the way home Lyle was very quiet, as if thinking of something to say, but he said nothing until they turned into the campground.

"Tomorrow we start getting things ready to hit the road. We have to make some money because all the money is going out with nothing coming in. The area has dried up for gold and silver and they have the story on our bandages. I bought a good supply of goods today, but we must be out of this state so we can make it and sell it. I'll be glad to leave this state. I have had nothing but poor luck and not a lot of time to loaf" Lyle said with an angry look on his face.

He stopped and got out, leaving Marie in the car. She had to manage the baby and step down from the high running board.

As she reached the house, Lyle walked by her and back out toward the car.

"I'm going to the store to settle up so we can leave in the morning," he said.

Marie took her time and fed the baby and settled in for a good night's rest. It was about dusk when she finally got to lay down. She thought about the wonderful "BLT" and fountain coke she had.

The mayonnaise taste still lingered even after she had her last cigarette of the day. She only brushed her teeth when she took a bath. She liked smoking, but Lyle had insisted she learn how to smoke home-made Bugler cigarettes because they were cheaper.

She worried about "taking to the road" again because of Leone. How was Lyle going to manage all the extra stops and expense? She felt a little better when she touched the bills she had hidden in her clothing as she drifted into a sound sleep. "This money is for Leone, and Lyle will never see it," she thought.

Morning came early as Lyle was preparing to "hitch and go." This is a common phrase was used to indicate that the travelers were "hitting the road." Marie was sad to leave. She had made friends with Juanita, Harold and other campers. She didn't like to be in a different place each day. She wanted the stability of a home to raise Leone in and ensure he had everything he needed. The "road" provided nothing but miles and miles of nothing but miles and miles. She liked the rustic setting of El Mercado and the neatness of the campsite. More often than not, Lyle would pick the cheapest place without bathrooms or any other conveniences. Things would have to change and she would ensure they did, even if it meant a major "blowup" with Lyle and his preconceived ideas. She thought, "Lyle is such an empty man and full of nothing but himself."

Lyle backed up the old Pontiac to the trailer and was trying to get the hitch in place. He was using a string of profanities that would turn the air blue, but they didn't seem to help. Juanita and Carlos were walking down the path to visit before the rig pulled out. Juanita gave Marie a box for El Bambino while Carlos went to help Lyle "hook up."

"Here is a small lunch for you when you got hungry," said Juanita.

Marie lifted the heavy back section and put the things away. Lyle had put some ice in the old chest and she put the goat's milk next to the ice. She was glad Juanita had brought her some milk because it would put off telling Lyle until the "timing" was right. Juanita gave Marie another small box.

"Open it Marie, it is for you," she said.

Marie pulled the brown meat wrapping paper off. It was a camera! She was so surprised she couldn't hold back and gave Juanita a hug.

"This little box camera is so you can always remember your baby with pictures."

"It isn't new, but the Brownie 620 Box Camera takes very good pictures," she said.

Marie was so grateful and she showed it to Lyle. He didn't say anything but she knew what he was thinking—more money for film. Regardless of what he thought, she was going to take as many pictures as she could.

She carefully put it in the car and waited for Lyle to check the car and fill it with water. He used some of the mixed water glass and black pepper in the radiator and it seemed to be working because it only took a little water.

Marie looked back and saw Juanita and Carlos waving as they slowly pulled out of the camp. It had been nice and she was going to miss it. She would have to wait and see what tomorrow would bring. She held Leone tightly as they turned on the hard road and headed south.

Chapter Four

The Journey

Late summer, Heading South

Lyle turned the old Pontiac right on old highway 25 and headed south, with the tear drop in tow. He finally managed to get it in third gear and settled into a towing pace of about thirty-five miles per hour. He felt like he was free at last! Lyle was a true vagabond and loved the independence of the open road. After he left his wife Anna in 1916, he was never able to settle in one place. He liked the adventure that took place at every turn of the road and with every new friend he met. The old Pontiac used so much water that he had to drive by the temperature gauge. The slow speed, adding water, and frequent stops for Leone made for a slow day. If they traveled 100 miles a day, they were very fortunate.

They rounded a large sweeping curve and workers had just finished installing a new Burma Shave sign. Lyle and Marie both loved Burma Shave signs and slogans.

LATHER WAS USED BY DANIEL BOONE HE LIVED 100 YEARS TOO SOON Burma Shave!

They waved at the workers as they passed. Everyone seemed to like Burma Shave signs. It passed the time and was fun on a trip, scouting and reading new and old signs. Burma Shave signs had been in vogue since 1927, when they had only two sayings. In part, Marie had learned to read English from these signs. She had no idea who Daniel Boone was, but she laughed anyway.

Marie put Leone in a makeshift crib in the rear, where a seat should have been. For practical reasons, Lyle removed the rear seat in every car he owned. The large space could be used as a truck if needed.

She found an old wicker basket in the camp dump and lined it with some of the muslin cloth Lyle had used on the tear drop roof. Leone fell asleep as soon as the car started to move.

It was Marie's job to read the map, road signs and other instructions so Lyle wouldn't get lost and could concentrate on his driving. He had almost no sense of direction, while Marie could find north in the dark on a rainy night. It was important they find a campground before dark because the old Pontiac had only one working headlight, no taillight, nor did the trailer have a red reflector like the law required. On top of that, Lyle couldn't see well enough to drive at night and Marie did not know how to drive.

With the advent of affordable automobiles, a new trend had developed in the American culture: The Road Trip. The flood of travelers forced on the road by economic conditions was staggering. Traveling became a way of life for numerous unfortunate people. Lyle and Marie fit well into this new cross section of American life: The Road People.

Travelers were weary of stopping every few miles to ask directions. The first road maps were given to customers by gasoline companies to increase business and promote customer loyalty. Travelers soon expected free maps. State and local governments promoted maps in hopes that the travelers would remain a few days more in their towns and spend money. Marie loved to read the town names and attractions because it gave her a much better understanding of English. Lyle and Marie had a copy of the first road atlas, printed in 1924. It illustrated old roads, campgrounds and trails. The new service station maps didn't show the back roads, only the main thoroughfares.

The Rand McNally auto road atlas was a good way to find directions and roads because the pages were in color and easy to read. Each state had a section so you could read about history, laws and most important, campsites. Lyle bought it from a fellow camper for a quarter. There were numerous handwritten comments in it about roads, camps and good places to do business. It was a valuable tool for the working traveler.

Hootentown, Kentucky was about thirty miles from Richmond, where they needed to stop for gas. Lyle knew of a nice place to park behind a Gulf station. Gasoline was 15¢ per gallon and oil was 25¢ a quart. Bulk oil was pumped from a large drum into a glass quart bottle, with a metal pour spout. Most oil came in thirty weight, which satisfied most cars of the day. Drum oil had a paraffin base to stand the pressure and temperature of an automobile engine.

Lyle used to carry oil bottles and ask the station owners if he could have used oil to put in his old car. On infrequent occasions, Lyle would change the oil and keep the used oil to put back in the car. He hoped someday to have nice car as his father Leon did. Both Leon and his brothers favored Franklins. They had the first air-cooled automobile engines, which were very dependable, but more expensive than the Model-T Ford.

Lyle was a dreamer and would sometimes drift off into an elaborate fantasy where he had plenty of money, beautiful women and a new Franklin car. He had driven a Franklin many times. He hated to be disturbed from his fantasy, but he had to ask the manager if they could camp out back. He agreed and charged Lyle 50¢ for the night, which included the use of the toilet and the outside water faucet.

Lyle and other travelers liked Gulf stations because everything was clean. Some services were free even if you did not buy gasoline. They were advertised all over the east coast and Lyle was correct, they were good stations. Another reason Lyle liked them was they would fill the old Pontiac with water, check the tires and clean the windshield and no tip was required.

Lyle was not very free with his money. He liked money and would hoard and save as much as he could. He would hide money in various places to keep Marie from finding it. He thought about Marie and the baskets. She could help a lot with the expenses, but he would have to watch her closely to ensure she did not hide any money. It was all right for him to hide, he rationalized, because he was the main source of income.

He wanted Marie to help keep the diaries. It let her think only about what was in the book and not question him about what he did. Marie was not fooled by his actions, but did what he wanted to "keep the peace."

"It is important to get out of Kentucky as soon as we can." Lyle said.

Marie suspected it was because he owed a large hospital bill in Lexington and she didn't know what else.

"Marie, chart a course so we won't hit too many mountains and pass through Chattanooga."

He had to climb steep grades in first gear. The old car would forever boil over. Sometimes it took all day to cross one mountain. He did not have that kind of time because of his impending schedule.

She selected old highway 27 because it ran close to Fort Mountain like Lyle wanted. It was sometimes called Pennine, but Lyle liked the old Civil War names.

He pulled the rig into the back of the Gulf station and set up for the night. There was a nice grassy spot with signs of camper's holes. He was comfortable with his selection. He wanted to meet George and Betty in Spring City, Tennessee in five days. There was a nice quiet place to park at Fort Mountain. They needed a secluded area so they could make their "mixes" for the new line he was going to sell. Lyle had used the old farmer's barn before. He would ask the owners if he could rent it for a week or two.

The only reason the barn was standing was the payment collected for the Rock City advertisement painted on the roof. The company also painted the entire area around the sign. If the roof needed fixing where the sign was painted, it was repaired free of charge.

The old barn was one of Lyle's favorite out-of-the-way campgrounds. The main reason was that it was well hidden from anyone curious enough to see what was going on. There was fresh water from an old spring fed well and a good outside privy. The old barn was solid and didn't leak where the signs were painted. He needed a good open area under cover to work out the new product. There was room to pull the tear drop and car inside the barn so prying eyes could not see what they were doing.

He wished they had started earlier that day but at least they were "on the road." He left the car hooked up so they could get an early start in the morning. Today was a thirty-five mile day; perhaps tomorrow would be better, he thought. He hated to stop for any reason, but the babe and car needed constant attention. In the back of his mind, he wanted to be in Florida before cold weather. He wanted to see Key West and what was left of Flagler's folly, the railroad that was destroyed by the hurricane of 1928.

Lyle had trouble going to sleep that night. He thought about how he was going to make the trailer bigger to accommodate the babe. He knew Ruth and Jerry would be coming south for the winter. Ruth was Lyle's daughter by his first marriage to Anna, and Jerry was her husband. She was about a year older than Marie and this bothered Ruth. They usually came south with just enough money to make the trip and depended on Lyle for support. He didn't like Jerry because of his association with the Detroit mob. Jerry bragged about how things were in "the business" during prohibition. He was a large, pushy person of German decent with a large scar on his face from a knife fight. He liked to push people around, but didn't bother Ruth while Lyle was around. Ruth's right leg was stiff at the knee from some injury she received. The story was she had "slipped on the ice." The stiff leg made traveling uncomfortable. With the new babe, he would have to stop loaning them money, which he never got back, and make Jerry work for what he borrowed.

He often thought about his father, Leon. He expected to meet him somewhere in Florida this winter but he never knew when or where. He loved to see his dad, but it created another burden on Lyle. He was drawing the plans in his head for the trailer conversion as he drifted into a deep sleep.

Marie and Lyle got along best when they traveled. Marie hated to admit it, but she enjoyed traveling, although she yearned for a place of her own without wheels. Both were up early and pulled the rig around to get some gasoline before they started on the trip. Lyle bought Marie a 5¢ cup of coffee with real cream. They both enjoyed a fresh sweet roll and store coffee together. When Lyle was on the road he was a lot easier to get along with and was not so tight with his money.

With Leone settled in his makeshift crib, they started on the road. On schedule, he went to asleep.

The next two days were pleasant and they didn't have any problems with the car or tear drop. Lyle was happy and talked a lot about his plans. Marie didn't always believe him and sometimes didn't listen to him. When he caught her looking away when he was talking, he would use one of his favorite words–"Hark!" Lyle was in the habit of planning too much to accomplish in a short period time. He rarely got all the work finished that he started.

They traveled through Danville, Stanford and stopped at Eubank. Lyle decided to buy some gold because there were some old antebellum homes. Sometimes the people were older and needed money. They were easy prey for Lyle. They parked on the outskirts next to a cemetery early in the afternoon. Lyle unhitched and went to try his luck. As "luck" would have it, he never got started.

The local sheriff stopped him and asked Lyle what he was doing parked there. Lyle told him he was planning on buying some old scrap silver and gold in Eubank. He asked Lyle for his license to buy and sell. Lyle didn't have one so the sheriff escorted him back to the campsite. He was going to make them move but he saw Marie and Leone sitting on the trailer step. He told Lyle to be out before nine the next morning. This incident frightened Lyle so bad he had to rest the remainder of the day. He didn't like any dealing with police or officials.

They started early the next morning so the sheriff wouldn't stop to remind them to leave. For some unknown reason, Lyle was frightened of anything to do with police or the law. It was as if he was always looking over his shoulder. Both Lyle and Marie were hungry because they didn't take time to make breakfast. Marie had some goat's milk in the ice cooler which she gave to Leone for his breakfast.

Both Lyle and Marie like to stop at diners. They served good food and usually were cheaper. They could eat breakfast for less than a dollar. Lyle knew of a nice diner just inside the city limits of Burnside, close to Prospect Mountain. He remembered a large parking lot where they could park the car and trailer. Travelers had special places all over the south where they could be comfortable and out of sight from prying eyes. So many people had taken to the road that most towns were suspicious of strangers.

After a very good breakfast at the diner, with several cups of coffee, they started south on highway 27 heading for a campsite at Parkers Lake. Lyle had a lot of figuring to do when he got to Parkers Lake. He had to bring his dairy up to date so he knew where he stood with his money. He liked to keep up with all the things he had to buy for his new project.

Marie would check and cross check her figures with Lyle's. Some of the time, Marie would use her "Schoty" for the addition and subtraction. She called her old abacus her friend because it would never lie to her if she told it the truth. Marie was taught to use the abacus before she could read and write. She had carried her old Schoty with her all over the world. It was scratched and battered, but she could work magic with figures.

Abacus comes from the Greek word "abax," meaning a calculating table. It can be used to perform all sorts of mathematical calculations. Marie used it mostly for addition and subtraction. She knew how to divide and multiply, but fractions and square root calculations escaped her. It was well worn and had to be placed flat so the beads would not slide, causing an error.

The calculating tool was invented over 5,000 years ago. It had changed very little over the ages. Some modifications were made to handle all kinds of calculations. Marie loved to use it and show Lyle how fast she could add and subtract. She was much faster but often let him win to "keep the peace."

They drove at a steady pace, singing little songs together with Burma Shave Jingles. Lyle stopped at Parkers Lake while Marie went in and shopped for a few things for the evening meal. She bought Lyle's favorite–cube steak and some day old bread. The clerk gave her a bag of potatoes with some bad spots. Marie didn't mind because she liked potatoes. It was one of her favorites from the old country. She returned to the rig and they headed to a favorite place between Parkers Creek and Flat Rock. There was an old garage and abandoned service station there. The owners allowed campers to stay a night or two. They ritually collected 25¢ as they talked over the evening fire. Lyle pulled around back and picked his place. He didn't have to worry about neighbors because they were the only ones there. Old Julius and Clerisy would be along in a while, so he set up in a hurry. Marie set the stove on an old table and soon had the supper meal cooked. They ate and settled Leone in the corner of the tear drop bed and he was soon asleep.

Julius and Clerisy were friendly older people. They lost their only son in the Great War. Their daughter had run away from home at 14 and never returned. Neither could read or write. They were anxious for news of the outside world. They had never been more than 25 miles from home in their life. Julius closed the business after their son didn't return from the war and they lived on their small pensions. They supplemented their income with campers and growing a few things to sell at their roadside stand. Lyle talked to them way into the night as Marie settled in for a good night's rest next to Leone. She didn't remember Lyle coming to bed.

They were on the road early the next morning after sharing a cup of coffee and homemade donuts with Clerisy. They wanted to travel as far as they could that day to meet with George and Betty as promised. Marie never understood the rush in doing things because Lyle was usually late. He had little concept of time and travel and depended on Marie to make all the plans. Marie knew George and Betty would wait because they knew how Lyle was and they had a lot invested in the new items to sell.

The road was good to the Tennessee border where they stopped for lunch at Isham. Lyle walked into town and bought a little gold from the local dentist. He also bought some gold from a hardware store and made a good deal. They had a used Coleman stove with an almost new funnel. Lyle, on a whim, bought the stove and funnel for $3.50. He knew Marie was tired of straining the gas through a chamois skin and the old stove was worn out. Lyle hid the stove in the back of the car and would give it too her at the right time when he could show off a little to his friends.

Regardless of what scheme he had working, he liked to buy and trade old gold and silver. Lyle rested for a while in the afternoon before they headed south again on highway 27. He wanted to make Pilot Mountain because there was a good old campground there. He was excited about seeing some of his old friends. He hoped Pope the Key Man would be there so they could swap some stories, but there was no such luck. Lyle and Marie arrived at "Pilot Camp" near dusk and hurriedly selected a place for the tear drop.

Marie started a fire and got supper going while Lyle went in search of old friends. Marie fed Leone and put him to bed. She washed and rinsed a few diapers for the next couple of days. She had problems drying them, so she hung them out of the window so they would dry.

"I'll wash his diapers in one state and dry them in another," Marie said out loud.

This became one of Marie's favorite sayings about traveling. She fixed his supper and covered it with a towel because there was no telling when he would be back. She finished her supper, washed the dishes in an old wash pan and went to bed. Lyle came back much later, ate his cold supper and went to bed angry. He had not washed or cleaned up. He reeked of stale cigar smoke, but Marie went back to sleep.

They had a short drive the next day to reach Spring City and the camp before dark. They left after a short breakfast of cold biscuits and bacon. Lyle insisted on hot coffee so Marie made a pot for both on the old Coleman stove.

The road out of the camp was rough and Lyle caught the hitch on the edge of a dry mud puddle. He tried to back and maneuver the old Pontiac but the clutch was too weak and the car started to boil over. Lyle asked some of men to help and they succeeded by digging around the hitch and rocking the rig until it cleared the hole. This set Lyle's temper on edge because of the ribbing the campers gave him about his driving. It would be a "hell to pay" day.

The rest of the day was occupied with putting water in the old car and nursing the badly slipping clutch. Lyle had ruined it at the last camp but kept saying there was nothing wrong with it.

They finally met George and Betty at a roadside park outside Spring City. Lyle followed them to the old barn camp at Fort Mountain. They negotiated with old Ben for the price. This was Ben's ritual so he could say he made some money on some "Yankee Travelers." They settled on $3.00 per week.

They parked on the outside of the barn just as the sun was setting. Everyone was very tired so they set up camp and went to bed early. They would get up early to prepare their camp and work area.

There was no need for an alarm clock because old Ben's roosters were crowing just as the sun rose. They roosted in the barn and were quick to crow at first light. Lyle was first up and ran for the outhouse. He had the "quick step" when he was afraid or nervous about something. He was probably a little of both, as well as excited about the new goods to package and sell. Marie was happy that Lyle had met George and Betty. When he had a project to work on, he left her alone. She was weary of Lyle and his attempts to bother her every night.

Marie and Betty started to fix breakfast so the men would be in high spirits for the remainder of the morning. Betty had no children but loved to take care of Leone. She gave Leone the remainder of his goat's milk and attended to him while Marie worked.

They moved an old kitchen table under a large oak in the back of the barn. There were the solid remains of an old lean-to shelter under the old oak. This would serve them well in case of bad weather. They raked the trash from under the shed and put the table in the back. They then went in the barn and gathered several old nail kegs they would use for chairs around their makeshift dining room. Lyle wanted Marie to set up the eating table in the barn. Marie didn't like the dark area he had selected. It smelled of various animals that used to live in the old barn. Marie placed her old Coleman on the end of the table and they were ready to open for business. Lyle decided to present her with the "new" stove and funnel. He liked to brag when he gave it too her. It didn't matter to Marie if he bragged or not. She was very happy to get anything from Lyle because he could be quite stingy at times. Lyle liked biscuits so Marie set up the "new" Coleman oven on the left burner of the new stove. She happily hummed an old Russian lullaby as she worked.

Lyle tried to move the old Pontiac but the clutch was slipping. It was too heavy to push with the outfit hitched up.

He asked Ben, "Ben, what can I do about my clutch?"

"Take out the wooden floorboard so I can get to the clutch housing."

Ben removed the inspection plate and looked in the hole.

"It smells like it was badly burned. Were you riding the clutch again?"

This angered Lyle but he didn't say anything. Lyle was not a person that could take a joke, but he could hand them out.

Ben was a massive man who was not intimidated easily. He went in the barn and brought out a can of pure white sand.

"My wife collected it at the riverbank. Lyle, get in and press the clutch."

He poured the sand between the clutch and flywheel.

"Lyle, start the car."

Lyle started the car as directed.

"Slip the clutch a little until you feel it grab."

It started to catch. He repeated the sand trick several times and the clutch seemed good as new.

"It is an old farmers' trick to remove the glaze for the clutch so it would grab. Stop slipping the clutch when you start. Get the car moving and let it out slowly. If you feel it slip, push it in and start over again. If you do that, the clutch will last a long time."

He charged Lyle a dollar and laughed as he left the barn, muttering something about "dumb Yankees." Actually, Ben had used this "trick" many times on his farm equipment and it had usually worked well. In this case, Lyle was lucky because it worked very well.

Later, Lyle kidded Ben about selling the place to him. Ben brought out an old for sale sign which read "For sale One Million Dollars, Cash" and put it in front of the barn to answer Lyle's question. Ben also had a sense of humor.

George and Lyle cleaned out the barn so they could park both rigs inside. George had a crude homemade tent on a trailer frame. He would fold it up for traveling and open it up when he camped. It was efficient, but in bad weather it leaked a lot. George was happy to have it inside for a change. The barn was about 50 feet wide, so Lyle put his tear drop near the door and George moved his to the back of the barn next to some old stalls.

One side had a long workbench that was used for repairing farm equipment. They decided it would be a good place to make their new product. There was an old well just outside the side door that would need some priming. Lyle and George got it primed and had a drink of the cool mountain spring water.

They looked at each other, shook hands and started to make plans to make and sell the new product. They talked, planned and decide on names for their new line. The names would be "No Smoke" and "No Knock," or something close to that. They hadn't decided on a firm name yet.

Their idea was to "invent" an additive for engine oil to stop old engines from knocking. The other was to add it to the cylinders to prevent oil consumption. There were many cars on the road that needed an overhaul. Most people could not afford engine work and oil could get expensive if a car used a lot. Their solution was an "overhaul in a can."

As mentioned earlier, George was a chemist out of work from the Depression. He had had several "scrapes" with the law, so finding a job was difficult. He had the knowledge to make the products but lacked the skill to sell the items. He had worked the formula out in his head while he served a little jail time for something he took that was not his. He had never tested it but the method was sound, at least in his mind.

Lyle told him he could sell an icebox to an Eskimo. Lyle really was a good salesman and could sell just about anything. They both had a "touch of larceny" in their blood, so they were well suited for each other.

If things worked out right, they could make a lot of money, but first they had to get the assembly rolling. Tomorrow would be a new beginning. Their traveling was placed on hold for a while as they worked out the details to get their "operation" started. Both sat and talked way into the night. Both Betty and Marie were sound asleep when the men went to bed.

CHAPTER FIVE

The Formula

Early Fall, Southern Tennessee

Marie listened to the peaceful sound of rain falling on the old barn roof. It was so pleasing to snuggle in a warm blanket and listen to the quiet sounds of nature. The rhythm of the rain made Marie feel secure. She knew she would have to face the distorted social fabric of Lyle's world in a few moments, so she lingered with the warm feeling as long as she could. The hill country of Tennessee was cool this time of year and she liked the feeling of the cool breeze. She knew the rain had a cold sting from the sound it made on the tin roof. She looked at little Leone. He was sound asleep, completely unaware of the world around him. She could hear the rooster ruffling his feathers, waiting for the sun to rise. She finally left her warm nest and dressed to tackle the day ahead.

George and Lyle left before daylight for Chattanooga. They were going to buy the ingredients to make the formula. Marie had heard so much about it; she was tired of the tête-à-tête about how they would be rich in a few weeks. She knew better because it was another one of Lyle's "get rich quick" schemes. She felt it would not work. The way George pushed the issue of doing it so fast bothered Marie. She could not put her finger on it but it bothered her. She liked Betty, but didn't trust George. He had a way of looking at people that made her skin feel creepy. Lyle was caught up in the new plans and nothing would stop him. She said a quiet prayer that he didn't get into trouble with George.

Betty was stirring outside, gathering cooking utensils and cleaning them so they could make some breakfast. She was an early riser and liked to cook breakfast while Marie was tending to Leone.

Marie and Betty found an old trash burner stove in the corner of the barn and hooked it up to an old tin chimney. It needed some repair and a good cleaning to make it ready to use. They put it in a sunny corner near the small end of the barn. On rainy days like this it was a good place to cook. They knew the weather was turning cooler and would be cold very soon.

Betty quickly had the fire going and some coffee brewing. Marie loved the smell and taste of her early morning coffee. She and her father used to drink coffee in the old country. He would make it very strong mixed with fresh cream and coarse sugar left over from the Japanese invasion.

They both sat at a makeshift table they salvaged from the loft of the barn. Betty had brought in the nail kegs from outside yesterday because she thought it was going to rain. They talked about covering the tops so they wouldn't be so hard to sit on.

"When you are always on the road you have to make a home any way you can," said Betty.

The thought of little frills made Marie happy.

Marie and Betty watched the cold gentle rain. The old Pontiac had little or no windshield wipers and the tires were so thin you could see the air through them. Marie knew Lyle would be grouchy after he returned and she wasn't looking forward to his fit of temper. He always took out his frustration on anything in his way. Maybe he wouldn't be so stingy and buy some new windshield wiper blades. He was too cheap to buy tires until they went flat and couldn't be repaired.

George and Lyle went to a well-stocked hardware store on the north edge of Chattanooga just off route 27. The first thing Lyle heard was Amos and Andy on a radio playing on the center counter. They were advertising the new Philco Model with smaller batteries that could be plugged into house voltage, either AC or DC. Lyle wanted a radio more than anything else. He wanted to listen to Lowell Thomas in the evening and hear Jack Benny jokes.

"If I make any money on this deal, I will get a radio," he said outloud.

It would have to be battery operated because most of the camps they used had no electricity. He daydreamed of tossing the antenna in a tree so he could hear distant stations. His daydream snapped when he heard George call him. Someone was always breaking up his special dreams.

George needed sulfur, lead oxide and heavy molasses. In addition, George's formula required flake glue, dried shellac and two funnels. He needed a large and small "cooking pot" to mix the formula. They asked the owner if he had any glass containers they could use to bottle and sell a "special product." He had a supply of pint and ½ pint bottles with no tops. They bought all he had and some cork stoppers to seal the bottles. They needed some heavy oil and selected SAE 140 transmission oil in a 5 gallon can. They also bought a gallon of motor oil. They decided that a gross of 144 bottles should be more than enough.

Lyle wanted to know who could print some labels. The owner of the store gave him the name of a local printer who did work out of his house. He lost his business several years before in the peak of the Depression.

"He's reasonable and would print any thing except money!" the owner said. Lyle paid $16.00 for the merchandise and they headed back to their "barn camp."

For the first time Lyle was anxious about what they were doing. He had just spent a lot of money and he didn't understand what the end result would be. George kept so much to himself that it made him nervous.

On the way back to Spring City, they drove by the rail yards at the end of 7th street and the Tennessee River. There used to be an enormous "hobo jungle" there until the Scottsboro trial of 1933. In 1933, some black men on their way to Alabama in a "hopped" freight train allegedly raped two women, who stayed in the jungle. It was a sensational trial. The "Scottsboro trial" went the Supreme Court of the United States. Since the unwanted publicity, the jungle moved to Erwin, Tennessee and out of the limelight.

Lyle missed the feel of the open road and security of the hobo camp. He was an amateur hobo but he traveled with them enough to know how they felt and acted. It was a carefree life with no responsibilities except to the fellow travelers. The rain had stopped and the countryside smelled fresh from the clean rain. He knew the "Knights of the Road" would appreciate the nice weather and warm afternoon sun. He thought the word on Dapper Dan had gotten around so he didn't stop.

George needed some fine saw dust to mix in the formula. They stopped at an old sawmill on the outer edge of town. It was a large mill partially closed due to the Depression. They made inexpensive furniture for the local community. They still did some logging when money allowed, but that was uncommon. Lyle struck up a conversation with a worker about logging. Logging was still in Lyle's heart but the work was too hard and dangerous. George bought what he needed from a furniture sawdust pile. He selected maple and oak sawdust. The oak was almost as fine as baby powder. The owner gave them all they could carry for 50¢ and invited them back for more.

George and Lyle never discussed how the formula would be made or the reason for the odd selection of ingredients.

George said, "In good time my good man, in good time."

Before they got in the car Lyle said, "We need to discuss the operation before we get back to Marie and Betty."

George was hesitant to tell Lyle how things were made and why. The first thing Lyle wanted to know is why he used powdered Minum (lead oxide or red lead) because it was poison. George finally agreed to tell Lyle how everything would work together. He explained all the procedures to Lyle as a chemist. He made it a lot more complicated than it should have been to confuse Lyle.

George had spent his time in jail for stealing from a chemical company in Idaho. Lyle was aware he had been in jail but he didn't know the reason. George wasn't about to tell Lyle all his secrets, only enough to keep him interested.

After about an hour of explanations, George asked Lyle, "Did you get your $16.00 worth?"

Lyle nodded, but wasn't very sincere in his acknowledgment.

George told Lyle, "If we play our cards right we can make a lot of money in a short period of time."

Lyle agreed and said he wanted to be involved in all the mixes and bottling. George reluctantly agreed. They continued toward their "barn camp," tired and hungry.

Marie walked to Ben's house and bought a fat hen for 25¢. She also bought some brown eggs for 1¢ each. Lyle liked eggs for his breakfast. It was cool enough to keep the eggs but she was worried because the ice was gone in the icebox. Leone's goat milk was about gone and she needed milk and ice so she could feed him. She would ask Lyle the minute he got home. Maybe she would wait until he had eaten. He would be in a better frame of mind. Lyle had given her a dollar. She still had the silver quarter in her pocket and some green backs pinned to her bra. Lyle wasn't the only one who could hide money.

She saw some goats across the road in a pasture. Perhaps Ben would know where she could get some milk. She made a mental note to ask him if Lyle refused.

Life was never easy for Marie. She had to fight every day to get what she needed to feed her family properly. Lyle kept insisting that Leone could drink real milk, not that smelly goat's milk. Marie "stuck by her guns" and got her way about that. Leone was 3 months old and growing like a weed. She had taken a roll of film that Juanita had given her with her Brownie camera. She wished they could stay in one place long enough so she could develop the pictures. They would be the first pictures she had of little Leone.

She walked the reluctant, fat chicken back to the camp on a string. She had to be pulled most of the way because she knew she would end up in a cooking pot. Marie chopped the chicken's head off with Lyle's ax and let it drain. Betty boiled some water to "pluck" the feathers. Betty had some potatoes pealed so they would have a good supper. They finished dressing the chicken and put it in the little oven on the Coleman stove. The pan fit the bottom of the oven but Marie had to stand the chicken on end so it would fit. After a while, it would cook down. She watched it until it turned golden brown. Marie dipped the fat from the bottom and made some delicious country giblet gravy. With all this, Lyle couldn't, or shouldn't, be angry. Marie knew that one way to a man's heart was through his stomach. She heard the old Pontiac bump and rattle as it turned in the driveway and her smile faded.

Lyle and George were very excited but held their excitement in check when they smelled the food. Both were starved and ate hardily as they talked excitedly about what they would do the next day. Marie and Betty didn't get a word in edgewise but at least Lyle was happy. They agreed they would begin the work the next day.

Early the next morning they prepared to make the formula. It wasn't really a formula but a simple mixture of common products. The idea was to make a product that the average person could add to their engine to stop oil burning and prevent engine knocks. George said he would work on the knock formula first.

He started heating a combination of transmission oil, motor oil, oak sawdust, dried shellac and some red lead in the large cooking container he bought. He cooked it until it came to a rolling boil. The mixture turned out to be thick, heavy, orange looking oil. The last step was to pour a bottle of Brilliantine hair oil to make it smell good. George wouldn't tell Lyle the amount of each ingredient or how they were mixed. The entire process took less than an hour to make.

George said, "Lyle we can make about $200.00 a batch after expenses for a $16.00 investment."

Lyle designed the labels and took them to the printer where he waited until they were done. The first batch was known as "Special Engine No Knock Formula." The instructions were simple. "Add one pint to the oil in any engine and it is guaranteed to stop most engine knocks or your money back." It was a white label with black and red letters. He had the other formula label printed as "Special Stop Oil Burning Formula." If the instructions were carefully followed, it was guaranteed that it would stop any engine from burning oil with a money back guarantee, also. He added the words Made in Chattanooga, Tennessee. The special instructions would be printed on a card and handed out with each bottle. George wasn't ready to make the oil-burning batch until he tested the first batch with Lyle as the salesman.

They bottled their first batch and labeled it. Lyle loaded ten bottles in the old Pontiac and headed for the sawmill where they bought the sawdust. He made his pitch to the owners. They liked the idea and bought 4 bottles for their sawmill engines. Lyle didn't wait around to see how it worked. He told them, "I'll be back in a couple of weeks."

He put the $8.00 in his pocket and headed for Fred's Garage a few miles down the road. He stopped and told the owner what he had.

Fred said, "If you can stop the knock in this old Ford, I'll buy all you have."

Lyle was frightened and his hands shook as he poured the contents of a bottle into the running engine. He didn't know what to expect but much to his surprise, the engine stopped knocking in a few minutes. Lyle was a little weak at the knees because if it hadn't worked he would've been in BIG trouble. George had been right! The formula worked! However, he still had no intention of returning to any place where he made a sale. Fred paid for the remaining 5 bottles plus the one in the engine. Lyle, with $20.00 in his pocket, drove the old Pontiac as fast as he dared to report the good news. He had forgotten about his mistrust of George because making easy money was in the wind. Lyle thought about the engine knocking. The knock should stop with all the sawdust and heavy oil. He vaguely wondered how long it would last but he didn't care, the money was burning a hole in his pocket. He had visions of a radio and a nice suit for himself. He never thought about Marie and Leone, only himself.

The barn camp was a happy scene that evening. Lyle stopped and bought some cube steaks (his favorite). Marie and Betty fried them with crisp fried potatoes. He wasn't thinking of Marie but of how good the steaks would taste. The wood burner was tied up with the formula so they had to use the Coleman stove. Ben's wife had given them some canned vegetables in mason jars. Marie opened a jar of lima beans to round out the evening meal.

Lyle and George were busy talking with their voices raised and an occasional bit of nervous laughter. Marie was worried that Lyle was getting in over his head because of the attraction of "easy money." She could hear them planning to make large amounts and sell as much as they could and "pull out." They planned to buy more material the first thing in the morning. Lyle would make the purchases while George worked on the other formula.

When Lyle left early in the morning, George began to make a batch of "No Oil Burn." He knew it would take Lyle all morning to buy the ingredients and return. He had ample time to make the mix. He would pass it off as trying to save time and he would tell him later. He knew Lyle was caught up in the money making and wouldn't question him about the product. It was George's time to do the things he knew best–make things to make money regardless of the consequences. He had been there before, many times.

George mixed all the remaining ingredients into the large container. He melted the glue before adding it to the mix. He left out the sawdust and large quantities of transmission oil. The main ingredients were molasses, fortified by the red lead, and dried shellac.

The instructions told the owner to "Get the engine hot, remove the spark plugs and add one teaspoon to the inside of each cylinder. Rotate the engine a few times and repeat the procedure. Replace the plugs and let the engine cool. Start the engine and it will no longer burn oil." The theory was sound. The sugar in the molasses would combine with the red lead and shellac and turn to hard carbon in the hot combustion chamber. This would seal the rings so it wouldn't burn oil. George wondered if it would work. Nevertheless, he didn't care as long as he had Lyle to make the sales and take the blame. George's name was nowhere on anything. He and Betty would leave if trouble arose. Betty didn't know about his schemes and he knew she wouldn't approve.

George was finished with the mixture when Lyle returned with the supplies. He told George that he could buy all they needed in Spring City and save the 2-hour trip to Chattanooga. This angered George because he wanted the supply area to be as far from their camp as possible. After a lengthy discussion they decided to rotate, buying at both places so suspicions wouldn't arise. This agreement satisfied both Lyle and George. Lyle knew something was wrong but again, easy money clouded his judgment.

When the formula cooled, George added some Vitalis hair tonic to give it a different aroma. He didn't want it to smell like molasses or the same as "No Knock." He and Lyle packaged the formula using the funnels they had bought. It was thicker and harder to bottle. The difficulty of making and packaging it would increase the price. They decided on $5.00 as the fixed price. They bottled and labeled 36 ½ pint bottles. If people complained, they would say, "Where can you get an engine overhaul for $7.00?"

They needed to find out how it worked so they decided on Lyle's old Pontiac. Lyle was very reluctant to try it. He agreed only if they would put in just a small amount and not the entire treatment. After an hour, they had completed the experiment. They waited for the engine to cool and took it on a short test drive. The old car stopped smoking and had more pick up. Lyle knew in his heart the old car was beyond repair or formulas, but was happy with the result.

Both Lyle and George were elated. They returned to the barn camp in time for a nice supper Marie and Betty had fixed. They had been there a little over a week. George had worked out the kinks in making the products and Lyle had perfected his sales pitch. Marie and Betty helped with the labeling and clean up. They used all the bottles and were ready to sell the product.

Lyle could hardly sleep that Sunday night. He was so excited about selling the formula. He knew he could sell the No Knock but he wasn't sure about the No Oil Burn. He decided on a plan. In spite of his better judgment, he would return to Fred's garage and see if he would try it.

Early the next morning Lyle drove to Fred's garage. Fred was very happy with the No Knock and bought another 12 bottles. Lyle talked to him about the No Oil Burn. Fred agreed to try it on an old Studebaker. The old flathead 6 cylinder was prone to burn oil. Lyle watched Fred "doctoring" the old engine according to the instructions. Fred wouldn't let him leave in case something went wrong. It took Fred about an hour to complete the job. It worked perfectly. The old Studebaker ran like a top with No Knock and No Oil Burn. Both Lyle and Fred were very happy. Lyle had 15 bottles of the No Oil Burn and Fred bought them all. With $99.00 in his pocket, he headed to the camp. To celebrate his excellent day he stopped by the Chattanooga Bakery and bought six 5¢ Moon Pies, 3 for himself, 1 for Marie and 2 for George and Betty. The Chattanooga Bakery was the home of the Moon Pie, one of Lyle's favorite sweets.

Lyle told George of his good luck and they decided to sell all they had before making any more. Over the next two weeks, they did just that. They made over $460.00 after expenses. They split the proceeds evenly. Of course, George didn't know that Lyle had increased the price on a few sales and put the "skim" money in his pocket. He had stashed over $90.00.

There were no complaints and everyone was happy. Disagreeable things started to happen when George tried to buy more supplies.

George went to the sawmill to buy some saw dust when the owner asked him about the No Knock. One of his sawmill engines had locked up and wouldn't run. George assured him it wasn't any fault of the additive but probably a bad engine. He said he would send a mechanic from Fred's Garage to check it out. George left and stopped by Fred's garage. An angry Fred and the local sheriff met him. The sheriff took him into Fred's office and questioned him at length about the No Knock and No Oil Burn formulas. He said Fred had complained about 2 engine failures and he blamed them on the formulas. George assured him it was not his fault and he let him go. He promised to return the next day and refund the money. As he was driving away, he saw the deputy write his license number down. This was a bad sign.

During the next two days, things went from bad to worse. Engines were failing right and left. Several people who worked in and around Fred's garage become ill. No one seemed to know what was wrong. George went immediately to the camp and told Lyle what was going on. He left out all the problems at Fred's and his talk with the local sheriff.

George started to pack. He was ready to leave as soon as Betty was in the car.

Lyle said, "George, it would be better to lay low for a few days until things cooled off."

George was stubborn and left early that afternoon. Instead of going away from Chattanooga, he drove through the town on his way north. He was stopped on the north side of town and arrested. Betty wasn't arrested and was allowed to follow them to the police station.

George was booked on several charges including criminal distribution of a poison. It seems that the lead in the formula had burned in the exhaust of the cars in Fred's garage. It had made a number of people quite ill. Most of the engines failed and he was booked on felony destruction of property. The last charge was selling without a permit.

The police interviewed George and Betty. George tried to blame Lyle for all his problems. Betty told them the truth about how George had been in jail and how he had suckered Lyle into selling the product for him. Lyle was a salesman and nothing more. Marie helped package the product but knew nothing about it. It was George's plan how to make the product. They accepted the story and escorted George out of the room in handcuffs. Betty told the police chief that she needed money to leave. He gave her all the money George had with him with instructions to leave town before sunset. She got into their rig just as the sun was setting over the Tennessee hills and headed north. George waved from a jail window but Betty didn't see him. It would be the last time he ever saw Betty, but he would see gray prison walls for a long time. His shady side had finally caught up with him.

Meanwhile, Lyle and Marie "laid low" in the confines of the barn. They stayed 2 days before venturing outside. Old Ben had given Marie some goat's milk for Leone and his wife let them have all the canned food they could carry. Old Ben knew what was going on but he felt sorry for Marie and the child. He returned early Sunday morning and said the coast was clear to leave and not drive back through town. Ben told Lyle they were looking for him and he had better leave. Lyle again was very afraid of any thing to do with police or the law, to the point that he became sick and had to sleep all afternoon.

Marie wondered if this close call would teach Lyle anything. She certainly hoped so. She would always wonder what happened to Betty. Ben told them that George was in jail and would be there a while.They were headed to De Funiak Springs, Florida to meet Lyle's father Leon and maybe his daughter Ruth. They left headed south toward Florida and put Tennessee in their rearview mirror forever.

The old Pontiac was burning oil again.

Marie remembered that Lyle was at his best when he was on the road. He was at his worst when he was camped and worried with nothing to do. He liked doing things with a touch of larceny. "What would he get into next?" she wondered. They had a little money and he would probably loaf for a while. She hoped he would work on the trailer so it would be more comfortable for Leone.

Lyle was thinking along the same lines, but he wanted a radio and a new suit. This time he gave Marie all the money except what he had skimmed from George. Lyle didn't give it a second thought that he had broken the law as much as George. The only difference was that he wasn't caught.

Marie was writing in the diary and Leone was asleep as they crossed the Tennessee border late that afternoon. She would miss Betty, but Georgia looked very good to them.

She looked at Lyle and saw a very new side of him. He was driving with a frightened look on his face and was very relieved when they got out of Tennessee. They would have a long talk very soon; she wasn't going to let any of his ways hurt Leone.

Chapter Six

The Irish Mule Traders

Late fall, Florida Bound

Lyle and Marie had just cleared the camp barn in time. The local sheriff sent a deputy to talk to old Ben about the road people who were renting his barn. Ben was cooperative but evasive. He showed him the pots and left over materials in the corner of the barn. He asked Ben which way they went.

"I don't really know but they talked about going north," Ben replied.

This was true because Ben overheard Lyle and George talking about selling the formula around Knoxville. The deputy thought he was correct because that was the way George Planter and his wife went. He picked up some of the pots and anything that looked like the stuff George and Lyle were making.

"What was Lyle and Marie's last name?" asked the deputy.

"I never heard him say and I didn't think to ask him. George told me his name when he introduced himself. Lyle and Marie stayed here a few times they both seemed like good people. This is the first time I saw their baby."

The deputy said, "I am going to issue a warrant using Lyle's first name only. It isn't a common name and he should be easy to find."

After making a few notes, he got in his car and headed back to town.

Old Ben looked at the leftovers that the sheriff didn't take and wondered how he could use any of the things they left. He took the remainder of the molasses and carried it to the cow barn. He would mix some with their winter feed so he would have a better supply of milk for the winter. He would mix the red lead with some paint for his farm equipment to prevent it from rusting.

The rearview mirror in Lyle's old Pontiac looked like the mirror in the tear drop. It was faded and broken. It was tied to the support bracket with some rusty wire. Lyle used a piece of the same wire he used to hang the mirror in the tear drop. It moved and shook with the vibrations of the old car and the road. The old Pontiac was nearing the end of its life span and the formula didn't help it. Regardless of the mirror movement, Lyle continued to look behind him. Marie thought it was funny watching his head move up and down and back and forth. She wanted to laugh but it would make him mad. It didn't do much good to use the mirror because the trailer blocked most of the view. As he rounded a gentle curve, he could see Lookout Mountain in the background. It loomed like an ominous shadow of his past. The thought of returning to Tennessee for anything made him sick to his stomach. It was a very close call with the law. He made up his mind to stay away from people like George. He had a premonition about George when they were selling bandages together but he was too interested in making "easy money." Lyle had a weakness for a sad story or tales of easy schemes to make money.

He told Marie, "This is the last time I will get involved with any shady deals."

"Lyle it better be or you will end up just like George and you won't like that. You have responsibility with a new baby. Think about that before you try any of your schemes again. Stick to what you know best and that's buying gold and sending it to Baltimore. It's sure money and we can make it on that."

"You are right Marie, I'll toe the line."

Lyle was frightened at the time and was rationalizing his reasons. When the effects wore off from the close call, he would be thinking about some new scheme but he would be careful and not involve Marie.

Marie put Leone to sleep in the back of the old Pontiac. She took their poke from her bra being very careful not to bother her personal stash.

She started counting their poke. She told Lyle they had a little over $500.00 cash on hand plus some gold Lyle had. This was a small fortune to them. She entered the amount in Lyle's diary in spite of the rough road. Lyle had almost $100.00 hidden and Marie had some from her sale of the brooms and baskets. Neither knew about the other's hidden money. For the first time in a long time, they didn't have to worry about money. Lyle was still thinking about getting a radio and Marie about the red dress in El Mercado. They both yearned for something they didn't have.

The area south of Fort Oglethorpe, Georgia was home to the Chickamauga and Chattanooga National Military Park. The September 1863 Confederate victory at Chickamauga Creek had turned the tide for the Confederacy on the western front.

Lyle enjoyed looking at old battlefields and was looking forward to the visit. He had visited most of the parks in Virginia but this was his first visit to a Georgia battlefield.

There was a nice wooded area a few miles south of the park. A local farmer would let a few campers stay for a few days. Most visitors were heading south for the winter. They could stay for a maximum of one week. The charge was one dollar for one day or the full week.

Lyle had forgotten all about his past troubles as he approached the park and spotted a number of tents pitched near Chickamauga creek. He immediately knew who they were. It was Pete Sherlock and the Irish mule traders. He could tell by their green tents.

They were a clannish and itinerant bunch that traded and sold horses, mules and any other things to make money. They preferred living in large tents and traveling in old trucks, towing wagons with their mules and horses.

Lyle had befriended them years ago. They wouldn't let many outsiders into their camp but Lyle was an exception. Lyle didn't speak the Irish Cant, but they all spoke English with a heavy Irish brogue.

Pete Sherlock was a bear of a man with large hands and a friendly smile. When he saw Lyle drive up and get out of his car, Pete rushed over and picked him up in a friendly bear hug. Lyle knew it was coming, so he relaxed and let it happen. The first time he had picked Lyle up, he bruised his ribs. He then looked in the car and saw Marie.

"And who is this fine lass?"

Lyle told him about Marie and the babe. Pete's wife Sheila walked up and scooped up little Leone in her big arms. She held him over her head and started to show him around. A blonde child was a rarity among the Irish. Marie was a little concerned but Pete quickly told her that everyone loved babies. That was immediately obvious as she saw many children of all sizes running around the camp. Sheila called Leone "Blonde" and the name stuck for a long time to come. Marie had called him Blonde before but Lyle didn't like it. This time he didn't mind.

They were just preparing supper and invited Lyle and Marie to join their camp. Most of their meals were prepared in a community kitchen by clan members who were designated as cooks. The clan numbered about 80, including children. All of the members had special jobs from raising the tents to driving. The selling jobs were left to senior male members like Pete and the elder McNamara.

After the wonderful meal of Irish stew Pete and his son, Penn, helped Lyle set up his camp. Marie stayed with the women of the camp talking about babies and the problem with Leone's milk reaction. They said they had a cure so he could drink regular milk. Apparently the sensitivity to cow's milk was a common occurrence within the clan.

Marie didn't have any idea who was who. She listened carefully but could barely understand the Irish brogue. For sure, she couldn't understand the cant. One old lady in the camp spoke Serbian, which was similar to Russian. This helped break the barrier and Marie fell into the rhythm of the women talking about their travels and children. Sheila brought a bottle of light brown liquid and gave it to Marie. She told her to mix the medicine with cow's milk and in a few weeks, Leone would be able to drink regular milk. Marie didn't believe it but was willing to try so Lyle wouldn't complain all the time. Marie was very tired and gave her thanks to the clan and returned to the trailer parked on the outside of the enclave.

Sherlock had selected a nice place by the creek under a maple tree that was turning colors with the coming of winter. Leone was already asleep and snuggled in his nest as Marie put him on his pad. The minute she laid down herself, she went to sleep.

Lyle stayed until the wee hours of the morning talking around the campfire with the men of the camp. She didn't hear him come to bed. Before she went to sleep, she knew Lyle had forgotten all about George and was looking for something new.

Early the next morning she heard the hustle and bustle of the Irish getting ready for the day. Lyle was already up having coffee with the Sherlocks. She could see them huddled around the campfire talking about the strategies of the day. They were a religious group with very strong ties to the Catholic Church. Marie was Russian Orthodox, which was similar in beliefs to the Roman Catholic faith. Their ties to the church didn't prevent them from indulging in the various shady operations they ran. They gave heavily to the church and asked for forgiveness of their sins every Sunday. Most of the time absolution was granted on Sunday and they started over on Monday.

It was a Monday and the camp was stirring to sell some mules to the local farmers. They also had some special hay they sold that would help lazy farm animals do more work. Lyle learned some of the secrets of their success and that was every one had several names they used. Pete had several printed cards with a number of names. The men dressed alike so it was difficult to tell them apart. Many of the women wore traditional long Irish dresses with beautiful embroidered tops and draping shawls and they spoke to no strangers. If asked questions from any member of the law community, they would speak only in the Irish cant.

Pete asked Lyle to go with him to deliver two mules and pick up some special cut and dried hay to sell. He agreed and went to the tear drop to tell Marie. She was awake and feeding Leone a mixture of the special herbs and milk. He looked happy and drank heartily.

Pete had asked some of the women to look after Marie and the babe while they were gone. Marie knew the Irish possessed a special gift of homemade herbal cures. She had learned many such cures from her mother in the old country. She felt in her heart that the herbal mix with Leone's milk would help to correct his reaction to cow's milk. The women got to the trailer about the same time as Lyle. Lyle was looking at a comely young lass of the Sherlock clan but he knew better than give it a second thought. They were a tight knit family and he didn't want to jeopardize a good thing. He did think about it long and hard but decided he would smile and say the proper hellos as Marie and the women headed for the largest green tent. Maybe Marie would be well soon.

Lyle and Pete left in an old Ford truck pulling a trailer with two nice looking brown mules. Two of the younger camp members rode with the mules to do the work. Pete was the senior member and made the deals and collected the money. The younger sat, listened and learned the work as Pete had from his father. They were headed for a large farm a few miles outside Lafayette, Georgia.

They arrived at mid-morning and stopped at a large modern farm complex. It looked like the farm had avoided all effects of the Great Depression. There was a large shed and what looked like a small factory building on the edge of the cleared area. Lyle saw several men busy around the buildings.

The farmer greeted them and shook hands. They walked around the trailer and looked at the mules. The farmer asked about the condition of the mules. Pete said they were the best he had. Fortunately, Pete was telling the truth. He didn't want to offend the farmer because he bought a lot of his special hay. The farmer looked at the mule's teeth and jokingly asked Pete, "What kind of enamel did you use on the teeth?"

Pete answered, "There is no paint on those teeth."

It was true, because he didn't want to "cheat" this man. Enamel was used to paint mules' teeth to hide the brown color of age. Pete did add a little brown hair dye to the face to cover some of the gray hair, but only a small amount. The farmer would never see it because he was very skilled in covering gray hair on mules. It made them look a few years younger.

Lyle never understood the difference between painting the teeth and dying the hair. Both were used to cover age and make more money. Pete on the other hand thought differently. It was all right to let the buyer think he was getting a good deal by not covering up the obvious, like teeth. He knew the farmer would never look at the hairline so he cheated him anyway. Lyle thought that was a very effective and subtle way of doing business. He thought to himself that he would have to figure a way to use this method someday if the opportunity arose. Pete was good to be around but he was far too slick for Lyle to understand all the devious ways he used. The Irish mule traders had been practicing their trade for generations. Lyle could pick up a few tricks but could never gain Pete's skill.

The farmer and Pete talked and argued trying to reach an agreement on the sale and trade price. Lyle listened intently to all of bickering and remembered it for future reference. There seemed to be at an impasse when the farmer's son walked up and talked to his father. The farmer asked Pete to follow him to a large barn where they ran their hemp operation. The farmer had a government contract to make hemp rope for the Navy. Most of the ships used hemp rope because of its flexibility and durability. The farmer had acres of the bright green plants. Some stood over 6' tall which looked like they needed to be harvested.

Recently they had purchased a new machine to process hemp and they no longer needed the vehicle that powered the equipment. It was a 1929 Buick with the rear wheels removed. They hooked a large belt to each wheel and used it to power one of the hemp separators. It wasn't very functional and was not used that much.

Lyle looked at the car and saw it was a series 121 model 41, 1929 Buick. It was dark green and appeared to be in good condition. The rear wheels were stacked near the front of the car. Lyle asked Pete if he could work a trade because he needed a car. He told him about the other car and the trouble he had had in Chattanooga. Pete dickered with the farmer and made an even trade for the two mules and 25 bales of the special hemp hay. The hay was about 25% hemp chaff and 75% field hay. They shook hands on the deal. That was a legal contract in Georgia and both men respected it. Several of the helpers started to put the Buick back together. Soon it was purring like a kitten and parked outside of the barn. The farmer put some gasoline in the tank so they could make it back to their camp. While the young men were getting the Buick ready for the road, Lyle and Sherlock reached an agreement. Lyle would give Sherlock $50.00 and the old Pontiac for the Buick. They shook hands and the farmer made out the bill of sale to Lyle. Some helpers loaded the hay on the empty trailer.

Lyle got behind the steering wheel of the big Buick and they headed back to Sherlock's camp. Surprisingly, the Buick ran like a top with its powerful 6-cylinder engine. Lyle was quite pleased with himself. The farmer had a ball and hitch on the back so Lyle wouldn't have to pay for any welding. They arrived back at the camp about an hour before dark. Lyle parked by the creek an asked some of the younger boys if they could wash the car. It was covered with a lot of dust and grime from the barn.

Lyle showed Marie the car, inside and out. They were both very happy with the deal. He asked Marie to put down the trade in the diary. Marie worked inside the car, cleaning out a couple of old chicken nests and a lot of dirt. They were both proud of their "new" car.

The police wouldn't be looking for this kind of car. Pete Sherlock was going to paint the old Pontiac blue before he sold it. Lyle knew he would make money even if the car were worn out. The clan members were skilled in treating cars like they "fixed" their mules and horses. Lyle didn't want to know how they did it. He suspected it would be "doctored" in the same manner as the mules: leave the obvious and cover-up the unseen defects.

Marie wouldn't let Lyle take out the back seat. She wanted a better place to put Leone when they traveled. Lyle reluctantly complied and agreed to build a flat platform over the seat so Marie could make a bed for Leone. This way she would be able to sit by him and ride in comfort.

She didn't like the rough feeling of the seats. It scratched her skin. It was made of a product called mohair which was made partially from goat wool. Sheila gave her a shawl to cover the seat so it wouldn't bother her. When she sat in the front seat, she could put it over that seat. She wondered if Lyle would ever build the platform. She didn't have to wait long. One of Pete's boys brought the lumber over for Lyle to build the shelf. He agreed he would start in the morning but Marie knew it would never happen because he was on a roll with the Sherlocks.

Lyle and Marie walked to the camp to eat supper and fetch little Leone. They talked about their good fortune since they left Tennessee. They wouldn't have to worry about their car being spotted and it was much safer and more reliable to pull the tear drop.

They arrived in the middle of supper and were invited to join Pete Sherlock in his large tent. It was beautifully decorated with a large high bed in the back and a nice table and chairs set up for their evening meal. The walls were insulated with carpets as was the floor. It was like walking into a picture show it was so quiet.

After the meal, the men joined in their usual conversations while Lyle and Pete discussed their plans for the next few days. Lyle didn't understand the reason they were interested in buying so much special hay. Pete explained to him that the hemp plant from was from Mexico. It was from the cannabis family and had low quantities of the same drug that was found in marijuana. The residue from the hemp plant had some of the same effects as marijuana except less intoxicating. When it was fed to cattle and other livestock it had a calming affect on the animals and for some reason the cows gave more milk. It was a good money-maker. They charged a good price for the hay and were able to sell all they could get their hands on. Pete said this information was between them and went no further because he was the first non-clan member that knew about the scam. This frightened Lyle a little because he didn't expect Pete to be so firm in his statement. Lyle also knew it was illegal in some states but he didn't know which ones. Pete told Lyle that he was glad that he had a better car.

He said, "I'll make good money on your old Pontiac because it is a popular car."

He hoped the baby would be healthy with the herbs Sheila gave Marie. He was headed for the Carolinas and hoped to see Lyle sometime soon.

It was nearing the end of the clans seven days and they were preparing to leave. Lyle felt he should be going soon, too. He would drive into town tomorrow and buy his license plate for the Buick. He went in the tent and told Marie it was time to get some rest. They went to their little tear drop, but not before admiring their new car.

Lyle said, "This car will run a lot better over the mountains, it won't use as much oil, and the lights work!"

Marie and Lyle settled in for a good night's sleep with nice thoughts of the next day.

It was late in the morning when they got out of bed and looked out of the door. The Irish had quietly pulled out during the night, leaving no trace that they had been there. This kind of moving typified the way they traveled: under a veil of secrecy. They were a clannish and cautious bunch but once a friend always a friend. Pete had given him some good ideas about making money. Lyle had already forgotten about the close call he had in Tennessee. Money and running the scam was very important to him now. He was interested in the plans Pete gave him. He would see the contacts in Florida if he ever got there. He was already two weeks behind.

He went to the creek and dipped some water with their bucket. Marie set up the stove and heated some for him to shave and get ready. He washed the parts that one could see and covered the rest with baby powder. Marie tried to wash the best she could with the leftover water. After breakfast, they started getting ready to "get on the road." The Buick was higher than the Pontiac so the trailer tilted a little to the rear. He said to himself, "I need to find a welding shop and have that fixed." Getting it done was a different matter.

Marie opened the passenger door of the Buick and found a large basket full of food and fruit. There was a note from Sheila and another bottle of the medicine for Leone's milk. Marie was very happy to get the things. In the bottom of the basket, there were a lot of boy's clothes that would fit little Leone. She liked Sheila and hopped she would see her again.

Lyle returned from town sporting a new Georgia license plate, an oil and grease job and a full tank of gas. Marie put Leone on the car seat in the back. Naturally, Lyle hadn't finished the little bed for him but the wood was strapped on the rear of the car. He promised he would do it soon.

He felt the powerful Buick engine under his foot when he returned from town. He knew he could travel 40 miles per hour and make better time. There were no oil or water leaks and this made driving a lot easier. They were both happy to be on the road again.

The Irish were hospitable people but he wasn't sure they could be trusted. Pete had been very good to him but he felt he had outstayed his welcome. They would meet again and share some tales of the road. They hooked up the tear drop and turned south on highway 41 heading toward Atlanta. Lyle wanted to visit Atlanta because he had heard so much about the Cyclorama, a Civil War round building that depicted the battle of Atlanta.

Lyle was a little miffed because he didn't get to see the Chickamauga battlefield. Marie never knew why he was so enamored with Civil War history. She suspected it was because of his Grandfather Freeman, who served in the 11th Michigan and would often talk about the "old days." It could have been because he wished he had served in the army at some point in his life.

Lyle didn't miss the old Pontiac or the broken rearview mirror he had for so many years. The Buick was high enough to just see over the top of the tear drop. He was glad he saw Pete and the clan but was also glad they left early that morning. He was happy to be on the road again headed south toward Florida.

CHAPTER SEVEN

Atlanta Area

Late fall, Florida Bound Continued

Lyle thought about the circumstances of his previous problems. He couldn't resist being a part of a well-planned scam. A touch of larceny ran in his bloodline.

"I will try and curb my first reaction and not jump in without thinking it through," He thought out loud.

These were good words and thoughts to live by, but Lyle would never follow through once he had the scent of money or a slick scam. He had to keep Marie from knowing any of his "extra" business.

He was thankful that he didn't have the old Pontiac because of the Michigan license plates. There was still a lot of animosity because of the Civil War, especially in the Atlanta area.

General Sherman's destruction of the city and subsequent march to the sea lay heavy of the hearts of many residents. Pulling a trailer and trying to sell or do business in the south with a "Yankee" license plate was not a good idea. Lyle tried his best to talk with a southern accent but somehow couldn't get the knack.

He told Marie to be quiet when they were in a store because the locals mistrusted foreigners almost as much as northerners.

Marie's speech had a very pronounced Russian accent. It wasn't so bad in larger cities where there was a cultural mixture of many races, but small towns held a lot of prejudices toward anyone or anything that varied from their way of life. They never saw anyone of color on the southern road circuit.

The highway from Chattanooga to Atlanta was crowded for the

middle of the week. Lyle and Marie chose Highway 41 because it was the most direct, though it would have been faster to take Highway 27 and cut into Atlanta by way of Rome. He was pulling the tear drop at a steady 40 miles per hour but traffic still backed up behind him. After about three hours of driving, he stopped at a roadside park. Georgia had many such parks for the convenience of travelers. They had large parking areas and modern restroom facilities. The grounds were dotted with picnic tables and water faucets. They usually had an area for people with trailers to park and enjoy a little rest. The state and cities didn't mind if travelers stayed overnight as long as they didn't abuse the privilege. Sometimes local venders would sell local products.

Marie and Leone were settled in their places and both were sound asleep. They didn't awaken when he turned the car off. Marie seemed to like to ride in the back seat while the babe slept. Lyle enjoyed the comfort of the new car. The seat wasn't torn and could be adjusted so he didn't have to stretch to reach the pedals.

He liked to dream about what he would do in the next few days. He wanted to work on the trailer and fix a place for little Leone to be more comfortable when they traveled but he just didn't have enough motivation to do the work. He felt a little guilty at times but the rush of the world quieted his feelings. He wished Marie would sit up front to keep him company, but his inner thoughts always kept him company more than she did. She was always asking him questions about getting things for the babe, which he usually ignored.

Lyle quietly opened the door and headed for the public facilities to refresh his body. Marie awoke with a start. She saw Lyle disappear into the washroom and decided to do the same thing. She quickly changed Leone and walked toward the facilities. She was about half way there when she noticed a policeman in an old Ford pull up next to their rig. Marie quickly returned and put Leone in his bed in the back of the car. He was a bit cranky and she went to the back of the trailer to get some milk for him.

"What are you doing here?"

"I am getting some milk for my baby." she said.

Lyle was just leaving the washroom when he saw the policeman. He literally froze in his tracks and turned white as a sheet. He had to hold on to the water fountain so he wouldn't fall as his heart raced in his throat. His first inclination was to run and hide. He looked around at the grassy hill behind the facilities and saw it was void of any place to hide and thought better of running. He usually didn't perspire but a cold sweat broke out on most of his body. He thought he was going to have a heart attack. He steadied himself and watched Marie talk to the policeman. He wasn't about to go down and talk to the officer. He would let Marie handle the questions as he watched the scene below him. Marie was gesturing with her hands and talking rapidly. He thought he saw the officer laugh. She was holding the babe in one arm and waving the other arm toward the north. Lyle was beginning to worry about what she was telling him. He remained out of sight because he didn't want to be involved with any kind of law enforcement.

After a short while, the officer got in his car. He looked at Marie, shook hands with her and drove out of the park. Lyle slowly walked down the steps using the handrail for balance.

The last time he had been that frightened was when he was waiting in Mexico for a member of Pancho Villa's army. He felt dizzy and wet with perspiration as he slowly walked to their rig. He sat down on the wide running board to get his breath.

"What was all that about, and what did you tell him?" he asked Marie.

"The officer was checking all travelers because they were on the lookout for some mule traders that were headed in this direction. They were suspected of stealing some mules from a farmer."

Lyle let out a long sigh of relief and wiped his face with a handkerchief. He thought they were looking for him.

Marie told the officer that she hadn't seen anyone that fit the description. She also told him that the trailer was too small for them, let alone any mules.

Lyle suspected that was when the officer laughed. She didn't like to lie, but she didn't want to be connected in any way with the Irish mule traders. She had a baby to raise and she valued her freedom.

"So that's why they left in the middle of the night. By the time they were caught and questioned about the theft, the mules would be working on some unsuspecting farmer's land. The mules probably would have painted teeth and dyed hair," Marie said out loud.

It was simply too much for Lyle to manage. If the officer had talked to him, he would have been too frightened to answer his questions. Lyle looked like he had something to hide some of the time, especially when he was nervous. He had to rest and get his strength back. He told Marie to fix something to eat while he went in the trailer and lay down.

Marie opened the back of the tear drop and placed her Coleman stove on a nearby picnic table. She fixed a light supper that Lyle hardly touched.

It was late afternoon by the time Lyle began to get his wits about him. He was still a little too shaky to drive.

"The first chance I get, I will teach you to drive," he said.

He wanted to leave this area but felt too bad.

"Marie, we'll pull up next to a nice tree at the edge of the roadside park and spend the night."

He felt relatively safe because there were a few campers already set up. He figured he would be alright after a good night's sleep and they would drive to Atlanta tomorrow. Marie cleaned the dishes by a water faucet and secured the trailer back for the night. She fed Leone while she smoked a cigarette.

She thought about her way of life and how close they had been in the last week or so to being arrested. It frightened her a lot.

Lyle was inside snoring loudly as the sun began to set. Marie hated this way of life but in a way, it was exciting. Sometimes Lyle worried her with his episodes of anger, illnesses and fear. He was not a stable man but he had enough drive to provide them with a fair living so far. She finished her cigarette and walked to the washroom. She returned and checked their camp to ensure it was secure. Road people seldom locked anything because of the trust they had for each other. They put things up in case of a wild animal or inclement weather. Lyle didn't own a lock for anything. It looked like she was beginning to be the stronger of the two. She agreed with Lyle, she needed to learn how to drive, but for a different reason. She wanted to be a little more independent. Lyle wanted her to drive so he could rest while they traveled, or in this case leave the area in case the police came back. She put Leone to sleep in his place and settled in for the night, being very careful not to awaken Lyle.

During the late evening, the officer returned and looked at the little tear drop. "I hope they will be safe and sleep well tonight," he said out loud.

He had no thoughts of anything wrong while Lyle was dreaming of a policeman putting him in jail.

The fields of goober peas were ready to be harvested as Lyle approached the outskirts of Atlanta. Georgia was a major producer of peanuts for many years. Peanuts were a staple in the Confederate Army diets. Peachtree Avenue was a beautiful street with old antebellum homes and striking stately oaks.

Lyle drove to the edge of Grant Park in central Atlanta and parked the trailer in a section designated for travelers. Grant Park was a 130-acre park donated by and named after Lemuel P. Grant, a civil engineer for the Georgia railroad. He was often referred to as the "Father of Atlanta." It was not named for Ulysses S. Grant as many people thought, as Georgia would never allow a major park named after a Northern General.

Lyle was happy to be there so he could see the Cyclorama at the other end of the park. He wanted to visit the Atlanta stockade and take Marie and Leone to the zoo. It was late in the evening and they set up their rig beside some travelers from South Carolina. They were not very friendly, so the conversation didn't last long.

Lyle and Marie walked around the park and bought some ice cream from a street vender. They both loved ice cream. Marie let Leone taste it and he started to cry because he didn't like the cold on his face. Eventually, they strolled back to their camp and settled in for the night. Marie used the public restroom to freshen up and give Leone a sponge bath so he would sleep better. It was a clear cool evening in Atlanta and perfect weather to sleep.

Lyle left early the next morning to see the Cyclorama. It was the largest painting depicting the battle of Atlanta in 1864. The 360 degrees, round building was made so the battle scenes unfolded before the viewers. It had been a major attraction since its construction 1921. He could spend hours looking at each item and reading every placard but he didn't take the time he wanted because he wanted to get on with his business.

Lyle loved the smell of old musty museums and forts. It was his style to read and study things that were of no interest to Marie. She wished he would stay all day.

Marie didn't like to visit old war museums or anything like them. She especially didn't want to see the stockade because it reminded her of the prison where her father Andrei was kept. It depressed her because she lived the turbulence of the revolution and the Japanese-Russian war. So, instead of going with Lyle she fixed herself a little breakfast and took care of Leone's needs.

Marie noticed there were a number of people selling products in the park on little stands and on the curbs. It was a nice clean way to make a little money. She thought about the baskets and brooms she had under the bed and hidden in various places. She was lucky to get the ones out of the old Pontiac before Lyle had traded the car. She put them behind the back seat of the Buick. There was a large storage area there that could hold a lot of things. She took Leone for a walk and looked at the things people had to sell. The prices, to her, were quite expensive. She priced one basket and it was $3.00 and not half as nice as hers. This gave her a good idea how much to charge.

Marie set up a little sales area on the hood and fenders of the Buick without asking Lyle. She put out several baskets and brooms. Before she finished setting up, a nice, well-dressed man asked her if she had a peddler's license.

"No, I don't have one and I don't know how to get one."

"You will have to get one before you can sell anything in the park," he said as he showed her his identification.

"Where could I get one and how much would it cost?" she asked.

"It will cost $2.00 a month and I can sell you one."

She went in the trailer, got the money out of her stash and gave it to him.

"What is the name of your business?" he asked.

"Marie's Arts and Crafts," she said after she thought for a minute.

He made out the license form from a booklet he carried. He signed it and gave it to Marie. It was a nice printed form with scrollwork around the edge. She was so proud of the little piece of paper with her name on it: "Marie's Arts And Crafts."

She clutched it too her chest and cried out loud.

"At last I have something of my own!"

She knew Lyle would be angry because it wasn't his idea, but she didn't give a whoop or holler what he said. She was in business for herself!

Marie looked behind the seat and found some of the bandages that Lyle and George had leftover. She put out a few pieces of costume jewelry that Lyle had bought.

She stood by the front of the car and said, "Hand made articles for sale."

This would become a hallmark for her sales pitch for years to come. The "set up" would become a way of life for them. It wasn't long before she had her first customer and sold a nice little broom for $2.00, which was $1.50 more than she thought it was worth. Before Lyle came home at 3:00 pm, she had sold over $30.00 worth of articles and still had a lot left.

Lyle was a bit mellow because he had enjoyed the day looking at all the sights of the park. He was too tired to go to the zoo. He sat down on the running board and asked Marie to fix some coffee. She made a big pot and gave Lyle a cup doctored with milk and sugar like he wanted.

A stranger walked up and asked if he could have a cup of coffee.

"If you have a cup I'll give you some coffee," replied Marie.

He reached in his tattered coat and pulled out an old tin cup. Marie rinsed it and gave him some coffee. He looked hungry and Marie gave him some leftover biscuits. He was very grateful.

"My name is Allan Sanders and I lost my job up north and I am a little hungry."

He and Lyle looked at each other.

"Are you from Atlanta?" Lyle asked him.

"I am from Michigan."

"So am I," Lyle said.

"I know you are," he said as he looked knowingly at Lyle.

"Where did I meet him?" Lyle thought. He figured it was probably at one of the hobo camps and dismissed the thought.

Mr. Sanders thanked Marie and walked to a bench and sat down to enjoy his little meal.

Lyle was angry with Marie for giving away good food but forgot about it when Marie told him about the way she made money. She gave him $20.00 and put $10.00 away in her poke. Lyle thought the $20.00 was wonderful because he didn't have to work for it. He didn't suspect she would have sense enough to hide money from him. He was happy that she had found a way to make some money until she showed him the license.

"Why wasn't my name on the license?"

"Because it's my business with things I have made, that's why!"

Lyle didn't say anything is response because he was still puzzled by the stranger.

Lyle soon forgot about his anger and sat down to eat. He was very tired of all the walking and looked forward to a good night's sleep. Tomorrow he would see the friend of Pete Sherlock's at the Federal bank. Lyle wanted to work the new scheme he had in mind but he didn't fully understand it. It was nearing dark so he settled in for the night. The only thing he took off was his shoes and socks. She could smell the stale clothes next to her but she was too tired to think about it and went to sleep as well.

The next morning Lyle arose early and dressed in his best clothes. He fixed his mustache and tie perfectly. There was a cool wind blowing from the north. He saw the leaves blow over the park and felt the chill of the wind through the cracks in the tear drop. It wouldn't be long before they would have to leave for warmer country. He had no heater in the tear drop and he hadn't looked to see if there was one in the Buick.

"Where are you going?" Marie asked.

"I'm going to see a man about a dog," he told Marie.

She didn't understand what he meant. "What kind of dog?" she asked.

"A money dog, what do you think?"

Marie didn't understand American humor or the nuances of the language. She was a long way from being fluent in English and Lyle didn't help her learn it, he only laughed when she made a mistake and didn't try and help her. He was trying to tell her it was none of her business where he went. Marie knew it had something to do with the idea Pete Sherlock had given him.

"Set up and try and sell the rest of the goods while I take care of business."

Lyle drove to the Federal Reserve Bank of Atlanta to see Pete's friend Mr. Archer who worked in the distribution department. Pete told him to see Mr. Archer about getting a federal license to buy gold and silver from banks across the country. Since the United States was taken off the gold standard in 1933, specially selected people were licensed to buy the silver and gold for the Federal Government from local banks. By law, they had to sell the gold to Federal banks and could make a small profit of no more than 10%. Lyle didn't trust banks at all but he thought it would be a good way to make money. He didn't know or understand how he was going to get the license. He would see Mr. Archer and see how it was done.

He asked the bank receptionist to see Mr. Archer.

"Please have a seat and I'll see if he can see you."

She came back to her desk and told Lyle he would see him in a short while, as soon as he finished a meeting. After about an hour Mr. Archer finally came to see Lyle. He wasn't friendly at all until Lyle mentioned Pete Sherlock.

"How is old Pete Sherlock? I'll bet he is as big and ugly as ever."

Before Lyle could answer, Archer invited him into his office and asked him to sit down.

"Lyle, how can I help you?"

"Pete was telling me about a license to buy gold and silver. He said you were the only one who knew how to get one."

"I know exactly what Pete was talking about. Let me see if I can get the right forms to fill out. You are the first one who has asked about it in Atlanta."

He found an application in his desk and started to fill it out. It was long and complicated with all sorts of questions. Finally, he had Lyle sign the form.

"Pete Sherlock helped save this bank after the Depression and I owe Pete my life and my business. He made several large deposits that got us over the surge of withdrawals," he said.

Apparently, Pete Sherlock was a very wealthy man, Lyle thought.

"Any friend of Pete Sherlock is a friend of mind!"

Mr. Archer made out an official looking license with a raised federal stamp. It said in effect that the bearer was licensed by the Federal Government to buy defaced silver and gold coins.

He further explained that the gold must be turned in to a Federal bank and he would be paid the metal value plus 10%.

He made Lyle sign an affidavit stating that he would only use the license to buy only from banks and not from private citizens.

Lyle couldn't believe his good fortune. It wasn't until Mr. Archer explained the license to him that he began to put the pieces together. He began to grasp the full meaning of what Pete had told him. Pete couldn't get a license because he had a criminal record and Mr. Archer knew it. He was a little confused at first about the law, but now he understood it perfectly.

"You must never abuse the privilege of the license or you could be fined and the license taken from you. It can also include jail time, so use it like you were an agent of the Federal Government."

Lyle readily agreed and asked how much it would cost.

"It would normally cost $25.00 but I am waving the fee because of Mr. Pete Sherlock, who is a major stockholder and depositor in our bank."

Lyle shook his hand and left the bank with the license carefully tucked in his coat pocket. He was floating on a cloud of joy. On the way back to the park, he was practicing his spiel.

"My Name is Lyle and I am licensed by the Federal Government to buy gold and silver."

He didn't give Mr. Archer's warning another thought. He would use it to buy as much as much gold and silver as he could from anyone that would sell him gold and silver. He would visit a few banks to make it look like he was doing right. He was going to make some money without a lot of work and he was licensed to do it! He felt of the license in his pocket and was very proud. He had a lot to brag about now. He would try it out the next day, first thing.

On the way home, Lyle was putting the pieces together about the federal "loophole" Pete Sherlock was talking about. In April 1933, President Roosevelt signed executive order 6102 which made it unlawful to hold gold coins, bullion or gold certificates. The sale of gold was prohibited except to a bank. The exception was if the Federal Government licensed an individual, and the holder could buy from one bank and sell to another.

President Roosevelt changed the price of gold from $20.67 a troy ounce to $35.00 a troy once in January 1934. A $20.00 gold coin was about one ounce and was actually worth $20.00 by the standard enacted in 1837. What this really meant was the government now owned all the gold in America and they had raised the price to $35.00 per ounce. This would raise the value of all gold in Fort Knox by over 40%. This was a very smart economic move made without lifting a finger, except to sign the order.

The federal license allowed holders to buy gold coin, bullion or gold certificates and sell them back to a Federal bank and make 10% on the deal.

What it meant to a dishonest license holder was to buy gold coins from people who still had them. Everyone knew it was against the law but a lot of people still were hoarding gold. The "Licensed by the Federal Government" could be used as a scare tactic. They would buy face value coins at $20.00 an ounce and resell them for $35.00 an ounce. The loophole was that the license said nothing about buying and selling from banks. It was like giving Lyle a key to Fort Knox. He was very happy but didn't quite know how he was going to pull it off.

He pulled into the camp and saw Marie talking to some people. Before he left, he made her "set up" on an old blanket near the sidewalk. She had sold most of the things they had. Marie said she made over $35.00, which meant she had at least $15.00 to stash. All that was left was one small broom and some bandages. Marie thought she would have to make some more as soon as she had a chance. Lyle told her to pack it up and fix some supper because he was hungry.

He turned up his collar and shivered a little against the wind. There were a few drops of moisture in the air. It was the late October and it was going to get cold very soon. The cold didn't bother Marie as she went about fixing supper.

After supper Lyle was so excited he couldn't relax. He wanted to tell Marie but he was afraid she wouldn't understand or would balk at the idea. He did show her the license.

"See, I got my own license today," he said.

Marie looked at it but didn't say a word because she sensed it was something that could get Lyle into trouble again.

Lyle was deep in thought planning his next move. The best idea was to leave early in the morning and drive south to escape the impending cold snap. Atlanta was usually nice in November but he didn't trust the weather. Before they left, he wanted to try out his new found skills in buying gold.

Early the next morning, they packed up their rig and parked it on Peach Tree Street heading south. Lyle looked at his watch and decided he would walk one of the near streets with the antebellum homes and try to buy some gold. Armed with $200.00, his license and gold testing box, he headed down Peachtree. He stopped at one house that looked the worst for wear. He knocked on the door and an old lady with a cane answered it.

"What do you want? Are you a Yankee carpet bagger?"

"No Mam," he said in his best southern accent. He started the spiel accenting "Licensed by the Federal Government."

"I have a few things to sell. Come in and I'll see what I have," the woman replied.

They stepped into the parlor of the great old house and he noticed a life size picture of Robert E. Lee on one wall. It had a tear from the upper left to the bottom right of the picture.

"What had happened to that beautiful picture?"

"My mother inherited the picture from a relative in South Carolina after she died. Some years after the war, a visiting Yankee officer sliced the picture for spite and I have hated Yankees every since."

She looked carefully at Lyle and wondered if he was a Yankee. "Have a seat and I'll be right back."

She returned with a sewing box and a small velvet bag.

"Can I be arrested if I have gold coins?"

"Not if you sell them to a licensed agent of the Federal Government," Lyle quickly answered.

She emptied eight $20.00 gold coins on the small table near the settee. He counted the coins and paid her face value of $160.00 and put them back in the bag. He gave her a receipt from the book given to him by Mr. Archer.

She handed Lyle the sewing box and asked him what he would give her for the contents.

Lyle set the box on the table and opened it. It was full of old watches. Lyle became a little excited but he didn't let it show. He carefully examined the watches an offered her $20.00 for the box.

"I'll take it! I am so glad to get rid of old memories. My husband had been a jeweler before he died and this was the last of the contents of his shop. They all need fixing and it is time I let them go."

Lyle paid her for the watches and went down the outside stairs to the street, tipping his hat as he went. She closed the door quickly behind him and disappeared behind a lace curtain.

He could see their rig down the street and he wanted to run but thought better of it. He had made his first gold buy and it worked like a charm! He was excited about the watches. He knew he could sell the 20 odd watches for a good profit. Even though it was cold, he was sweating by the time he reached the rig. Marie was ready to leave and Leone was asleep in the back seat. She had the diary and was ready to bring it up to date.

Lyle carefully put the box of watches in the back floor board, started the car and pulled out on Peachtree headed south on highway 41. He felt the gold coins in his pocket to make sure they were still there. A mist of cold rain hit the windshield and the leaves blew across the street as they weaved their way out of Atlanta. There was a Federal bank in Griffin he wanted to visit to collect his money. He would tell the bank he paid $35.00 for each $20.00 gold piece when in actuality, he had only paid twenty.

He laughed to himself after a quick mental calculation of making about $150.00 on the coins. He had a good idea that he could make a good profit on the watches also.

Marie looked at him as he quietly talked to himself and she knew they were in for a rough ride.

CHAPTER EIGHT

Gold Fever

Winter, Finally Heading South

Lyle was thinking about how much they had in the poke and what he had in his stash as they left Atlanta behind them. He answered the questions "correctly" so Mr. Archer would give him his federal license without checking out his answers. Some of his answers were outright lies, especially if the question asked about police or any kind of trouble. He knew they wouldn't check and besides he rationalized that it did no harm. All of this subterfuge pleased Lyle. He liked to make people think he was someone or something he wasn't.

The first day he tried his new scam, he made a lot of money. Making money intoxicated Lyle, so his thoughts were beyond reason and bordering on fantasy. He thought he would stop in Griffin, Georgia and see if he could buy some more coins before he traded them in to a Federal bank. He also had some scrap gold he wanted to send to Baltimore. He thought he would stay a few days if the weather didn't get too cold. Lyle also wanted to get a radio as soon as he could. He didn't know where he would keep it because there wasn't much room in the trailer. He would work that problem out as soon as he could. Maybe he could build a shelf and work on the trailer so the radio would fit. Marie shouted at him and broke his dream in a snap.

"Wake up, Lyle! You're driving over the middle of the road and a truck is coming!" He swerved the car back into their lane to avoid the truck.

"Lyle, are you day dreaming again? You can't daydream and drive the car at the same time!" Marie said angrily.

"You are right," he said and he slowed the rig a little and concentrated on his driving.

It didn't help much because he liked to dream about all the things he wanted to do. He was especially susceptible today because he had a new scam working. He rationalized that it wasn't really dishonest because he had the license. He forgot about the affidavit he signed in Atlanta and his words he had given.

He hoped he would find some more old ladies like he did in Atlanta so he could "scare" them into selling some gold coins. He would make over $200.00 on the coins and watches. Making a hundred dollars in one afternoon made Lyle drunk with power and anticipation. It was like he was driven into a wild mental frenzy counting all the money he would make.

It began to rain harder, mixed with bits of ice that made clinking noises on the windshield. Lyle was too busy driving and dreaming to think about the cold.

"I'm cold in here. Can you turn on the heater? Leone and I are both cold," Marie asked.

He didn't know anything about the heater controls so he pulled over and looked at the dashboard. He found the temperature lever and pushed it to the right. He turned the blower switch to the right and they felt warm air on their feet. He moved the upper lever and felt warm air on the windshield. He then moved it in the middle so it blew some warm air on the windshield and their feet.

Marie wiggled her toes in the warm air.

"If it gets any colder, we won't be able to stay in Griffin and I will miss out on my contacts," Lyle said out loud.

The inside of the Buick was comfortable now and Lyle pulled back on the highway and drove toward Griffin. They arrived in the outskirts of the town in mid afternoon. Lyle knew of a nice place to camp in Orchard Hill a little south of Griffin. They drove to the old campsite and parked in his favorite place for 25¢ a night. The rain had stopped but the weather was still a little chilly. They unhooked and set up the tear drop. Both Lyle and Marie were hungry so they drove back to Griffin and stopped at a diner. Lyle didn't like to spend the money but he didn't want to eat outside in cold weather. They both ate well and Leone had his milk and a little oatmeal that Marie ordered, though he didn't like the oatmeal until she added some sugar. The Sherlock medicine was working well for Leone. He was able to handle cow's milk a lot easier.

They finished and Lyle paid the bill. Lyle liked to work the "dirty food" scam when he was alone. He carried a match box in his pocket filled with a combination of dirt and dead bugs. Sometimes, when he was serious about not paying the bill, he would gather some live bugs or ants. Once he had a baby toad in the match box. When he was alone, he would order some food and just before he finished eating, he would put either some dirt under the food or one of his choice bugs. It worked every time but he wouldn't use it while Marie was with him because he was afraid she would tell the manager it was a trick.

They left the diner and got in the Buick to look over the town and case some proposed work areas. They drove around the town and scouted for some areas to work. There were a lot of mills that made hosiery and clothing. The town was busy for a small town. He found a few old houses on the south side of town that he would try the next day, weather permitting. He drove by both local banks and neither were Federal banks. He did see a lot of uniformed police patrolling the town both in cars and on foot. He wondered why there were so many. He was going to think about working Griffin after they got back to the rig.

The next morning Lyle and Marie arose early and hooked up their rig.

"I think it's better to drive on to Macon, Georgia. They don't have a Federal bank here," Lyle said.

In the back of his mind he was thinking about all the uniformed police he saw. He wondered how many were working undercover and he wanted to leave town as soon as he could.

He knew there were a lot of old homes in Macon. Because it was larger, he expected he would find a Federal bank to sell his coins. He really didn't want to run into a policeman. He also wanted to stay somewhere for a few days so he could send his gold to Baltimore and get the money back at general delivery.

They arrived on the northern outskirts of Macon early that afternoon. Upon Marie's insistence, they looked for a nice campground where she could wash diapers and clean the trailer. They stopped at

Chalmers Cabins and Campground on the Okmulgee River, a little north of town. It was a very nice place, just what Marie wanted. There was a nice communal bath with hot water and each campsite had a water faucet. Lyle had never stayed there and he was concerned about setting up in a strange area.

The owners met their rig and seemed to be very friendly. "How much is it to camp for a night?" Lyle asked

"With your rig camping cost 75¢ a night or $1.00 with electricity."

He reluctantly decided to stay at Marie's insistence. They even had a place to wash clothes. Lyle paid for 75¢ for 3 nights to keep Marie quiet. He didn't have to worry about electricity because they didn't have anything that needed it. He selected a nice site overlooking the river. They parked at the edge of some willow trees.

"I can make some baskets from the limbs if the owners don't mind," Marie said. She walked to the bathhouse to see what they had.

"They have a nice shower with hot water and you can take a bath tonight," she told Lyle after she returned.

"I'll take a bath as soon as I have a little time," Lyle said.

Marie knew better, unless she pushed him to take a bath. After Lyle took a bath, he usually felt better but complained about catching a cold. She didn't know what it was about Lyle and baths.

She set up the Coleman on their picnic table and started to fix some supper. Lyle was hungry so he went to the store at the front of the campground and bought some cube steaks, green grapes and a loaf of bread. Marie was busy fixing the meal when Mr. Chalmers and his wife Sarah walked up and started talking to Lyle. They were friendly and the conversation worked its way around to what Lyle did for a living.

He told them the spiel about being a federally licensed buyer and added a few small lies to make it sound better.

"Really!" They both said, almost in unison.

"We have some coins we have been saving and were afraid to take to the bank because the grace period ended in January. Can we show them to you and not get into any trouble?"

"Of course I'll look at them for you. Do you want me to go to your house or do you want to bring them here?" Lyle graciously asked.

"Please come to the house so we won't be bothered with prying eyes," Sarah said.

"As soon as I finish eating supper, I'll come to your house," Lyle said.

Marie didn't understand what Lyle was doing but she said nothing. In time, she would find out.

Lyle was so nervous he couldn't finish eating. He smoked 3 cigarettes before he finished and was still nervous. He offered Marie one of the new store bought "Wings" cigarettes. They weren't as strong as homemade Buglers, but they tasted better. She liked to smoke Sweet Picayunes, but Lyle didn't buy any. Lyle finished supper and got his gold assay box, money and his precious license and walked toward the Chalmer's house at the front of the campground.

They were waiting for him on the porch, rocking in identical old wooden chairs. Lyle stepped up on the porch and they invited him in.

"Please have a seat in the living room while we get our gold and coins," Sarah asked.

Mr. Chalmers brought out a chamois skin bag and gave it to Lyle. He had a small cardboard box, which he placed on the table by the couch.

Lyle carefully emptied the coins in his left hand. There were 10 coins of various values in almost new condition. The face value amounted to $210.00.

"I will give you $200.00 cash for the bag of coins," Lyle said.

The Chalmers readily agreed as if they were getting rid of stolen property. Lyle started to make out a receipt.

"We don't want or need a receipt," he said.

Lyle agreed and put the coins and the receipt book in his coat pocket. That was all the better for Lyle.

"Please look at what's in the little box for us," Sarah asked.

Lyle opened the box and found it full of a mixture of gold articles and old costume jewelry. Lyle acted like he was checking the pieces with his gold scratch and the acid.

"You have about $25.00 in gold and a lot of old worthless jewelry," Lyle said.

"See, I told you your mother's junk wasn't worth anything," Sarah said.

They agreed on $25.00 and Lyle paid them. Lyle was again very nervous and needed a smoke. He knew the value of the box was many times more valuable than what he paid.

"Do you mind if I smoke?" Lyle asked.

"Let's all go out on the porch and have a smoke," they both said.

They sat in the rocking chairs and lit their cigarettes and were silent for a while, rocking in the old chairs. They made a rhythmic sound on the old hardwood floor. Lyle remembered the rhythm and sound from his childhood when Estella, his birth mother, would rock him. Lyle was dreaming again and snapped back to reality as Mr. Chalmers started to talk.

"You and your wife and child can stay as long as you want at no charge. We are very appreciative of the way you helped us. I'll even give you a drop cord in case you need it."

Lyle was flabbergasted with their kindness after he had cheated them out of a lot of money, but they didn't know it. This was the kind of deal that Lyle was at his best with. He was very pleased and he felt a tiny bit guilty, but he had given them a small fortune for the gold he bought. The sad part was that they were happy with the deal and were willing to help Lyle and Marie all they could. Sarah left and came back with an electrical cord and a small clip-on lamp with a 25 watt bulb and gave it to Lyle. "This will make Marie very happy," Lyle thought, "and keep her from asking so many questions." Lyle thanked them as he started to leave.

"If you have some friends that can be trusted with your same problem, please keep me in mind," Lyle said.

"We would be glad to."

They both said good night as Lyle walked off the porch and doffed his hat. He walked back to the trailer carrying his new electrical cord and the light.

Marie had fed the babe and put him to sleep. She cleaned the stove and dishes and was smoking as she looked down at the river. She enjoyed these quiet times without the hectic days of travel. She hoped they could stay a few days. Lyle showed her the box of jewelry he bought and but not the gold coins.

"Look at the light and cord I got for you!"

He plugged in the cord and hooked the light on the inside vent of the tear drop. He turned it on and for the first time Marie had a light to see.

She was very happy and gave Lyle a hug. She looked through the box under the light and picked out the gold that needed to be prepared for their next shipment to Baltimore.

"I'll save the costume jewelry and sell it at our next set up," Marie said.

"That's a good idea," said Lyle.

Ordinarily Lyle wouldn't agree so easily, but he wanted Marie to stay out of any business to do with gold coins. Lyle remembered the old Chinaman who taught him how to make more money from gold coins. He got the other coins from the trailer and put them in the chamois skin bag. He gave Marie the nice velvet bag as a rare kind gesture because she had expressed interest in it. It was colored deep purple and that was special in Marie's religion.

Lyle sat on the bench by the table and started to shake the coins in the bag up and down in the chamois skin bag. The gold coins made a flat tinkling sound as they rubbed together. He put them down for a moment and lit a cigarette, and then started shaking them again.

"What are you doing Lyle?" asked Marie.

"I am going to make a little more than the $360.00 face value from the coins. The ones I got from the Chalmers were almost new and could stand a little wear. I can collect the gold dust from the chamois skin bag and send it to Baltimore."

Marie still didn't understand stand why he was shaking the coins, but she knew it wasn't right.

He shook them for about an hour, checking the surfaces every so often. He then put the bag down and lit another cigarette. He was tired from the stress and worry of buying the coins. "I'll put them down and finish in the morning," he decided.

He was exhausted and so was Marie. The babe was already

asleep and they crawled in beside little Leone and Marie went promptly went to sleep.

Lyle lay awake for a long time thinking about the way things were going. He would send the gold to Baltimore tomorrow and cash in the gold coins at the Federal bank. He was excited and worried at the same time. He finally went to sleep with the gentle noise of the river below, dreaming about the new radio he would buy soon. It was a little chilly but he didn't notice it.

He was awake early and headed for the bathhouse. He was going to take a rare bath because he wanted to be clean and neat when he went to trade in the coins. Before he left, Lyle asked Marie to shake the coins while he was gone.

Marie took the bag and began to shake it like Lyle. He was back in about 45 minutes and she gave him the bag.

"I am tired of shaking this silly bag. Why don't you do it?"

Lyle took the bag and looked inside. It was covered with tiny particles of gold. He filled his wash basin with water and sat it on the table. He then carefully emptied the contents in the water, filled the bag with water and tuned it inside out. He carefully rinsed the bag until he couldn't see any specks of gold, then let the water settle and removed the coins one by one. He carefully rinsed them all so the gold specks would fall to the bottom of the pan. Gold was much heaver than water and all of the gold settled to the bottom. He then carefully poured off the water until there was only gold covering the bottom.

"Marie, hold my handkerchief over the neck of my coffee cup."

He poured the remainder of the water and gold in his white handkerchief. The water passed through and several ounces of gold remained. He twisted the cloth so the water would drain out leaving almost dry gold flecks.

They sat down and drank their coffee while the gold dried.

"Marie, this is how you get a little more for your money. No one in this part of the country knows anything about this old Chinese trick. I expect we have about 3 ounces of gold we can send to Baltimore. At $35.00 an ounce that is an extra $105.00 we made."

Lyle wanted to go to the bank early that morning while Marie was packing the rest of the gold for shipment. He felt confident about the visit to the bank.

"After all, what could go wrong?" He said.

"Marie, make sure you put all the gold dust in the little medicine bottle with the screw on lid."

"That's what I am doing now," Marie told Lyle with an impatient tone in her voice. "How many times do you have to tell me?"

Marie finished feeding Leone and put him to sleep. She left the door open so the cool breeze could air out the little tear drop. She then sat down on the table bench and looked out over the gentle, flowing river, enjoying the peace and quiet of nature. As she smoked her cigarette, she relaxed a little thinking about her daily life. The stress of the past few weeks had been difficult. She didn't know what Lyle was doing but she was going to get to the bottom of it very soon. Whatever it was, it was on the outside of the law. She didn't like to be left out in the dark. As soon as he got home today, she was going to confront him and get the answers she needed.

She needed to wash all the diapers she had in case Lyle decided to leave when he got back. She never knew when they were going to stay the next night. He was always running from something or some person. She didn't know which but it concerned her.

At least they had a little money and were eating well. Leone was almost over his reaction to cow's milk. She had been very diligent in mixing the medicine with his milk. Each day she had put in a little less like the Sherlock's told her. In another week, he would be fine. She was also supplementing his milk with baby food and he seemed to do a lot better.

Sarah said it was alright for Marie to trim some willow so she could make baskets. This morning she cut a large bunch and tied it under the trailer. When it dried, she would make some more baskets. She liked to "set up" and sell things. It was an honest way of making money and she liked it. She never knew when Lyle might not come back to their camp. She felt her independence growing as she wrapped the gold for shipment. Lyle told her to have the money sent to general delivery, Lake Park, Georgia. At least she knew where they were going.

Sarah walked up with some fresh fruit she bought from the store.

Marie loved oranges. She pealed one and ate it immediately. She had never seen an orange until she came to America and she loved the taste and texture. It smarted her lips a little, but she ate them anyway.

"It looks like the cold snap missed us," Sarah said.

"I'm so glad. We don't have a heater and not many blankets. I'm happy the car has a heater, though, although I think we'll be going to Florida very soon and won't need a one," Marie said.

"I think I have something you can use," Sarah said.

She walked to a near by storage building and returned with a small electric heater.

She gave it to Marie and said, "We have no use for it. We found it in a camp space after some campers left. We kept it for over a year and now it's yours."

"Thank you so much! It is so kind of you to help. It will help us a great deal. Lyle will be very pleased and little Leone will sleep a lot better."

She took Leone and they walked to the post office about 3 blocks away. She mailed the package to Baltimore. She knew Lyle would be happy about it.

Lyle arrived at the bank and parked in the side parking lot. It was a huge, official looking building in the middle of Macon. He was apprehensive about going into any kind of office building; it seemed to remind him of a jail. He walked to the side door and went in the bank building.

Lyle had $360.00 face value in gold coins in his pocket, which would be worth over $600.00 plus the commission. a

He wasn't sure how to figure it but he knew he was going to make some money. This, added to the $150.00 he had left, would make a tidy sum. He would send the rest of his gold to Baltimore and would have about $200.00 coming back including the gold dust. He would have enough to buy his radio now. He was very upbeat when he walked into the Georgia Federal Bank. It would be more money than they ever had. The business was working well.

"I am looking for the manager of the gold purchase department," Lyle asked the secretary

"May I please see your license?" the secretary asked.

Lyle showed her the license and she directed him to an office at the far side of the bank.

"Ask for Mr. Forsyth," the secretary said.

Lyle did as instructed and was asked to wait. In a few moments, a large gray haired man appeared.

"May I see your license please?" Mr. Forsyth asked.

Lyle presented him his license and he studied it for a while.

"How may I help you?" Mr. Forsyth asked.

"I have some gold coins that I purchased from banks that I need to turn in," Lyle said.

"May I please have them?" Mr. Forsyth said.

Lyle gave him the gold coins.

"I'll have to determine the amount we owe you. I'll be right back," said Mr. Forsyth.

He left through a rear door. Lyle saw him call another person to come to the office with him. It seemed like he was gone forever. Lyle fidgeted and was very nervous. He smoked several cigarettes by the time he came back. Mr. Forsyth invited him in his office and sat down in his chair behind the desk.

"Lyle, please take a seat." Mr. Forsyth said.

"We have your money for the coins, but I am afraid they didn't weigh out to be as much as we first thought. I think the banks you bought them from should have weighed them before they sold them to you," he said.

"What do you mean Mr. Forsyth?"

"We have been running into this quite often with our agents in the field. There is a group of Chinese who have been shaving the coins so they can sell the gold dust. Mr. Archer should have briefed you on that. I am afraid you have been the victim of a Chinese scam," said Mr. Forsyth.

He handed Lyle one of the coins and described how he could tell there was a problem. "Look at the edges of the coins, they are almost smooth. Because the edge is rough, they jingle the coins in a sack and gather the dust and resell it," Mr. Forsyth said.

Lyle looked at the coin and saw the edge was smooth. He returned the coin to him.

"What does this mean to me?" Lyle asked.

"It means you are going to be short over $100.00 because they weighed short. We can only pay you the weight of the gold. After we weighed the coins, they were about 4 ounces short in face value. We have the difference amount plus your 10% commission. We are sorry that you lost almost $150.00 in the transaction, but please be careful next time. It is business and I have no choice but to give you what the gold weighs." said Mr. Forsyth.

Lyle gazed at the floor and looked very dejected. Nevertheless, in his heart he wanted to get out of there as soon as he could. He was very nervous and put on a very sad face. He still had made a lot of money because he had paid face value for the coins.

"We have a new rule starting the 1st of next month. All money turned in to a Federal bank must have a receipt of purchase from the bank of origin," said Mr. Forsyth.

"I will make sure I have a receipt next time," said Lyle.

"Not any receipt, but one of these," he said. He showed Lyle a book of printed official looking receipts. "They are numbered and have to be accounted for," he said. "Please sign the ledger for the receipts and you can be on your way."

He handed Lyle an envelope with the money. Lyle carefully counted the money and looked dejected to impress Mr. Forsyth. He checked his signature with the license and gave Lyle his license and the very official looking receipt book. They shook hands and Lyle started to leave.

"Don't be a victim of the scam artists again. It'll always cost you money," said Mr. Forsyth.

"You are very correct and I thank you for showing me the tricks of the trade," Lyle said. Little did he know, Lyle thought.

"You are quite welcome!" he said

Lyle heard him say to an associate as he left, "There goes another victim of the Chinese gang. I hope we catch them soon. What they don't realize is they can't sell the gold dust. All of the gold houses have been warned about not buying any flake or gold dust."

Lyle stopped in his tracks when he heard that part of conversation. He hurried out of the bank and sat in his car. He was exhausted from the ordeal. He had no idea they would weigh the coins. He had no idea the gold houses wouldn't accept dust anymore. Things were changing too fast for him to keep up.

He had wasted all that time and energy shaking the coins. He was very glad the bank officer hadn't suspected him or he would be on the way to jail. He had a bigger problem now. He needed a receipt from the bank so he could sell the coins. He didn't like that at all. He hurried back to the camp. He was hungry and wanted to eat. When he got back to the camp Marie was talking to Sarah and feeding Leone. Lyle slowly drove up so he wouldn't create a lot of dust. They had a little rain but not enough to settle the dust.

"Have you fixed something to eat?" Lyle asked.

"No, I haven't. I have been washing diapers and feeding Leone. What have you been doing besides running around?"

"Nothing really. Let's go to the diner and get some supper," Lyle said.

"There is a nice diner about 5 minutes down the road. You can't miss it with all the lights on the edge of the sign. I'll see you a little later," said Sarah.

Marie loved to eat out so she hurried and got in the car with Leone in her lap.

"Have a nice supper. We talked to some friends and they have some gold to sell if you can come by after supper," Sarah said.

"I'll stop by in a couple of hours and talk to you and Mr. Chalmers," Lyle said.

He drove out of the park and headed toward town. Lyle wanted some mashed potatoes and roast beef. Marie could already taste the bacon, lettuce and tomato sandwich.

Lyle didn't go back to look at the gold. He prepared the rig to leave early the next morning as Marie had predicted. He gathered every thing and hooked up the Buick so they would be ready early the next morning. He very carefully wound up the 50 foot extension cord. He wrapped the little heater in an old shirt so it wouldn't be damaged. Now that he had an extension cord, he could get a radio that operated on house voltage and batteries. Marie was getting used to his unplanned way of life, but it didn't mean that she had to like it.

"Did you finish the gold shipment?" Lyle asked.

"I wrapped and mailed it this morning," Marie said

"You mailed it!" Lyle said loudly. "I wished you hadn't done that, I wasn't supposed to mail the dust," Lyle said as he took the receipt from Marie. "We'll have to wait and see what happens, now."

"You asked me to wrap it for mailing. I was only trying to help; I can't read your mind!" Marie said.

Morning came early as they headed south on highway 41 toward Lake Park, Georgia. Lyle knew it as a nice quiet town close to the Florida line. "I have enough money so I won't have to work for a while and I can loaf. Maybe I can build a shelf for a radio," he thought.

"Lyle, we have to talk about what is going on and what you are doing."

"Let's get a few miles under our belt and I will explain everything." Lyle said.

Lyle took the next several hours explaining what he was doing. Marie said nothing until he was completely through.

"How could you get us in such a mess? You have a baby to think about! I don't understand why you have to cheat people. We can make a nice living with our set. With the gold and silver you by we will have a good living."

It was obvious she was hurt and angry but there was noting she could do.

"We'll work our way through it and I'll stop buying gold coins from people," he replied.

This satisfied Marie for a while as they drove on toward Florida. Lake Park was only a few miles north of the Florida line.

Lyle was wondering what kind of trouble he would be in with Fishlows in Baltimore. He had been doing business with them for a number of years and never had any problems except an occasional short check, which they corrected. He didn't need any more things to worry about.

The excitement of buying and selling gold coins was beginning to fade. He still had a few silver tricks in the bag with the federal license, but he wouldn't try them until later. Gold fever had been cured.

CHAPTER NINE

Lake Park

Winter in Georgia

After 3 days on the road and 2 flat tires, Lyle was ready to find his camp in Lake Park, Georgia. He was tired, grouchy and otherwise ill tempered. Much to his dislike, he had to purchase 4 new tires. The old tires were dry and rotted from sitting in the warehouse for so long. It cost him almost $40.00 to have them mounted with new tubes. He didn't get them balanced because it would have been another 50¢ per tire. When Lyle was this way, Marie was very quiet and said nothing unless asked.

Lake Park, Georgia was located about 15 miles south of Valdosta and a few miles north of the Florida line. Stately pines and crystal clear lakes that stretched as far as the eye could see made Lake Park one of the most beautiful spots in all of sunny south Georgia. Since 1890 it has been a quiet and out of the way community. The sunsets were spectacular, outlining the magnificent live oaks and magnolias. The people were charming and friendly. They went out of their way to spend time talking with strangers and neighbors. The only bank closed in 1929 and never reopened. The A&P grocery story was the largest business in town.

There were several small cafes where the locals gathered and talked about their community and friends. The food was excellent and very southern, with fried fish and hush puppies. Lyle didn't like hush puppies. If he was served grits, he would eat them with butter and sugar like he did corn meal mush. The locals would shake their heads in disgust.

The town had changed in the 6 years since he was there in 1928.

Lyle and his father Leon were on their way to Key West when the hurricane of '28 stopped their trip. They stayed for a few weeks and went back to Michigan.

His favorite old campground was gone. In its place were some single tourist cabins with tiny carports. The lake looked the same as well as the old trees. Lyle pulled into the Lake Park Tourist Court and parked under a huge Oak tree next to the road.

"What is that beautiful tree with the shiny green leaves?" Marie asked.

"That's an old Magnolia tree. In the early fall it has beautiful white flowers that have a nice fragrance," said Lyle.

Lyle got out of the car and met a nice looking young man walking toward him.

"My name is Jim Allen, may I help you?" he asked.

"Is your dad home?" Lyle asked.

"Dad passed away over 4 years ago. He had a bad accident on the lake and never recovered," said Jim.

Lyle knew it was Bill Allen's hobby of fishing with explosives to catch fish the easy way. He would mix soda, vinegar and lime in a weighted mason jar and drop it in the lake. It would explode several seconds later. The stunned fish would then float to the surface. He would gather them in and have a fish fry. What he didn't need, he sold.

"Was Bill fishing when the accident happened?" Lyle asked.

"So you know about his fishing habits," Jim said.

"I used to eat a lot of his fried fish. We would sit around a bon fire and tell stories about the old days in Michigan. He liked to brag about his big fish hook and pole," said Lyle.

"I forgot dad was from Michigan once we moved south. I stayed with my mother because she didn't want to come down here in 1918 when he got out of the army. He was tired of cold weather and working as a logger. We came down when he got hurt so I could help him finish the cabins. I am glad we did, it's so beautiful and peaceful here. Both Ruth and I love it here," said Jim.

"Are you the one who used to talk about Mexico and how pretty it was?" asked Jim.

"Your dad and I would spend hours talking about going to Mexico. The last time I was here, my father Leon was with me. They got along very well. Both had been in the lumber business in Michigan and knew a lot of the same people."

"I got out of the business in 1916 and never looked back," said Lyle. "I used to stay here when it was an Auto Park. My camp was by the large oak in the back."

"I'm glad you stopped. Dad told me to give you a place to park or a cabin to live in and not charge you anything," said Jim. "The old tree is still there. Come on, let's walk back and see if we can find you a place to park."

Lyle liked him instantly. He was like his father—always trying to help people.

They walked to the large Oak tree behind the cabins. There was an old boat shed where Bill used to keep his boats. The indentations were still there where Lyle had parked years ago.

Lyle told Jim about his plans to work on the tear drop so it would have a little more room. He also told him he might try and sell a few baskets on the road while he was working on the trailer.

"There's an electric plug in the shed. Pull your rig and park it where you want. There's also a water faucet by the shed," said Jim.

"We really appreciate it. I need to do some work on the car and trailer. Marie and I both need some rest from all the traveling we have been doing," said Lyle.

"Stay as long as you want. There's plenty of room. This time of year, we don't get many visitors. Lake Park is off the beaten path to Miami. Most of the Northerners use US 1 to go south," said Jim.

"I don't know what to say, Jim. It is a God-send to stay here while I finish the repairs and rest up," said Lyle.

"I'll bring you a key to cabin 8 so you can use it while you work on the trailer. It has a sink and toilet. The bathhouse is in the middle of the cabins. If you need to wash clothes, there is a laundry behind my house and you're welcome to use it," said Jim. "When you get set up, come up and have supper with us and meet my wife Ruth."

Lyle walked back to the car and told Marie about their good fortune. It really made Marie happy when he told her about the cabin. It had been so long since she had slept in a real bed with sheets, she didn't know what to say.

Lyle started the Buick and made his way to the new camp. He positioned the tear drop in the same holes he had used years before. He had a good feeling about this place and the pretty lake. He didn't like to go in the water because he couldn't swim, but he really liked the view.

Marie set up her stove on a small table in the boat shed. Lyle ran the extension cord and hooked up the light. Then he put blocks under the wheels and got the car unhitched.

Marie was happily humming a Russian song. Lyle usually told her to stop but this time he didn't seem to mind. She fed Leone and changed him, and then put him down to sleep in the trailer.

"Don't put him to sleep. We're going to Jim's house and have supper," said Lyle.

About that time, Jim walked up and gave Lyle the key to number 8. "Don't forget, we'll have supper ready in a hour or so. I'll come and get you when it's ready."

"Marie, here's the key to number 8. Why don't you go and see how it is while I finish setting up our rig," said Lyle.

Marie took the key and with Leone in her arms and walked the few feet to the cabin. She inserted the key like she was going into a mansion. She was so happy she couldn't get her words out correctly. When she got excited, her Russian accent grew a lot worse and today she was excited. She opened the door to a nice cozy one bedroom cabin. It was bright and warm with nice windows that overlooked the lake. There was a small table with two chairs next to the side window. The sun was shining on the white enameled top of the table and reflected on the white lace curtains. There were "pull down" blinds for privacy. She had never seen them and pulled them up and down to see how they worked. She laid Leone in the center of the bed and continued to look around the room.

The room felt so warm and cozy to her. There was a little bathroom in the corner with a sink and commode and a large mirror over the sink. She looked at herself for the first time in a long time. She jerked back and looked again. She hardly recognized herself. Her hair was a mess and she had dark circles under her eyes. It frightened her to the extent that her knees grew weak. She sat down on the commode top and tears came to her eyes. She held her face in her hands and sobbed quietly to herself. Lyle hated to see anyone cry and right now, she hated Lyle.

She hadn't slept on clean sheets since Leone was born, and that wasn't really sleeping because of the hospital setting. The tear drop had a J.C. Penney's cotton blanket on the bottom. The old surplus mattress was lumpy and smelled from the dampness it collected. The old pillows were chicken feather filled. The feathers would poke out and add a prickly feel to the pillows.

"I haven't had a good bath since we left Kentucky and I'm so tired," she said out loud. She made up her mind as she walked out of the cabin.

"Lyle, you watch Leone while I get a bath and wash my hair. I don't want to hear any excuse. He'll be asleep in the trailer and all you have to do is check him," Marie said in a huffy voice as she gathered her stuff and walked to the bathhouse.

Lyle knew when to keep his mouth shut. He watched Marie as she walked to the bathhouse. It was best he kept his mouth shut, now. He had seen her this way before but not quite as bad. She really had a bee in her bonnet today.

He sat down at the table under the boathouse shed and lit a cigarette. He looked out over the calm waters of Long Pond Lake. The lakes in the region were sinkhole lakes. It was strange to him to sit outside in November in shirt sleeves. The lakes in the region were warm which affected the air temperature by the lakes. It was several degrees warmer by any of the lakes.

Balboa Lake was the largest and deepest. The last time he was there, a team of scientists from Canada was trying to determine how deep the lakes were. He asked about it at a local café but they didn't know. They never found the bottom of any of the spring fed lakes but it was estimated to be over 300 feet deep.

As the story goes, one team lost a deep probe with a lead anchor. It was snatched out of their hands and nearly sunk the boat when it approached 300 feet. On occasion, you could see bubbles of gas escaping from the bottom. At night, it created a strange spectacle when the gas bubbles reached the surface. They were accompanied by strange moaning noises.

These stories about the lakes created an aura of mystery surrounding them. Lyle had seen and heard the bubbles at night or late evening. Sometimes you could see small flashes of light when the bubbles rose to the surface. Lyle wondered what caused them and was a little frightened of them or whatever caused them. He was afraid of anything he didn't understand. The locals would refer to it as "them bubbles." Just the sound of it made Lyle have goose bumps.

The trailer door faced the shed and he could hear the babe if he cried. He hoped he didn't cry because he didn't have any idea what to do if he did. He didn't tend to his daughter Ruth and wasn't about to start with this one.

He mailed a card to his father Leon a few weeks ago and said he would be in Lake Park at the old campground. He was a couple of weeks late getting there and wondered if his dad had come and gone. He would ask Jim after supper if he had seen or heard from him.

His daughter Ruth was another thing. His dad was very close to Ruth. He would tell Ruth that Lyle was in Lake Park and ask her to take him there. He didn't want her around for a while, especially if he was doing work on the trailer. He didn't want to pay for another cabin and they always needed money.

Marie and Ruth didn't get along very well because their age was nearly the same. Ruth was about a year older and resented Marie. For Lyle's sake, Marie avoided getting into an argument with her. She knew blood was thicker than water, or so the saying went.

Marie was heading back to the cabin and drying her hair. She didn't stop or say anything to Lyle. Instead she went into the cabin and closed and locked the door.

"Open this door Marie, I want to talk to you!" shouted Lyle.

"Watch Leone while I get ready and leave me alone so I can have a little privacy. I'll be out as soon as I'm ready."

This angered Lyle to no end as Leone started to cry.

"Marie, the babe is crying. Come and see to him!" Lyle shouted.

"Pick him up and pat him gently on the back. He should go to sleep again. He's hungry and needs changing," said Marie through the door.

Lyle was standing on the top step with his face almost on the door talking to Marie. It was a funny sight as Marie looked through the side window and saw him. He was holding Leone in one arm and waving the other like he was a crazy man. Leone was sound asleep from all the rocking motion. Lyle saw he was asleep and rushed to put him down. He looked at his arm and it was all wet. He turned on his heel and sat down quickly, lighting a cigarette as Marie laughed at him through the window.

Marie came out 30 minutes later with her hair in a nice curled bun in the back. She was clean and had on fresh clothing.

"Lyle, get ready while I feed and change Leone. The next time he gets wet you better learn how to change him," said Marie.

Lyle said nothing as he went to the wash room to get ready. "What has happened to Marie?" he thought. "She never would talk to me like that. It must have been Betty talking to her. Yes, Betty is the problem. I'll put a stop to that as soon as I get a chance. If it isn't Betty, what else could it be? I just don't understand."

"Why don't you use the cabin sink Lyle? It would be a lot easier. You never take a bath anyway and the sink will work fine," said Marie.

"I don't want anything to do with that cabin," said Lyle.

"I don't care where you sleep, Lyle, I'm going to sleep in the cabin between the nice clean sheets," said Marie.

Flaring her nostrils a little, she turned away from him. She did that when she was getting angry. It took to a lot to get her angry but when she did, watch out!

About 30 minutes later Jim ambled down the path. He was big like his father and walked in a similar gait. Lyle could tell he was used to hard work and didn't mind it. His gentle personality was very nice to be around. He made people comfortable when he spoke.

"Come on folks, supper is ready. I hope you're hungry and like fried chicken and mashed potatoes! Ruth is a good cook and likes company. We don't have any kids and we make it up with friends. Here, let me carry the baby. What's his name?" Jim asked.

Marie told him "Leone," and she looked a little worried as Jim cradled him in his big arms.

They went into the back of Jim's house. They entered a large well lit, screened in back porch. It was decorated with fall leaves and colors. They had a red candle lit on the corner table. The dining table was next to the wall facing the lake. It was set with nice plates and silverware. There was a big plate of fried chicken in the middle.

Marie was hungry and couldn't wait to eat. It seemed like years since she had had a good meal, but it was only a few days ago.

Ruth came in the room and Jim introduced her to Lyle and Marie. Jim laid Leone in a basket-like crib and pulled it next to Marie.

"Sit here and you can watch him. He's a heavy scudder. I bet he'll be a big man," said Jim.

"His grandfather is a big man, well over 6 feet. He has blond hair like him," said Marie.

"I like children. Jim and I never had any but we still have hope someday. He is as cute as a cats meow. What's his name?" asked Ruth.

"His name is Leone after his Grandfather. I sometimes call him Blonde because of his almost white hair," said Marie.

Her Russian accent was very evident but she was able to speak very clearly and everyone understood.

"Let's eat before the food gets cold," said Jim.

Everyone dug into the meal. Lyle and Marie ate well because they were relaxed and very hungry. Lyle was a light eater but he outdid himself with a large piece of sweet potato pie with whipped cream.

After the meal was over, Marie and Ruth cleaned the table and were washing the dishes. Lyle and Jim went outside where Lyle could smoke. Neither Jim nor Ruth smoked and didn't allow smoking in their house.

"Lyle what kind of work is planned for your trailer?" Jim asked.

"My first thought was to enlarge it so I could add a radio. I want to make it a little bigger for Marie and the babe. I can see now she isn't very happy with the way things are. I didn't realize it until she went in the cabin," Lyle answered.

"I built a lumber storage shed behind the boathouse. My father bought enough lumber to build 12 cabins and we completed only 8. I'll give you the key to the shed. You're welcome to use all the lumber you want to work on your trailer," Jim said.

Lyle was flabbergasted. He had planned to spend at least $100.00 on lumber for the expansion. It would be a great help and he was very grateful.

"That is very good of you Jim. I know your father would be proud of you for being so kind. Jim, he was also a very kind and generous man and you are just like him," said Lyle.

What he was really thinking was how much free lumber he could get without him getting suspicious. He needed to build a table so Marie could do her "set up" on the road. He hoped Jim wouldn't mind how much he used.

"Jim, is there a jeweler in town? I have some watches that need repairing." said Lyle.

"There is old retired jeweler in town. He retired and sold his shop in Valdosta a few years ago. He does some work in his home. I'll take you to see him tomorrow. He is very slow but does excellent work," said Jim.

Lyle was thinking money again. He wanted to pay for the repair by giving some watches in trade. He hoped he could work a deal because he wanted to sell some of the watches before he left town.

"When you have time we'll go see him," said Lyle.

Jim pulled a key from his key ring and gave it to Lyle.

"This is the key to the lumber shed. Use all you want. The nails and some hardware are in the back cabinet. He had some tools on the back shelf," said Jim.

"Much obliged to you!" said Lyle.

"I want you and Marie to move in number 8 until the job is finished. There is no use being cramped and uncomfortable when you can sleep in the cabin. It is the last one we built and has only been rented 3 times. I think you'll find it very comfortable for you and your family," said Jim.

Marie and Ruth came down the steps and chatted a bit about the meal and weather. Marie looked very tired and Leone was asleep in her arms.

"There are blankets and some extra towels in the closet. Feel free to make yourself at home," said Ruth.

"I think we'll turn in for the evening and get some rest. We've been on the road since Leone was born in August and we're road weary," said Lyle.

They headed toward the cabin after saying good night and thanking them for a nice home cooked meal. Lyle didn't say much except that he wanted to get his stuff so they could stay in the cabin. He didn't say anything about staying in the trailer.

"I should ask him why he isn't going to stay in the trailer since he had been so firm about it earlier," thought Marie. But, she thought better of it and left it well enough alone.

She got Leone's basket out of the Buick and put it on the floor of the cabin. She got a blanket from the closet and spread it on the floor where she placed the basket. She was going to let him sleep there for the night and see how it went. She put Leone in the basket with his bottle and he went sound asleep. He had been sleeping all night for the past few days since he could now drink straight cow's milk. She was glad she didn't have to bother with the medicine or goat's milk.

Lyle and Marie lay down on the nice comfortable bed and slept the sleep of weary travelers.

They awoke when Leone wanted his breakfast. Marie was up feeding Leone and Lyle went outside to check the weather and use the bathroom. He selected the Oak tree for his morning relief and forgot about the bathroom in the cabin. Marie reminded him and he grudgingly came in and closed the bathroom door behind him. After they ate the breakfast that Marie had fixed on the Coleman stove, they sat under the shed and looked out on the water.

"I am going to build you a table to use as a set up. Make some baskets and brooms so we can make a little money while I build the new parts our trailer," Lyle said.

Marie made a mental note-it was the first time Lyle referred to anything as "ours." He was acting very out of character. Maybe he was mellowing, but Marie really didn't know.

"Lyle I don't want you to pull any of your schemes on the Allens.

They are too nice and have been very generous with us. You know how to do all the things you do but don't do it here!" Marie said angrily.

Lyle reluctantly agreed. He opened the Buick and got out his tools and began to plan what he was going to do with the tear drop. He looked in the wood shed and found most everything he would need. He selected the right lumber and set it outside. The saw horses were still usable and he set them up near the wood shed just under the shade of the oak. He set about building a table so Marie could use it as a set up on the highway.

Marie got out her basket molds and set them on the shed table. She selected the best willow from under the trailer and started trimming it like she learned from old Mr. Fletcher at the Kentucky camp. She soon had the right pieces and she started to weave the willow around the molds.

Jim walked up and asked what they were doing in a friendly tone. Lyle told him what they had planned and Jim thought it was a good way to start.

"Lyle, I am going into town to get some supplies. Would you like to ride along and see about getting your watches repaired?" Jim asked.

"I'll meet you in few minutes after I clean up and get the watches," Lyle said.

He quickly washed his hands and face in the cabin and put on a coat. He brushed his hair and checked his moustache. He wanted to look good for the trip up town.

Jim and Lyle left in his 28 Model C Ford truck. He needed a few groceries and some things from the hardware store. It was next door to the A&P.

"Lyle, the jeweler lives on the next block. I'll drop you off and introduce you to Mr. Minor. I'll meet you at the A&P in a little while," said Jim.

Lyle agreed and they stopped at Mr. Minor's house. Jim introduced Lyle to him and then excused himself and told Lyle he would meet him a little later. The old man invited Lyle to have a seat at the kitchen table. Lyle agreed and started to explain what he wanted.

Mr. Minor asked to see the watches. He examined 4 of the better ones and told Lyle he would fix the 4 for $20.00. Lyle agreed and left the watches with him.

"Mr. Minor, what will the watches be worth once they are fixed?" asked Lyle.

He looked at each one very carefully. "They would be worth about $15.00 to $20.00 each," he said. "Don't be in a big hurry, mister. I'm old and a little feeble. I don't get around as good as I used to. I should have them in a week or so."

"That should be fine Mr. Minor. I'll be at Jim Allen's for a couple of weeks working on my rig," said Lyle.

Lyle left by the front door and walked toward Jim's truck in the A&P parking lot. He had wanted to show the jeweler his federal license but resisted the temptation. He knew he was on the edge of his good fortune and he didn't want to spoil it. He would try and do everything as legal as he could while he was in Lake Park. Of course, this didn't mean he wouldn't try and make a little extra once he was set up on the highway in front of Lake Park Tourist Court.

"How did the visit go with the jeweler?" asked Jim.

"I left the watches with him and he said he would let me know in a couple of weeks. It'll take me that long to get my rig fixed and rest from the long trip," said Lyle. He and Jim Lyle headed back toward the camp.

"Jim, I need to stop at the post office and see if I have anything at general delivery," said Lyle.

"The post office is on our way to The Court. I'll stop and let you check the mail. You can use our address if you want to. It won't be any problem at all," said Jim

Lyle thanked him and said he might do that. In his heart, he wasn't about to let Jim know any of his business. He didn't let Jim know how he felt but kept it to himself.

He went in the old post office building and asked for his mail at general delivery. He had a registered letter and some money sent registered. He signed both receipts and gave them to the clerk. The clerk counted out his money. Lyle was a little surprised that it was about $150.00 short. Maybe it would be in the next letter. Baltimore sometimes did that. He took the money and put it in his pocket, thanked the clerk and left. He put the letter in his pocket and would read it when he got back to his camp.

Lyle was very surprised to see Marie had made several baskets. She had found some more willow on the lake shore and was drying it in the sun.

"If you want me to sell these things, you had better make a table," said Marie.

Lyle busied him self with making the table the rest of the afternoon. Finally, around dark, he was finished. It was about 6 feet long and 2 feet wide. It was perfect for a good set up. He had forgotten about the letter until it fell out of his pocket. He sat down at the boat shed table and read it. When he finished, he was white as a ghost.

They stated that they could no longer accept gold dust from any agent. They were required by law to send it back to a Federal bank with a letter of explanation. They had to include Lyle's name and an explanation of why they kept the gold. They included a receipt for 4.25 troy ounces of 22 karat fine gold dust.

Lyle clutched the letter and thought about all the trouble he could get into. He had just lost $150.00 and received a threat of getting into trouble with a Federal bank. He knew he could no longer use his license to turn in gold to a Federal bank. He still had the silver angle to work. He would let things ride for a while before he tried it.

Lyle and Marie cleaned up, ate supper and retired for the night with Leone sound asleep in his little basket. Marie wondered what the next day would bring as she fell into a sound sleep. Lyle laid awake for a long time wondering about what he should do and how much trouble he was in. He could hear the bubbles of the lake and wondered what caused them at night. It frightened him a little thinking about the noise they made, as he fell into a fitful sleep.

CHAPTER TEN

Cabin Number Eight

Late Winter, South Georgia

Lyle didn't sleep very well the first night in the cabin. He wasn't used to a soft bed so far off the floor. He had problems sleeping when he had plans on his mind. He was trying to do as little as he could in the tear drop trailer and still be able to make a place for his radio. He knew he had to make room for Leone because he was growing like a weed. Marie was starting to ask questions about the size of the trailer.

She already said something about the mattress because it smelled. She also complained about the storage space for Leone's clothes. He was tired of her complaints.

"At least you have a place to sleep," Lyle said out loud.

"What did you say, Lyle? I was sound asleep. Don't be so loud, you'll wake up Leone."

"All right, I was just talking out loud, I'll be quiet. Go back to sleep, Marie."

"I'd completely forgotten about getting a radio. I'll ask Jim if he knows where I can get a good used radio that will play on batteries and house voltage," thought Lyle.

He was dreaming about listening to Amos and Andy and how they made him laugh. He was thinking about listening to the news so he could be up with world affairs and hear what that Roosevelt fellow was doing in Washington. Lyle thought it was against the law to marry a cousin. He thought Eleanor was his cousin but wasn't sure. Her last name was also Roosevelt.

"Who are you talking to Lyle? You have been talking for the last half hour and there's no one in the cabin except me and Leone," said Marie

"I was making plans to change the trailer so we will have a little more room," said Lyle

Marie didn't say anything. She got up and tended to Leone and herself before he got out of bed. She looked at her old wooden handled tooth brush. She had a mixture of soda and salt in a little jar that was almost empty. She wet her tooth brush and poured some of the mixture on the brush and brushed her teeth. It tasted awful and made her gums bleed.

"The last time I went to the store, I saw a sign that advertised tooth cream. It said the cream was refreshing and cleaned the teeth better than any other product. There was a picture of a cute little baby on the poster, too. I'll get some the next time I go to a store. Lyle doesn't need any because he has those ugly red store bought things he calls teeth," Marie thought to herself.

She knew Lyle would be hungry and went outside to start fixing some breakfast while he used the water closet. It was a little cool outside but refreshing to feel the cool air and the warm breeze from the lake.

"If it gets any colder, I'll have to move the stove inside and cook. I can open the window by the table and use the Coleman," Marie said out loud. "Here I am talking out loud, just like Lyle. What's the matter with me anyway? What in the world I am doing? I'm getting just like Lyle, and talking out loud to myself is a bad habit," she thought.

Breakfast was over and Lyle had gone into town with Jim to look for some material to fix the trailer. Marie would be glad when he started. She knew it wouldn't be fixed like she wanted, but anything was better than they had. She opened the door to the trailer and laid Leone down to take a nap. He was getting pretty big now and slept well at night. He liked his morning naps, which gave Marie time to do her chores.

She wanted to make some more baskets and brooms if she could find some pine straw. While she was looking for straw next to a big pine, she saw a pile of what looked like logs with small roots. She asked Ruth what they were. Ruth told her they were palmetto logs left over from clearing the area to build cabins. They tried to burn them but they wouldn't burn so they left them in a pile.

Marie had an idea. She brought one of the logs back to the camp and pealed off the outer husk. She could see the root was made of thousands of tiny bristles embedded in a soft woven like wood. She worked the root wood from between the bristles and saw it would make a nice stiff brush. She used one of Lyle's small saws and cut a piece from the root. She worked with the root and soon had a nice brush trimmed and shaped. She found some sandpaper in the shed and sanded the handle until it was smooth. She trimmed the edges with her sewing scissors and she ended up with a nice brush with perfect bristles. The bristles were stiff yet pliable. It seemed like it would last a long time.

Marie opened Lyle's can of 40 cut pound shellac. She found an old paint brush and shellacked the handle of the brush. It made a nice looking brush. The handle was shaped like a scrub brush. It looked like it was purchased from a dime store.

"I can make some of these in different sizes and sell them on the set up along with my baskets," said Marie out loud. "There I go again, talking out loud like Lyle," she thought.

She didn't know it, but the Seminole Indians in south Florida had been making palmetto brushes for many years. However, Marie's brushes were a little different and a lot nicer. She couldn't wait to tell Lyle, but on second thought, she wouldn't say anything and would see if noticed them.

Marie made 5 brushes in a short time. She wondered how much to charge for them. The brushes and baskets would make a nice set up when Lyle moved the table down to the highway. She had some sorted pine straw she was weaving into a small whisk broom when Ruth walked up.

"What are you making, Marie?" asked Ruth

"I'm just finishing some straw brooms for my set up. How do you like the palmetto brushes I made?" asked Marie.

"You made these! Marie, they're beautiful!" said Ruth. "Are you going to sell them when Lyle sets up the table out front?"

"I hope to sell a few if anyone will buy them," said Marie.

"How much are you going to charge for them, Marie?" asked Ruth.

"I was thinking about 75¢ for all the items. I'd like to make a little sign that says 'Marie's Home Made Articles.' I'll get Lyle to help me because I can't write English very well," said Marie.

"Marie, I used to be a school teacher in Michigan. I'll help you with the sign. I'll make it out of wood so it will last a long time."

"Oh! Ruth that would be so nice if you could do that for me."

"Marie, you should charge a little more for the baskets. They are so well made and are very pretty. You could get at least $1.25 for them," said Ruth.

"Maybe you're right, Ruth. I'll think about it while I get ready to set up."

"I want to buy one of the brushes so I can try it out on my floor. Marie, here's 75¢ for the brush."

"No Ruth, that's a gift for being so kind to me. A lot of people don't like foreigners, especially Russians. I'm happy you don't have those kind of feelings."

"Thanks Marie, I appreciate it a lot. I'll always remember you when I use the brush. I need to go back and start cooking for supper. Jim and Lyle should be back very soon. Jim is always hungry," said Ruth.

"Let the shellac dry over night before you use it. It should be fine in the morning. Thanks for everything," said Marie.

They waved at each other as Ruth went back to her house. Marie thought she was a very nice person and liked her a lot. Most of the people Lyle knew were thieves or crooks. It was a nice change to meet the Allens. They were down home folks and pleasant to be around.

Marie decided she would put some shellac on a few of the baskets to see how they looked. "It really helps the look and feel of them. I will charge $1.25 for them as Ruth had suggested," thought Marie.

She heard Jim's old truck turn in the drive way. It seemed to backfire every time he shut it off. On schedule, it backfired as they got out of the old Ford.

Lyle got out carrying a brown box under his arm and walked toward the cabin.

"Marie, I finally bought a radio like I've always wanted. Jim knew a man who had some used radios for sale and I bought this one for $10.00. It's a 1932 Philco Model 16B with 6 tubes. They call it a tombstone radio because it looks like a tombstone. It has 4 bands! I can listen to overseas broadcasts and everything!" said Lyle.

"Just look at you holding the radio like a baby under your arm. I wish you liked Leone as much as you like that radio."

Lyle didn't answer but looked at Marie with a hard look. She knew he would fuss at her when the Allens were out of sight. She knew he paid more than $10.00 for it because it still had the new tag on it. "Let him lie if it makes him feel better and it only hurts Lyle," thought Marie.

"Look Marie, it has a new battery with a charger! Look at the aerial. All I have to do is throw it up in a tree and get all the stations I want," said Lyle.

In 1931, RCA sold the patent for Super Heterodyne radios to other manufactures. The difference between the old style TRF (tuned radio frequency) and the new Super Heterodyne radio was it only needed one dial to tune. The old TRF had 4 or 5 dials. It made it a lot easier and much more sensitive to pick up stations. It was a lot easier to tune with one knob.

"Have fun with the thing Lyle. I have to work on my set up," said Marie.

Lyle saw the gallon of shellac sitting on the table with Marie's baskets. "What are you doing with my shellac? That stuff costs $2.00 a gallon!" shouted Lyle.

"Don't get your underwear in a knot, Lyle, I used it to waterproof my baskets! They'll be easier to sell if they look nicer," said Marie.

"Stop using my stuff to make your baskets, Marie. The things probably won't sell here anyway," said Lyle.

"Look Lyle, I'm going to use the shellac. If I sell some I'll give you your precious $2.00 for the shellac!" shouted Marie.

She was getting ready to throw his radio battery in the lake because she was so mad at him but Jim walked up and they stopped arguing. Marie started to calm down when he complimented Lyle on the nice brushes he made. Marie spoke up and let everyone know she made the brushes and it was her idea.

"They really are nice brushes, Marie. I know they'll sell very well. It's nice the way you shellacked the handle. It makes them look store bought," said Jim. "Let's move your set up table on the road tomorrow and display your homemade articles. Ruth is working on your sign and it will be ready in the morning,"

Lyle finally got around to asking, "What brushes?"

Marie showed him the 8 nice brushes she had made. She actually had made 10 and gave one to Ruth and kept one for her own use.

"I gave one to Ruth for making the sign for my set up," said Marie.

"When you are working the set up, Ruth will watch your baby so you won't have to worry abut him all the time," said Jim

"That's very nice of you. I'll let her know when I'm ready to start my set up," said Marie.

Lyle wasn't part of the conversation between Jim and Marie and it made him feel a little funny. He didn't like the idea of Marie giving away anything, but he kept quiet because Jim was there. "Marie is getting too independent. She gets her own way too much. I'll have to put a stop to that. I just don't know how," thought Lyle.

He walked to the shed and started to set up his radio. He hooked it to the electric plug and turned it on. All he could hear was static mixed with an occasional music sound.

"Lyle, don't you need to hook up the aerial to make it work?" Marie asked.

"Mind your own business, this is my radio!" said Lyle.

He thought about it a minute and got out the coil of aerial wire. He tied a piece of wood to one end and threw it over the lowest limb of the Oak tree. It caught and held. Lyle didn't know it, but he would lose most of the aerial because he forgot to tie a slip knot on the end of the aerial wire. He took the other end of the wire and sat down next to the back of the radio. He touched the back of the radio and it shocked him so bad he ended up flat on his back next to the table.

Marie was laughing so hard she was doubled up watching Lyle work on his Philco. He was about to get up when she walked over and helped him. He was a mixture of angry, frightened and embarrassed to end up on the ground by an electric shock. It was his first and he didn't like the jolting tingling sensation a shock produced. It frightened him more than it hurt.

Marie was still laughing to herself as Lyle sat down and had a cigarette. She turned the radio off and looked at the back of the radio.

The instructions, printed in red, said to "Always shut the radio off before connecting the antenna." Marie read them aloud.

"Lyle, read the instructions before you operate the radio and you won't get knocked on you back side!" said Marie, laughing.

After Lyle got up, he brushed his clothes, though he couldn't brush off his hurt feelings like he did the dirt. He was quite angry, but didn't hold his anger very long. He was angry one minute and calm the next. Marie was the opposite. It took her a long time to get angry and she stewed in her anger for a long time.

He got his tools and started to get the supplies from the lumber shed to start on the trailer. He measured the radio and battery pack and added the dimensions to his plans.

He had decided to remove the back trunk portion and extend the length by 2 feet. He wanted to make a place to put a bed that wasn't on the floor. He could use the underside for storage. The tear drop section of the back would be rounded and a widow put in the back. The area were the outside kitchen was would become the inside bed area without a raised back.

Lyle planed to widen the trailer by 6" inches on each side. He would do that by moving the wooden frame over to the passenger side 6" and building an extra 6" on the driver's side.

The rounded portion of the roof in the center would be leveled out and made tall enough to stand beneath. The window and small kitchen area in the center would be on the passenger side. On the opposite wall, the storage cabinet would be extended and made taller.

He would make a small eating area and a crib for Leone where the old bed used to be. He planned a nice shelf over the eating area where he could mount his Philco radio. He would add a couple of electrical outlets, one in the kitchen area and one for the radio. He was also planning to add a 6' x 6' square storage tray under the trailer to carry long items such as willow and fishing poles.

Lyle was a master planner but a very poor finisher. He told Marie of his plans and she made some small changes, such as a small sink with an outside drain and maybe an ice box for Leone's food. Under the sink, she wanted a small cabinet for her kitchen utensils and dishes. Lyle reluctantly agreed.

He went to the cabin to ask Jim if he could help move the table to the front so Marie could make her set up. Jim brought the truck around and they loaded the table and drove to the front.

Marie selected a nice area under the big oak in front. It had plenty of shade and a good parking area. She would see how it went when she made her first set up. She could hang her new sign on the tree so travelers and locals could see it. Ruth gave her an old white bed spread to cover the table. It really looked nice with all her articles set up on a white background.

Jim suggested she use his old wooden wheel barrow to carry her set up to the front. She was welcome to store it at night under their garage. He assured her it would be safe from any harm. Marie though it was a good idea and agreed.

"Lyle, I want you to help me push the wheel barrow in the morning while I take Leone to be with Ruth," said Marie.

"Ok Marie, I'll help with moving the set up to the front. But it will be your job to put it in the garage at night," said Lyle.

She agreed and planned what she would bring to the set up. Lyle got the wheelbarrow from the garage and pushed it back toward their camp. It was an old thing with a welded metal wheel, flat-bottomed and a vertical back next to the wheel. The handles were old tent poles with a carved grip. The wheel made a crunching sound on the gravel path to cabin number 8.

Earlier that day Marie had made a fishing line. She took an old nail and bent it in the shape of a hook. Then she tied some heavy construction string to the nail and fastened some left over chicken skin she got from Ruth to the nail as bait. She tied a heavy nut to the line about 2 feet up and then drove a stake in the ground and tied the 50' piece of string to it. She stood by the shore and circled the line over her head and threw it out as far as she could. She had forgotten about it until she neared the lake and saw the line twitching in the water and moving back and forth.

"A fish, a fish, I've caught a big fish!" shouted Marie.

She and Lyle hurried to the edge and started to haul in the line. It fought hard against Lyle's hands and cut his palms. Marie could see the outline of a big fish as it came near the shore.

Lyle finally pulled it up on the grass after several minutes of a hard fish fight.

"What in the world is the thing!" shouted Marie loud enough for the whole camp to hear. "It doesn't have any scales and what are the funny whiskers around its ugly mouth?" she asked.

The fish flopped toward Lyle and he jumped back, falling in the water. He made a big splash as he landed near the edge with his feet still on the shore.

"Help! Help! I can't swim!" Lyle shouted.

For the second time that day, Marie stood by and laughed at Lyle.

"For goodness sakes, Lyle, the water's only a few inches deep where you are. Pull your feet under you and stand up!" she said.

About that time Ruth, Jim and several other travelers came to see what happened. Marie and Lyle both had been very loud with the fish and Lyle falling into shallow water.

"Come on Lyle, take my hand," Jim said.

He stepped in the shallow water and gave Lyle his hand and helped him out of the lake.

Lyle looked like a drowned rat with his salt and pepper black hair covering his face. His glasses were hanging on one ear with a wet cigarette drooping out of the corner of his mouth. The entire camp had a good laugh.

Lyle's instant reaction was to be angry, but he saw all of the smiling faces and started to laugh at himself. This broke the ice and everyone was talking and laughing at the same time as they looked at the strange fish.

"What kind of beast did I catch?" asked Marie.

"Marie you've just caught the biggest cat fish I have ever seen out of Long Pond Lake. It must weigh 25 or 30 pounds," said Jim.

"Do you eat it?" asked Marie

"Eat it! It is the best tasting fish you'll every have!" said Jim. "I tell you what. I'll take the fish to the house, skin it and get it ready to deep fry. That is, if it's alright with you Marie," said Jim.

"It's alright with me but I'll be hanged if I am going to eat any-thing that looks like a cat," said Marie.

Jim picked up the struggling catfish and cut the line close to his mouth. Typical of catfish, it swallowed the entire hook, bait and line. He carried it toward his house with the rest of the people following. They all wanted to see how much it weighed. It was 38 pounds.

Marie didn't give a tinker's dam how much it weighed or what kind of cat it was. She was determined she wasn't going to eat any. She sat down on the cabin step as Ruth brought Leone to her.

"He's been fed and given a nice hot bath and he's ready for bed," said Ruth.

"Thanks a lot Ruth, I really appreciate it. It has been a long days" said Marie

Marie took Leone and put him in is little bed in the cabin. As Ruth said, he went fast asleep. She thanked Ruth again and excused herself as she needed to clean up a bit from the fish catch.

"We'll see you at the fish fry, Marie," Ruth said as she left.

"Not if I can help it," she said to herself. She was still a little rattled from catching such a large and strange fish. She had never seen or heard of a catfish.

Lyle changed his clothes and hurried back to Jim's house to join in the excitement. Lyle liked a crowd around him so he could exercise his ego. He would brag about Marie catching the big catfish although he wouldn't tell her that.

He had brought the Philco radio in and finally got it hooked up. He put it in on the little table in the cabin. "It looks like a big brown tombstone," thought Marie. She had no experience with radios but it looked simple enough. She turned the large knob on the left like Lyle did. It made a loud click and buzz. Marie jumped back because it frightened her a bit. Soon, she could hear voices and music but she couldn't tell what it was. She read the center dial. It had 4 settings: Broadcast, short wave Europe 1, Europe 2 and The Far East. Listed under the Europe 1 setting was a list of countries including Russia. Marie selected Europe 1 and turned the tuning knob. She heard a distant static filled with a Russian song. She was fascinated by the sound and sat down to listen.

It seemed like minutes when Lyle came back from the fish fry and saw Marie at his radio.

"What are you doing Marie?" asked Lyle.

"I'M listening to some Russian music on the radio," she replied.

"Let me see it," said Lyle as he sat down. "I wanted to listen to the 8 o'clock news with Walter Winchell." he said.

He tuned the radio until he found the station he wanted.

"Hark! I want to listen to the news," said Lyle.

That was his way of telling everyone to be quiet. Marie would hear this word many times as he listened to his radio. Hark was his favorite "shut up" expression.

"At least he's quiet, and doesn't fuss at me, and leaves me alone when he has his radio," thought Marie.

Hours later, Lyle came to bed and immediately went to sleep and started to snore. Marie moved a little and started to dream about dancing to the music she heard on the radio. She loved to dance but never had an opportunity to since she met Lyle.

Marie was having a lot of success working her set up. It was Sunday afternoon about 1:00 pm when a number of cars stopped to look at her homemade articles. They were well dressed and Marie thought they probably came from church.

"Jim and Ruth told us about your nice things and we thought we would stop by and see what you have," said a nice, well dressed gentleman.

By late that afternoon, Marie had sold most of her things. Ruth had given her an old wooden cigar box to use as a cash box. Marie loaded the wheel barrow and parked it under the shed along with her sign. She was very proud of her sign.

Marie went into Ruth's house and picked up Leone and headed back to cabin number 8. She was very proud of herself and for the first time she felt contented with her life. She liked the area and the little cabin. It reminded her of her father's cabin in Russia where she would spend happy times with him.

She opened the door to the cabin and found Lyle sitting next to the radio listening to some kind of program that made him laugh.

She put Leone in his bed and washed her hands and face. Lyle didn't acknowledge them when they came in the cabin and she spoke to him. She was tired and fed up with the way Lyle acted. "He acts like he is the only person in the world," thought Marie, almost out loud.

"Lyle, I want to talk to you!" she said in a raised voice.

"As soon as George Burns is off," Lyle said.

Marie walked over and turned off the radio. Lyle got up with an angry look in his yes. Marie pushed him back in the chair. Lyle's eyes got very big looking up at Marie. He knew she was mad but he didn't know why.

"Lyle, when are you going to work on the trailer instead of spending all day listening that radio?" asked Marie.

"I'll listen to it a much as I want! It's my radio!" answered Lyle.

"That's fine with me, Lyle, if that's what you want to do. I'm telling you this one and only time that I won't stay another day in that little trailer unless you make it livable. I can make a good living for myself here. I've talked to Jim and Ruth and they'll rent me this cabin for a good price. I can make a good living for me and Leone by selling my things at the set up," Marie said vehemently. "Look at the money I made today while you have been loafing and listening to the radio!" she said, as she opened the cigar box and showed Lyle the money.

She had over $30.00 and a lot of change.

He looked at the money box but didn't think of the money. He saw the deep set anger in Marie's dark brown eyes.

"If you don't do something now, you'll be going to Florida with only the old Buick and the little trailer for company," said Marie.

She picked up Leone from a sound sleep and went outside. She sat at the table under the boat shed and lit a cigarette.

Lyle was flabbergasted. He reached over and turned off the radio and sat for a while in deep thought.

"I didn't think I did anything wrong. I did like I always do and she shouldn't get so mad at me," Lyle said out loud. He sat for a long time to think about what Marie had said. He got up and went outside and looked at Marie and Leone.

"I guess you're right, Marie. I'll start on the rig tomorrow and fix it like you want," said Lyle.

Marie looked at Lyle with wet eyes.

"You know exactly what I want, Lyle. You need to make a better place for our child and treat me better. I don't mind traveling but we need to have a better place to live. Leone will be getting big pretty soon and he needs his own place to sleep," she said in a soft voice.

In one way, Lyle was glad he could stay a while longer. He wanted to get his watches and make some money on them. He wished he could buy a little gold in the town so he could send it to Baltimore. He had a good stash but he wanted more. He thought about going to Valdosta and buying some silver, but he'd wait until he was in Florida.

The trailer was putting a stop to a lot of his plans and he was confused about making money. It was easier for him to figure a way to make quick money but, he didn't want to hurt Jim and Ruth. He didn't really care, but it would get him into more trouble with Marie.

Lyle couldn't think of a good way to make an honest living but for a while he would try. Marie was doing well with the baskets and brushes. That would help them for a while until he finished the trailer.

It was a good way to keep out of sight and work a few ideas he had. Lyle spoke to a man at the lumberyard about linoleum for the trailer. He told Lyle about a special grade he could buy and sell to people and make good money. Lyle had to think about that because it would require work. He got the name of the product and would check into it later. "Right now, the important thing is to finish the trailer as soon as possible and head south for the winter," thought Lyle.

He wanted Marie to stop being so demanding. Maybe fixing the trailer would help. He was going to do the best job he could and finish it before they left.

"I wonder what that man wanted I saw in the park In Atlanta. What was his name? Oh! Yes, I remember. It was Allan Sanders. There is something familiar about him. I wonder if he was kin to the Sanders in Detroit. Jim and I saw him drinking a cup of coffee where we were having a late breakfast. He looked right at me. I wonder what he wants," said Lyle out loud, with a little worry in the back of his mind.

He sat in the other chair and looked out at the lake in the dark.

They both could hear the bubbles of the lake as the light from the cabin door shed a soft light on Lyle, Marie and Leone.

Lyle looked at the eerie glow of the cabin light on the lake. He wondered if cabin number 8 had anything to do with all the problems he had in Lake Park.

Marie wasn't the same person before Leone was born. He wasn't sure if she ever would be. Maybe tomorrow will be a better day, Lyle thought.

For the first time since she left Mother Russia, Marie looked at the North Star and wondered if anyone she knew was looking at the same star. She smiled quietly to herself and walked into cabin number 8 for a good night's rest.

Chapter Eleven

Christmas Season

Sanford, Florida

Highway 17 & 92 makes a gentle curve around Lake Monroe on the northwest side of Sanford, Florida. Lake Monroe is the basin for the headwaters of the St. Johns River. The actual headwaters are St. Johns Marsh. It flows north to Jacksonville and is one of the few rivers in the United States that flows north.

The new bridge over the St. Johns River was high enough to see the edge of Sanford. The lake had a seawall surrounding it on the south side all the way to the St Johns River. It was an excellent place to fish.

The history of Sanford went back to 1870, when Henry Sanford bought 12,500 acres and established Sanford. It was incorporated into a town in 1877. Seminole county was established in 1913 with Sanford as the county seat.

Lyle liked Sanford because it was a beautiful old town with friendly people. Many of the streets were brick with old beautiful homes. There were large parks and wide streets. It was a nice Florida town, warm and friendly.

There was a nice, well kept public park where they could park the trailer. Lyle wanted to rest a few days and then see if he could do a little business in and around Sanford.

Marie was finally satisfied with the new additions and changes. It wasn't exactly a tear drop anymore, but it had the general shape without the steep back curve or lid that lifted. It was the same old tear drop with a lot of changes that took Lyle 6 weeks to finish.

Lyle had done a surprisingly good job considering he rarely finished anything he started. He knew in his heart if he didn't Marie and Leone would be back in cabin number 8 in Lake Park, instead of traveling to Key West with him.

At Marie's daily insistence, the trailer had a real ice box built under the sink with an outside drain. She had enough cabinet space to store the items she needed to make her life a little easier.

The full size bed in the back was a nice addition to the inside. It was elevated about 12" with 4 nice pullout storage drawers underneath. They were portioned into compartments. She could store clothes and other things she needed. One side, without compartments, was for dirty clothes with holes for airflow. Lyle left the old WW1 mattress on the pile of old palmetto roots in Lake Park and replaced it with a new bed he bought there.

Leone's bed was in the front next to the eating dinette. It could be folded against the wall to make more room during the day. Leone would take his naps on the bed. Of course, there was a shelf for Lyle's Philco radio. He would use the batteries when needed so he could listen to the news when there was electricity. He had to buy a new aerial because he left the original aerial hanging in the Oak tree at Lake Park.

Marie's favorite part was her little kitchen area. She had a small sink that drained outside with work space next to the kerosene 2 burner stove. Lyle had moved the roof vent so it would be over the stove. Marie liked the Coleman better because she could regulate the flame a little easier. Kerosene, or "coal oil," as Lyle called it, didn't burn as clean as white gas. Most of the time, she would use the Coleman stove until Lyle fussed. He wanted her to use the coal oil stove because coal oil was cheaper.

All in all, it was a far cry from the old tear drop. This one resembled a compact home on wheels, especially with electricity wired to the inside. A lot of the better auto parks offered electric hook ups. The main reason for the electricity inside was to provide current for Lyle's precious Philco radio.

Lyle turned south on 17-92, which was named French Avenue, and pulled into the city park on 4th Street. It was nice, small, shady park about 1 block square. There was a bathhouse on one end of the park, which offered the necessities for short term camping. There were no electricity but anyone could stay for one week at no cost to the camper. After one week, the city charged $2.00 a week.

Lyle picked out a nice shady place on the far side of the park away from French Avenue. It was a busy street with the opening of the new farmers' market. It was within walking distance of downtown and the market.

"Marie, how about getting some supper while I look around the park. There's a little store on the corner of 1st and French. We need some Buglers," said Lyle.

"All we have are some cold cuts from yesterday and we need ice. Get some bread while you're there," said Marie.

Lyle left for the store and Marie started fixing supper. She put Leone on a blanket and listened to him make little talking noises. "I'll bet he'll be a noisemaker when he gets older," thought Marie.

She heard the tinkle of little bells and she instantly thought about old Boris the horse. The sound was almost the same as when her father used to take her on sleigh rides in Russia. She looked up and saw an ice wagon pulled by an old gray horse.

"Ice by the pound! Ice, fresh ice!" the iceman called out.

Marie walked to the street and waved at him. He pulled up next to the curb.

"Need some ice, lady?" the ice man asked.

"How much is it?" Marie asked in her quaint Russian accent.

"It's 10¢ for 12½ pounds or 15¢ for 25 pounds," he said.

"I'll take 12 ½ pounds, my ice box is very small," said Marie.

"Where do you want the ice?" he asked as he got off the wagon seat and walked to the rear.

"Put it in the trailer, you'll see the little box. How often do you come by?" asked Marie.

With a practiced swing, he grabbed a small piece of ice from the back with ice tongs and slung it over his shoulder. His back and shoulder were protected by a thick piece of rubberized canvas to keep him from getting wet.

Marie opened the door to the trailer and he put the ice in the top of the ice box and closed the door with a resounding click.

"This is a nice set up you have here, mam," said the ice man.

Marie gave him a dime and he put it in the open pocket of his apron. "I'll stop by when I come this way. I run this part of town every other day," he said.

"What does 'fresh ice' mean?" asked Marie

He sat back in his seat and took a long puff on his old pipe.

"The city built a new ice plant out on highway 46 to support the new farmers' market. When I pick up ice from the plant it is freshly made ice," he said.

Marie heard the clip clop of the horses' hooves on the brick street as he left. It reminded her so much of her home that she was beginning to get a tear in her eye.

"What was that all about?" asked Lyle as he walked up.

"The ice man will stop by every other day and deliver us ice," said Marie.

Lyle didn't say anything but sat a small bag on the outside table.

"Fix some supper Marie and let's walk downtown to see a picture show. The man at the corner store said there was a good Tarzan picture on tonight," said Lyle.

"What in the world is a Tarzan? I haven't heard of that place. Maybe we'll get some popcorn. I love popcorn!" thought Marie.

They hurried through supper, bundled up Leone in a little blanket and started to walk toward town. The park was a short 5 blocks form the center of town. They walked to 1st street, turned right and sauntered toward the clock in the center of the street.

Lyle asked a passerby where the picture show was. He told Lyle it was the first street on the right past the clock. They were both getting a little exited as they turned the corner and saw the Ritz Theater with a sign on the Marquee that said "Tarzan The Ape Man with Johnny Weissmuller and Maureen O'Sullivan."

"So, Tarzan is an ape-man and not a town," thought Marie.

Lyle bought the tickets and they all went in to see the movie. Leone was sound asleep in Marie's arms. It was the first jungle movie Marie had ever seen. The animals and jungle scenes of deepest Africa fascinated her. Little did she know that the movie was made in Silver Springs, Florida, about 80 miles north of them.

Marie and Lyle shared a big bag of 10¢ popcorn, though he couldn't eat very much because of his false teeth. Marie's eyes were glued to the screen as Tarzan raced across the jungle trees. The excitement made Marie a little nervous as she ate popcorn by the handfuls. The salt stung her lips but she didn't care.

Marie liked to watch movies. She had seen a few in China with her first husband, Howard. She and Lyle had watched only one movie since they had been together. Maybe this would be the beginning of a new trend with Lyle and Marie. Lyle appeared to be absorbed in the movie and didn't say anything except "Hark" when someone was talking.

The lights came on at the end of the movie and they waited until most of the people left before they went out the front door.

"Lyle what are all the colored people doing coming down from upstairs?" asked Marie.

"That's a hard question to answer, Marie. Look at the sign on the corner. People of color must be off the streets by dark and in your own town! Unfortunately, it's a way of life in the south. That's one of the reasons the Civil War was fought. I don't like it, but if we want to live in the south we must accept it," said Lyle.

Marie thought about what Lyle said. "Lyle, I have never been in a place where colored people are separated from whites. Maybe I have, but I haven't noticed it," said Marie.

"Lyle and I don't go out very much. It's a shame," she thought.

"Like I said Marie, it's a way of life in the south. Keep your mouth shut and you'll stay out of trouble," said Lyle

They walked up 1st street and stopped in the corner drug store. Lyle was a little melancholy after seeing the Tarzan movie and stopped in to get a soda. He ordered two vanilla sodas with whipped cream.

Marie had never tasted such a great drink in her life. They sat at a booth and drank their sodas. Marie made a slurping sound through the straw as she got to the bottom of the glass.

"Lyle, that's the best drink I've ever had. I hope we can have some again," said Marie

"I don't mind getting out occasionally and having a soda when we have a little extra money. We're getting a little low so enjoy it because we won't be able to do it anymore until I make some money," said Lyle.

Marie thought a long time about what he said as they walked back to the park and their camp. The past few weeks had been a turning point in her life. She knew she could make a living making baskets and brooms and that gave her a warm feeling inside. She also had seen and done a lot of new things. Lyle had kept her in the dark about everything except traveling in the trailer. He wouldn't take her anywhere except to eat at a diner and buy groceries. Now that she had seen some things, she felt a lot better.

She liked Florida in one way but she didn't like the attitude of people had against anyone who wasn't southern. When she spoke, people looked at her and often whispered, "That's another foreigner."

She also saw the blank stares of the colored people when they left the balcony of the picture show. "I'll just have to wait and see," thought Marie, sadly.

"Where do these people live?" she asked Lyle.

"There are several colored towns around Sanford. They work in the fields and small businesses. There is a barbeque stand in the colored section of 13th street. It has the best food you have ever eaten. How did you like the Tarzan movie Marie?" asked Lyle, trying to change the subject.

"I thought it was good but I think Jane should have had on more clothes. You could see about everything, especially when she was swimming under water. I didn't know that there was a tribe of colored midgets!" said Marie.

"Marie, that's just a story and nothing like that ever happened. Don't believe everything you see at a movie," said Lyle.

He didn't care much for the African scenes but he liked the underwater scenes.

"I liked it anyway and it did so happen! Nothing you can say will change my mind!" said Marie

"I know when to be quiet. Marie is very set in her opinions and a tidal wave couldn't change her mind," thought Lyle.

They were both smoking as they walked back to the park. Marie stopped and looked at some beautiful red flowers growing on a large bush. They looked like a little hat with a yellow center. She stooped to smell them.

"Those are native hibiscus. I didn't plant them; they just grow on their own accord. They don't smell, but the bees like them. Watch out or you might be stung on the nose," said an old lady sitting on the porch.

"Thank you, I don't like to be stung by anything," said Marie.

"Where are y'all from?" asked the old lady in a friendly tone.

"We're from Georgia on our way to Key West," answered Lyle.

"You're not any more from Georgia than I am and you have a foreign wife. I lost a husband in a foreign land fighting someone else's battles," she said.

She was still talking as Lyle and Marie continued to walk down the street.

"That's the attitude a lot of people have. It's the same as up north except they don't like people from the south. The best thing we can do is stay out of the way of people like that," said Lyle.

"What is that strange smell in the air? It seems like it may be coming in on the east wind," said Marie.

"Which way is east?" asked Lyle.

"Toward town," answered Marie.

"The smell is from the fields. It is probably celery because Sanford grows a lot of celery. It won't be long before they are the celery capital of the world," said Lyle.

"I don't like celery but it smells good on the wind," said Marie.

It was dusk when they got back to their camp. They settled in for a good night's rest with all the new things in the trailer. Lyle listened to his radio and commented about all the bad things going on in the world. The storm clouds of war were forming over China. The Japanese were on the move and Lyle didn't like it. Roosevelt was trying his best to get the economy going but Lyle didn't like the way he was doing it.

Federal income tax was something Lyle didn't understand. All of his business was cash except an occasional check from Baltimore. Without a permanent address, he was hard to find. Lyle never had anything good to say about the world situation.

After breakfast the next morning, Lyle asked Marie if she wanted to go the zoo and take Leone so he could see the animals. Marie agreed and they got in the Buick and drove to the Sanford zoo. It was at the foot of Park Avenue right on Lake Monroe. They really could have walked but it looked like it might rain. Florida was subject to rain showers all the time with water on both sides of the state.

"Lyle, what is the funny looking building that looks like a turtle shell?"

"That's a band shell. It is used for special occasions when a band plays. The music is reflected out from the shell-like structure. Everybody can hear them playing," said Lyle.

Marie had never been to a zoo but she had read about the animals in her homework. They walked toward a round area with a water moat about 10 feet across. It was a monkey island surrounded by a cement wall with about 25 monkeys of different types. They were having a great time with a ball someone had tossed in. Some were swinging on ropes and others were begging for food from the people standing around the moat wall.

"I've seen prisons and prisoners in the old country. I hate to see all the animals caged, with no future. The monkeys almost look human," thought Marie.

They walked up to a cage to a huge silver ape with his back to them. Lyle made a noise and the ugliest thing Marie had ever seen jumped at them. It scared Leone and he started to cry.

"What is that thing with the blue face and yellow fangs!" shouted Marie.

"The sign states it's 'Jiggs the Mandrel.'" said Lyle

"Let's get out of here, Lyle; I can't stand the way the animals are treated." said Marie.

They got in the car and drove down the edge of the lake street. They stopped and got out to watch some colored people fishing. It looked like they had a huge clump of worms on the end of their line. She liked to see people fish with cane poles.

"What is that dark log thing a little ways out that's moving?" asked Marie.

"Mam, that there is a gator." answered an old colored fisherman.

"What's a gator?" asked Marie.

"It an alligator," said Lyle

"An alligator! Let's get out of here! I don't want him to eat my baby!" shouted Marie.

"There ain't no need to fret about that ol gator, mam." He's been here since I was a just able to fish as a little un. He sits and waits fo an ol bird to land on his snout and then he catches it fo dinner. That's ol Methuselah. Directly he'll git tired and go and finds him a warm place to sleep. He dun et 2 birds today," said the old colored man.

Lyle and Marie got back in the car and headed to their camp. Marie was tired and Leone needed changing and she didn't want to see anymore "gators."

They got back in late afternoon. Marie tended to Leone and Lyle walked to the corner store. They had a checker board and he wanted to play. He hadn't played since he left Carlos and Juanita's campground.

He brought two of the repaired watches with him in case he found someone that needed a watch. He had traded the older broken watches to the jeweler in Lake Park for the repair. He ended up with 4 good watches.

Marie was thinking about what a nice place to live and raise a child this seemed, in spite of alligators and problems with people not liking most outsiders. All she wanted now was to get a good night's rest. Traveling and sightseeing had made her tired. This was the first time since they left Indiana that they took time from work and travel to have a little fun.

Lyle sat down with a few of the "good old boys" for a sociable game of checkers. They all played well and Lyle won a few games but a man named Mr. Kendall won most of the games.

He worked for the city of Sanford as a heavy equipment operator and whatever else they wanted him to do. He was a WW1 veteran with a good sense of humor. He went through the war without a scratch. He fell while returning home and broke his leg aboard ship. It didn't heal quite right and he had a slight limp, but it didn't hurt him to walk. During the evening of playing, a few stories came to light. He said he had helped design the mechanism so a machine gun could be fired through the rotating propeller of an airplane. Lyle thought that was a real accomplishment.

Lyle really enjoyed himself although he didn't win many games; he enjoyed just talking to the men. After the games were over Lyle wanted to know if anyone needed a watch.

"I'm staying over at the French Avenue Park with my wife and baby. I've been running into a little hard luck and I want to sell my grandfather's watch to get a little pocket money," said Lyle.

He took one of the watches out of his pocket and sat it on the checker table.

Mr. Bradbury, a local garage owner, picked it up to see if it ran. It was a nice silver plated Elgin and seemed to run fine.

"I need a watch, my son Brad took mine and lost it. How much do you want for it? I don't think I caught your name, sir," said Mr. Bradbury.

"I'd like to get $20.00 for it if I could. My name is Lyle," said Lyle.

Mr. Bradbury passed it around and everyone looked at it.

"I'll give you $20.00 for it if no one else wants it," said Mr. Kendall.

"Just hold on a minute. I've got first choice because he let me see it first," said Mr. Bradbury.

"Mister, I'll give you $22.00 for it," said Mr. French, who owned a plumbing business across the street.

The price went back and forth until Mr. Kendall gave Lyle $25.00 for it. Lyle gave him the watch and everyone had a good laugh. He didn't dare to take out another watch and try to sell it.

They all shook Lyle's hand and wished him well. They invited him back to play checkers even though he didn't play checkers very well. Lyle smiled at that joke but didn't like it. It hurt in his ego to be laughed at. He couldn't stand to be out done. He said good night and thanked them as he started back toward his camp.

The men all sat down and started playing checkers again. Mr. Kendall passed the watch around for everyone to see. He was very proud of his treasure.

Lyle felt good about selling his "grandfather's watch." He made a quick $25.00 on a watch that was worth about $10.00 and it didn't belong to any member of his family. He felt good running any kind of scam. There was something about making a little money and fooling people that seemed to make him feel alive again. It had been a couple of months since he had sold anything and he was happy again.

"If those are the kind of people around here, I'll make a killing as long as they don't talk to each other. They seemed like they knew everybody in town and their business. I'll have to be very careful," Lyle said out loud as he walked back to the trailer.

The next morning, while Lyle was gone looking for a place to set up, Marie walked around the park. There were a few campers from all over on their way south or north. Sanford was a good place to stop because of the nice park and friendly people.

She heard the tinkle of small bells again and saw an old covered truck with the name "Roth's Bakery" on the side. She walked over to the truck as several children were gathering around. The man got out and opened up the back. He had a wonderful display of all kinds of cakes and cookies. He sat out a small box and let the children pick their choice of broken cookies. She heard him speak with a heavy accent. She thought it might be German. He was a big friendly man and all the children liked him. Several campers were buying things from his wagon as well. She walked up and looked at what he had to offer.

She purchased an apple pie and a loaf of self risen bread, which Lyle liked. She paid him 35¢ and went back to her camp. Apples were very expensive in the old country and she loved the taste of them. The baker had added white icing on the top and called it French apple pie. She couldn't wait to taste it. She went in the tear drop and poured herself a cup of luke warm coffee and ate a piece of the pie. She wondered what Lyle would think of her eating some of the pie before he got back. She decided she didn't care and ate another piece. Lyle would have to settle for what was left.

"I've been on the road for a long time with Lyle and I haven't seen anything except campgrounds and the inside of the car and trailer. As soon as we find a place for a while I'm going to learn how to drive. I want to go shopping alone so I can buy what I want and not what Lyle thinks I want. I just have to figure out how to do it. I can see Florida is a pretty place and I want to see everything I can," thought Marie.

After a week of looking around town, Lyle decided to move his rig south of town at an intersection. He thought it would be a good place for a set up so Marie could make and sell some of her brushes and baskets. He was able to park his rig behind a City Service gas and service station, which had a water and electric hook up. The road divided into a "Y"; one way went north as French Avenue and the other went into town as Park Avenue. It was a good place for a set up as people going both ways could see it easily.

It was especially nice because there were some covered tables from an old fruit stand. He paid the owner $5.00 to set up for a week. He wanted to work the idea of the linoleum while Marie worked her set up, but he never seemed to have the time. Lyle was thinking about renting the small building behind the old fruit stand to set up shop buying and selling old scrap gold and silver. He hadn't used his federal license since the run in with the bank and the Baltimore gold company. He had lost over $150.00 and was afraid to buy anymore gold coins. He loved the challenge of buying and selling gold coins, but was afraid he would be caught. There was no law against buying scrap gold but he was worried that Fishlows in Baltimore had sent in his name to the Federal Government after he sent in his gold shipment with the gold dust.

Marie had to put on a sweater in the middle of the day. There was cold north wind blowing as she prepared her set up. There were two nice bench shelves that held the remainder of her goods. Marie had just finished when the Seminole County Sheriff stopped and got out of his car.

"Afternoon, mam," the sheriff said.

"Good afternoon, sir. Do you need some brushes or baskets for your wife?" she asked.

Marie wasn't afraid to talk to anyone although her English was heavily accented. She liked people and enjoyed talking.

"No mam, but they are very nice. Did you make them yourself?" he asked as he picked up a basket and looked at it.

"I do need to see your business license," he said before Marie had a chance to answer.

"Officer, I didn't know I needed one," she answered.

About that time, Lyle was coming back and saw the police car.

He continued to drive down the block to avoid talking to him. Marie saw him and was about to wave but thought better of it.

"I'll tell my husband as soon as he gets back. Where do we buy the license?" she asked.

"If you follow Park Avenue almost to Lake Monroe, it's on the left side near the zoo. In the mean time, I'll have to ask you to stop selling your goods. Maybe in a couple of days I'll come back and get some things for my family for Christmas," said the sheriff.

Marie thanked him for being so nice as the he was leaving. She started to pick up her goods as Lyle drove up.

"What did he want?" he asked with a nervous tint to his voice.

Marie told him they needed a license to sell things in Sanford and Seminole County. She continued to pick up and store her brushes and baskets in the trailer.

"I don't think we should stay here, Marie; the weather is turning cold. I wanted to go south and see Key West. I've wanted to visit America's most southern city for a long time and see the old Flagler Railroad, what was left of it," said Lyle.

"But Lyle, I like it here. We could get a little land after we make some money and build a nice place to live and sell our goods. I had forgotten it was almost Christmas and we need to stay here until after the New Year," said Marie.

"All right, we'll stay here until after the 1st of the year and then head south," Lyle reluctantly agreed and went to the car to get a jacket because he was also getting cold.

"We'll stay here since I've paid for a week. Besides, we have electricity and I can listen to the radio and charge the radio battery at the same time. Fix us some lunch and let's take a ride and see the Big Tree," said Lyle.

After lunch, they rode south on 17 & 92 toward Orlando. The road was very narrow through a swampy area about 10 miles south of Sanford. There was a sign to turn right and "See Florida's Big Tree."

They took a narrow road for about a mile and turned into a small parking area. They parked and got out of the car. The north wind wasn't so bad there because of the dense forest. They followed a dirt path that led to the big tree. The sign said the tree was ¼ mile.

They rounded a sharp turn in the trail and the path opened up to the largest tree Marie had ever seen. It was a huge cypress tree so tall it hurt Marie's neck to look up at it. The sign read: "The Senator, Florida's Big Tree. Largest cypress tree in the U.S.A. President Calvin Coolidge dedicated it in 1929. It is 3500 years old with a circumference of 47' and 126' tall."

"Hold Leone while I take some pictures," she told Lyle.

Lyle reluctantly held him while Marie took almost a roll of film of them and the big tree. Lyle was getting tired and he told Marie it was time to go. He was too tired to fuss about the cost of the pictures but he would get to it later. He had threatened to throw the camera away more than once.

The evening was cool and comfortable as they went to sleep early. Lyle wished he had picked another place because the traffic was kept him awake. He finally went to sleep dreaming about the great rail-road that went to the Florida Keys. Tomorrow he would try and buy a little gold. Because of the license requirement, he would have to be careful.

It was Christmas Eve and the first one for little Leone. Marie wanted a little tree to celebrate the season but Lyle wouldn't hear of it. He didn't believe in Christmas or anything about the birth of Christ. Marie didn't want to hear such nonsense. She had it in the back of her mind to change his way of thinking about Christmas for the sake of Leone. She went in the back area of the station and cut a small cedar after asking the owner. He gave her a few feet of leftover ice cycles and some red garland. She was so happy. It was about 18" tall and she sat it up on the dinette next to Leone's bed. Lyle didn't like it because he had to reach over it to turn on the radio. He didn't say much but Marie knew he was not in a good mood.

Marie walked to a corner store and bought some oranges and a few nuts. She stuffed them in one of Lyle's old socks and put it at the bottom of the tree.

"It isn't much but it will be Leone's first Christmas. He likes oranges and I'll feed him a little of one tomorrow," said Marie.

She listened to Christmas carols and recognized some of the hymns. There was a little church about a block away and she wanted to go. It was not her kind of church but it didn't matter; it was Christmas Eve. She told Lyle she was going to the church to listen to the Christmas music. He told her she couldn't go.

Marie wrapped Leone in a blanket and went anyway. She sat in the very back and looked at the beautiful Christmas tree and saw all of the happy people exchanging gifts and singing carols. As a child, it was a very special day. She felt very sad and lonely and hugged Leone tighter.

An elderly lady came up to her and stood for a moment looking at Leone. She held out her hand to Marie.

"Come join us around the tree while we sing Silent Night," the lady asked.

Marie went with her and stood with the people while they sang. She had tears in her eyes listening to the beautiful organ and the voices of the people. At the end of the song the lady reached under the tree and handed Marie two white paper bags tied with a green and red ribbon. At first, Marie didn't want to accept them.

"It's our way of giving thanks to the Lord on his birthday. As the Lord said, it is more blessed to give than to receive," said the lady.

Marie took the gifts and held them close to her as they sang "Hark the Herald Angels Sing." Marie knew the song and sang with them in Russian as the tears now ran freely down her cheeks.

She went back to the trailer and quietly slipped in. She got out the leftover apple pie and had a big piece as she watched Lyle snore. Leone liked the sweet flavor of the icing and gurgled like he wanted some more. She hadn't told Lyle about the pie and she was glad. It was Leone's first Christmas and she was happy as she quietly finished the French apple pie.

CHAPTER TWELVE

Silver Time

Winter, South Florida

Marie saved the old cracked mirror from the trash pile before Lyle rebuilt the trailer. Lyle threw it out and replaced it with a round shaving mirror he bought at the drug store. Before they left Lake Park, she made a woven frame from willow and pine straw and attached it with some of the wire she used on the brooms. For some reason, Marie was very fond of the old mirror. It had seen her reflection during all the long 9 months of her pregnancy. She wanted to remember to never get into the same problem again. This was her last child and she meant to keep it that way regardless of what Lyle wanted.

Marie hung the mirror over Leone's bed to remind her of better times to come. The old broken mirror was reborn from a discarded piece of glass to a nice looking addition to the trailer. Her reflection still lived in the mirror. She no longer saw Lyle's angry face in it as she had before on many occasions. She wasn't afraid of him like she used to be. At last, she saw a little hope in the future as she had gained a skill and could take care of herself.

She was busy cleaning the trailer after the holidays had passed. The old light bulb had been connected and turned off and on with a string cord. She wanted to find a shade so the light wasn't so bright, although it did help her do her housework in the trailer. She knew Lyle would be moving soon but she didn't know how soon. She had to be ready every day.

Lyle had met a family of gypsies the previous week. Years ago he had helped this clan in some form or another. They considered him

"Romani," or "a true friend." He said he was going to help them set up a fortune telling business on French Avenue. There was no law against it but they were closely watched due to the bad reputation of gypsies.

Their main way of making money was to set up in a small town and open a fortune telling business. The elder women of the group would be the ones who told fortunes. They would charge a few dollars to tell some poor soul if he was going to be successful or any number of things he wanted to hear.

As a rule, the older women were pretty good at what they did. This was due in the most part because they were a very good judge of character. There were different steps in fortune telling. A person's palm was read and the more money they gave, the better their "tale." The gypsies would tell in lofty, familiar or homely ways depending on the client. For a few dollars, they could piece together a pretty good fortune, or at least one that the customer wanted. All of the money was made and controlled by the eldest woman in the clan and passed on to the "Kapo," or chief of the tribe.

Marie's mother Anna once told her, "Gypsies are one scattered race like stars in the sight of God."

"I wonder what Lyle is doing for so long? He's been gone most of the day. I have Leone all cleaned, dressed and ready to travel early today," Marie thought.

Lyle came back just as the street light on the corner of French and Park came on. He'd been trading with the gypsies and was happy. He liked to be around them because they were very good at making money.

"We're going to the Gypsy camp in the morning, Marie. I want you to meet some of the people. They have some good ideas about making money and traveling," said Lyle.

Marie remembered the old days when she lived in Russia and her father traded with Gypsies. She liked the way they dressed and were a very close family group. As a child, she often played with the children of one family.

About mid-morning the next day Lyle took Leone and Marie to the gypsy camp. The leader, Kapo Popoy, and his wife Lyuba met them with open arms. They liked children and took to Leone immediately.

"What is the boy child's name?" asked Lyuba.

"His name is Leone, after his grandfather," said Marie.

"His Gypsy name is Purrum. Do you know what that means Marie?" asked Lyuba.

"I don't know, but I think it means some kind of onion," said Marie.

"In this camp, you will be called Maria and you are right, it is a special kind of onion. How did you know this?" asked Lyuba.

"I remember my father talking about a special onion from Iran but it was spelled a little different," said Marie.

They all sat down to a large table and were treated to a huge meal. Marie was very hungry and ate some of the food, which she remembered from the old country.

After the meal, the men gathered together and were talking and smoking. The children ate separately, somewhat like the Irish mule traders. At the meal, everyone was speaking English. However, during the meal clean up they all started speaking in their language, which was a combination of English, Armenian and Iranian. Some of the words could be traced to the ancient Sanskrit.

Marie listened very carefully and could understand most of it. One old woman was not happy with the strangers in the camp. She believed they would bring bad luck. The gypsies were a superstitious lot. They wore a lot of jewelry, some of which was to ward off bad spirits. Jewelry also represented their wealth. The women of the tribe carried all the money and acted as a bank when needed. Red was never worn because it denoted a dishonest woman. The exception was that red could be worn at a wedding by the bride for one day, indicating she had never been with a man.

Marie listened to their conversation, pretending not to understand until one woman started talking about her and Leone. She didn't say anything bad but made a comment about her facial scars from the old country. She was wondering how she got the marks. The conversation went back and forth when the old woman said they could only come from one part of the world and that was a province in Turkistan. Marie acted like she was interested in cleaning a pot and spoke in a very clear voice.

"I was born in Ashkhabad, Russia and I am proud of these marks on my face. I also know that your young ones don't know anything about it. I lived and played with the Romani as a child and I like you all. But don't make the mistake that I am a fool like someone just said. I learned to speak your language when I was a child. I am not as good as I use to be but I understand every thing you say," said Marie in their Roma language.

The area was instantly silent. Even some of the men turned around when they heard Marie speaking. Lyuba came to Marie and gave her a big hug.

"When I first saw you, I knew something was familiar about the way you spoke. Your English wasn't very good and you had those marks on your face. You are welcome in our camp anytime Maria," she said. "See those men out there talking? They think they are the bosses. I hold all the money and I make all the decisions. They provide what men provide. If there is anything you want to know, just ask me."

Lyle walked up about that time with several of the men. They started taking to Marie at the same time, Lyle in English and they in Roma.

Marie held up her hand. "I can't hear all of you at the same time," she said.

"Let Maria speak!" said Lyuba.

"I have nothing to say except it was very nice of you to invite my Romo (Man) and my O Nevo (Baby boy) to your tribe camp. We go as friends and hope to never be a Gaje (non gypsy) to your tribe ever again," said Marie.

"Spoken like a true Romani. Let's have a toast of Rakia (plum brandy) before our friends leave," said Popoy.

Marie was glad to get back to their camp. She liked to feel at home again but it made her very sad and lonely. She thought a lot about Mother Russia and tried to put it out of her mind. She knew her place was here and not with the gypsies.

Her Russian name Maria stuck in my mind. She liked the sound of "Maria" and not the way Lyle said "Marie." It sounded like he was calling a herd of wild goats, but although she didn't like it she never said anything to Lyle.

"Lyle, my real name in the old country was Maria and I would like to be called Maria," she said.

"Marie was your name when I met you and your name is still Marie. I won't call you anything but Marie and that's that," said Lyle with anger in his voice.

Marie knew she would gradually work Maria into being her name but for the time being, she would settle for Marie. She also knew what Lyle's problem was; he didn't like her to be better at anything than he was. Marie spoke several languages and liked to be with people. Lyle was pushed aside when the gypsies found out she cold speak Roma (Gypsy). She decided she would be quiet and not bring it up, though.

"Where in the world did Marie learn how to speak Gypsy? It really put me on my heel when I heard her speak. She never talks to a lot of people. I'm going to have to keep her out of the way. She could cause me problems when she starts talking to people," thought Lyle.

The next morning Lyle went to the post office and got a general delivery note from his father. It was a postcard that had been forwarded several times. It said that he was going to meet Lyle at Vero Beach in a month at the old beach campground. Lyle looked at the postcard and saw that it was dated 3 weeks ago. He put it in his pocket and drove back to their camp.

"Marie get ready, we're going to hit the road. We have to meet dad in Vero Beach," said Lyle.

"I'm ready when you are, Lyle. I'm always ready to go because I never know when you're going to move again," said Marie, with a little sarcasm in her voice.

Lyle was anxious to try the gypsy idea of using silver coins to make money. They didn't have a federal license and couldn't use the scheme except in a very small way. He still had his license and he would try it in Vero Beach. He was happy to try another scheme and he was happy he had his license. It was time to move anyway. Lyle did like the town and area. He thought maybe he would come back again some day, but he dismissed the idea as he hooked up the rig and got ready to go.

He decided to take highway 46 to Titusville and then pick up US 1 to Vero Beach. He liked the area on the Florida east coast. There was a lot of traffic and plenty of room to find a place to set up for Marie.

"Why does Marie want to be called Maria? It's a foreign name and sounds too much like a Mexican name. I don't want to think of Mexico every time I use her name. It will be Marie and that's all there is too it," Lyle said to himself.

Marie was watching him talk to himself but said nothing. She shook her head. She was wondering what kind of scheme he was working now. He said nothing as she put Leone in his bed in the back of the Buick. He still hadn't fixed a place for him. He used all the lumber on the trailer.

When she asked him about it, his answer was "I haven't got time to fool with it now, maybe later." Later never came.

The road to Mims was rough and narrow and it took most of the day to get there. They camped in a small park just before the road ended at US 1. Lyle could see a lot of cars going north and south and wondered if this would be a good place for a set up. He dismissed the thought when he saw a police officer stop at the gas station and talk to some people. He looked in his direction but said nothing. Lyle looked away immediately and tried not to act suspicious as the officer left and turned south on US 1.

Lyle saw a sign that read "To The Dixie Highway." He later learned that the Dixie Highway was a wandering road which took several directions from Ontario, Canada to south of Miami. It was a name that brought back some of the Civil War memories told by his father and his tales of the 11th Michigan, of which he was a member.

After supper, Lyle and Marie walked to look at the Econolockhatchee River. It was a wide black river with some people fishing from an old pier. They were catching a variety of fish.

Marie looked across the river and saw some cows grazing on the river bank. She couldn't believe her eyes at first. She saw a large gray bull that was a cross between a camel and a cow.

"Lyle! What kind of cow it that gray thing . . . or is it a cow?" shouted Marie.

Lyle looked at the large animal and saw it was indeed a cow with a large camel-like hump behind its neck. The cow was gray with horns that curved downward. Lyle had no idea what it was.

"What kind of animal is that across the river?" asked Lyle of a fisherman who was leaving.

The fisherman looked around to see what Lyle was talking about.

"Those are Brahma cattle imported from India. They are tick and flea resistant and not as easy to get sick as the other cattle. Many people don't like them because they eat a lot more. And I am one of the people who don't like them. My Name is Duda and I own a cattle ranch around Rockledge. I like to come up here and fish and get away for a while," said the fisherman.

"Thanks for the information, sir. My wife and I were curious about what kind they were," said Lyle.

"I don't plan on having any on my ranch," said Duda as he put his tackle and a string of fish in is truck. "I have Herefords and Black Angus. They sell better as beef animals. The Brahmas don't taste as good as the other breeds do."

Lyle thanked him and started to walk away.

"Wait a minute! Have you ever tasted largemouth bass?" Duda asked.

"No we haven't, but I'd like to try some," said Marie.

Mr. Duda unstrung a nice size fish, wrapped it an old newspaper and gave it to Marie. "My family and I have plenty to eat. Fry it in hot grease and you'll have a feast," he said as he got in his truck.

"Thank you, sir!" said Marie as she looked at the fish.

They walked back to their camp and Marie fixed the bass like she was told. It tasted wonderful and they ate every bit except the bones and head. Marie was beginning to like Florida better and better.

Vero Beach was about 100 miles south on US 1. The vicinity was a tourist area even in Depression times. There seemed to be a lot of northern money traveling south to Miami. They saw many places to have a good set up all along the road the beach. The area was called Indian River country because of the name of the inland waterway. It was also home to some of the nicest citrus groves in Florida. They passed miles of orange groves. There were many fruit stands, each advertising the best Indian River fruit. Lyle stopped at one that said "All The Orange Juice You Can drink for 10¢."

Lyle and Marie got out of the car and each bought a cup of ice cold orange juice for the 10¢ as advertised. Marie liked the taste of the juice. It was a little sweeter than what she used to get in Ashkhabad. They both finished their cup and asked for more.

"Mister, that's all you can drink for a dime. Read the small print at the bottom of the sign," said the clerk.

"One cup is all you can drink for a dime." For once Lyle had been had by his own greed. Marie thought it was funny and laughed at Lyle's red face. The clerk was also laughing with Marie. Lyle got very angry and got in the car and started it. He almost drove away without Marie.

"What's the matter with you, Lyle? It's only a dime and it was a big cup. See, the clerk gave me the cup. It says 'Indian River Juice,'" said Marie.

Lyle was so mad he reached for a folded road map and drew it back to hit Marie.

"Lyle that would be the biggest mistake of your life if you ever touch me with that map!" said Marie in a cool, collected voice.

He thought better of it and hunched over the wheel and drove on toward Vero Beach.

Vero Beach was a nice community founded about 10 years earlier to support the growing citrus industry. Lyle was supposed to meet his father at the small campground at the edge of town near the Indian River. It was easy to find because it was the only one in town.

They checked into the camp and Lyle paid $2.00 for a week. He hoped his father would be there so he wouldn't have to wait on him. He parked next to a tall row of Australian Pine trees. They had needles like a regular pine except they were dark green and segmented. The wind made whistling noise as it moved the pines back and forth. The pinecones were small and had small burrs about the size of a marble. Marie liked the trees because they made her feel secure. They were planted in a solid row that blocked the view on the back side of the camp. The front side faced the Indian River. It was nice view and she felt comfortable. The camp was shady and had electricity and water on each spot. Lyle wasn't very good at backing but he maneuvered the trailer into spot number 8 after several tries. Marie could smell the clutch like she did in

Tennessee. She hoped he didn't ruin it. Old Mr. Ben wasn't here to put sand in it.

"That's strange, it's the same number as the cabin in Lake Park," said Marie.

Lyle walked up and down in the camp looking for his father. He asked the owners if they had seen him. They shook their head, "No."

"Marie, I'm going to the local bank in town. Fix some lunch. I should be back in about an hour," said Lyle.

Marie knew the hour could be from 1 to 4 hours. Lyle had no concept of time. He tried to do too many things in a short period and never got anything done. His idea of 10 hours of work was to hire 10 men and work them for one hour. This time idea put Lyle behind all the time. He would never catch up on his work.

Lyle easily found the bank in the center of town. He knew what he had to do. He walked into the bank and asked for the manager who handled scrap silver. The lady directed him to an old well dressed man in the rear of the small bank. Lyle introduced himself and gave him his federal license.

"How may I help you, sir?" asked the manager.

"As you know, I'm licensed by the Federal Government to buy scrap silver from non-Federal banks. I will in turn take the silver coins to a Federal bank. It is a service the Federal Government provides to you. As you know, the current price of silver is 44¢ per ounce. I have been directed to give you 1¢ over market value for defaced coins that are taken out of circulation," said Lyle.

"I'm glad you came along. We have a lot of coins we need to get rid of. It looks like you got here just in time. We were going to have them melted at our expense and sent to a Federal bank," said the manager. "If you will excuse me I'll get my assistant and we'll get the coins out of the vault."

"Of course, take all the time you need," said Lyle as he got up as a courtesy to the manager.

Lyle sat down and took a deep breath of air. He was so nervous that his hands were wet. He had planned the speech to the bank manager and it went off without a hitch.

"As long as he goes to the vault, I'll stay. If he heads for the door I'll leave and he won't see me again," thought Lyle.

The manager summoned his assistant from behind the counter and accompanied him to the vault area. In a short while, the manager came out carrying several cloth bank bags on a small 2 wheeled dolly. He motioned for Lyle to come with him.

"These are bags of defaced or unusable silver coins. We'll weigh them so you'll know how much you owe for them," said the manager.

"We don't have a new scale but this one we use to weigh money should be alright. We weigh all bags coming in to see if they have the correct amount of coins," said the assistant.

They began weighing the coins and marked the weight on each bag. The total for 3 bags was almost 35 pounds. Lyle paid him the specified amount and gave him a receipt.

"You don't have to report the sale of silver, only gold," said Lyle.

"We know that; it's no one's business what we do with the silver," said the manager.

"May I use your dolly to take them to the car?" asked Lyle.

"My assistant will help you. We collect that much silver in about 6 months. Many of the coins come from the orange pickers who work in the orange groves. They drill holes in them and put them around their necks. For some reason they believe silver will ward off evil spirits. When they leave, they pass the coins to the local merchants who bring them to us. Frankly, we are glad to get rid of them. The inspectors don't want us to keep them very long," said the manager.

The assistant loaded the coins in Lyle's Buick. Lyle waved goodbye and with a shaky hand drove back to the camp.

"I hope this scheme works like Popoy said. I need to stop at a hardware store and buy some liquid solder and mercury. I hope the gypsies know what they are talking about and I hope it works for me," thought Lyle.

He was able to buy what he needed and he headed back to the camp. He was anxious to see what he had in the bags. He knew it would be a lot of coins. He hoped most of them had holes. He knew some would be completely destroyed by fire or kids putting them on a railroad track.

He got back to the camp just in time to see his dad drive up in a new 1934 Buick sedan. He would keep the coins secret and not let anyone see them for now. He wanted to be sure about every thing.

"Dad must be living high on the hog to have such a nice car. I like the new colors cars have this year. The light tan make the car look wonderful," thought Lyle. The last time they talked about cars was when Lyle "borrowed" his Franklin and took it to Mexico.

They both got out of their cars at about the same time and shook hands with each other. Leon was a tall, well built man with broad shoulders. He dwarfed Lyle when they stood together. His hair was a beautiful silver gray and was always well groomed.

"Good to see you son! How are Marie and my namesake doing?" Leon asked in a deep bass voice.

"They're doing just hunky dory like I said in my last letter," said Lyle.

"That's a different car than you had last time. Where is the old 28 Pontiac you bought in Detroit the last time you were there?" asked Leon.

"Dad, it gave up the ghost and I traded with some Irish mule traders for the Buick. It runs good. I had to put 4 tires on it when I had 2 blowouts, but it pulls the trailer very good and has plenty of power," said Lyle. "How did you get such a nice new car? The last I heard you were driving that old Hudson."

"Do you remember that old house and few acres we had in Charlotte? I sold it to the people who own the sawmill down the road. The house wasn't much and the back of the property was full of rocks," said Leon.

"I'm glad it's gone; there were a lot of bad memories in that house," said Lyle. "That's were we lived with my mother. You decided you wanted to live with another woman and leave us alone. I don't want to get into an argument with you dad, but someday I'm going to say my peace."

"What's cooking, Marie?" asked Leon. He ignored what Lyle had said as if he wasn't even there.

"Just a few things I threw together. I didn't know you'd be here so soon," said Marie.

"Hey, your English is a lot better that the last time I saw you!"

"I've been working on it."

Marie watched as Lyle and Leon walked off and were talking with a lot of hand waving which was Lyle's way and appeared to be Leon's way also. Lyle was smoking and Leon had his chew of "Red Man" in his jaw.

"They are so different. Lyle is tiny beside Leon's 6'2" height. They look like father and a small son. I guess Lyle mother was small," thought Marie.

After supper, Lyle and Leon got in his new Buick and drove off. They didn't say much to Marie except "We'll be back in a little while." Marie wanted to ride in the new car but she stayed and took care of little Leone.

"I wonder what Lyle is up too. He was gone a long time today and wasn't angry when he came back. Something is going on. He hasn't written in his dairies for several months. I'm going to ask him what he's doing," thought Marie.

She had finished with the supper clean up and had little Leone ready for bed. He was sitting on a blanket chewing on a rubber toy Marie bought for him.

Lyle and Leon drove up about that time. Both got out of the car and were apparently very angry and were exchanging profanities, Marie noticed.

"What's wrong Lyle?" asked Marie.

"Dad wants me to go back up north and help him with the lumber business. I don't want to go and he's arguing with me about all the money we can make. I told him I didn't like the cold winters anymore and I was going to stay south as much as I could," said Lyle with an angry tone on his voice.

"I don't want to go up north in the winter. We have only a small electric heater and little Leone doesn't have any winter things. The way he's growing, he'll be walking soon," said Marie.

"I've got some good things going and I want to finish them. Maybe in the summer we'll go and visit, if we have the money. I don't want to be caught and have to pick raspberries again like we did after we got together last time on one of his "big deals. I'm going to stand my ground and let dad go back up north," said Lyle.

"I've got my bed fixed in the back of the Buick and I'm going to hit the hay," said Leon.

Marie walked to his car with him and he played with Leone. "He's going to be a big fellow." said Leon.

"I think he'll look like you and will be as tall," said Marie.

Leon opened the back door to the car and Marie saw a bed in the back. The seat was missing and he had built a bed in its place. "That's where Lyle got his idea about taking out the back seat of all the cars. His car looks like a trash dump in the back," thought Marie.

"I like to go to bed with the chickens," Leon said as he got in the back of the car and Marie walked back to the rig.

"I don't want to go up north. I'm happy here in Florida. I want to go on to Key West and see all the things I want to see. I've never been any farther south than Orlando. There are a lot of money people in Miami and I want to work the area. This isn't a good time for dad to meddle in my business like he always does," said Lyle.

Marie agreed with him and they went to bed, both tired after a long day.

Marie heard Leon rustling around the camp way before daylight. She knew he was an early riser but he didn't have to make so much noise.

He was probably making his coffee. He carried a stove and things to cook with. He was like Lyle, too cheap to pay for his food at a restaurant unless it suited him. "I wonder where his wife Carrie is. She never travels with him," she thought. Marie didn't care much for her because she was so loud and crude. She was a big woman and didn't like company and kept a sloppy house. "I've been to her house once in Grand Rapids and I don't want to go back. I don't blame Leon for leaving her at home," thought Marie as she drifted off to sleep listening to the wind in the Australian pines.

After breakfast in the morning, Leon and Lyle went for another walk leaving Marie to clean up the mess as usual. Leon left some of his dirty clothes for Marie to wash and she resented it.

She took a load of clothes to the bathhouse and put them in the big wash tub. She looked at the row of washing machines in the washroom but didn't know how to use them. She started to wash them by hand.

The owner of the camp came in and asked what she was doing. Marie told him she was washing clothes.

"That's what the machines are for," the owner said.

"I don't know how to use them and besides I don't have any money with me," said Marie.

"Let me show you," said the owner as he explained how to operate them and use the roller wringers to dry squeeze the clothes when they had rinsed.

"Here, I'll give you some free time so you can get all those clothes clean," said the owner as he recycled the timer with a special key.

Marie busied herself with learning how to operate the machines. She had a lot of mechanical ability and learned very quickly. Her father had taught her a lot of "man" things when she was growing up. Her two sisters weren't interested in working and besides that Marie was his favorite. She finished washing in about half the time with the help of the machines. She took the clothes out and hung them on the clothesline provided by the camp.

It was almost noon when she got back to their camp. Lyle was sitting at the table looking at a lot of silver coins.

"Where's your dad?" asked Marie.

"He got mad and went back up north. All he wanted was to borrow some money. That car isn't his; he borrowed it from the owner of the sawmill to come down here. He did sell the old place but Carrie got it all for her kids. I loaned him $100.00 so he would go home and leave us alone," said Lyle.

"I thought something was funny about the way he talked yesterday. What am I going to do with his clothes?" asked Marie.

"Wrap them up and I'll send them to him at his home. He was having a lot of trouble with Carrie and wanted to get away. There's no use being around dad when he has troubles. He drags everyone into them. I'm glad he's gone for a while. He tries to tell me what to do all the time. I think he's still mad about me taking the Franklin, even though I paid him back long ago," said Lyle.

"Like father, like son," Marie thought.

Lyle continued to sort stacks of silver coins on the table. The table was behind the trailer, in the shade of the Pine trees. It was out of sight and Lyle was comfortable with sorting the coins although he was looking around like he expected someone.

Marie finished putting the clothes away and made a pile of Leon's clothes on the trailer hitch. Lyle added two supporting steels rods from the outside center to the hitch for strength. These bars came in very handy when she had to dry Leone's diapers.

"I'm glad your dad left, too. He made me nervous the way he acted. What in the world are you doing Lyle, and where did you get all that money?" asked Marie.

"We've hit the mother load! said Lyle.

"What do you mean?"

"Look at these coins and tell me what's wrong with them," said Lyle as he handed Marie a handful of silver dollars.

"They all have a hole in them," said Marie after looking carefully at the coins.

"Watch what I'm doing," said Lyle. He placed a silver dollar on a piece of cloth, opened a tube of liquid solder and very carefully filled in the hole. The solder dried almost instantly. I was almost the same color as the coin but you could still see the hole outline and Marie told him so.

"Now watch what I'm doing," Lyle said as he poured a drop of mercury on the coin. He rubbed both sides with the mercury and the coin became very shiny, like it was new. He wiped the coin with a piece of jeweler's cloth to take some of the shine off and handed it to Marie.

"Now look at the coin," he said.

"It looks like a regular coin and you can't see the hole anymore," said Marie.

"That's the beauty of it. I buy the coins for 45¢ on the dollar. I fix them and pass them as "good money," said Lyle with a big smile on his face.

"Isn't that against the law? I thought you were supposed to turn in the money at a Federal bank like you did the gold," asked Marie, quite concerned.

"It's foolproof Marie. There's no trace of the silver back to the government and the coins look like new. We can't miss with this one," said Lyle, with a proud arrogant smile on his face.

"There are no perfect schemes anywhere in the world. My father always said that. I remember when he would tie a string to his wallet and laugh when some on tried to steal it. This looks like it has the long string of the law tied to it," said Marie.

"I don't want to spend any of the coins here because I bought them here. I'll sell the smashed coins to a Federal bank to make it look good," said Lyle. "We'll pull out in the morning and head south. Dad has gone back north and I don't have to worry about Ruth and Jerry, my daughter and her husband until spring. Dad said they wanted to meet us somewhere in South Carolina when the weather warms," he said.

"Let me show you how to make up the coins," said Lyle.

They continued to work on the coins for the rest of the day. Marie didn't like doing the work because she felt dirty cheating someone out of money. She didn't know who was being cheated but someone certainly lost money. However, she felt she really didn't have a lot of choice as she continued to work on the coins.

"I wonder where we'll be tomorrow," thought Marie as she filled in a coin with solder. Lyle applied the mercury and put the last of the coins away.

CHAPTER THIRTEEN

The Heart of Dixie

Late Winter

The road to Lyle's promised land of Key West was long and hard. Nothing would have it until he visited the southernmost point in the continental United States. The Dixie Highway was a concrete ribbon of small town after small town from Vero Beach to Miami. Unless you were from a particular area and knew the locals, it was difficult to have a set up of any kind.

Lyle and Marie used the "doctored" silver coins whenever they could and were quite successful. They found that using small amounts were a lot more successful than large amounts. Marie usually passed the coins because a woman looked less suspicious than a man. Once Lyle tried and he caused a commotion in the grocery store because he tried to buy $8.00 worth of groceries.

"Lyle, what in the world are you trying to do, get us caught?"

"We have a lot more dimes than we have of the larger coins and I was trying to get rid of them."

"Next time let me shop and you stay out of the store! I don't like doing this because it makes me feel dirty all over. If you have to spend money, use common sense and mix up the denominations so it won't look so suspicious. All someone has to do is look at you and you look suspicious."

They were working their way through the 50¢ and $1.00 coins because it was easier. Lyle didn't know what he was going to do with all the dimes he had. "Next time I'll let Marie shop and I'll stay in the car or sit on a bench," he thought.

Lyle looked at the coins he had and noticed that the mercury was starting to wear off and you could see the outline of the liquid solder. He rubbed a few of the coins and the coins brightened. He put them back in his pocket and wondered if he should tell Marie.

He found a nice shady place south of West Palm Beach. It was an old souvenir store and partial fruit stand. It was for rent and for a reasonable $25.00 per month.

Lyle negotiated with the owner, Mr. Blanchard, an old retired railroad engineer. They agreed on a price and what he could use. He paid 2 months rent and pulled the trailer behind. It had a nice bathroom with a big crow's foot tub and shower combination. There was a stove and ice box in the small living quarters behind the store. It was all one building with a covered outside display area and the location was perfect on the southern edge of West Palm Beach. The road had two lanes and a good parking area to catch both north and south bound traffic on US 1.

The problems began when Lyle went to town to have the lights turned on. He was told he must be a Florida resident to qualify for a minimum hookup charge. A non-resident cost $50.00 to have the power turned on and a resident was only $5.00.

The qualifications to be a resident were simple: Get a Florida drivers license and a tag for the car and trailer. The car and driver's license were no problem but he had no title or bill of sale for the trailer. It was homemade and Georgia didn't require a license on a trailer.

Lyle was caught between two difficult situations. He would have to provide identification and addresses to get his drivers license. He would have to contact an attorney to get a legal bill of sale for the trailer. The police know that the trailer didn't have a license and it couldn't be moved until it did.

"Marie, I don't know what to do. We're in a spot and I don't know how to get us out of it," said Lyle.

"I don't understand what you mean; explain it to me so I can help," said Marie.

"You won't understand what the problems are and you really don't need to know."

"Very well Lyle, figure it out for your self. You usually get into more trouble when you don't listen to me."

"Alright Marie, if you must know. We have to have a tag on the trailer and we have no bill of sale because it is homemade. I'll get us out of this if it's possible without spending too much money. We're set alright with the help of the silver but we can't waste it. It's the weekend and I'm going to ask around and see if anyone knows a cheap lawyer. The power will stay on a few more days in the owner's name so we can use the cabin. Tomorrow I'll see the landlord and ask if he knows anyone that can help me with the trailer tag."

"It's like I said Lyle, if you do things right and legal the first time you won't have to do it over. Remember, in Lake Park Mr. Allan asked you if you were going to get a license. They aren't required in Georgia but other states do. It would have been easy."

"Don't remind me Marie, I don't want to hear about it. I didn't want to tag the trailer, but this state is tough on outsiders who want to conduct any business. I'm going to see Mr. Blanchard and see if he knows anyone," said Lyle.

Marie had a lot of washing to do. Leone used a lot of diapers. She would be so glad when he was out of diapers.

"Like my other two son's, I'll have him trained as soon as he begins to walk," thought Marie.

The weather was warm but not the stifling hot like it was in the summer. Marie hand washed all his diapers and was able to get some of Lyle's underclothes from him. She wished he would change more often but it was like asking a goat to swim.

Marie finished her washing and hung it out to dry on a clothesline behind the trailer. There were palms and Australian pines in the yard that provided a lot of shade. The line was between two old iron posts that looked like they would fall at anytime. She cleaned the wire and hung them to dry using some old push-on wooden clothes pins left on the line.

She looked over the area for the first time. Lyle kept her so busy she had very little time to do anything for herself. She liked the quiet times when he was wandering and doing what he did best–nothing. She knew he would figure a way to get a license, legal or illegal, though she hoped it would be legal because the local police knew what he was doing.

There was a large covered shed in the back of the house with a wide swing out door. She pulled on the handle and opened the door. It was full of old garden tools and stacks of lumber. Several green lizards came scurrying out, a little upset at being disturbed.

"Now, now Mr. and Mrs. Lizard. I won't hurt you, I just want to look in the shed."

Marie was a person who loved all kinds of creatures. She liked to pick up the little lizards. They would open their mouth as if to bite. She would put the open mouth on her earlobe and they would bite down just hard enough to hang on. She would just let it hang on her earlobe. It would anger Lyle to no end because he was afraid of everything in the animal kingdom.

She called it "showing their money" when the lizard would open his mouth and let the red skin under its neck puff out. It was red and about the size of a dime. When Lyle saw this, he would run away.

Marie also liked to look through old things and see what people left from the past. She noticed a handle attached to a wicker-looking basket. She moved some tools and old lumber and found a nice old wicker baby stroller with large wheels and a convertible cover. After considerable work, she had it out in the open. It was dirty from the years it had been stored. The inside padding was long gone and the handle loose.

Marie cleaned on the old stroller for several hours until it looked like new. The handle was easy to fix with a piece of her broom wire. She folded an old blanket in the bottom so Leone would be comfortable.

She put Leone in the old stroller and followed the path to the ocean. The path was part hard shell and wood planking but it was smooth enough for the stroller. The stroller had good springs that supported the weight and was easy to push.

She topped at a sand dune and saw the beauty of the Florida Atlantic coast with a wide beach and green waves breaking in the surf. It was such a wide expanse of beauty that Marie was awe struck; she had never seen such an expanse of natural splendor. She had seen oceans and seas all over the world but nothing as majestic as what she saw there.

She looked for a long time before she picked up Leone and walked on the sand barefooted.

In the northern waters she visited there were very few shells. Here she saw more shells than she thought possible. She picked up as many as she could as she waded in the warm water and listened the gentle surf.

"It's time I get back. If Lyle finds I'm gone, it'll be hell to pay and I'm not interested in that today. It has been too nice a day to listen to his ranting and raving," said Marie out loud.

She tucked her shells in Leone's stroller and headed back the 3 short blocks to their camp.

"Where have you been Marie?"

"I found this old stroller and cleaned it up. We took a little walk to the beach and it is so pretty," said Marie in the nicest voice she could muster.

Lyle wasn't angry but surprisingly happy, and this confused Marie.

"Mr. Blanchard knew a retired lawyer and we went to see him. He can do all the paperwork for $50.00 if I give him all the receipts and a letter from someone who saw me build the trailer. I'll write to Jim and ask him to send me a letter. Mr. Blanchard said he would keep the power on until we got the mess settled," said Lyle.

Lyle then got busy writing a letter to Jim. He asked Marie to look in the car and trailer and get all the receipts together. He quickly finished and went to the post office to mail the letter. He checked general delivery and he had no mail.

"I guess I shouldn't have any mail because I didn't tell anyone I was here. I need to drop Ruth and dad a line and let them know where I'll be for a couple of weeks," said Lyle out loud.

"Were you talking to me? I don't cotton to strange men talking to me!" said a lady in the post office.

Lyle said nothing and as he left he doffed his hat to the lady. He noticed she was writing down his license number.

"I had better get the license changed before I have a cop on my tail," he thought.

He drove back to the camp and saw Marie sitting on a bench, rocking Leone in her newfound stroller.

"It's getting late Marie. Let's go to the diner and get some supper. I want to go to bed early so I can turn in this defaced silver to the bank tomorrow. There's probably close to $50.00 worth and I don't want the price of silver to go down. I'm not making any money, so any income will help. This outlay is killing our stash. I'll have to look for a Federal bank in town. There should be one with all the businesses I see in the area" said Lyle.

Marie was happy Lyle didn't fuss at her. It was good that he was occupied with something. When he wasn't, it was very hard on her because he always found fault with anything she did. The only thing he didn't fuss about was Leone. In fact, he didn't pay much attention to him except when he cried. "Can't you shut him up? I can't think when he is crying," was Lyle's often repeated quote.

He arose early and put on his "bib and tucker" as Lyle would say. He was clean-shaven and well dressed with one of his better, frayed ties. He left after a quick breakfast of corn meal mush in search of a Federal bank to sell the defaced silver coins. He looked at all of them carefully before putting them in a bag. He selected a few that might possibly pass in a crowded store and by someone who didn't look closely.

He left without saying goodbye, which was his way. He thought only about which road he was taking that day and about nothing else. Today his road led him toward the bank and making some more money.

Marie never got used to him leaving without so much as a simple wave or goodbye. Her family, in the old country, was very close and everyone was courteous to everyone else. It wasn't like that with Lyle. Marie felt a combination of anger, frustration and relief when he left.

This morning it was more of a relief than anything. She planned to go the beach and collect some more sea shells. She had an idea how to make some things out of the shells and maybe use them in her set up. The sea made her feel relaxed and secure. She had very little of that feeling anymore. She hadn't since she came to America some 7 odd years before.

Lyle found the bank he wanted to visit but it was almost 30 minutes before it opened. He stopped at a small café across the street from the bank. He went in and ordered a cup of coffee and two of the homemade donuts they had in a glass case on the counter. He was just dunking his first donut when a group of policemen came in for breakfast. He almost choked on his donut when they sat down. He continued to dunk his donuts and tried to be as inconspicuous as he could. They ordered and were talking among themselves except for one officer who looked his way several times. This made Lyle feel very uncomfortable as the hair on the back of his neck hackled. He finished his coffee and donuts and got up to pay at the register by the door. He passed by the officers and tried not to look in their direction.

"Excuse me mister, where do I know you from?" the officer asked Lyle.

"I think you are the officer who tried to help me register my homemade trailer so I can get a Florida tag," said Lyle as he grew weak in the knees.

"Did you get your tag?" asked the officer.

"No sir I didn't, but Mr. Blanchard took me to a retired attorney to help with the paperwork," said Lyle.

"Oh, you must mean Mr. Board. He was in practice for many years and retired several years ago. He's a good attorney and should help you get the matter straight very soon," said the officer.

"Yes, I think he will. I'm waiting on a letter from Georgia to submit with the rest of the paperwork," said Lyle.

He paid for his coffee and donut and started to leave.

"Have a good day sir!" the officer said.

"You too!" said Lyle as he left the café.

The officer watched him carefully as he walked toward his car. Lyle needed to pick up the money bag and go to the bank. It was going to open in a few minutes. As soon as he picked up the bag and headed toward the bank, the officer came out of the café toward Lyle.

"Stay where you are!" the officer shouted with his hand on his pistol.

Lyle stopped in his tracks as the officer approached him with two other officers spread out on each side.

"What's in the bag sir?" asked the officer.

Lyle was so frightened he couldn't talk. He stuttered and tried to answer but couldn't.

"Drop the bag and put your hands up," said the officer, very calmly.

Lyle did as he was told and stood very still, his heart almost beating out of his chest. The officer picked up the bag and looked inside. He held some of the silver coins in his hand.

"What are you going to do with these?" he asked.

Lyle was still very scared but he regained his composure enough to speak.

"I am licensed by the Federal Government to sell gold and silver to Federal banks. I have a license in my right inside pocket," said Lyle as he started to reach for his pocket.

The two other officers drew their guns and went into a crouch position.

"Hold it sir; I get the license for you so no one gets hurt," said the officer.

He reached into Lyle's coat pocket and got the license. He signaled to the other officers to lower their guns as he carefully read the license.

"Is this you? Do you have any other kind of identification?" he asked Lyle.

"I have a Michigan driver's license in my wallet. It's in my left rear pocket," said Lyle.

"You can put your hands down while I look at it," said the officer. He carefully examined the papers and returned the bag and papers to Lyle.

"What's this all about?" asked Lyle nervously.

"We're so sorry to upset your morning but we had a special alert yesterday. As you know, John Dillinger was killed in '33. We were advised that his gang was headed to south Florida, so we are being extra cautious," said the officer. "Let me help you to the bank, you look little upset," he said as the other two officers went back to the café.

"I could use a little help to the bench where I can rest a bit. I have a bad heart and this scared me so much I thought my heart was going to bust," Lyle said as he walked to the bench.

"Sorry for the inconvenience and we apologize sir, but we have our job to do. You fit the description of one of the Dillinger gang. He escaped in '33 and is still at large. You are about the same height and build. You were acting suspicious with the bag under your coat," said the officer.

Lyle thanked the officer as he walked away. He lit up a cigarette and smoked it with shaking hands. "It isn't my day to do any business," he thought.

He picked up his bag and went to his car. He could feel the officers still watching him as he drove away. He drove slowly around the block and returned to the camp as fast as he could.

"Marie, I've had a terrible time in town," he said as he got out of his car.

He explained what happened while he was in town He was so upset he couldn't hold anything on his stomach.

He went in the trailer and lay down. He was so exhausted he didn't wake up until the next morning. He had a light breakfast and sat down to think things over. Then he decided he needed a little more rest and went back to bed.

Marie went about her business of taking care of Leone and a little shopping at the country store. She bought some cube steaks and fried some potatoes. Lyle hardly touched his food. He was still in a state of nervous exhaustion and he went back to bed again. Police had a devastating effect him. He hadn't been that worried since he was in Mexico many years before. It was the second time in his life he had a gun pulled on him and he didn't want it to happen again.

For the past weeks, Marie had been watching Lyle start and drive the car. Lyle wasn't very good with the clutch because he jerked the car most of the time. He was especially bad towing a trailer. Marie could smell the clutch burning. She wanted to learn to drive but Lyle wouldn't teach her. He didn't like the idea of a woman driving a car just like he didn't think women should vote either.

She sat in the driver's seat, grabbed the steering wheel and looked out over the long Buick hood. She looked at the gauges and saw water temperature, oil pressure and generator. In the center was a large round dial indicating miles per hour. She adjusted the seat her so feet would reach the pedals. It didn't need much adjustment because Lyle was so short. Marie looked down at the position of the brake, clutch, emergency brake, gas pedal and gearshift. She practiced shifting gears from 1st to 2nd and then to 3rd like she was driving the car although the engine wasn't running. There was a small line of perspiration as she contemplated whether or not she should start the car. She was afraid Lyle would wake up if she started the it. The keys were left in the ignition because they wouldn't release from the switch. No one ever locked cars anyway.

She tapped the gas pedal twice as she had seen Lyle do, pressed the clutch in with the gearshift in neutral and engaged the starter. It scared her when the engine sprang to life and settled into a smooth idle. She quickly turned the key off and looked over her shoulder to see if Lyle was awake. There was no sign of him.

There was a large open area in the back next to the sand dunes. She got out of the car and walked back and looked it over to see if she could maneuver the car on the little road. Finally, she got up the courage and started the car again. She carefully pushed in the clutch, grabbed the swirled marble handle of the shift lever and pulled it into 1st gear.

"So far so good," she thought as she looked at the trailer to see if Lyle was awake.

She let out the clutch too fast and the Buick lurched and died. It frightened her. She turned the key off and got out. She walked around the car and thought about it. Leone was asleep in his bed and she had some time before Lyle woke up.

She settled back into the driver's seat and started the car again. This time she let the clutch out very easy and the car moved forward. She gave it a little gas and drove around the road and came back to the camp. She drove around again and felt very good turning the wheel and judging distance.

"Now for the big one. I'll try to back her up and see how it feels," she thought out loud.

She put the gearshift lever in reverse and slowly backed up. She was about to stop when the right rear fender bumped a palm tree. The car quit and she got out and looked at the damage. It was only a skinned place on the palm tree. She put the car back exactly where it was. Lyle and Leone were still asleep.

"All I need is a little practice and I bet I can pass the drivers' test. I know all the road signs because it helped me to learn English. I'll ask Lyle to get a copy of the driver's book and I'll study it. My only problem is to get somebody to teach me how to drive on the road and shift gears." thought Marie.

Around dusk, Lyle finally got up and was pretty well rested but he was hungry.

"This has been one more day for me. Marie get me something to eat, I need some food and fix some coffee," said Lyle.

Marie heated up the potatoes and cube steak and gave it to Lyle. The coffee was done when he was half through eating. She poured him a cup and he finished his supper.

"Marie, I learned a lot today. I fully intend to stay away from all cops. I want to avoid another run in like I had today. It scared the heck out of me!" said Lyle.

"I hope it taught you a lesson! It never pays to do anything dishonest. If you don't, then you won't have to be afraid of the police," said Marie.

"Get the babe and let's take a ride. I want to see if I can find another bank that's not in an area that the cops use. They like the café and seem to be watching that bank," said Lyle as he got up to go to the bathroom.

"As soon as I get back we'll go," said Lyle.

Marie put Leone in the back seat and sat in the passenger seat waiting for Lyle.

Lyle came back out, closed the trailer door and he got in the Buick.

"What's wrong with this seat? It's set too far forward! Have you been messing with my seat?" asked Lyle.

"I want to drive and I took a little practice drive in 1st gear around the back of the lot. I know how to start the car and use the clutch but I need to know how to drive on the road," said Marie with a defiant tone in her voice.

"I told you I'd teach you how to drive when I have time. Leave the car alone! I don't want it to be damaged, understand!" shouted Lyle.

"Don't use that kind of voice to me Lyle! I'll learn how to drive with or without you!" said Marie.

Lyle didn't say anything; he just gripped the wheel and drove. He knew when to be quiet. This argument could turn into a big fight and he wasn't up to it after the strain of the day.

He drove down the drive and turned on US 1 toward Palm Beach instead of West Palm Beach. He thought there might be another bank there. He stopped at a gas station to get some gas and air in the left rear tire. It apparently had a slow leak.

"The tire shouldn't leak. The guy who changed the tires at Western Auto probably pinched the tube. I have to get it fixed before I start on the road down to the Keys . . . 19¢ a gallon is a more than I paid in Georgia. It looks like everything is different down here," said Lyle as he put air in the tire.

He paid the attendant who was an older man in bib overalls with a name tag that said "Bob."

"Do you know of a Federal bank in this area?" Lyle asked.

"The closest one is West Palm Beach, but there is one a few miles down the road in Lake Worth. It was closed for a long time and just reopened several months ago," said Bob.

"Marie, there isn't a bank in Palm Beach. It's getting dark and I don't like to drive in the dark. I'll drive to Lake Worth in the morning and finish my business," said Lyle as he got in the car.

They went to their camp with Lyle in a sullen mood. It was after dark when they got back and by that time he was really grouchy. He didn't like to drive at night and he was tired and aggravated from the happenings of the day.

Lucky for Marie he went straight to bed without even so much as a good night or single word. Marie had fixed the fold out bed in the little house. She put Leone to sleep in the wicker stroller and watched the sky for a long time. It was a clear and cool Florida evening that the state was famous for the world over. Marie saw a shooting star and made a wish.

"I hope with all my heart that Lyle would find something honest to do and stop treading on the edge of disaster all the time," she wished with a sincere prayer mixed in.

She knew he could do most anything with his hands if he put his mind to it. Her father told her that making money without working was a sure way to trouble.

"The more money you make that way, the less you want to work. You wake up one morning with the idea not to work again. Nothing that comes easy in life is worth what it seems at the time," he had said.

The fold out bed was soft and comfortable as Marie settled in after a nice tub bath. The water was warm enough from the tank on the roof. Many Floridians had a tank on the roof and let the sun heat the water during the day. It was a very practical way of getting free hot water. She went to sleep quickly after checking on Leone tucked in the stroller. Her dreams were a mixture of running in the ocean sand and driving the Buick.

She heard Lyle as he started the car and pulled slowly out of the driveway. She knew he was going to a Federal bank to try and sell the silver that was too defaced to spend. She didn't like to spend the "doctored" money but she really had no choice. So far, it spent well with no questions, especially the 50¢ pieces. Everyone looked at a silver dollar but they didn't pay any attention to the smaller coins, especially half dollars.

Lyle stopped at a diner on the way to Lake Worth and got a good breakfast. He was still a little nervous from the day before. He didn't want any more encounters with the cops for any reason.

"May I have a little more coffee," he asked the comely young woman who was waiting on him.

"Certainly, sir. Where you from?" she asked.

"I'm from Michigan and on the way to Key West. I'll be here a few days. What's your name?"

"Can't you read? My name's Melissa, or so it says on my name tag."

A large man with a dirty apron came out of the kitchen. His dirty, floor length apron barely covered his huge belly that shook when he walked.

"Lissa is that Yankee drummer bothern you?" he asked.

"No Frank, I just getting him some more coffee," Melissa said in a gruff tone. "Git back in the kitchen and fix that order I hung on the clip," she said.

Lyle heard some cussing in the kitchen and got up to leave. He knew he wasn't wanted and didn't need anymore trouble. He left one of the "holy" dimes as a tip and paid his bill. He turned and looked back as he was leaving. Melissa was watching him every step of the way. He was glad to get out of there and just in time as Frank grabbed her and pulled her back in the diner.

"I'll never stop there again; that girl is 20 miles of bad road," thought Lyle.

The bank opened a few minutes before Lyle got there. He parked in the front and gathered his bag and checked to make sure he had his credentials so the transaction would go smooth. He walked in the door and asked the receptionist where he could find the bank manager.

"If you will wait a moment, I'll get Mr. Atkins."

Lyle sat in a green leather overstuffed chair and was admiring the trim when Mr. Atkins walked up.

"I'm Mr. Atkins, how may I be of service?"

Lyle went through his usual spiel about the license and the Federal Government. It seemed to impress Mr. Atkins as he looked carefully at the license.

"Come with me and let's see what you have." As they passed the receptionist desk, he waved at her behind his back. As soon as they were out of sight, she picked up the telephone and dialed a number. Lyle didn't see any of that interaction but continued to follow Mr. Atkins. He was thinking only about the money he would get and nothing else.

Mr. Atkins took the bag of silver from Lyle as soon as they entered his office. Lyle took a seat while he examined and weighed the silver. It took a while because there seemed to be something wrong with the scales and he kept reweighing it over and over.

"You have 43½ troy ounces of silver. I'll have to call and get the latest silver prices from our main office in Miami. We do very few silver transactions here at this branch," said Mr. Atkins.

He left his office and asked the secretary to call the main office and see what the price of silver was; at least that's what Lyle thought. She actually made a call to the local police to come to the bank.

Mr. Atkins had received a letter as all Federal banks had yesterday to be on the lookout for Lyle. He was wanted for questioning by the Secret Service for questionable gold transactions over the past few months.

"The price of silver is 46¢ a troy ounce. I'll have my assistant get the money for you. Please sign this receipt that we paid you for the silver we received, plus your commission," he told Lyle.

The assistant bought in some bills and change. Mr. Atkins counted the money and paid Lyle.

Lyle was seated, counting the money, as two police officers came into Mr. Atkins' office.

"Is this the man we need to hold until the Feds get here?" the sergeant asked as he looked at Lyle.

Mr. Atkins nodded and looked at Lyle.

"Stand up and empty your pockets," the officer told Lyle.

"What have I done wrong? I just came in here to turn in some silver that I am licensed to do," said Lyle in a high pitch voice.

"Just do as you're told. Turn around and put your hands behind you back," he said as the other officer handcuffed Lyle's hands behind his back.

About that time, two well dressed men came in the bank. The receptionist directed them to Mr. Atkins' office. They thanked her and walked toward his office. They identified themselves as Secret Service agents.

Lyle looked up and saw somebody he had seen before. It was Allan Sanders, all dressed up and looking the part of a "G man." The men didn't speak to Lyle but asked Mr. Atkins if he had a room where they could speak take him.

"I have a conference room on the 3rd floor that isn't being used. You're welcome to use it," he told Mr. Sanders.

"Take the cuffs off this man. He's not a criminal, we just wanted to question him," said Mr. Sanders. "Let's take a little walk, Lyle," he said as he helped a very shaken Lyle out of the chair. "Atkins, bring some coffee and donuts to your conference room."

He led Lyle to the 3rd floor conference room and asked him to sit. He had the license that Mr. Atkins gave him and was studying it carefully. It looked genuine and handed it to his partner.

"It looks real to me Allan," his partner said.

Lyle started to tell them that of course it was genuine.

"No need to talk right now, Lyle. We'll get to you in a minute as soon as we have some coffee," said Sanders.

Lyle relaxed and slumped in the chair with a million things racing through his mind. He didn't know what to expect or what he had done. He had to wait and find out and he couldn't stand it. He had learned one thing over the years–keep you mouth shut unless you are asked a question.

About that time, there was a knock on the door and Mr. Atkins brought in the coffee and donuts.

"Pour yourself some coffee Lyle and let's get down to business," said Mr. Sanders.

Lyle didn't budge an inch. He was so scared he couldn't move a muscle. A picture of Robert E. Lee over Mr. Sander's head transfixed him. His concentration was divided between fear and the need to go to the bathroom.

"I need to use the bathroom," said Lyle.

"It's at the end of the room on the right. Don't get lost," said Mr. Sanders.

Lyle returned to a cup of coffee and two powdered donuts. He felt a little better and sat down. He took a sip of the coffee and picked up a donut.

"You don't know who I am, do you Lyle?" asked Mr. Sanders.

"I remember you in Atlanta and Lake Park. There is something familiar about you, but I can't place you," said Lyle.

"In both places I was doing undercover work to try and catch the people who were "shaving" gold coins. That falls under the jurisdiction of the Secret Service. Of course, every one thinks that our job is to protect the president but that is only one part of it. We follow the money trails if there is counterfeit or any attempt to defraud the government with gold and silver coins. It was a job given to us by the President since we went off the gold standard in 1933," said Mr. Sanders.

"Think a little farther back, Lyle. Let's go back to Detroit, say about 1915. Can you remember that far back Lyle?" asked Mr. Sanders.

"I can remember working in Detroit and the year but what has that got to do with you?" asked Lyle.

"Think a little harder. Do you remember the name of the company and what the owner's name was?" he asked.

Lyle thought about the time when he was having all kinds of problems with Anna, his ex wife. He thought about the company and suddenly remembered. There was a Sanders who was one of the owners of the company he worked for.

"So that's it!" thought Lyle.

Mr. Sanders saw the look on Lyle's face. "So, you do remember my father," said Mr. Sanders. "What else do you remember, huh? Do you remember the large amount of money you and your family swindled out of the company? Do you know what that did to my dad? No, I guess you don't because you left the country and couldn't have known," he continued.

"I remember now and I am ashamed to admit it," said Lyle.

"Unfortunately, there is nothing that can be done on that count because of the statue of limitations governing that kind of default and it has expired," he said.

Lyle was beginning to get real nervous as Mr. Sanders sat on the edge of the table.

"He's looking right at me and it makes me feel uncomfortable," thought Lyle.

"It almost killed my dad. They had a bad year and coupled with the loss from your family, he had a serious heart attack and had to retire. He's gone now but he always liked and trusted you Lyle, and he was ashamed of what you and your family did," he said.

"I know what they did to me. I had full intentions in paying the money back, but my dad and uncles ran away with the money and I left for Mexico," said Lyle.

"It's over and done with Lyle. Dad passed away in '29 after the stock market crashed. He was able to get an injunction on the property your dad put up for the loan. It is now 600 acres of prime Sanders' timber land. We plan on developing it in a few years or selling the property. I hear Ford Motor company is planning to expand their plant. We'll just have to wait and see," he said.

"Allan, don't you think we should get on with it," said his partner.

"Your right, that has nothing to do with this investigation. I just wanted Lyle to know who I was and how I knew him. It's over and forgotten, for now," said Mr. Sanders. "Lyle this is my boss, Mr. Walsh, and he wants to talk to you about your federal license."

They asked all about his activities and how he got the license and how he used it. After about 4 hours of interrogation, they were through.

Lyle hadn't been very honest with them about buying the gold coins but they didn't know it. He also lied about the silver coins he altered so he could pass them at face value. They also didn't know that.

"Their main concern was shaking the coins and trying to sell the dust to Fishlows in Baltimore. They couldn't prove where I bought the coins or anything about the silver," thought Lyle.

"We must assume you bought the coins from a bank. If that is correct, you paid the correct price for the coins. You were shorted when you turned them in to the last bank but you sent the gold to Baltimore. They in turn withheld payment and sent a letter to us. We are required by law to issue you a voucher for the money that was shorted by the gold agent in Baltimore," said Mr. Walsh.

If I had anything to do with it I would have put you in jail and you know it!" said Mr. Sanders.

"Allan, that's why I am making this decision–because of your bad feelings toward Lyle," said Mr. Walsh.

"Lyle, this is what we're going to do. You signed an agreement with the Federal Government that you wouldn't abuse the privilege of the license. Effective immediately your license is revoked. Furthermore, you are forbidden to buy any more gold coins. You may continue your practice of buying old scrap silver and gold. However, you must sell it only to Fishlows in Baltimore because we will keep track of what you sell. It that understood!" said Mr. Walsh.

"I agree with everything you want me to do," said Lyle.

"Very well; wait here while I draw up an agreement," said Mr. Walsh.

They went outside and wrote an agreement and returned it for Lyle to sign. The old Underwood had made a few errors and had some strikeovers, but he ignored them and willingly signed the paper. They gave him a copy and a voucher for the money he lost on the gold dust. He was very shaky as he got up and went downstairs. The bank was ready to close but they cashed his voucher and paid him for the silver coins. Lyle was shaking so bad he could barely sign the voucher and put the money away. His knees were continued shaking as he went outside in the cool of the late afternoon.

The agents both turned to Lyle and Mr. Walsh said, "This is the last time we want to see you. The next time we'll send you to the pen."

"This is a turning point in my life," Lyle told the agents, "and I thank you for being easy on me."

Mr. Walsh shook Lyle's hand but Mr. Sanders didn't as they walked to their black Ford.

"I'll be very careful about spending the rest of the silver coins. I still have some things I want to do with the linoleum I looked at in Lake Park," thought Lyle.

He drove home very slowly, thinking about the events of the afternoon. He was very shaky and extremely tired. "In a way, I am glad I met Mr. Sanders. I finally found out what happened. When I went back to Michigan in 1921 to settle the divorce with Anna, I didn't see anyone or talk to anyone. That part of my life has finally been put to rest. I didn't know it had a statue of limitations or I wouldn't have been so scared all the time," he thought to himself.

The camp looked good to him as he pulled in behind the little house and saw Marie and the babe sitting at the old table.

"What's wrong Lyle; you look as white as a sheet?"

"Marie, don't bother me now it has been a long day! I'll tell you tomorrow when I'm rested. Draw me some bath water so I can take a good bath."

She looked at him with a quizzical look but did as she was told.

"Wonder of all wonders! Lyle must have had a very bad day to come back to his camp and take a bath! We'll see what happens tomorrow," she thought out loud as Lyle was taking his bath.

She looked out at the evening sky and was somehow happy this evening. She thought Lyle might be at a turning point in his life, at least she hoped so.

Chapter Fourteen

Southern Florida, Key West

Late winter

Lyle awoke in a daze, wondering if all the things that happened were a dream or they actually occurred. He was in a deep dream about loafing in Mexico and the servants were serving him wine and food. Lyle didn't care for alcohol and he wondered why he had had a dream about wine. Maybe it was sign of something. Marie often spoke about dreams and their signs but he didn't believe in it. When he awoke, he thought he could taste the stale residue of food in his mouth, but all he had were the donuts at the bank. He was so scared then that he didn't even taste them.

Lyle often daydreamed he had stayed in Mexico, married a pretty senorita and raised a family. He couldn't and wouldn't form a relationship that didn't have a quick way out. He thought many times that he should marry Marie, but it would close the door on his life and he wasn't ready for a commitment like that. He was almost 50 but the adventure of the free and open road still flowed heavily in his veins.

This last incident with the law frightened him to the point that he wanted to keep driving and leave the troubles behind. He did that once to the life with Anna and his daughter Ruth, by running away to Mexico. Seeing Allan Sanders brought him back to the time when it was very difficult for him and he took the easy way out. This time he would try and stick it out for the sake of Marie and the babe. Time would tell, but he wasn't going to box himself and be tied down in one place or to one person for the rest of his life. The lure of easy money and the vagabond way of life was too strong for him to resist.

Shortly before noon, Lyle drove to the post office to see if he had any mail. The letter was from Jim Allen. He took the letter and the receipts to Mr. Board so he could get a legal bill of sale. Mr. Board said it would be a couple of days and he should have his trailer license.

The last thing Lyle wanted to do was to stay there one day more than necessary. He was dreaming about the adventure ahead in Key West. Lyle didn't care how many bridges he burnt behind him or who he hurt in the process. He never learned that this would present more problems than he could handle. It was very evident when Mr. Sanders confronted him, but he had no remorse.

He was looking forward to driving to the Keys and seeing Flagler's Key West Extension of his Florida East Coast Railway. He was particularly excited about seeing all the railroad bridges

Henry Flagler was a successful entrepreneur who built the Florida East Coast Railroad. In 1905, he began the connection of a railroad between Miami and Key West, which required the construction of a 7-mile open water railroad bridge. Storm and torrential rains took their toll of workers and construction. With Flagler's health failing, the crews worked day and night to fulfill his dream. Finally, it was completed in 1912 and on January 22, 1912 Flagler found himself in his private rail car, Rambler, traveling the Key West Extension that he lived to see come true. In May 1913, with his project complete, Henry M. Flagler passed away. His dream of train service between Miami and the Keys was a reality. This was the time when a "Key Wester" could travel round trip for $4.75.

Lyle especially wanted to see the great 7-mile bridge, which was in daily train use. For some reason he had made up his mind to make the trip regardless of how Marie felt. She didn't want to go but Lyle would have his way. He was a little concerned about the ferry trips but he would face that when he got there.

Mr. Board came to their camp the next day and gave him the required paperwork to get his license. Lyle started to pay him $50.00 but he thought about the last watch he had. He talked to Mr. Board about it and he agreed he would take the watch for the work he did. Lyle looked to be a winner and this time; he had swindled an attorney into taking an old watch for his fee. Lyle was happy.

"I'll have to find some more watches. They make good trading material," thought Lyle out loud.

He went to the courthouse in West Palm Beach and bought tags for the trailer and Buick. He didn't get his Florida drivers license because he was afraid to take the driving test. He knew his eyes were bad and he couldn't judge distance very well. The police didn't think to ask him. They wanted to see him leave as much as Lyle wanted to leave.

"It's too bad that Lyle had to be caught up in the gold and silver schemes. I like the area and the place we rented. I especially like the ocean and mild winter weather," thought Marie.

Mr. Blanchard was a nice man and would have worked out a way so they could buy the building and property. Since his wife died, he had closed the fruit stand and moved into the cabin on the next street over. He was looking for some responsible people to buy the place, but obviously Lyle didn't fit into that category.

Lyle stopped at Boca Raton and Fort Lauderdale to buy some old scrap gold. It was different here. There were no old mansions that Lyle liked to visit. The homes were new or just a few years old. The doctors and dentists had no interest in selling any of their gold. He had no luck at all. He couldn't understand or speak the Cuban brand of Spanish. They spoke a lot faster than he couldn't keep up with and this hurt his ability to buy anything.

The outskirts of Miami were crowded with morning traffic. Lyle hadn't seen so much traffic since he lived in Detroit. It was still a nice drive through the heart of a great city.

Many of the residents were Cuban. They stopped at Coral Gables to buy some groceries. It was Lyle's intention to pass some of the silver coins at the store. The owner was Cuban and spoke limited English. Lyle put the silver coins on the counter as he tried to speak Spanish to the owner. The owner ignored his attempts at Spanish and spoke in broken English. He picked up the silver dollars and looked at them very carefully. He shook his head and said "no good."

"What's wrong with the money?" Lyle asked.

"I see this many times in Cuba. The women make holes in the coins and wear them around their neck for good luck or to ward off evil spirits. When they need money, they try and patch them. The bank won't take them and I won't take them," said the owner. "See the hole at the top; someone has tried to fill it and didn't do a good job. I'll have to have a good coin or paper money," the owner continued in broken English.

"How did you have American money in Cuba? I thought you had your own money," asked Lyle.

"We do have our own peso, but the dollar works better for us. U.S. Dollars have been used in Cuba since your army went to my country and fought. I know all about how you are," said the owner, getting a little red in the face.

Lyle thanked him, paid with paper money and left the store in a hurry. He didn't want to get into an argument with any of these people. They obviously didn't like anyone in their community that was American.

"That's very odd. They live here but don't like us, how strange," thought Lyle as he and Marie left the store.

Marie was embarrassed.

"I told you about those coins. The mess you put in the holes is coming out. We can't use them anymore," said Marie.

Lyle looked at some of the coins very carefully. The dimes were the only ones with a hole that couldn't be seen.

"I'll have to fix them when we have a chance. This time I'll buy some better liquid solder. The stuff we used was old and kind of dry," said Lyle as he got in the car. "Let's find a camp so we can fix some of the coins," said Lyle.

"We need to stop soon. Leone needs a bath and I'm tired," said Marie.

They drove though Coral Gables and on to Homestead. It was a nice small town on the edge of the everglades. It had a main train station for the Key West run.

They found a city park with water and a bathroom. It was a beautiful grass park. Marie had never seen grass that was so green and closely woven.

"What kind of grass is this?" asked Marie.

"It's green grass, everyone can see that. What a stupid question," said Lyle.

"You said that because you don't know. I'll ask the park manager," said Marie.

Later, when they had eaten and she finished giving Leone a bath, Marie went to the park office.

"What kind of grass is that in the park?" asked Marie of the lady in the office.

"That's native Bahia grass mixed with centipede. The Bahia is used for cattle feed but grows well if you cut and fertilize it. The centipede grows wild and gives it that rich green color. It would go back to the wild in no time if we let it grow," answered the lady manager.

Marie left with a thank you and pamphlet about the everglades.

"Lyle, it says the everglades is a river of grass that flows from Lake Okeechobee to the ocean. I bet it is pretty but very wild," said Marie.

"It's full of snakes and alligators. Besides, the Seminole Indians control the area as part of their reservation," said Lyle. "Did you know that the Seminoles are the only Indian tribe that has never signed a peace treaty with the government?"

"I hope we get to see some of it from the road," thought Marie, ignoring Lyle's statement about the Indians.

"Tomorrow we'll see the Florida Keys. I want to stay at Key Largo tomorrow night and drive the rest of the way the next day. I hope the ferry doesn't hold us up too long," said Lyle.

"Where is Key Largo?" asked Marie.

"It's the first big island on the way to Key West," said Lyle.

"Lyle, why don't we take the train? It costs only $4.75 each and Leone rides free. We'll be there in a few hours and we don't have to worry about driving, especially on the old ferries," said Marie.

"Then we'll have to rent a room and it will end up costing us more money. We'll drive and see all the sights," said Lyle.

The sun was shinning on the water as Marie and Lyle drove on the first bridge headed to the Keys on Florida 4A. The water was a different color on each side. The eastern side was the Atlantic Ocean and the western side was the Gulf of Mexico. They drove through Tavernier and looked for the campground. There was a nice park just on the edge of town.

Lyle pulled over and looked at the old atlas they had. The next place to camp was at Long Key, about 35 miles. He would have to take a short ferry to connect with the road.

"Let's drive to the Islamorada Key area and see how it looks. I want to spend some time looking around," said Lyle.

"Lyle, I need to use the bath room. It looks like the one in the park is open," said Marie.

She walked to the bathroom and started to go in. She felt something biting her legs but she couldn't see what it was. After she was finished, she started back to the car. She had several more bites and started fanning her legs. She started bites on her scalp under her hair. She hurried and got in the car and rolled up the window.

"I am being bitten by something I can't see. Whatever they are there're about to drive me crazy!" said Marie.

"Let's get out of here," said Lyle, as he put the car in gear and headed south.

The bugs finally stopped biting as they got to the ferry crossing to Long Key. There was a nice auto campground with several campers parked waiting on the morning ferry. The state of Florida provided water and electricity for 50¢ a night.

They selected a nice spot by a palm tree with a view of the Gulf of Mexico. Lyle got the wheel blocks in place and the electricity hooked up. He turned on his radio and was looking for a station. The palm tree wasn't tall enough to extend the aerial very far. He picked up a lot of Spanish stations and finally got one out of Miami. Amos and Andy were broadcasting their afternoon play and he was glued to the radio.

Marie took Leone to the water, sat on a large piece of coral and put her feet in the warm water. She sat Leone down in the shallow water to play in the wet sand. He was happy and content to be where it was warm. He would laugh and look at Marie as the waves washed over his legs.

"This is so nice and comfortable, but I still feel the things biting me. I wonder what they are. I can feel their bite but I can't see them," said Marie out loud.

She got up and picked Leone out of the water. He was starting to cry from the bites. She washed him off under the overhead outside shower to get the sand and salt water off. Marie was itching a lot when she went to the trailer and told Lyle about the bites.

"Hark, can't you see I'm listening to the radio!" said Lyle in a mean voice.

"Lyle, watch Leone; I'm going to the office see if I can find out what these bites are," said Marie.

"Take the babe with you. I'm listening to the radio," said Lyle.

"Like I said, he stays here with you. I'm not going to take him out in this bug storm," answered Marie in a hostile voice.

Lyle knew better than to provoke a fight so he kept his mouth shut as Marie closed the door and went to the office. She asked the man in the office what the bugs were that were biting her and her child.

"Mam, those are called "no see ums." They come out of the sand when the weather turns a little warm. Down here, we call them sand fleas. "No see ums" is a Yankee word because they are so small that you can hardly see them," answered the man. "They come out after a cold snap and last a few days. As soon as it's hot or after dark, they don't bite. The Indians in the glades used a special plant to keep the bugs off. We got the idea from them," he continued.

"Is there anything I can do about them? They don't seem to bother my husband but they are eating my son and me alive. We need something to stop them from biting," said Marie.

He laughed and reached under the counter and gave Marie some dried leaves that looked like long blades of grass.

"Break these up and rub them on your skin. It'll keep the critters off."

"What kind of plant is it? It smells terrible," said Marie.

"That's the idea. It's called citronella and has a kind of oil in it that bugs don't like. Take some more and light a small fire with it. The smoke will drive them away," said the man.

Marie thanked him and left for the trailer with an arm load of the plant. She made a small fire with some dried palm fronds mixed with the dried citronella leaves. In the old country, Marie learned a lot about plants and how to use them for medicinal purposes and food, but this was the first time she had ever used a plant that kept bugs off.

The fire was going well and Marie stood in the smoke. Gradually, the bugs got the idea and were not as plentiful as before.

"Lyle, the bugs are about gone. You can come out now," said Marie.

Lyle came out and Marie explained what the bugs were and how to handle them. Lyle half listened because they didn't bother him very much. Marie suspected it was his body odor, which kept anything away.

Marie saw some other campers wading in the shallow water and catching small lobsters by hand. She walked over and watched them. She asked what kind they were because they were a lot smaller than she had seen in China. They told her they were Florida lobsters and were very good for eating.

She went back to the trailer and got a pot. She waded in the water and caught 3 nice ones and brought them to the shore. She told Lyle to get the Coleman out because she was going to cook supper. Lyle reluctantly got the stove and sat it on the picnic table at their campsite.

In a short while, Marie had a lobster supper fixed with a few potatoes thrown in the boiling water. They were bright red when they were cooked. At first, Lyle wouldn't try them. Marie told him it was fine, that left more for her. He finally tried them and together they ate all 3 of the lobsters.

After supper, Lyle got out the remainder of the silver coins and tried to re-patch the holes. It was difficult because the liquid solder left a smear.

"Let me show you how to do it right, Lyle. The ones that are bad are the ones you did. Look, clean out the old solder from the hole and let it set. Use a small piece of my broom bristle and clean the hole. We still have some rubbing alcohol that we can use to clean the hand grease from the coins," said Marie as she finished cleaning the table.

She threw the lobster leftovers back in the water and watched a myriad of small sea creatures eat them.

"What comes from the sea, goes back to the sea," thought Marie out loud.

Lyle was cleaning the silver and Marie was applying the liquid solder. She was glad he bought a new tube because it worked a lot better.

They finished a little before dark, about the same time Leone awoke and wanted something to eat.

Lyle watched the beautiful red and golden sunset as it sank into the western sea. It was one of the rare times that he took a little time to watch the sun set and he marveled at its beauty. He was not prone to be affected by any of the beauty of nature, in direct contrast to Marie. The beautiful purple plants and bougainvilla flowers added a tint to the landscape. The area was named "The Purple Isles" for the beauty of the plants.

Marie sat with him and said nothing as the sun set. She didn't want to disturb the beauty of the moment. It would be hectic soon enough.

After 2:00 pm, more ferry rides between on Long Key and Marathon Key they were within site of Key West.

"Key West at last! Look at all the boats, Marie. It probably costs a lot to go fishing on one of those," said Lyle.

They found a place to park almost at the end of the key. Lyle set up the trailer and decided to go for a walk around town. It was small city and he wanted to see the sign that signified the most southern point in the United States. The bottom of the sign said: "Cuba 90 miles."

"Marie, you stay here while I look around the town. Later, we'll go into town and get some Cuban food," said Lyle.

She looked at all the people walking and looking at the small souvenir shops and displays. The train from Miami brought tourists every day, if they could afford the fare of $4.75 for a round trip. The actual trip by ferry had cost a lot more but they had a place to sleep.

"Why not!" she thought, as she got all of her brushes and baskets and fixed a set up on the Buick. Almost immediately, people started to crowd around and look. They had never seen brushes like that. They loved the baskets. In a short while Marie had sold most of her goods. She went in the trailer and got the costume jewelry and put in the set up. It sold like hot cakes. In less than an hour she sold everything she had, even some broken jewelry. In this part of the world people were isolated and didn't get to see any hand made brushes or baskets from willow. Word got around that she was set up and several people wanted to place orders for her things. By the time Lyle got back she had closed her set up. She had sold over $60.00 in that short time.

"Lyle, this is a wonderful place for a set up. I sold everything I had and took in over $40.00," said Marie, leaving out the $20.00 she had tucked away. "I even sold most of the junk jewelry you had," continued Marie.

"I'm glad Marie; we really need the money now that it is hard to pass the silver. We still have some money in the stash," said Lyle. "Let me have the money you made, I don't have very much on me."

"Let's wash up and get something to eat. I saw a nice Cuban restaurant in town and I am hungry," continued Lyle.

"I've never eaten Cuban food and I'd like to try it," said Marie as she picked up Leone and started after Lyle. "He never waits on me and I'm always in a hurry," she thought.

Good to his word, they went to a nice café with tables on the outside and inside. They picked one on the outside and sat down. As soon as they were seated, a tall man dressed in an immaculate black and white outfit brought two glasses of water with ice. Marie was very thirsty and she drank the entire glass. The waiter waited patiently until Marie finished the glass and poured her another one. Without a word, he gave them their menus and walked off. Marie could see him out of the corner of her eye as he waited on other tables.

As soon as they made their selections he appeared as if out of nowhere. He took their orders of yellow rice and shrimp for Marie and beef stew with mashed potatoes for Lyle. He didn't write anything down. Marie didn't know how he could remember all the orders from the tables he served.

Their order came exactly as ordered. They ate and watched the people wandering the quaint streets of Key West. Marie didn't like the area because it was so isolated. If a storm came it would cut them off from the mainland. One the other hand, Key West fit Lyle's vagabond personality. He liked the way people had a lot of time to loaf and the weather was nice even in the winter.

On cue, as they finished their meal, the waiter cleared the table and put out a clean napkin and silverware for them. He snapped his fingers and a boy pushed a cart to their table. It was loaded with wonderful Cuban sweets. Both Lyle and Marie were stuffed, but each picked a small desert.

"These are so good . . . I wonder why Lyle is spending so much money eating in a fine café?" thought Marie.

Lyle finished his desert quickly and asked for the bill in Spanish. The waiter gave him the bill on a small silver tray. It came to a little over $3.00. Lyle put 4 silver dollars on the tray and waved his hand.

Marie's heart froze. She was frightened that the silver dollars wouldn't be accepted by the café. And, true to Lyle's character, he got up quickly and left. Marie looked back and noticed the name of the café. It was called "El Requerdo," or "Souvenir" in Spanish. At the same time, she saw the waiter and an older man walk into the street looking in both directions. They were obviously looking for them as they faded into the crowd.

"Lyle, why do have to spoil a nice evening by passing the bad silver coins? I was enjoying the food and Leone liked some of the things and he was quiet most of the time," said Marie.

"I don't know Marie, it seemed like a good way to get rid of the coins and we had a good meal, didn't we? Stop complaining and let's get back to our camp. I want to leave in the morning," said Lyle.

Marie kept looking over her shoulder as they walked back toward camp. She was afraid the police would be looking for them. Lyle seemed preoccupied with the passing crowd. He wanted to look at everything but seemed too tired. He went to bed as soon as they got to the camp. This kind of pressure and excitement was too much for him. He was tired all the time.

Marie washed herself and Leone in the warm water of the bathroom. She put Leone to bed and sat on a bench, watching the long colorful twilight in the west. She remembered the sunsets in Siberia. The twilights there were very long because there was little daylight in the winter. The sun would rise about 10:00 am and set about 2:00 pm. She didn't miss that part of her life but she did miss the colors of the sunset. She put out her cigarette and headed toward the trailer in hopes it would be a nice day tomorrow. She saw the storm clouds brewing in the west and it looked like a storm was coming, as she could feel it in her bones.

Winter was not hurricane season, but you could have fooled Marie. The waves were crashing over the sea wall as Lyle was getting the rig ready to roll north. The rain was light but horizontal because of the wind. Lyle hated wind ever since his experience as a small child in Michigan. He was trying hard to not look scared as his cigarette blew out of his mouth.

Marie didn't mind heavy weather except when it looked dangerous. This morning it was kind of fun to watch the heavy surf and people dodging the waves. Marie liked to play in the surf as she often did in China. She was a strong swimmer.

"Leone is going to be a good swimmer when he gets a little older," thought Marie.

"Marie! Let's get out of here before the storm hits!" yelled Lyle over the sound of the wind.

"All right Lyle, don't get your underwear in a knot. I'll be there in a minute," said Marie as she put out her cigarette and got in the car.

"Where are we headed?" asked Marie.

"I don't care, but north for sure and see if we can get out of this storm," Lyle said as he drove out of Key West heading north on Florida 4A.

They stopped at Marathon Key to get gas and use the restrooms while they waited for the ferry. The weather was getting better as they had left the storm behind. It was a little blustery, but the rain had stopped. The wind had blown the sand fleas away and it was going to be a nice day as Marie wished for.

"We'll have to spend the night because the water is too rough for a ferry to make the trip," said Lyle, seeing the ferryboat at Key West tied up at the landing with a sign that said it would run in the morning.

Marie fixed a sandwich for them out of some ham she bought in Key West. The Cuban bread was a little hard but very tasty. The bottled coke tasted very good with the sandwiches. It was rare they had bottled drinks because of the cost and bottle deposit. Lyle didn't like to pay it even though he could get it back. They ate and settled in to spend the night.

Leone had his bottle and was making small gurgling noises as they drove. He liked to ride and was happiest when they were moving.

The old Buick acted like a rocking crib for him. He was asleep very soon. They were both glad to get off the Keys and out of the rough weather. Lyle didn't like the boats. He knew one had burned the year before.

They camped in the same place in Homestead as they did on the down trip. There were no sand fleas because the wind and rain had washed them away. The evening was warm and comfortable as Lyle and Marie talked about where they were going.

"Some campers told me about Kissimmee. They said it was a friendly small town with wide streets and a nice campground on a large lake. I think I'll try there. I would like to stay south until spring time," said Lyle.

"Anywhere is better than down here. The people all seem to be in a hurry. I don't speak Spanish and I don't care for Cuban food. The black beans we had with the meal tasted like warm, hard dirt," thought Marie.

"Let's bring the dairies up to date. We haven't been keeping up and I want to settle and count our money and write down expenses," said Lyle.

The next several hours were spent writing down the events of the past 2 months. There was a lot of bickering and arguing but it was finally over. Their stash money was a little over $500.00. This included about $75.00 in silver coins, which they put away. Marie had about $100.00 in her private saving and so did Lyle.

"It looks like we are pretty well set for a while. I want to try and open a small store to buy old scrap silver and gold. Maybe we can do that in Kissimmee," said Lyle. "Look at the map and see what's the best way to go."

Marie looked at the old atlas for a long time. She selected state road 26 to South Bay on the edge of Lake Okeechobee. She knew Lyle wanted to see the lake.

"Let's hit the hay; I'm tired after the drive from the keys. It's only a little over 125 miles but it was a hard drive. The ferry rides made me nervous. I'll be glad when the bridges are built," said Lyle.

South Bay was a small town on the southern edge of Lake Okeechobee. It was a center for the sugar cane industry, which they raised in the rich soil around the lake. There were no campgrounds so they drove a little farther and found a roadside park on the edge of the lake. They stayed the night and Lyle and Marie walked on the edge of the levee early the next morning to see the huge expanse of water. It was the largest freshwater lake in Florida and the headwaters of the everglades. It was almost impossible to see the lake because of the high levy on the southern edge. The hurricane of '28 had killed over 1800 people and many were buried in a mass grave, not far from where they camped. The levy had flooded and caused the great Lake Okeechobee flood.

Lyle looked out over the water and then to the flat land south of the lake and thought how terrible it must have been. He and his dad were in Lake Park, Georgia when the storm hit. If they had been a week earlier, they might have been caught in it. His dad wanted to see the lake and they were planning on seeing it before they went to the Keys.

"It's strange how life deals the cards and I am still alive today and I could have been in that mass grave," thought Lyle out loud.

Kissimmee was exactly like Lyle expected–quiet and isolated. They stopped in a nice shaded, grassy city park on the edge of Lake Tohopekaliga. It was affectionately called "Lake To Hope The Hell You Like It." The locals referred to it simply as "Lake Toho."

Kissimmee was a Caloosa Indian word that meant "Heavens Place." The town was initially a trading post on Lake Toho. In 1883, the citizens incorporated and changed the name to Kissimmee from an old 1752 Spanish map, which named the town Cacema. They pronounced it phonetically and it became Kissimmee.

The town was small but had a wide divided street with a nice flower garden area between the boulevards. Kissimmee was off the tourist route and depended on cattle, lumber and sugar cane for its livelihood.

Their camp was on the edge of the lake and there was a covered picnic area adjacent to the trailer. There was also a nice central bathhouse with water and electricity at each site. Lyle could never figure out why they put in such a nice park except to attract some travelers. They were the only occupants except for a very old rundown trailer a few spaces away.

Lyle set up the rig and plugged in the line to the power outlet and nothing happened. He asked a worker what he should do. The worker told him he had to go to city hall and buy a permit to park and they would turn on the power. Lyle got a permit for 2 weeks for $10.00, which included turning on the power. It would be $4.00 a week after that. The people were very friendly and helpful. Lyle felt good with his first contact with the locals.

"Lyle, don't do anything wrong in this town. Don't try and pass any of the silver. We have enough green backs to live fine. If you decide to do any business, do it legal and above board. Do you understand what I am telling you Lyle?" Marie said in a strong voice.

"Ok, Marie, I'll play it straight in this town. It seems like a nice place to spend the rest of the winter. In the morning, let's look around and see if we can rent a little store so I can do some business. You can make some more brooms and baskets and we can sell them," said Lyle.

After breakfast, with Leone settled on the back seat, they decided to drive to St. Cloud, a few miles away. It was a smaller town built on East Lake Toho. It was a real logging town as Lyle recognized the logging equipment that was clogging the roadways. There was a small café and a hardware store but little else to start a little shop.

They drove back to Kissimmee and looked around the town. It really wasn't necessary to drive because their camp was only 2 blocks from downtown.

One of the few federal highways, 17 & 92, ran through the center of town. There was a lot of traffic and activity but he didn't see any vacant buildings or stores. They drove back to the camp to think about their situation.

"Marie, I'd like to stay here a couple of months, or at least until the weather warms in the Carolinas. I want to meet dad there. I noticed a stand of willows around the edge of the lake and there are a lot of palmettos growing in this part of Florida," said Lyle.

"Somebody has to dig those things up. I saw some along the road where they were doing some work. If you think I'm going to get a grubbing hoe and dig them you have another think coming," said Marie in a strong voice.

"I think I'll take a walk up town and see if I can talk to some men about finding a place to set up," he said.

"I wonder what set Marie on such a bias. She was usually calm about such things. I worry about her getting too pushy," said Lyle to himself as he left the camp. "One thing I don't need is another pushy woman."

He decided to try a different tactic. Some years ago, he had seen a small jewelry store in the back of a drug store. He stopped at a drug store and sat down at the lunch counter. He looked at the short menu and ordered the blue plate special, which was a hamburger steak and mashed potatoes.

While he was eating, he looked around the store. It was very typical of most drug stores except for one thing; it had a good selection of automobile parts. There were spark plugs, points, condensers and a variety of hoses and belts.

"This is very unusual for a drug store," thought Lyle as he continued to look around.

He noticed a small cubical with a counter in the rear of the store. It was walled on three sides with a counter in the front. The shelves were bare of any goods.

There were a lot of people coming and going in the store. There was a register in the front and one in the back by the pharmacy and the back door. He finished his food and paid the waitress at the front register.

"Where can I find the owner or manager," asked Lyle.

"He's one in the same and you'll find him in the pharmacy. He is also the druggist and the landlord for the two upstairs apartments next door. Ask for Mr. Robinson," said the waitress.

Lyle spoke to Mr. Robinson at length about the space in the back of the store. He showed Lyle the area and how the display case worked. He was interested in Lyle's proposition yet somewhat suspicious of what he had to sell. He asked him to bring in some of the brooms and baskets. As for the gold and silver business, he would have to think about that.

There didn't seem to be a lack of money in the town. The businesses were thriving with a lot of people on the street. He looked both ways on Broadway and saw no evidence of a Depression.

"The lumber business was always good to me up north. I don't know the cattle business, but there seems to be a lot of ranchers by the way they dress," said Lyle out loud as he walked back to the camp.

"Marie, I made a deal with the druggist at the drug store. We can put our goods in the store. He has an inside set up where we can sell your brooms and baskets," said Lyle.

It actually wasn't a "deal," only a conversation with the druggist to see some of the things Marie made. He implied that the gold business was going in the store but it wasn't so, at least not yet.

The next day, Marie gathered a bunch of willow growing by the lake and cut it to dry. There were several piles of old palmetto roots in the area where people had been digging up their yards or from road repair. They were glad to get rid of them because they wouldn't burn.

Marie set about getting things ready to make her baskets and brooms. She thought about doing some knitting and sewing to add to her set up.

"It's very odd. Lyle isn't doing any of the work and I'm getting my set up ready to support us all this winter while Lyle loafs. I just hope he doesn't start any schemes," thought Marie.

CHAPTER FIFTEEN

Central Florida

Late Winter

Marie worked for 2 weeks and finished making a large supply of baskets, brushes and brooms. Her hands were so blistered and swollen that she could hardly use them. She doctored them like she learned from Harold Fletcher in Kentucky.

"It seemed so long ago that I learned the trade from him. He was such a nice old man. I wonder what happened to him," thought Marie out loud, as she rubbed her hands.

They were still blistered and very sore. It was almost impossible for her to do simple things that required use of her hands for any period of time. She was exhausted from all the work making brushes from the palmetto roots. The roots were a lot more difficult to cut and strip. It angered her inside to think that Lyle wouldn't help her. He seemed pre-occupied with his gold buying and trying to figure out another scheme.

Lyle worked out the arrangements to have a set up for Marie in the drug store. He rented the area with the counter for $25.00 a month. The agreement was he had to keep records of all sales and pay Mr. Robinson 6% of them. They agreed on a hand shake. Lyle was already figuring out a way to get away without the 6%, but he didn't know how as the employees were instructed to watch all sales.

Mr. Robinson wouldn't let Lyle operate his gold business out of the store. He agreed to let Marie sell some of the items he bought, but not before he examined them to ensure they were priced correctly. He had some experience in selling gold jewelry and he didn't want his store to get a bad name. He was very honest with his customers and wanted them to keep coming back.

Lyle hired a lady by the name of Mildred Clark to watch Leone at the campsite while Marie tended the set up in the store. The shop was to be open Tuesday through Saturday from 1:00 pm until 6:00 pm.

Mildred had been stranded in Kissimmee after her husband left her for parts unknown. She had a small decrepit trailer that was parked several spaces from their rig. She was originally from Wisconsin and was a very tall person with a good personality, but there was something about her that Lyle didn't trust. She agreed to watch Leone on those days for 50¢ a day plus meals. Lyle told Marie to carry all her money and things with her. Marie wasn't particularly happy with the situation but Leone seemed to like Mildred and that was some comfort.

Her hands were still too sore to do very much on the first day the set up opened. She put out some of the hand made articles on display to see how many she could sell. A lot of people looked the 1st day but she sold only 3 articles. She went back to the camp a little disappointed.

Before she went home, she had asked the druggist to look at her hands. He was upset that Lyle had let her hands get in such a bad condition. He gave her some soothing ointment to help with the blisters and told her to wash her hands often to prevent infection.

"Lyle, it wasn't a good day. A lot of people looked at what I had but I don't think they liked me because they could hear my accent," said Marie.

"I'm hungry, how about fixing some supper," said Lyle, avoiding the conversation about the store and her hands.

"Lyle, can't you see I'm dog tired. I've worked all day and you did nothing but loaf. If you want anything besides cold cuts then you better go in town and bring us something. My hands hurt so bad I can hardly close them and make a fist, which is what I'd like to do to you right now!" said Marie in a husky tired voice.

Lyle decided it was best if he went to town and bought some supper. He stopped at a café and brought home some fried chicken with gravy, mashed potatoes and corn bread.

It was the first time Marie had ever tasted corn bread. It had bits of corn in the bread and was warm and very tasty. Lyle didn't like it and gave Marie his piece. He didn't buy any for Mildred, so she went back to her old trailer. Marie knew she had some food because she gave it to her the day before.

"I don't like this southern cooking. It cost me almost $1.50 for this supper. I hope you enjoy it Marie," said Lyle in a disgusted tone.

"I'm going to get a bath. Watch Leone until I come back," said Marie.

Leone was asleep and didn't require any care. This pleased Lyle as he didn't want to be bothered with the babe. Out on the lake, he noticed a number of people fishing in the late evening. They were catching a lot of fish.

"They must be fishing for supper," thought Lyle out loud.

"Go ahead and take your bath, Lyle. The water is warm and you need to get clean and take off those clothes so I can wash them," said Marie.

He reluctantly did what Marie asked and headed toward the bathhouse with his toilet kit in hand.

"I don't know what's wrong with her. It's not Saturday and I don't feel like a bath," Lyle thought.

Marie liked to watch people fish. The water was calm, with a hint of moon low in the sky. The grass grew right to the edge of the water. The bottom was a beautiful crystal white color. Marie guessed it must have been some kind of special white sand.

She looked back at the town and saw some pretty lights in the window of a dry goods store. She massaged her hands with the cream the druggist gave her. It was soothing and took some of the pain away.

"I need to get some clothes so I can look better in the drug store. I want to be able to sell as much as I can. Lyle won't let me buy any new clothes. He likes to go to a used store or the Salvation Army. I can't stand the smell of those old clothes," thought Marie out loud.

Lyle came back about that time after a bath. He seemed in a little better mood.

"I didn't do so well today in the set up. There were a lot of people looking but not very many had cash to buy. Some wanted to trade me things for the brushes and brooms. No one looked at the baskets. Several people wanted to know if they bought something if they could charge it to their store account," said Marie. "I watched the customers who came in the store. Most of them went to the back and put what they bought in a little receipt book with their name on the top," she continued.

"I noticed there were a lot of people waiting for work near the back of the town. They seemed to be gathered there early this morning. What looked like a boss came out and called off names. About half went to work and the other half was asked to come back in the morning," said Lyle.

"When we first got here, I thought there was a lot of money. I think there are several people who are controlling what few jobs there are. The Depression is affecting everyone," Lyle continued. "Tomorrow, I'm going toward Orlando and see if I can buy some gold. Marie, I want you to try and sell as much as you can. Get Mildred up early and get started soon," said Lyle.

"My hands hurt so much, I don't know if I'll be able to do anything tomorrow. I'll doctor them this evening and see how they feel. I'm not going to take a chance of hurting them anymore," said Marie.

Lyle didn't say anything; he just looked at the ground and mumbled something to himself. He didn't like it one bit, but there was nothing he could do. He got up without saying a word and went to bed.

Marie loved the quiet evening and the fresh smell of nature. Even though it was winter, the grass and flowers smelled wonderful to her. She could see some distant lights across the lake and she wondered what or who it was.

"People in this town act different. They act like they're looking for something but I don't know what. I'll have to watch them and see what I can find out," thought Marie as she got into bed and covered with a light blanket to ward of the evening chill.

Lyle was already somewhere in a deep sleep, snoring and moving his lips like he was talking to a crowd of people.

Lyle took the Orange Blossom Trail early in the morning. He drove toward Orlando looking for old homes or dentists offices. He stopped at a gas station and asked if there were any dentists in the area. The operator told him there were two a little ways up the road.

He found the first one and stopped asked if he had any scrap gold he wanted to sell. The dentist brought out a box of old gold teeth, crowns and several pairs of old eye glasses.

"What are you doing with these old frames?" asked Lyle.

"Some of my patients didn't have enough money to pay me so I took anything they had to trade. Times are tough so I took what I could get," said the dentist.

Lyle weighed and checked all the gold he had and made the dentist an offer, which was considerably lower than its actual value.

"If that's all it's worth, I'll take it," said the dentist.

"Do you know of anyone else who has scrap gold for sale?" asked Lyle.

"Everywhere you go, businessmen have gold and jewelry they have taken in payment. It's hard to sell because no one has the money to buy it," said the dentist. "Check with my brother at the 1st store on the right. Tell him I sent you."

Lyle took $150.00 with him and bought at least $300.00 in gold from several places, including a gas station. It was a good place to work as long as long as he had the money to buy things. He would send it in tomorrow and see how long it took to get his money. He didn't know how Fishlows would respond after the problems he had. He had rented a post office box in Kissimmee so he had time.

"Besides, Marie is making good at her set up and it gives me time to loaf," thought Lyle out loud.

He stopped at a roadside café and got himself a good meal. Lyle liked to eat and he knew Marie didn't feel like cooking because of her sore hands. He looked out the window and saw the workers putting up another Burma Shave sign. It read:

Every Second
Without fail
Some store
Rings up
Another sale
Burma Shave

"My cash register was ringing up today. Those businessmen didn't have any idea what they were doing with all that gold. I could have really gotten some good deals but I had to be careful. I did do a good business and didn't lose any money," thought Lyle in a happy mood.

Lyle was happiest when he was scamming someone. These people needed money and Lyle gave it to them, but not in the amount he should have. He bought some gold that was 18 karat for 14 karat prices. He also used the copper penny trick and under weighed a lot of items.

Marie was busy in the store showing people her goods. It had been a little better day and her hands felt better. The druggist gave her some Apinol. It was the oil of the southern pine and it helped heal quicker. It smelled like pine oil but no one noticed or cared; this was a lumber town. It had been a patented medicine for a long time, especially in the south. It was used for aches and pains and as a very good antiseptic.

She had a talk with Mr. Robinson about people charging her goods to the store. He agreed he would let his better customers charge her goods. He would pay her at the end of each day from her receipt book. He was a little reluctant to do so, but Marie told him it was the only way he was going to get his 6%.

"Marie, I'll charge the goods for you but I'll have to charge you 10% instead of 6% because it will tie up my money. I'm also taking a chance that someone won't pay me. It's all business and that's the way it has to be," said Mr. Robinson.

"I agree with you, but I want to be paid every day. It's the only way I do business," she said.

"You're a hard woman to do business with, Marie. I have respect for anyone that stands up to me," he said.

Even though it hurt her right hand, Marie was determined that it would be a handshake agreement with a witness, so she wouldn't lose any money.

"My father taught me a long time ago when I was a very small girl in Ashkhabad. He was a good businessman and I learned from him. He told me 'A handshake is just like you signed a piece of paper, especially when you have a witness,'" said Marie.

"This was the first time I put it to use and it worked," she thought to herself. "It's too bad I didn't have sense enough to shake hands with Lyle and let it go at that. If I had it to do over again, that's exactly what I would have done. It's too late now, I'll have to grin and bear it," thought a very pensive Marie.

Lyle sent the gold the next day to Baltimore. He figured he had about 9 oz total gold. They usually shorted him some because it was the company's way. His new address was a good thing, especially since his dad wanted to get in touch with him.

The last time his dad visited, something was going on with the women folk in his life. Lyle thought he was about to jump from one to another very soon. He recognized the way he talked.

He had some old scrap costume jewelry that he gave Marie. He told her to put it in the set up and see how it would sell. She liked some of it and insisted she wear it. Marie kept the books on the set up and Lyle didn't question her. Unless she sold something "under the table," all the money was accounted for.

Lyle got his gold money in about a week. True to their way of doing business, he was about 1 oz short, but at least he finally had some money coming in and they didn't say anything about the previous incident. The gold dust was a worry in the back of Lyle's mind and he was glad it worked out in his favor.

At the same time, he received a letter from his dad telling him he needed some money and he would meet him in Fort Pierce, Florida in about 3 weeks. He also said he had just gotten married but he didn't say to what woman. That was the way with his dad, always broke and going with a lot of women. This was the first one he married in many years. He would court them and move on to another one after a couple of years. It was a wonder Lyle didn't have a lot of brothers and sisters he didn't know about. He reluctantly sent him $25.00.

"Marie, we're in a pickle. I want to go and see my dad in Fort Pierce in a few weeks and we are doing so well here," said Lyle.

"We're not doing that well. I've sold almost all my goods and my hands still haven't healed well enough to make some more. The druggist tries to short me on my sales but I have him figured out. I keep my abacus with me and he can't cheat that. You said he was honest, but not to me. I think he has the people all tied up with his charging scheme. That's why he has so many different goods in the store," said Marie.

"I don't know, Lyle, but I think there may be something in the southern willow or palmetto that hurts my hands. They break out even when I handle the dried baskets, but not as bad as when I make them from fresh wood," said Marie.

"What are you putting on your hands?" he asked.

"The Apinol helps but it doesn't keep them from hurting. If it hadn't been for Mildred helping with Leone, I wouldn't have been able to go on," continued Marie.

"We need to keep an eye on Mildred. I've been missing some small change I keep on my shelf. Not much, just a little bit each day," said Lyle.

"I thought the same thing when I saw her in the drug store a few days ago. She was looking at a Baby Ruth candy bar. I thought she put it down but I think she put it in her pocket. There was one missing from the counter," said Marie.

The next day Marie awoke with a sharp pain in stomach. She thought it might be gas from the food at the drug store. The cooks didn't care how they fixed it. They never washed their hands and wiped the grease on their dirty aprons. She had only eaten there a couple of times and decided it wasn't a good idea.

"Mr. Robinson, I have an upset stomach from too much grease at your lunch counter. I'm not used to that kind of food," she told him.

"Here Marie, take some of this. Put three drops in a glass of water 3 times a day for 3 days and your stomach should be all right. I'll put it on your bill," he said.

"No, I'll pay for it. I don't want my name on one of your books. What is it?" she asked.

"It's called paregoric and it does wonders for stomach ailments," he said.

Marie paid him and went toward her set up. She turned and thanked him but he was already busy with other people and didn't pay any attention.

Every morning she checked her set up and this morning there

several pieces of jewelry missing. She saw the lady who worked the floor and motioned her over to her counter.

"Have you seen anyone going through my set up?" she asked.

"I saw the cooks looking at your jewelry late yesterday. I told them to leave your things alone," said the lady.

Marie walked over to the counter and saw the older cook wearing a broach that she had in the case.

"Excuse me, but I'd like to see the pretty broach you're wearing. Where did you get it?" asked Marie.

"Oh, it's my mother's and some times she lets me wear it," said the woman.

Marie walked back to the drug counter and spoke to Mr. Robinson. He listened very carefully.

"That's not true. That lady has been working for years and she wouldn't steal a penny," he said.

"But sir, I had that broach in my case last night and today she's wearing it," said Marie with a positive tone.

"Let me tell you something, lady! What makes you think you can come in here and accuse one of my employees of stealing? You are nothing but a drifter and a vagabond and I want you out of my store! Get you stuff together and get out!" shouted Mr. Robinson. "Your month's rent is up today and I want you out!"

"Before I go I want my money from yesterday," said Marie.

"As far as I'm concerned, I don't owe you anything. Get your stuff and get out. You have 30 minutes to clear out or I'll call the police," he said in a loud voice, attracting the customers' attention.

Marie put her things in a box behind the counter and left with the heavy load as quickly as she could. It hurt her stomach as she carried the box to their camp. Mildred was there playing with Leone in the grass.

"I wonder what 'vagabond' means. I've never heard the word but it doesn't sound good. In a way I'm glad to be out of the store. I like outside set ups a lot better. I guess Lyle will be mad, but I don't care. I'm tired of Kissimmee anyway," thought Marie.

Mildred saw her carrying the box and came to help her. Marie felt so bad and angry about the drug store incident that she went in and laid down.

"Mildred, would get me some water so I can take my stomach medicine the druggist gave me," asked Marie. "It tastes terrible. As bad as it tastes, it should help something; it sure isn't helping my mouth," said Marie.

"What's the matter with your stomach?" asked Mildred.

"I have a lot of gas and pain. I think it was the food I have been eating at the drug store," answered Marie.

"Why did you bring the box back to the camp," asked Mildred.

"I got into an argument about some missing jewelry and one of the women was wearing it. They were covering for each other and the druggist asked me to leave," said Marie with a depressed tone to her voice. "Watch Leone until Lyle gets back. I'll rest and I should feel better in a little while."

Marie slept the better part of the day. She awoke about the time Lyle returned. He didn't have any luck buying gold near Haines City. There were a lot of people out of work. He drove up just as she was sitting down to a cup of coffee she made. She lit a cigarette watched him drive in the camp.

Lyle got out of the car carrying his gold bag with a dejected look on his face.

"Lyle, what does 'vagabond' mean?" asked Marie.

"It means a drifter or someone who wonders from place to place without a home," answered Lyle.

"I guess that means us, doesn't it?"

"Yes, I guess it does. Where did you hear that word?"

"The druggist called me a vagabond as he was asking me to leave his store," said Marie.

Marie told him the story of what happened in the store and about the stolen broach. They both agreed it would be best to leave well enough alone. She also told Lyle she wasn't feeling very well.

"We'll leave in a couple of days. I'm expecting a letter from dad and maybe one from Ruth and Jerry. I need to get the oil changed in the Buick and get it greased. I'll also get the tire patched and then we'll leave for Fort Pierce," said Lyle.

Marie thought for a long time about being a vagabond. The sound of the word made cringe. The way the druggist said it made her feel cheap. She knew she had accepted that way of life and had to live with it. "Maybe someday I'll get a home so I can plant some flowers and raise a little garden," thought Marie as she fixed supper for all of them.

"Mildred, we're going on to Fort Pierce in a couple of days. What are you going to do?" asked Lyle.

"I'd like to tag along and help Marie. She isn't feeling well. I could watch the babe and help with the chores," said Mildred.

"What are you going to do with your trailer and where will you sleep?"

"An old fisherman offered me $50.00 for it to make a fishing shack. I can sleep in the back seat and ride there with Leone."

"Fair enough. I want it understood that if you cause any problems of any kind I let you off wherever we are!"

"I won't cause any trouble and I'll do what I can to help. I'll need a little money from time to time."

"I'll give $5.00 you every week plus your food. Here's $5.00 in advance."

Mildred looked at the bill with a strange expression on her face as she put it in her apron pocket.

"Is that alright with you Marie?"

"That's fine with me Lyle, at least until I feel a little better. One thing is for sure: I'm not going to make any more goods until my hands get well and I feel better," said Marie.

"Good, it's settled," said Lyle.

Marie wasn't feeling much better when they got to Fort Pierce. It was a town like Vero Beach, but a little nicer. They found a camp away from the water and settled in for a short stay in anticipation of Lyle's dad joining them.

"Lyle, I need to see a doctor. I feel very bad," said Marie.

"I'll take you to a druggist and see what's wrong."

"No Lyle, I need to see a real doctor. I think I'm pregnant and something isn't right."

"Pregnant! Why in the world are you pregnant? We don't need another babe! We have enough trouble with this one!"

Lyle paced and ranted and raved about all the problems a new baby would bring. Marie sat quietly and watched him talk. He looked like a puppet with his arms waving. It almost made her laugh at his gestures.

It reminded her of going to a circus in Russia and watching the puppets perform. All the children would sit and boo the mean ones and laugh at the funny ones. Lyle was a combination of both and she laughed out loud.

"I don't feel like arguing, just find me a doctor. You know perfectly well why I'm pregnant!"

Lyle went to the camp office and asked about a doctor. They told him about a Dr. Devine. He had an office a short ways down the road. Lyle asked them to call him and ask if he could bring Marie to see him.

"There's the phone, go ahead and call him. I'll get the number for you," said the manager.

"Please call for me, I don't now how to use a phone. I've never talked on one."

"Here, I'll call for you and you can speak to the doctor or nurse."

Lyle made an appointment for the next morning for Marie to see the doctor. He didn't like it one bit, but he would wait and see what the doctor said. He hoped it would be a stomach ache like Marie had complained about and that she wouldn't be pregnant.

Marie went to bed and rested while Lyle drove to the post office to see if there was any mail. He got a postcard from his dad saying he couldn't come south and could he meet him in Quitman, Georgia in two weeks. The card was dated 2 weeks prior and his dad should have been there now. At least that would save Lyle from looking for him here.

The visit to the doctor's office went as scheduled. He gave Marie a complete physical and said she was indeed pregnant and had been for about 3 months. He wasn't pleased with the position of her womb. He gave her some vitamins and instructed her on how to handle her pregnancy. He wanted her to see a specialist as soon as she could.

"Marie, you must take it easy for the coming months. This is going to be a difficult pregnancy and you must not do a lot of heavy lifting or traveling," said Dr. Devine. "I'm just a family doctor and I want you to see specialist as soon as you can. I'll make the arrangements.

Call my office tomorrow and we'll have an appointment scheduled. I've delivered a lot of babies but yours is a special case."

Lyle paid the receptionist with 5 silver dollars. She took them without hesitation and gave Lyle a receipt.

"Lyle, why did you do such a thing to the doctor? He was only trying to help me," said Marie.

Lyle didn't reply, but only laughed as Marie got in the car and they went to the camp.

"We'll be leaving in the morning and go to Quitman, Georgia and meet dad. I hope he's there this time," said Lyle.

"Lyle, I can't travel feeling this bad. The doctor said I needed rest and not to travel. Why don't we stay here and you can work the doctors around here?"

"I don't care what the doctor said, we're going to meet dad in Quitman and we'll leave in the morning. Mildred can help you with your work and it should be easy."

"But Lyle, he wants me to se a specialist about the way the baby is being carried. I don't want to lose this baby!"

"It doesn't matter to me about any special doctor. We can find one in Georgia if you need one. I don't want to hear any more about it! We'll leave in the morning just like I said."

It was 2 ½ hard days of bad roads and cold weather before they got to Quitman. It was an old town not far from Lake Park. The town had limited industry and depended on agriculture for its existence. It was not far from the Withlachoochee River.

"Why on earth would your dad want to meet you here? There's nothing except a few old houses and cotton fields. There isn't even a place to park," said Marie.

"I know of a place down by the river. Some hobos told me about it a long time ago. Maybe we can stay a few nights and see if we can find dad."

There was a small area where children swam and some people fished that offered enough space to camp. There was no water or electricity. An old outhouse was their only convenience. Lyle parked the trailer and unhitched the car.

"Mildred, help Marie get supper ready I'll go in and check the mail."

Lyle came back about 2 hours later with a sour look on his face.

"Dad will meet us in Eufaula, Alabama in a few days. He had car problems and his new wife didn't want to drive so far south so he left her at home. We'll stay the night and drive on to Alabama in the morning. Let's hope he'll be there; I'm tired of chasing him all over the country," said Lyle in a tired, disgusted voice.

"Lyle what we have to fix is ready to eat. You didn't give us much time to stop and get groceries because you were hell bent to make it to Georgia. Well, here we are and what do you have to show for it? Nothing! Your father still isn't here to meet us," said Marie.

"Mildred, fix Lyle a plate and feed Leone. I'm going to bed. I don't feel very well. All that traveling isn't doing me any good," said Marie.

They drove through Moultrie and Albany, Georgia and across the Alabama River into Eufaula, Alabama on the 3rd day. It was a hard trip for Marie. She rode in the back seat and didn't eat very much. Mildred did a good job of taking care of Leone and keeping up with Lyle's wishes.

They found a nice camping place close to the river on a high bluff. This part of Alabama was very pretty with high river bluffs and gentle rolling hills.

They had water and a nice bathhouse that was shared with the boat people. They were a group of people who made their living fishing and hauling supplies up and down the Alabama River. They were an isolated, friendly bunch that liked to talk and tell stories about their adventures on the river. They would pull into the landing, off-load their supplies and pick up another load. Most of the goods were delivered to isolated farms and communities along the river. They made a fair living but were exposed to the whims and currents of the Alabama River.

Lyle bought a little gold from them, as they had it for the same reason the businessmen in Florida had gold–they often were paid in it. This time of year, their only business was delivering daily use items for the people. They also hauled the mail under a federal contract.

"Lyle, I am not feeling very good. Could you get me some more of my medicine the druggist gave me? It seems to settle my stomach when it rumbles so," said Marie.

Lyle gave her the medicine and waited until she was asleep. He told Mildred to watch her and Leone and walked down the trail to toward the boat people's camp. He wanted to talk with them. Earlier, he had noticed an old woman who was tending a large cooking pot. She was smoking a corncob pipe and singing an old sea song. Lyle recognized the tune because he heard his Grandfather Freeman sing it often.

"Hello madam, how is the sun shining today?"

She looked up rather surprised and looked in the sky.

"If you're not selling anything, the sun is shining just fine," said the old woman.

This was an old sea faring way of greeting people. He wanted to ask her about Marie. Maybe she could help or knew someone who could.

"My name is Lyle and I come seeking advice about my wife from the wise woman of the camp," he said with a very humble tone in his voice.

"My name be Matilda, and what's your wife called?"

"She is called Marie and she comes from a far off land."

"All of us come from a far off land and we meet in one place to befriend the needy. What kind of sickness does she carry?" asked Matilda.

"She is with child and has a lot of pain. The doctors don't know what is wrong and all they want is money."

"Do you have any money for Matilda?"

"I have some silver coins for you. They once had holes for good luck and I give them to you." He handed her some quarters and 10¢ pieces. She looked at them and put them in her apron pocket.

"Take me to you wife."

She picked up a ragged old leather black bag. There was some faded gold lettering on the side but it was not legible. She fell in behind Lyle and followed him to their trailer. Marie was asleep and Lyle tried to awaken her, but she was groggy and didn't wake up but stayed in a semi-conscious state.

"Leave us be; this is woman business!"

Lyle walked down to the edge of the river and smoked a cigarette as he thought about Marie. He waited and waited in a nervous state. He paced like he did in Lexington, but he didn't take out his watch and leave it on a windowsill. He thought about how her being sick would slow down doing what he wanted.

After about an hour Matilda and Marie came out of the trailer.

"She is with child and it isn't in the right place. I gave her some herbs to take so she can sleep. I will think on it and come back tomorrow, if you have some more silver."

"When you come back, I will have some silver for you."

"No paper, just silver! The paper money drowns and goes away with the currents, but the silver lives forever."

"Marie, what did she say?" asked Lyle after she had left.

"She told me that the baby was growing in the wrong part of my body. She gave me some herbs to try and help it find its way home. I don't understand it all, but she'll be back tomorrow and tell me what I have to do. I don't know how all the baby stuff in the body works."

"Do you believe that old woman? I think she is a little crazy."

"She is crazy, but like a fox who knows the ways of nature. My mother was like that. She couldn't read or write but she could cure most ills."

The next day Marie was feeling a lot better when the old woman came to visit. Lyle gave her some silver coins and she was happy to talk to Marie. Again, she ran Lyle off and talked to her alone.

"She told me, if I take it easy and don't jar my belly or travel, I should be fine. The baby is trying to go to its natural home with her help."

"If dad gets here, we're going to Albany, Georgia and buy some gold. We'll be here a couple of days so take it easy, but we'll have to travel."

Marie lay back in her bed and thought about what the druggist had called her. She got out her old mirror and looked at herself. She looked a lot worse than when she was carrying Leone. She wished in her heart that it hadn't happened, but the time for wishing was over. She carefully put the mirror back.

"I guess I am a vagabond, but I don't want to be. I want to keep this baby and make Lyle stop traveling. I don't have much faith in that, though. I feel in my heart something is wrong inside of me and the baby will never live," thought Marie sadly as she drifted off to sleep.

CHAPTER SIXTEEN

Southern Georgia

The last letter from Lyle's father said he would meet them in Eufaula, Alabama. Lyle's father was, in effect, no better at managing his life that Lyle. He was continually borrowing money and never paid it back. They would meet Leon, if he showed up, and travel to the campground at Albany. Marie didn't like the idea of Leon using Lyle as a source of money. Sadly, there was nothing she could do, except to keep her mouth shut and not anger Lyle.

Lyle could never make a decision when he was under pressure. It all depended if he ready to move or not. He was out trying to buy some gold but his luck was spotty. He would buy a little in an area and then the well would dry. Money was a fickle enemy. If the farmers made a little money on their crops or other things, they wouldn't sell their gold. Several times people wanted to buy their things back but Lyle wouldn't sell, mainly because he sent the goods to Baltimore.

It was a confusing time for Lyle. He was torn between seeing his dad and the problems Marie was having with her pregnancy. The fear of Ruth and Jerry, Lyle's daughter and son-in-law, visiting him was another concern. He knew he would be in for a hard time with Jerry. Ruth was alright when Jerry wasn't around, but they both were lazy and didn't like to work for the money they borrowed.

Jerry never worked outside of the Detroit mobs and driving a truck. He was too crude and clumsy to help Lyle with any of his business deals. He had a strong Detroit accent that offended Southerners. The bitter pill of the Civil War stuck in a lot of throats and they didn't like "Yankees." He had a big mouth and violent temper that could get him into trouble with the law. He had already spent some time in a Michigan pen and he had that hard bitten prison way about him.

"Mildred, I feel so bad. Can you get me something to eat?"

"We don't have a lot to fix. Lyle won't take me shopping and you feel too bad. I think Lyle eats while he's out and doesn't think about us," said Mildred.

"Go see, what's her name, oh yes, Matilda. Go and see if she has some food to sell. Take a few silver coins with you."

Mildred walked carefully down the path to the boat people's camp. She was afraid of anything she didn't understand and she was sure they had magical powers with all the singing she had heard the night before.

"I'm Mildred from the camp on the hill. I take care of Marie and her baby. Can I speak to Matilda?"

"I be Matilda, what you want?"

"Marie is sick and her man isn't home. She needs to eat and pretty soon! I have some silver for you, from Marie."

She didn't say anything when she took the coins but winked her eye as she turned and walked toward the cooking area. There were a number of people seated in various places eating. Matilda returned with an old blue enameled pot. It had a curved wire handle and wooden grip.

"This be supper for your family. Wash the pot and bring it for supper tomorrow. Bring more silver or thar be no supper."

Mildred walked up the hill, carrying the pot by its long curved handle. She was glad the top of the handle was wood or she would have burned herself.

"Marie, I think we'll have supper. It smells wonderful and I'm starved."

Mildred dished out 2 bowls of the food. It was a mixture of many vegetables and meat. Marie noticed some strange bones, but she ate it anyway. They both wiped their bowls clean with the last pieces of bread.

Leone liked the taste of the juice on bread. He ate, drank his milk and was about to fall asleep when they heard Lyle drive up. Marie was ready for him regardless of how bad she felt. She was about to give him a piece of her mind.

"Marie, I brought supper for all of you. I forgot about getting groceries. I hope you both like hot roast beef sandwiches and mashed potatoes," said Lyle as he walked in.

Marie looked at the roast beef sandwiches on a paper plate, covered by a gravy stained newspaper. She touched the meat and it was cold.

"Where have you been? I've been hungry all day! Look at what we had to eat! It's some strange stew from the boat people's camp," said Marie.

Lyle gave the food to Mildred to put up. It was cold at night so it would keep.

"Mildred, give that nasty mess to the dogs. There're a lot of loose dogs around and they need a meal. I wouldn't eat it after seeing the newspaper dipped in the gravy. Besides, it's ice cold and we are out of coal oil. The weather is too cool outside to set up the Coleman," said Marie. "We need milk and ice," she continued, "and it's time you went shopping if you expect to live in this camp or any other one with me!"

"I'll take you and Mildred to the store in the morning. But we have to move to Albany. Ruth, Jerry and dad are going to meet us there in a few days," said Lyle.

"That's just what we need–Ruth and Jerry mooching off of us. I remember the last time. You loaned Jerry $25.00 and they left for Racine, Wisconsin without a word of thanks."

"It's going to be different this time. I'll set up work rules so no one will be in doubt about how I feel. Jerry will have to work to make his living. Ruth can't work because of her crippled leg, but she can help you with cooking and cleaning."

"They always have a dog of some kind. The last time it was a dirty little cocker spaniel who drooled and shed dirty hair all over me!"

"Let's see what happens. We'll stock up on supplies tomorrow and get on the road. Albany isn't far and there's a large campground near the Muskalee River. I think it's called Chehaw. I hope there are some people we know when we get there. Maybe we'll see Pope the Key Man."

The trip to Albany went well. After they crossed the Alabama River, the road was smooth and well marked. Marie felt a little better and she rode in the back with Leone, who was doing quite well. He was growing and very active. He didn't sleep as much and liked to watch the passing scenery.

She bought a supply of herbs from Matilda, with more silver coins of course. Marie wondered why she was so attached to her coins. She also gave Matilda one of the broaches Lyle bought. She told her goodbye and wished her well. As she looked back, she saw her clutching it to her chest like it was worth a million dollars.

They found the auto park a little north of town on the river, as other travelers had stated. There were several other campers in the park but Lyle didn't know them. He selected a nice place close to the bathhouse so it would be convenient for Marie.

He was setting up the trailer for a lengthy stay. He knew he would have to take Marie to a doctor soon. The pain wasn't getting much better and the herbs only helped her rest. Whatever old Matilda was trying to do with the medication, it wasn't working.

"Marie, let's go into town and get some groceries. I noticed the park office had ice. We'll get some when I stop to pay. Mildred, stay here with the babe and get the trailer cleaned out while we go into town. We shouldn't be gone for over an hour or so. I need to check the mail and see where dad is."

The post office was in a crowded section of town. Lyle had to park a good ways from the main entrance. He wanted Marie to check general delivery but she wasn't able to walk very far without pain. She got out anyway to keep him from being mad.

As she got out of the car, she tripped on the high granite curb. She fell on her left side and was too stunned to get up. Lyle watched her for a moment as people started to gather. He got out and went around the car to see if he could help her.

"Lyle, I'm sorry but I can't make it to the post office. It hurts so bad I can't stand it! Call some help, I think I'm bleeding."

"I'll get some help," he said as he spotted a policeman on the corner directing post office traffic. He told him the problem.

The officer went to a black police emergency phone box and

called the police station. He told Lyle that an ambulance and escort would be there soon. The officer went to Marie and told her every thing would be all right. He moved all the pedestrians back so she could get some air. She appeared to be having difficulty breathing.

"I'm a nurse, step back and let me help. Where do you hurt?" said an older lady as she stooped down to help Marie.

"I'm pregnant and the pain is in my lower stomach. I can feel something warm and wet. I think I'm bleeding."

The nurse touched her stomach and felt the muscles tighten with the slightest pressure. She checked and Marie was bleeding. The side-walk started to get a small red stain.

"It hurts so bad I don't think I can stay awake much longer."

"How many children do you have?" She asked as she took Marie's rapid pulse.

"I have 3 children, all boys," said Marie as the ambulance drove up, escorted by an Albany police car.

Marie was speaking in a very low tone of voice. Her English was barely audible and was mixed with Russian words and phrases.

"What hospital are they taking her too?" asked Lyle in an excited voice.

"Memorial, it's just a few of blocks away," said the ambulance driver as they loaded Marie into the back.

"Get in your car, mister. I'll hang on the running board so you can follow the ambulance to the hospital," said the policeman.

The 3 short blocks seemed like an eternity as the ambulance weaved in and out of traffic. The officer was hanging on the inside of the passenger window and blowing his whistle to warn traffic.

Lyle could see the reflection of the red ambulance lights on store windows. The blood on the sidewalk flashed thorough his mind and he almost became sick.

"Phoebe Putney Memorial Hospital Emergency Entrance" was painted on a large white sign in red letters. "Emergency Vehicles Only" was written on the bottom.

"Pull up behind the ambulance and go with you wife. I'll park your car and meet you inside," said the officer.

The attendants were waiting at the door and put Marie on an

emergency gurney. They wheeled her down a short hall into a brightly lit room.

"Sir, you shouldn't go in there. The doctors will take care of everything. Please come with me so we can get some information on your wife," said a kindly nurse in a sparkling white uniform.

Lyle saw the doctors move her to a table as the doors were closing. He could smell the antiseptic odors of the hospital. He was rapidly becoming ill from the odors and his lack of food for the past couple of days.

The nurse sensed he was having a problem and called a male orderly, who escorted him to the men's room. Lyle used the bathroom and washed his face. The orderly got a glass of orange juice and made Lyle drink it. In a few minutes, he felt better.

The nurse was waiting for Lyle and took him into a small room with a large desk and a lot of hospital equipment.

"Please sit down and let me check you out before we do any paperwork," she said.

"How is Marie doing and how much is this going to cost?"

"You wife is in the very best of care. The best specialists are with her now. Roll up your sleeve and let me take your blood pressure."

She ignored his question about the money and put the blood pressure cuff on his arm. Her eyebrows raised and she took it 2 more times.

"Mr. What's your name?"

"Lyle, a very old name."

"Where are you from?"

Lyle told her and she wrote the information on a form.

"Sir, you have very high and erratic blood pressure. Sit here a minute while I ask some questions."

The policeman came in inquiring about the woman who came in the ambulance. He gave the keys to the orderly to give to Lyle. He found Lyle in the nurse's office and gave him the keys.

"The policeman said to tell you he hoped everything would work out alright," said the orderly. "He also said your car was parked in the east parking lot," he said as he handed the keys to Lyle.

Lyle thanked him and wondered how he got the keys out of the ignition switch. He thought they wouldn't come out.

The nurse completed all the paperwork and had Lyle sign the 3 different documents. One was a declaration of inability to pay.

"What does this mean, 'inability to pay'?"

"Sir it's very obvious that you don't have a lot of money and you live in a trailer. We are a state regulated hospital that has funds for cases like yours," she said as she walked him down a hall and into a room an empty room with only a table and chair inside.

Lyle's heart rate immediately began to slow down and he started to feel better. He told the nurse on the questionnaire that he only had $80.00.

"So that's why they'll pay for the bill. I didn't tell them about the money we had in the stash. I hid it under the trailer so Mildred couldn't get to it while we were asleep," thought Lyle.

"Hop up on this table and let me listen to your heart," said a nice young doctor who walked in the room. "The nurse said you had erratic blood pressure," said the doctor as he took his blood pressure.

He introduced himself as Doctor Armstrong, a resident cardiologist, and asked the usual barrage of questions about diseases and family history. He stopped short when Lyle told him he had rheumatic fever when he as 12.

"How did it affect you? Were you in bed the entire 2 weeks or did you get up and down?"

"I didn't stay in bed very much. I had chores to do. I would sleep some in the morning but get up and help dad in he lumber mill in the afternoon."

"That's what I was afraid of. I can hear a leaky valve and your pulse is erratic. How long have you had this condition?"

The nurse stepped in and asked to speak to the doctor. They stepped outside in the hall way.

"His wife was just taken to emergency surgery. They almost lost her in the emergency room. Be careful how you tell him. I am concerned about his heart and blood pressure," she said.

"I'm also concerned about his heart. He has a very erratic pulse and a leaky heart valve. It makes a loud noise when he breathes. I'll tell him something when he asks."

The doctor stepped back into the room. "Lyle, what kind of medications do you take?"

"I don't take anything. A doctor in Mexico gave me some bitter powder I had to mix with water. It tasted so bad I only took it twice. I've had this problem since I was about 20."

"I am going to prescribe the same medication for your heart. It is in pill form and you must take it every day without fail! How about your pain? Do you have much chest pain?"

"Occasionally, but it goes away."

"I am giving you some small white tablets for your chest pain. Put one under your tongue and the pain should stop very quickly. It's nitro glycerin and it instantly enlarges your blood vessels and the pain will go away. It can stop you from having a heart attack."

"How is my wife doing? I haven't heard anything."

"I want you to take one of the nitro pills and lay back and relax. I'll come back in a little while. I'll check on your wife and let you know."

Marie was taken, unconscious, to emergency surgery. She was bleeding uncontrollably and had lost blood pressure. A term of obstetric doctors performed a complicated operation that involved the removal of all her female organs. The pregnancy had occurred in the fallopian tubes and remained there. This caused severe complications for Marie. It was necessary to abort the pregnancy because of the complications caused by the position of the baby.

After almost 8 hours of surgery, Marie was taken to the intensive care unit. She was in very critical condition. Lyle could only see her through the window because of the fear of infection, so he went back to the camp to tell Mildred of the surgery and the complications she suffered.

"Was it a boy or girl?"

"It was a tiny girl with the beginning of soft blond hair just like the babe, the doctor said."

"When can I see her?"

"The doctor said I can see her late tomorrow if she regains enough strength to wake up. They put her in a deep sleep so she wouldn't wake up and start bleeding," answered Lyle.

"I still didn't get any groceries. Here's $10.00, walk up to the camp store and get some food for us. Get some ice for the ice chest, too."

"Look Lyle, I'm not Marie. The ice is too heavy. Either drive me up or get it yourself!"

Lyle drove her to the store and they got what they needed. Leone's diapers and all his dirty clothes needed to be washed. Lyle bought all the necessary supplies to take care of them for a few days.

Marie hung between life and death for the next week. An infection had set in and she had to be fed through a tube. She couldn't keep her food down and it caused her to bleed.

Finally, on the 10th day in the hospital, she opened her eyes and said she was thirsty. That was a good sign.

For the first time, Lyle went to see her. She was pale and on her back with a mask over her face.

"You have 5 minutes sir," said the nurse in charge, "and I mean 5 minutes."

"Yes mam, I'll do as you say."

"Lyle, how is Leone? I worry about him with that Mildred," said Marie.

"He's fine but not to worry. Ruth and Jerry will be here tomorrow and I am getting rid of Mildred."

"Maybe Ruth can watch him until I get out of here. I hate green Jell-O and that yellow mush they give me."

Lyle and Marie talked for the rest of the 5 minutes. They waved at each other as he left the room.

The doctor stopped and talked to him for a while.

"Your wife has had a very complicated surgery. It will take another 3 to 4 weeks in the hospital and a long time to recover, maybe as much as 6 months," said Dr. Miller.

"How are you feeling? Doctor Armstrong said you had a bit of problem with your blood pressure and your heart. Are you taking the medicine he prescribed," asked the doctor.

"I haven't been doing as good as I should because of all the worry," replied Lyle.

"Come in my office and let me take your blood pressure and listen to your heart," said the doctor.

"How is it?"

"Your heart rate is erratic but stable. Wait here while I get another doctor who specializes in your kind of problems."

In a few minutes, he returned with another doctor.

"Lyle, this is Dr. Schultz. Let's let him listen to your heart."

"I don't have a lot of money for special doctors. I don't know how I'm going to take care of Marie once she gets out. We live in a trailer."

"One thing at a time," said the new doctor, Dr. Shultz. "Let me listen."

Dr. Schultz examined and listened to his heart for a good 5 minutes.

"Come with me, I want to run some tests on you. We have a new machine called an Electrocardiogram machine. It measures the rate and beat of your heart in 8 different places on your body. The machine records the heart action on a graph so we can study it. We call it an EKG for short. It was developed in the twenties but we just got ours last year. They are quite expensive."

"Will it hurt much? I can't stand a lot of pain."

"No, the worst you'll feel is a little cold where they put the pickup leads. It will take about an hour to complete the test."

The test results showed an abnormality of the aortic valve. Lyle's heart was trying to beat before all of the blood was pumped out of it. This caused some pain and an erratic heart rate.

"I understand you had rheumatic fever as a child. I suspect that was the cause of your heart damage. Your blood pressure is a different issue all together. You have a very high top number and a very low bottom number, which is a little unusual."

"What can I do about it? I don't want to be admitted to the hospital. I have a baby boy that I have to take care of. Marie is still in the hospital and I want her to get well and be released," said Lyle.

"I'm going to put you on some new medicine that should help

your heart. I'm afraid the blood pressure we measure is probably your normal pressure. The human body is trying to correct for a problem and in this case it's a leaky heart valve."

A few days later, Marie was transferred to a regular room and could receive visitors. She couldn't walk but she was allowed to be pushed around in a wheel chair. On Sundays, visitors were allowed to bring their children either in the cafeteria or outside.

Marie was beginning to get her appetite back and gain some of the 30 pounds she had lost after her surgery. Her color was good and she was able to sit up for a couple of hours before she went back to bed. She perked up as Lyle brought Leone to see her. She couldn't hold him because of the operation but she played with him while Lyle held him.

They took Marie back to her room and she ate a light supper. She was allowed to smoke and she enjoyed a cigarette after her meal. She opened the window and looked out over Albany.

"I wonder what Lyle will do now that I can't travel for a few months. He lives for the road and running his scams on everyone he meets," thought Marie out loud.

Lyle and Marie didn't talk about the surgery at first, though Lyle did mention he was given some medication that made him feel a lot better and his heart was doing better. But finally, late one afternoon, they talked about the surgery and its consequences on their life.

"Lyle, you know I'll never be able to have any more children. They removed everything that would cause any more problems or me to have children. It's very sad for me to lose the little girl. With my 3 boys, I always wanted a girl."

She got a tissue from the side of the bed and cleared her nose. She was the closest to crying that Lyle or anyone had ever seen. She had lost most of ability to cry when she left Russia in all the turmoil.

"The doctor told me I have lost all my sex. Lyle, that means Lyle you have to leave me alone. I'm not interested in you or any other man that way ever again . . . Do you understand what I just said Lyle?"

Lyle nodded his head but he really didn't hear her. What he heard was a woman in the hospital complaining about her surgery and that she couldn't have any more children. That was fine with Lyle because he didn't want any more kids. He didn't hear what she said and never would understand.

"Ruth and Jerry are coming in tomorrow. I need to find a place so you can be comfortable and Ruth can take care of you. I have been having a lot of problem with Mildred. She's very lazy and doesn't want to work. As soon as you get out and we get settled, I'm going to tell her to hit the road! I have been doing a lot of gold buying and we are pretty well set. Don't say anything to the hospital staff because they aren't charging us anything for all the things they did because we live in a trailer and don't have a permanent address."

Lyle forgot to tell Marie that he told them he had only $80.00 and that put him in a poverty bracket. He left with Marie staring at the ceiling as a tiny tear rolled down her cheek. She didn't wipe it off but thought about what would happen now. She and Ruth didn't get along very well and the trailer was getting too small for all of them. Leone would be walking very soon. In one way, the surgery would make her life easier because she wouldn't have the constant worry of more children. On the other hand, the next few months would be very hard on her. Lyle would try and make her work and she wasn't going to do that anymore. If he would find something that wouldn't hurt her hands so much, she wouldn't mind.

Marie went to sleep, watching the night grow darker. She would be glad when she got out of the hospital. She didn't understand how Lyle had worked a scam on the hospital without paying., but she was too tired to worry about it. She tried to picture what her little girl would look like but her face was a mixture of people and kept changing from one face to another. She finally went to sleep until the night nurse woke her for her evening medicine.

Ruth and Jerry showed up late that evening in an old green Dodge, which kept smoking after they shut it off.

"Dad, how are you! I haven't seen you in so long! You really look good! Come on Jerry, get out of the car and say hello to dad."

Jerry got out and stretched his short, pudgy body. He yawned and spit on the ground. As he stretched, his shirt pulled up and he scratched his hairy fat stomach and passed wind. He had his usual 5 o'clock shadow and needed a shave.

"Hi, Lyle! How are you," he said as he waved his hand.

He headed toward the bathroom with out saying anything.

"This is going to be "one of those" visits. I can see it now. When he gets back from the water closet, he wants to eat and then ask for money. I'll cut him short before he asks," thought Lyle.

"How is Marie and little Leone?"

"I guess you didn't get my letter. She's in the hospital from a serious female operation. She lost the baby, a little girl."

"Dad, I'm so sorry. How is she doing?"

"She should get out in about 10 days or so. We can't travel for a couple of months."

"Jerry, did you hear what dad said?"

"No, I heard him talking but I didn't hear what he said," said Jerry.

She told Jerry about Marie's surgery and all the problems they were having. He didn't seem to care or make any comments.

"Marie's operation and hospital stay has left me in bad shape. I have enough money to buy a little gold, but I'm almost broke. I had to send dad a little money and that left me without very much," said Lyle.

Ruth and Jerry looked at each other and didn't say anything. They were expecting to get some money for the trip back. If they wanted money, Jerry would have to work for it.

About that time, Mildred walked up with Leone on her hip. He was crying for some reason. Lyle introduced them and Ruth took Leone in her arms.

"What a big boy! You and your blond hair. I wonder where that came from. Your dad and mother both have black hair."

"I guess you forgot, Ruth. Your granddad had blonde hair and so did your Grandma Estella."

"Yes, I guess I forgot. Leone, you're wet! Mildred, where are his clean diapers?"

Ruth changed Leone and gave him a bottle and put him down to rest. All the time Mildred was watching with a hard, looking in her eyes. She didn't want Ruth to take over what she was doing.

"Let's hit the hay. We'll go and see Marie tomorrow and try and figure out what to do," announced Lyle.

They went to see Marie in the morning. While Ruth and Jerry were visiting her, Lyle went to the nurse's station to find Dr. Miller. He waited in the waiting area and a few minutes later he came to see Lyle.

Lyle told him about the small trailer and the problems he had with money. He needed to rent a cabin or small house to take care of Marie and provide a place for his daughter and the nanny to sleep.

"Go in and visit with Marie. I may have an answer to your problem. I have to check with somebody and I'll see you before you leave," said the doctor.

The doctor came into the room a little later and asked Lyle to step into his office so he could talk to him.

"Lyle, I think I have an answer to your immediate problem. I have an associate who has his mother's house for sale or rent. I told him about your problems and he said to come and see him. Here's his name and address. I told him you would probably see him sometime this afternoon. It's his day off and he should be home. If Marie keeps improving, she should be out by this time next week."

Lyle thanked the Dr. Miller and shook his hand. He went back in the room and got Ruth and Jerry. He said goodbye to Marie but didn't walk over and say any more. Ruth kissed her on the forehead and patted her shoulder.

Lyle came back in briefly and told Marie he was looking at a place for them to stay for a while after she got out. Marie didn't pay much attention to him because he was always planning and did nothing. She turned over and tried to go to sleep.

Lyle left Ruth and Jerry at the camp to figure out a place to sleep instead of their car. With Ruth's stiff leg, it was hard for her to get comfortable in their old Dodge. It was a big, old 4 door sedan with little pull down jump seats for extra people. Jerry had built a bed that covered the entire back of the car. It was big enough for them both but Ruth always had trouble because of that leg.

Lyle arrived at the doctor's house in the middle of the afternoon. He was surprised to see Dr. Armstrong, the one who had checked his heart and gave him medicine.

"It's you, Lyle. I was wondering who Dr. Miller was sending over to see my mother's old house. If you look at the top of the hill just beyond the tree line, you can see the chimney. Let's ride over and see it and we can talk on the way. Here, get in my old shay. I need to exercise old Dobbin. He's getting up in age but he likes to sashay with the old shay," said the doctor.

"The old house is over 100 years old and was one of the first farms in the area. They fought Indians, floods and famine to build the farm. My house is on the southern 400 acres. Her old house sits on about 20 acres of cleared land with a small creek in the back."

It took just a few minutes to get to the old house. It was a large, two story, well built house. There was a sizeable barn in the back. The well was one that you had to draw water from but it looked clean.

They went inside and found a large home, completely furnished. There was electricity to all the rooms and it had a modern kitchen with running water and a modern bathroom. Lyle wondered about the old well but didn't say anything about it.

"If you need hot water, you'll have to fire up the old boiler in the basement. There's plenty of wood."

"Before we go any further Doctor Armstrong, I can't afford a place like this. It's way over my head."

"Nonsense! I am a pretty good judge of character. I thought about you when I checked your heart. I need someone to look after the place and make some repairs to the barn and paint the house. I'll provide all the materials if you can do the work. It won't cost you a dime if you agree to rent it under those terms."

"Let me look around and see if I can do the work. My step son is here and it may be a way for him to help out."

They walked the grounds and looked at the barn. It was a little like the barn in the Tennessee hill country, but smaller. The house needed a lot of work, with broken shutters and almost no paint left on the outside. They went back inside and looked at the upstairs. The stairs needed work and so did several doors.

"I'm glad there's a downstairs bedroom for Marie and the babe. The upstairs will be fine for Ruth and Jerry," thought Lyle out loud.

"Doc, I'll give it a try. I'll do the very best I can to make the old house like you want it," said Lyle as he offered his hand to Doctor Armstrong.

"Fine, come by my office and well sign a rental agreement so there won't be any misunderstandings," said the doctor as he left the house. "Here's the keys. The power and everything is turned on, even the natural gas for heat and cooking. Go ahead and move in so you can get the house ready for Marie."

Lyle thanked him and shook his hand with both of his. This was a gesture of sincere thanks and appreciation.

Lyle's mind was alive and racing with all kinds of plans as he drove back to the camp. He would talk to Ruth and Jerry about his good fortune but he wouldn't tell them everything. He wanted them to do all the work and live in the house for nothing. It was typical of Lyle's ideas and he didn't care how he used people for his own gain.

Ruth was busy cooking supper when Lyle got back. She was a good cook and had a pot of her Irish stew on the stove. There were biscuits in the small oven and a fresh pot of coffee.

Mildred was watching Leone with a sour look on her face. She didn't like the idea of Ruth stepping in and taking over. She liked Lyle and in her tiny mind was hoping something would work out for them. Lyle wouldn't give her the time of day, let alone any idea he was interested in her. Mildred was still hoping until Ruth showed up. It ruined all of her plans and she was angry and frustrated.

Lyle told Ruth and Jerry about the house and what they had to do to have a place to stay and help Marie. Mildred was listening but didn't say anything.

Ruth and Jerry thought it was a good plan and said they would help all they could. Ruth was asking a lot of questions about the house and where it was. Lyle told them all he knew.

"Let's ride up to the hospital and tell Marie the good news," said Ruth.

"Mildred, we're going to take Leone to see Marie. You cleanup and we'll be back in an hour or so," said Lyle as they got in the Buick.

Mildred looked a little miffed because she wanted to see Marie. She watched the Buick leave the camp and she went to the trailer.

She searched the trailer and found about $25.00 in silver coins. She took the coins and got her and some of Marie's clothes and went to

Jerry's old Dodge. The keys were in it and she started it up and drove off down the road, hoping to find a better life.

They returned from the hospital to find the trailer door open and Jerry's car gone. They looked for a note and found none. They asked some of the campers and they said they saw her driving out of the camp a couple of hours ago.

Lyle reported the theft to the police who took down the information and would call the neighboring towns and see if they could pick her up. Lyle and Jerry signed the papers so a warrant could be issued for her arrest.

Lyle was nervous and upset because it meant he was now responsible for Ruth and Jerry. He didn't know what he would do except to see what the morning would bring. He was very tired and they all went to bed early. Lyle slept in the back of the Buick and Ruth and Jerry slept in the trailer.

Lyle could smell Mildred on the bed clothes and didn't like it, but he was too tired to do anything about it until tomorrow. He hoped it would be a good day tomorrow so he could move into the house.

Early the next morning the police knocked on the trailer door. They told Jerry they had found the car abandoned with a flat tire about 25 miles away. He asked them to wait while he woke up Lyle and told him the news.

"We'll take you to the car so you can drive it home," said the first police officer.

"Lyle, let me have a little money so I can get the tire fixed. I'm flat broke."

Lyle gave him $5.00 and Jerry left with the police officer.

The other officer asked Lyle if he wanted to continue with the warrant for her arrest. Lyle told him it wasn't necessary if his car wasn't damaged. He didn't want to see anyone in trouble.

Jerry drove up with his Dodge just as Ruth had finished breakfast. They all ate in silence.

Jerry looked very angry and displeased with the entire situation. He told Lyle it was his fault that Mildred took his car and he wanted to be paid for a new tire.

Lyle ignored him and turned the Buick around so he could hook up the trailer.

Jerry gradually calmed down and got the idea of what was going on. He helped Lyle hook up and gather all of the things he had out of the trailer.

Lyle wound up the electrical cord and put it in the Buick.

"Follow me and I'll take you to our new home. It is about a 20 minute drive. Take Leone in your car; I can't watch him and drive. I'll pull the trailer around toward the barn so I can work on it, you park out front on the gravel road area when we get there."

Lyle was very glad to be rid of Mildred. He knew it would make Marie happy to let Ruth take care of Leone. He was happy he dropped the charges because there was no damage to Jerry's car except a flat tire. He didn't want to see anyone in jail but he never wanted to see her again. She would probably get into trouble anyway, passing the patched silver she had stolen.

Later that evening they were settled in the house with Ruth and Jerry moved in upstairs. Ruth had fixed a good meal and they were all ready to go to bed. She found an old baby crib in one of the upstairs rooms and put Leone to sleep in it.

Lyle laid awake a long time in the large downstairs bedroom. The sheets felt cool to his body but the blanket was warm to his touch. He would be glad when Marie got out of the hospital so they could hit the road again.

CHAPTER SEVENTEEN

The House

Spring in Georgia

Lyle left early the next morning to see Doctor Armstrong to negotiate and sign the rental and repair agreement. Lyle had a list of repairs for Jerry to fix on the house. He wanted to talk to the doctor about the repairs and how he could get supplies and what was to be fixed first.

He arrived just in time to walk with the doctor to his office. They signed the agreement and he gave Lyle a copy. They discussed the list at length and the doctor added a few things to be done.

"I've arranged for you to get supplies from the lumberyard just down from my house. Keep all the receipts and a list of what you do. Here's $100.00 for any supplies they don't have. I'm so glad you agreed to help me with the house," said the doctor as he started on his rounds.

Lyle walked a little ways with him as they chatted about Marie. He wanted to know when Marie would be released so he could surprise her with the house. Lyle knew it would help her heal quicker to get out of the hospital and be with Leone.

"Come on, I'll take you to see her," said the doctor.

"Lyle, I'm so glad to see you," Marie said as he walked into her room. "I've been talking to Doctor Armstrong about his mother's house. He said you had an agreement to sign and we could rent it for the repair you would do. Lyle, he's been very good to us. I don't want you to do anything to him. Do you understand what I mean?"

"I just signed the papers and he gave me $100.00 for supplies that I can't buy at the lumberyard," said Lyle. "He must trust me with all the things he's doing for us," he thought, almost out loud.

Lyle told her about Mildred and how she took $25.00 in silver from the trailer. He told her the stash was safe under the trailer and he would leave it there because he didn't trust Jerry either.

"Marie I didn't pursue the warrant against her because Jerry got his car back. I was worried that he would be arrested and Ruth would have to stay with us."

"That was a good choice; I don't want Ruth staying with us, she will bleed us dry. She is good with Leone but I expect that will come to an end as soon as Jerry gets some money to go back north. I'm glad that Mildred is gone from our life. She wasn't very clean with Leone. How is my little man doing? Is Ruth taking good care of him?"

Lyle assured her that he was fine. He told her about Ruth finding the crib and fixing it for Leone. It had rockers on the bottom so he could be rocked asleep.

"It will be good to see lights in the old house. I'd always know when mother was up," said Doctor Armstrong as he walked in the door.

Lyle and Marie continued to talk a while as the doctor was checking her. Lyle told him about using the crib and asked if he minded if Leone used it as a bed.

"Mom rocked me many a time in that old crib and I turned out alright. I hope you and your son enjoy it. Bring him in sometime and let me look him over. Has he seen a doctor since he was born?"

Marie looked down and said a quiet, "No."

"If you keep improving, you'll be out of here in no time. When you get to feeling better and are out of the hospital, bring him around and I'll give him a good checkup."

The weather looked a lot better than it had been for the previous week. Lyle thought he saw a few buds on the trees and spring was just around the corner.

He felt good with the new crisp $100.00 bill tucked away in his wallet. He was thinking of ways to use it to his advantage without letting the doctor know what he was really doing. As soon as he got to the house, he would get Jerry busy on the repairs. He'd give Jerry the list of the things that needed to be done.

Lyle knew the doctor wanted to see progress. The first thing he would do was repair the shutters and paint the outside of the house. He was also formulating another plan in the back of his mind but he didn't have it all together yet.

"Jerry, let's you and I look at the outside of the house and see what it needs. We have to get started on it soon. The doctor wants to see some progress if we live here with only a little rent to pay."

Lyle told Ruth and Jerry that he had to pay half the rent for the work they were doing. In that, Jerry had to work to pay the other half. Because he was so lazy, it was the only way Lyle could think of to get the house fixed without doing any work himself. He rationalized that he was getting Jerry to pay back some of the money he owed.

They went to the lumberyard and picked up the necessary supplies to begin the house painting. Mr. Heifer, the manager, was aware of what colors the doctor wanted. He selected the correct primer and color for the entire house.

"We don't have any ladder or way to paint the upper areas of the house," said Lyle.

"I already thought of that. The doctor and I talked it over. We have a set of ladders and scaffolding you can use," said Mr. Heifer. "I'll have it and the materials delivered later today."

"Do you know of anyone who can help with the painting?" asked Lyle. "My heart won't let me climb ladders and Jerry can't do it by himself."

"I'll call the doctor and let you know tomorrow. In the meantime you can replace the shutters and start priming the lower part."

Lyle could see that Mr. Heifer was going to be a problem. He was acting as a supervisor for the doctor and it would be hard, but not impossible, to get away with anything. Lyle loved a challenge to make a little money and get away with something. It didn't matter how much because it was the "challenge of the chase," as his Grandfather Freeman used to say.

Ruth was cleaning the house and taking care of Leone. She seemed to enjoy her dad's Company. It had been a long time since they had a chance to sit and talk about old times. He asked about Ruth's mother, Anna. Ruth told him she remarried a retired banker and was quite happy. She had a half sister and brother that she had never met.

Lyle was a little despondent when he heard that. He always cared for Anna. She was Bohemian and had a nice, easy going personality. To this day, he couldn't think of a good reason he didn't come home in '21 when she sued him for desertion. Lyle was a wonderer and thought of himself as a renaissance man and couldn't help it. The only thing he could do was to rationalize his way out of the dilemma. He knew in his heart that the causes and actions only seemed valid, and they actually weren't true. He knew he was not honest within his heart but some unconscious cause drove him to do the things he did. In actuality, doing things correct and honest were often easier than his way. It all started so long ago that is became a way of life for Lyle.

He often thought about Juanita and her son Juan Carlos. He didn't know for sure it was his son until Juanita had told him it was. Someday he'd like to see him, but he didn't know when.

Sitting in an open patio and listening to the Mexican troubadours sing their love songs was Lyle's favorite pastime. Being alone was not one of his better ways to pass time.

"How do you want these shutters fastened? They have different hangers," asked Jerry.

"Don't put them up before you prime and paint them. It's a lot easier to paint shutters off a house because of all the slats," said Lyle. "Jerry is just a little bit smarter than some of the rocks in the flower bed," thought Lyle out loud.

"I don't feel like doing all the work and I won't. I'm holding money over Jerry's head so he'll finish the job. He can't go anywhere without some money. We don't have a lot of time, but I'd like to be done about the same time Marie feels like traveling," thought Lyle while he watched Jerry work.

Lyle was having a problem trying to figure out a way to convince Marie to return to traveling. She had been in the hospital 3 months and she would be recovering another 3 months.

"Ruth, tell Jerry I'm going to visit Marie and stop by the campground and see if there is anyone I know."

"I'll make sure Jerry works and doesn't come in and sleep on the couch," said Ruth.

Lyle decided to stop by the camp first and see if there was anyone he knew. As he drove, he was thinking about a way to fix the trailer a little better. It had to be bigger for Leone and Marie. He thought about building a new one but he didn't know if he wanted to take the time. A lot depended on Marie and where his father was and when he would visit. A lot also depended if he could keep Jerry working.

He was putting a plan together as he turned in the drive. The camp appeared deserted until he saw two old trailers he didn't recognize. At the end of the last camp area, he saw the old familiar green Hudson of Pope the Key Man. He was so glad he was there. He would have all the news of the trail and what the people were doing.

He got out of his car and walked up to Pope's old car. He was sitting by an open fire, drinking his tea and talking to several of the campers. He saw Lyle and got up to greet him.

"Lyle, you're a sight for sore eyes! I haven't seen you since we were at Juanita's in Kentucky. Where have you been and what's happening in your life? How is that beautiful wife of yours?"

They shook hands and Lyle sat down on the running board of the old Hudson and put his hands out to the fire to warm them. Lyle didn't like tea very much but he took a cup of strong tea with cream when it was offered, as he didn't want to hurt Pope's feeling.

They exchanged seeing this one and that one. Finally, Lyle told him about Marie being in the hospital and losing her baby.

"It doesn't seem right you staying in a house Lyle. I've never heard of you and a house getting along very well."

"I didn't have a lot of choice. Ruth and Jerry are here and they don't have any money. They were sleeping in their car."

"I remember them a couple of years ago. Wasn't he the fellow from Detroit who got into problems with the mob?"

"He's one and the same. He's older, fatter and lazier. He doesn't have a lot of skills that I can use. He's helping with the house so I can get it rent free."

"Lyle, you always have a way of coming out on the clean end of the stick. I heard about your escapades with George Planter in Tennessee. He got 5 years and here you are talking to me!"

"I was lucky on that one. What happened to his wife, Betty?"

"She went back north and took up with a drummer out of Wisconsin. The last I heard they were selling cheap Mexican pots and pans in Texas."

"Pope, how do you keep up with all the people and things that happen?"

"I like all the road people and I like to know what happens. For instance, you lost your federal license in Florida. Didn't I tell you a long time ago that Florida wasn't a good place to do any kind of shady deals?"

"Yes you told me more than once. I should have listened to you and it got me into trouble," said Lyle. "Have you been back to see Juanita and Carlos?"

"No, but I heard that Carlos got really sick and went back to Mexico. They weren't married you know."

"I guessed they weren't married but I was never sure. He used his last name, Marron was it? Who's helping with the camp and store?" asked Lyle.

"The last thing I heard was that Harold Fletcher, the basket maker, was trying to help. He isn't in good health and the old mustard gas burns bother him a lot. I think she'll give up the camp and go back to Mexico. She has a kid she left in there when she came to the states with Carlos. I think she'll go back and be with him. I heard she was sad and lonely now that Carlos went back to Mexico."

Lyle stared at the fire, as Pope put on some more wood to help with the chill of the evening. He thought about what Pope said about Juanita and felt a small tinge of guilt, but it didn't last long. Most of the campers had gone to their camp when he and Pope were talking about people they didn't know. One boy, about 13, listened carefully to everything.

"Boy, go fetch us some more wood for the fire before it gets dark. There's some over by the river bank," said Pope.

"What's going to happen to us, Pope? We're travelers with no home except the road. We take our home with us every where we go."

"I don't know the answer to that one Lyle; I left my home so many years ago. I've forgotten what it feels like to sleep in a real bed. This old Hudson has been my bed for many years. The keys put me to sleep at night. No matter how you turn or move, they tell you about it."

He looked at Lyle for a long time. He was looking through him, into the distant dark of the night. He was quiet for a long time as Lyle stirred the fire and watched the sparks float up in the crystal clear night sky.

"I love the open road. Me and my keys are a way of life. Somebody will find me one morning sitting by the embers of a fire with my tea cup in my hand. It's the way I want to catch the East Bound."

"It's harder when you have a family like I do. I have to make enough money to take care of them. I don't know about Marie. She's been very sick and would rather have a house than a trailer."

Both men looked at the crackle of the new wood the kid put on the fire. They followed the sparks as they climbed into the night sky. The kid went back to his camp and left the two old men thinking and looking at the glowing embers of the fire.

"Lyle what are you going to do when Marie gets out of the hospital and is able to travel again?"

"I don't really know for sure. I've been thinking about building a new and bigger trailer while she's getting better. I've got a perfect place to build it in the barn behind the house. With Jerry here, he could help with some of the heavier stuff and I could make a nice rig."

"How long do you think it will be before Marie can travel?"

"I figure about 4 to 6 months. A lot depends on how she feels about things. I'll have to make a nice rig so she'll be willing to give up that house. We've been talking so long, I forgot about seeing Marie!" said Lyle as he jumped up.

"It's too late now, Lyle. You can see her tomorrow. Sit down and let's finish our talk. It doesn't happen very often that two old vagabonds like us can solve the problems of the world in one night."

"Pope, one thing's for sure: I'm not going to settle into a house and get a job. I'm going to stay on the road as long as I can and work my gold racket and other things to make money," said Lyle as he lit another cigarette and settled in for a long talk.

Both old travelers went to sleep by the fire in the wee hours of the morning after talking about everything under the sun. Lyle was happy and content and had worked out a lot of things in his mind. He knew what he had to do and how he was going to do it.

Garland Pope was a living legend among the road people. He had no enemies and helped everyone he could.

"I'm glad we had our nice long talk and caught up on everything," Lyle thought as he drifted off into a peaceful sleep.

After a good campfire breakfast and hobo coffee, Lyle drove back to the house. It was mid-morning and Lyle didn't see Jerry working. He went in and found Ruth taking care of Leone. Jerry was still in bed.

"Ruth, I'm going into town and see Marie. I need to check the mail and see where dad is."

"Dad, where have you been? I had supper fixed–a nice tender pork chop and mashed potatoes. When you didn't come home? Jerry ate it. Are you up to some of your old tricks again?"

"No Ruth, I spent the evening talking with Pope the Key Man. We talked about everything under the sun around a campfire. You remember him don't you?"

"I think I do. Did he drive an old green car?"

"That's him. He is one of my oldest and best friends on the road. He keeps up with everyone and passes on information to all the campers. He also settles a lot of legal issues because he is trusted by all."

"Well, in that case. That's alright then."

"Get Jerry up and make him go to work. We need to show some progress on the house every day or we will be booted out of here. The lumberyard manager is keeping an eye on us."

Jerry heard Lyle come in and was angry that he woke him. He came down stairs looking for an argument.

"Ruth, you better tell your dad to have some respect when people are sleeping! I need my rest if I'm going to work on this house."

Ruth didn't pay any attention to him. Most of the time, he was all bark and no bite unless he could sneak up from behind.

"Jerry, it's after 10:00 in the morning and you needed to be up and working before 8. We have no money and you won't work. Just how do you think we're going to get back to Detroit, rob a bank?"

"You know, I thought about that," said Jerry, as he poured himself a cup of coffee. But I don't want to spend any more time in the pen."

"Shave and get dressed in your work clothes while I fix breakfast. I want you outside working when dad comes home!"

When Lyle got home, Jerry was busy priming the new shutters on some old saw horses he found in the barn. He was moving slow and had paint droppings everywhere but where he was painting.

"It looks like Ruth got him busy. I need to see what kind of things I can find to start on a new trailer," thought Lyle out loud.

He went inside to talk to Ruth about it. He had a proposition he wanted to present to them.

"Jerry, stop working and come inside and let's have a cup of coffee. I want to talk to you and Ruth."

Jerry willingly came in to get out of the chill of the day. He had on old coveralls that truck drivers wore and they were covered with gray/blue paint. He washed his hands and warmed them over the stove in the kitchen.

The kitchen was a large bright room with a bay window overlooking the rolling fields of the farm. It had once been thousands of acres but was now down to 20, where the house stood.

A bright red and white checkered table cloth decorated the kitchen table. Ruth had made some biscuits early that morning and they all sat down to have some coffee and biscuits. Lyle liked leftover bacon and Ruth put some on his plate. It was a comfortable, warm setting as the three drank their coffee and looked out over the warming spring scene.

"I have a proposition for both of you. It will require a couple months work from you two. It's my plan to build a new trailer to replace the one we have. It's good for two people but with the babe, it gets crowded. We need some more room so the babe can grow. He'll be walking pretty soon and he needs his own bed."

Jerry stared out the window and looked like he wasn't paying any attention. He knew it meant he had to work and he didn't like that.

"Jerry! Pay attention to what dad is trying to tell us. I think he may have an idea to get us out of this jam."

Jerry sat up and turned his chair so he could look at Lyle.

"Sorry Lyle, but my mind was somewhere else. Go ahead and tell us your plan."

"I want you to help me finish working on this house and help me with some of the heavy work on the trailer."

"In turn, I'll give you my trailer free and clear so you will have a way to travel. It has a Florida bill of sale and is legal in any state. In addition, I'll give you $100.00 travel money. How does that sound to both of you?"

Ruth and Jerry looked at each other in total surprise. They both thought he was going to ask them to leave. They nodded to each other in complete agreement.

"Dad, I think that's very generous of you. We'll help any way we can, won't we Jerry?"

Jerry nodded his head in agreement and stood up as Lyle extended his hand to seal the agreement.

He took Lyle's his hand in a firm grip.

"Lyle, we appreciate your offer very much and we won't let you down. I'll work as fast as I can to finish the house. When you need help with the new trailer, I'll be there," said Jerry in a sincere voice, while Ruth nodded in agreement.

"Ruth, I can't stand sleeping in a house. I'll sleep in the trailer until Marie gets home. Jerry, I need some help to move it closer to the barn so I can hook up the electricity and listen to my radio. This radio doesn't go with the trailer. You'll have to get your own," said Lyle.

Ruth and Jerry went back in the house and both were talking and waving their arms at the same time. Lyle looked at them and knew he had a good deal. He got in his car and drove down the driveway.

He visited Marie in the hospital. She wasn't in her room but sitting at the end of the hall in the waiting room talking with some people. She looked at Lyle and gave him a weak smile.

"How are feeling, Marie? I'm glad to see you're getting around a little better."

"I still have a little infection in my scar. I'll have to wait another week before I can be discharged. I'm sick and tired of the food. I like the people and the doctors, but the food is horrible."

"I'll see if I can find the doctor and find out what's going on," said Lyle.

Lyle told her about his long talk with Pope the Key Man and

about Juanita and Carlos. Marie was sad to hear about all the bad things going on. She wasn't surprised about Betty; she had told Marie about an old boy friend who lived in Wisconsin.

"You know Lyle, Betty wasn't legally married to George. They were sort of like we are, living together common law. Have you ever thought about us getting married?" asked Marie.

"It wouldn't make any difference. We're married in the eyes of the law in most states. You and the babe have my last name."

"The difference would be that I'd have a piece of paper saying you and I are husband and wife. In case anything happened to you I would have something to prove it."

"Let's wait until you get out of here and we can talk about it," said Lyle. I need to get back to the house and see how Jerry is doing on the work. When he sees me leave the driveway he stops working."

He waved at Marie as he left the room. He was glad to get out of there. He had no intention of marrying Marie or anyone else, for any reason. What they had was good enough because common law was an accepted practice in the south. He didn't want the door closed on his future because he still didn't know exactly what he wanted to do.

He stopped by the post office and there was a postcard from his dad. He wasn't coming south until later because his wife didn't want to leave Pontiac, Michigan. Lyle thought they were still in Cresse. He would never understand what his dad was doing. He asked for more money. Lyle sent him a card that said he was flat broke and couldn't send him any money. He told him that Marie was still in the hospital and couldn't travel for several months.

Later that evening Lyle was settled in the trailer. He was listening to his radio and writing in his dairies. He hadn't kept them up to date since Marie was sick.

Amos and Andy were doing their usual back and forth comedy routine. Lyle was sitting at the dinette and smoking a ready made Camel. He didn't like them as well as Sweet Picayunes, but they were cheaper. He was tired and decided to go to bed early. He didn't like the house because it was too big. He was used to the bed in the trailer and felt more comfortable.

"Let Ruth and Jerry have the house for now. I don't want to run into them tonight," thought Lyle out loud.

He had no idea how he was going to convince Marie that they needed to be on the road. Once Marie was in the house, it was going to hard to get her out. Maybe the new trailer would help convince her.

Ruth and Jerry were convinced that the plan proposed was a good thing for them. They both worked very hard at doing what Lyle wanted. Jerry was very careful about his painting and soon had all the shutters fixed and the front of the house painted.

Lyle picked up Marie at the hospital 2 weeks later. She was able to walk to the car with no trouble. She had lost a lot of weight but she looked good.

She said goodbye to all the friends she had made. The head nurse gave her a bouquet of flowers from all the staff.

"Lyle, I'm so hungry." Let's stop at a diner and get some food. I want a hamburger and French fries so bad," said Marie as she got in the car.

"Good idea. I know of one on the way to the house."

Marie was so happy to be out of the hospital and able to eat again. She ate all her food as she talked to Lyle about the house and how Jerry was helping paint and do the repairs.

Lyle didn't tell her about building the trailer. He would tell her when they got home. She was anxious to see Leone and Lyle knew it. She didn't like Jerry but she did like Ruth. She knew Ruth was a little older than her and they had their problems about it, but she hoped it would be better this time.

Leone was crawling on the hardwood floor of the kitchen when Marie came in. He saw Marie and stated to make talking noises. She stooped down but she couldn't pick him up, so she just sat on the floor and played with him.

"Marie, I'm so glad to see you! Leone has been good and very easy to be around, but I could tell he missed you. I think I almost have him potty trained. He can stand and try to walk. I think he'll walk pretty soon," said Ruth. "Let me help you up, Marie. I'll take you to your room so you can lie down."

"I've been on my back for 3 months! I want to look at the house and fix me a cup of good strong coffee!"

Lyle and Marie went to bed early. Ruth pushed Leone's crib into the room so Marie could watch him. Leone was sound asleep and would sleep all night. Marie was happy with the bed and house.

"I can't sleep in a house, especially in this big soft bed. I'm going to the trailer and get a good night's sleep," said Lyle.

"You sleep anywhere you want. I'm going to sleep in this big bed and enjoy every minute of it," said Marie.

She got up and checked Leone to make sure he was ok as Lyle walked out of the house to his beloved trailer.

"I've been sleeping by myself for the past three months. I don't need him keeping me awake with his snoring," thought Marie out loud, as she got back into bed.

She thought to herself about all the pain she endured with the surgery. She had made some good friends at the hospital and was glad she did. She knew Lyle would try and bother her as soon as he got a chance but she was firm in her conviction. The doctor said she had "lost her sex," and that was the way it was going to be. She thought about the nice feel of the bed and all the things a permanent home offered. This was the longest she had been in one place since she took up with Lyle and she liked it.

Lyle went to the trailer and turned on his radio and listened to the news about the Japs in Manchuria. He felt in his heart they would be at war soon. He was happy he wouldn't have to go because he was exempt. He went to sleep after turning off the radio and putting out his cigarette. He went into a deep sleep with no thoughts or dreams of tomorrow.

Marie was settling into the routine of the house. Between her and Ruth, the house chores were going well. It was the first time Ruth and Marie ever got along for an extended period of time. They had a common bond and it was Leone. Ruth loved the little boy and Marie could see she really tried to do her very best in spite of her stiff leg.

Leone was starting to climb on everything and say a few words. Marie still couldn't pick him up, but he didn't mind. They would go outside with Ruth's help and watch the birds fly in and out of their gourd nests in the front yard. He would laugh at their antics.

"I am going to teach this boy everything I know about nature so he will grow up loving the earth and all that lives in its boundaries. My mother taught me all about the earth medicines and about how to get along in the wilds and I am going to teach Leone the same way," thought Marie.

Jerry was helping Lyle finish the outside work. They had painted as far as their ladders would reach and were waiting for the doctor to send over some help to complete the top part. Jerry did most of the heavy work and Lyle worked the fine trimming. He had an artistic manner about small things he did. If he took his time, he could make the lines almost invisible.

Lyle had figured a way to get his trailer built with little or no money. He would buy a little more lumber than he needed each time he ordered for the house and hide it in the barn. In a month or so, he would have enough material to start the trailer. He needed a suitable frame and flooring before he could start. He had plywood in various sizes to build the roof, sides and floor. He had the lumberyard split larger wood pieces into smaller sizes to fit the trailer.

The trailer would be about 18' long and 6' wide, depending on the frame and axle he would get. It would have a bed in each end with a nice kitchen in the center. There would be a dining area adjacent to the kitchen with a nice window over the dinette. Under both beds would be a large storage area. He would use the old curtains he found in the attic as his bedroom privacy curtain. Leone didn't need one.

Lyle was supposed to replace a lot of the electrical sockets in the house, but he diverted the supplies to his own use, though he did enough in the house to impress the doctor favorably.

Lyle used some of his own money to buy romex to wire the trailer. He was going to have double walls on all sides and the roof and the wiring would go in between the walls. There would be an outside connection so it could be hooked to an electrical socket. Double walls gave more sound protection and they were good to hide the wiring. In addition, they would act as a temperature barrier if he put in insulation. It was expensive and Lyle wanted to use all he could for nothing. Jerry was good at electrical work so he would wire the trailer as soon as Lyle was ready.

Near the middle of summer, the house was almost finished and Lyle found a nice trailer frame from a junk yard. A New Moon trailer had been wrecked and Lyle bought the aluminum frame with hitch and tires. The sides and top were gone but the floor was intact, complete was linoleum flooring. Lyle bought the frame for $100.00. It was an excellent start to build a nice trailer.

The doctor visited only once, a few days before, and was very pleased at the progress. They only needed to repair the upstairs doors and they would be finished.

Marie helped by telling Lyle where and what she wanted in the trailer. She was firm about the beds and kitchen.

Lyle built the outside walls first and included an extension on the back that would serve as storage and a fold-down work bench. The design was similar to the kitchen in back of the old tear drop, including a section of the back that would open and be used as a cover for the work area.

Lyle bought some piano hinges for the house but kept them for use on the trailer. So far, the doctor had paid the bill and said nothing about any of the supplies Lyle was diverting to his trailer.

The doctor provided some help and they finished painting the top part of the house in one day. It looked very good and Lyle was proud of his work.

On one visit to the house, the doctor checked Marie and Leone. He pronounced her ready to travel and Leone a healthy young boy. He liked the way the house was refinished, especially the outside paint and new shutters.

"Lyle, you and your family have done a great job. I am very pleased. I think you deserve a little more than just the rent," he said as he gave Lyle $200.00. "This is for a job well done. I sincerely appreciate all you have done."

"He hasn't mentioned the other $100.00 he gave me. I still have it tucked away," thought Lyle.

Lyle put the money in his pocket before Jerry could see it.

"You folks stay here as long as you want. Just let me know a couple of weeks before you leave. This house and land is for sale. I could make you a good deal on it and carry the paper myself."

Marie heard him say that and appeared to be very happy. She wanted to stay and Lyle knew it. He wished she hadn't heard the doctor make the offer.

"Doc, you know I don't have much money. I can't afford a mortgage as big as this one."

"You'd be surprised how little it'll cost you. Let me know if you want to talk about it," he said as he got into his new red Cadillac roadster.

All four of them got together late one evening and talked about what they had done.

"Jerry, you've done a good job for me. I am about finished with the trailer. As soon as it's finished, I'll let you have the old trailer, like I said. I'll give you the money I promised but you must stay until my trailer is finished."

They all stood up and Lyle and Jerry shook hands. They all laughed at their good fortune and went in the kitchen to have supper Ruth had fixed earlier.

Marie still had hope she could get the house as her own. She didn't know how to convince Lyle to stay; he had a very hard head about living in a house. On the other hand, she had to admit that the trailer looked very nice and Lyle had put in everything she asked him so far. Time and time alone would tell.

CHAPTER EIGHTEEN

The New Trailer

Georgia mid summer

Lyle was making good progress with the rough work on the new trailer. He had gathered some old flooring left in the barn and built a vat large enough to soak the marine plywood so he could bend it to conform to the curvature of the trailer. He then sealed the floor with a thin layer of cement. It would accommodate a 4 x 8 sheet of plywood.

Building the jig to bend the plywood was little short of genius. He made a wooden mold that could be shaped to the exact curve of the plywood on edge. He would insert a piece of wet wood, bend it to the correct proportion and let it dry for a few days. When the mold was removed, it held the exact curve that was set. It was a method used by old shipbuilders. His father had taught him and it was passed down from generation to generation.

The work was very time consuming, but Lyle was driven by a strong desire to have a nice place for Marie and the babe and to get away from the house. He knew he was in strong competition with the house and its setting. Marie liked to plant and tend to flowers. She had planted some tomato plants and was looking forward to eating fresh garden vegetables. It was all in direct competition with Lyle's desire to travel the roads and work his schemes.

Regardless of how hard Lyle worked on the trailer, he was constantly planning and scheming how to make a little money. While Marie was in the hospital, he worked the Albany area and bought all the gold he could afford. The Baltimore company was shorting him a little more each shipment. He would usually get his money back, but the process was lengthened by weeks. Lyle could sense the gold market was drying up.

Jerry was not used to doing fine work, but he had the brute strength to help with the heavier items. He was needed only a few times a day, as building the trailer was akin to building a boat. It had the same curves and fine lines of a boat and required hours of skilled carpentry to make al the pieces fit together.

Lyle worked only a few hours a day, mostly in the morning. He liked to take his afternoon siesta and go back to work late in the afternoon.

Because the house renovations were complete, Lyle could no longer get supplies from the lumberyard charged to the house account. He had to dig into his beloved stash to buy necessary hardware and small things to complete the trailer. He estimated it would take another 6 to 8 weeks to finish the job. This time he was saving receipts, especially from the trailer frame, to get a license. It had a serial number and could be registered. He even had plans to connect the wiring to his car so there would be rear lights. The wiring was attached to the frame so it wasn't too hard with Jerry's help. Jerry was good at wiring and had been a help hooking up the inside electrical connections.

To prevent any problems from happening in the future, Lyle took the bill of sale for the frame and copies of the material receipts to the tag office. They sold him a $2.00 license plate for a Blue Moon. He tried to tell them it was only a frame but the clerk just said, "Next." Lyle left with the plate and attached it to the back of the new trailer.

Marie was tending to Leone, with Ruth's help. The clean air and bright sunshine of a beautiful Georgia spring sped up her healing. She could do most everything except pick up Leone, but she was working on that.

Her tomato plants were doing well and she tended them daily. She liked to walk around the house and feel like it was her home.

She also knew in her heart that Lyle would be finished with the trailer one day and they would have to leave. For that reason, she wasn't getting too attached to her surrounding, but she wouldn't let Lyle know it. She continued talking about the house and he continued to sleep in the old trailer. Every night she could hear his radio and see him sitting at the table listening while he smoked and drank his coffee Marie had fixed.

Marie had a path she walked around the farm to get her strength back. Ruth would watch Leone while she walked every morning. Her walks took her out by the main road and down an old cow path to the creek at the back of the property. It took her a couple of hours to make her rounds.

At the creek she would sit on an old log and watch the squirrels play in a large hickory tree. Marie loved animals and the natural beauty they added to the land. She could never bring herself to even think about hurting an animal.

One morning, she decided to walk the same trail back to the road and then to the house instead of the creek trail which came out behind the barn because she didn't want to walk by the new trailer and encounter Lyle. He would stop and talk to her about leaving and traveling again. She wasn't up to the foray of words this morning.

On her way back on the cow trail, she noticed some movement on the side of the path. She stopped and parted the tall grass and saw a small white cat, barely half grown, lying on its side breathing heavily. It had blood on its head and side.

Marie carefully picked up the cat. She emitted a small low cry like a small child. The cat was badly hurt either by a passing car or someone had tossed the cat out. Marie wrapped her in her apron and gently carried her back to the house.

"Hillbilly, you look like you are a little worse for wear. I'll clean you up and get some warm milk under your nose and you should feel better," said Marie, talking to the cat.

"Hillbilly is a good name for a cat who wanders and gets into trouble. You'll have to learn how to be careful if you live under my roof," Marie continued.

The cat answered with a tiny meow as Marie cleaned her cuts. The more she looked at the cat the more she realized that she was the victim of a lot of bites, perhaps from an angry dog or another cat. Marie feed her some warm milk and put her on an old towel at the end of her bed.

Leone saw the cat and made little noises and pointed at it. He was beginning to pull himself up and walk by holding things. At ten months, Marie was pleased with his progress. Since she had been in the house, she had potty trained him so he could sleep all night and not wet his diaper. It would be easy to teach him how to walk because he was trying so hard. Leone was so bowlegged he looked like an old cowboy trying to get on a horse. Marie thought it would be nice to walk her path with him and start to show him about nature. The cat was a very good step toward his future.

Over the next week, Hillbilly got better. She had a penchant for potatoes. She especially liked bits of fried potatoes. She even liked to eat potato peelings, which surprised Marie to no end.

During the day, Hillbilly liked to sit in the sun by the bay window. The window had a wide sill and Marie put an old soft pillow on it so she should sleep in the morning sun. She was very good in the house and would let you know when she wanted to go out. Hillbilly became part of the family, at least to Marie and Leone. Lyle didn't like cats but he would have to put up with her.

"I don't care what you think, Lyle, this cat is coming with us wherever we go. I brought her back from near death and Hillbilly is part of the family."

Lyle looked at Marie and started to say something but he knew better. He lowered his shoulders in resignation and went out to work on the new trailer.

Jerry didn't have a lot to do when he wasn't helping Lyle. Marie talked to him about learning how to drive a car.

"I used to teach drivers how to drive trucks and I think I can teach a woman how to a drive car," said Jerry.

"Jerry, I don't want Lyle to know. If we drive anywhere you drive out of the area and then I'll take over."

"Whoa, hold on. You don't know anything about driving and already you're behind the wheel!"

"I do know something. I drove the car while Lyle was asleep and I can use the clutch pretty well."

"I'll tell Lyle we're going to the store to get some groceries."

"Ruth, please watch Leone while Jerry takes me to the store."

Marie got behind the wheel of the Jerry's old Dodge with the confidence of a seasoned driver. Jerry was a lot of things, but he was an excellent driver. He had the patience to teach someone to drive with the proper balance of road skills. His years on the road as a truck driver complimented his natural ability to handle a car.

Marie sat in the driver's seat, put in the clutch and started to drive like she had been doing it all of her life. She took to driving a car like a duck took to water. They drove on back roads and into parking lots. He taught her how to parallel park and sense to feel of the car and the road.

They came back home after a few hours on the road with Marie behind the wheel. She drove to the barn and blew the horn. Lyle came out of the trailer and his eyes almost fell out of his head when he saw Marie behind the wheel of the old Dodge.

"What in the world are you doing? You don't know how to drive! Your going to get into a wreck and kill somebody," said Lyle in an angry voice.

"Lyle, in all my years behind the wheel, I've never found anyone with the 'seat of the pants' ability to drive a car. She is a natural. I'm going to take her to get her license as soon as she studies the book so she can pass the written test. She can pass the driving test today."

Lyle threw his hammer down and struck his trot for the house. He used the bathroom and came out a little calmer.

"Ruth, pour me some coffee and scramble me an egg. I have to think about this driving business with Marie."

"Dad, there's nothing to think about; It's already happened. Marie can drive and she's going to get her license. You might as well face facts."

Lyle sat down with a sullen look on his face and lit up. Marie sat down across from him and also lit a cigarette.

"Lyle, me being able to drive will be a help to you. I can buy groceries or take Leone to the doctor. You won't have to stop working when I need something."

"Jerry, you and Ruth leave us alone a minute," said Lyle.

"Marie, I guess I was wrong. You're right; it'll help me if you drive. I don't know about you pulling the trailer, but we'll make that another lesson that doesn't need to be learned right away. You need to get used to driving car for a while before you try and pull a trailer."

Two weeks later, Marie had her first driver's license and she was very proud of it.

Jerry was a little bored with all the time he had on his hands. He had made fiends with one of the workers at the lumberyard, Robert. Robert was one of the lead drivers for the company. Jerry was short on money and went looking for a job driving a truck for the lumberyard. They hired him based on Robert's recommendation. It was a good way to keep Lyle and Jerry apart. They hadn't been getting along so well the past month. They would argue about the trailer and money–Jerry always wanted money and Lyle wouldn't give him any.

Actually, Marie gave Jerry $20.00 from her personal stash for teaching her how to drive. This didn't help Jerry very much but it kept him quiet for a little while.

Robert was a little like Lyle in that he liked to do small jobs for quick money. He told Jerry about a slick scheme to make some extra money.

The lumber company had received a truck load of linoleum. It was labeled 40% cork and was made in La Grange, Georgia by a company that was now out of business. In fact, the linoleum was barely a good grade of tar paper with designs painted on the surface. A good twist of a shoe heal would make a mark.

Robert bought the entire truck load for little of nothing. It actually cost him about 2¢ on the dollar. He wanted Jerry to help him sell and install it at a cut rate price to the customer.

"Robert, I want to talk to my paw-in-law. He knows a lot about these kind of deals. He's been doing them for a long time."

Jerry went back to the house and found Lyle working on the inside trim of the new trailer.

"Lyle, I want to talk to you about a beautiful deal I ran into."

Jerry told Lyle about the deal and asked what he thought.

"I ran across the same deal in Lake Park and in Sanford. It looks like the company sold a lot of bad product and went belly up. The boys in Lake Park offered me the entire load for less than 1¢ on the dollar. All they want is to get rid of it. I'll let you know how we can do it. The problem as I see it is neither you nor Robert could sell water to a man dying of thirst."

Lyle went back to work on the new trailer and thought about the scam. He would also like to try out one that Pete Sherlock, the Irish mule trader, told him about. He needed a few supplies to tie it in with selling a linoleum job.

"It's just what the doctor ordered. Robert and Jerry have the muscles and I have the brain to sell the jobs," thought Lyle.

He went in the house and asked Jerry to come out. He wanted to talk to him.

"Go get your friend Robert after he gets off work. Meet me here tonight and we'll talk business," said Lyle.

Marie knew that Ruth and Jerry were going to get the old trailer, so she went there and unloaded all her belongings and stored them in the barn tack room. It was waterproof and the things wouldn't ruin. Ruth helped her unpack everything except what Lyle would need to sleep at night.

"Ruth, I'll give you one set of bed clothes so you can have a place to sleep. Get your clothing out of the old Dodge and store it in here."

Marie carefully took her old mirror down. She wrapped it in a dish towel and carried it to the house. She put it in her bedroom for safe keeping.

"I love that old mirror. It reminds me of the good and bad things that happened in the old tear drop. I'll keep it forever to remind me never to get in such a fix, ever again," thought Marie.

"Better yet, I'll go hang it in the trailer right now," said Marie out loud.

She stopped and looked at the trailer as she was walking to the house. A flood of sadness flowed over her. Suddenly, she thought about the little baby that wasn't to be. She thought about her surgery and the long stay in the hospital. She wasn't the same woman now that she was a few months ago. She wished in all her heart she could have had the little girl. She would have named her Anna, after her mother. Thoughts of little pink things for a girl passed through her mind. The thoughts were broken by Leone's first words. He was trying to say Hillbilly but it came out as "Hee Bee." Marie was so happy he was starting to say things she could understand.

Hillbilly rubbed against her leg and wanted to be petted as Marie walked in the house. She looked at Marie as Marie stroked her head. She had one blue eye and one green eye. Marie thought it was so pretty. She bought her a pink collar with a tiny bell so she could hear her around the house. The only thing Marie could tell from the injury was Hillbilly didn't hear very well.

Lyle met with the "boys" and he laid out a plan to make some money.

"Let's take a ride tomorrow and select some good places to sell the linoleum and I'll put on the touch. We want to be a good ways away from here so when it does come apart we can be long gone," said Lyle.

"There are some little towns like Putney, Pretoria and Leesburg," he continued." These people are mostly peanut farmers and they'll all need our special deal to put linoleum in their kitchen. It has been a good peanut year. My selling plan is to offer them a good installed price at least ½ of what the regular dealers install it for. We'll throw in a stove cleaning and blacking."

"What do you mean 'blacking'?" Jerry asked.

"While I was with the Irish mule traders, they taught me a way to black stoves to make them look as good as new. I'll mix up the blacking and let you two do the work. I'll do all the selling and you two follow me up to make the installation. One other thing, I'll get 1/3 of the profits and each of you gets 1/3. Is that agreeable?"

Robert and Jerry looked at each other and nodded in agreement.

"Have either of you ever laid linoleum?"

"I did a lot of it when I worked for a carpet company," said Robert.

"That's good. Jerry can help with the installation and you both can black the stove. The mix is simple. You mix coal oil, coal black and add a touch of Brilliantine so it smells nice. You wipe the stove with a rag and get off most of the grease and dirt. Let it cool off and then use a paint brush and paint the stove with the stuff. Put some old newspapers down so it won't mess up the new floor. Then you collect your money and leave!"

"Make sure you tell them to wait until the stove dries before they fire it."

For the next two weeks, they worked the surrounding areas and did very well. They sold all of their goods and made a very good profit. They didn't sell any close to their camp. They had enough left to complete 3 or 4 floors.

"Jerry, you and Robert can sell what's left of the goods. I'll make up some more blacking and we'll be done in this area." I think we should lay off selling because something might come back to haunt us. Our story will be what the carton says: '40% cork and other natural materials.' We don't know anything about the tar and paint. That'll be our story. Understand?"

Robert and Jerry nodded in agreement and then went off to talk and count their money.

"I know how to sell this stuff better than Lyle. In the next couple of days, we'll drive to Moultrie and sell the rest of it. We won't tell Lyle how much we made and only cut him in for a small share," said Jerry.

"Maybe nothing," said Robert.

Lyle was busy finishing the trailer while Ruth and Marie drove into town to do a little grocery shopping. Jerry had finished running all the light for the outside. The inside needed a little more finishing and Lyle was busy with the counter top. He promised Marie that he would finish everything he started. It wasn't his nature, but he was doing his best.

He made a nice little kitchen for Marie. He had found some new type counter top on sale at the lumberyard and cut it to fit the cabinet. He installed the sink with a nice kitchen work area on the side.

The sink was a leftover from the Blue Moon trailer. It had a hand pump to pump water in the sink and Lyle connected it to a 20 gallon fresh water tank under the frame. It was a nice touch for Marie. The ice box was a trade-in at the lumberyard as some people were buying the new electric ice boxes and turning in their old ice boxes. It was just like new and would hold 25 lbs of ice.

The frame had a dirty water tank. It was once hooked up to a toilet and sink in the old Blue Moon. Lyle was trying to figure a way to use it instead of a thunder mug. He would go to the place where he bought the frame and see how it worked.

Lyle stood back and looked at the almost finished trailer. For once in his life, he had made up his mind to completely finish an entire job.

He painted the outside two tone. It was black on the bottom about half way up and the roof and top side were silver. The roof was made of marine plywood covered with heavy canvas and painted with 4 coats of waterproof silver paint.

"This one won't run silver when it rains! I won't have to listen to Marie about everything turning silver after a rain," said Lyle out loud.

He walked toward the house to get a cup of coffee and rest. He looked back at the trailer and was very proud of himself. Lyle was an artisan but didn't like to finish anything he started. This was an exception. It would be completed in a couple of weeks and they could be on the road again, if he could convince Marie, it was the right thing to do.

"She has that cat and pays more attention to Leone and the cat than she does to me. One thing is for sure, that cat stays here if we travel. I'm not going to haul a cat in a trailer and that is my ruling," thought Lyle.

He still had to put on the 2nd coat of varnish on the inside and finish the storage cabinets. He wanted to get some of the sink topping to put on the dinette. Everything was coming together with the help of the new scam. It brought in good money and he didn't have to work a lot, but it put him behind schedule. Right now he wanted to go inside, have some coffee and rest a bit.

Early the next morning, Jerry and Robert loaded up the old Dodge and headed for Moultrie. It was about an hours drive to the farm country north of the town. They stopped in Sigsbee and went into a small country store. It had a coffee pot and biscuits for the locals to eat and drink while they talked over the world situation. They both got a cup of coffee and a biscuit, sat down and joined in the conversation.

Robert, being from Georgia, asked the proprietor if he knew of anyone who needed some linoleum put in his or her house. He had a sample book and showed them to the men around the old stove. The stove wasn't lit but it was where they always sat.

The proprietor was scratching his head while he looked at the sample book.

"In a show of honesty and good faith, we'll black your stove free of charge if you can give us the names of anyone who would be interested in a new floor," said Robert.

"Let me think now," said the proprietor, as he scratched his hairy chin.

Jerry went out to the car and brought back the stuff to clean and black the stove. He and Robert started cleaning and within an hour, they had the old stove looking like new.

"Say mister, I need some flooring in my old house. If I get some, will you black my stove for a good price?" asked an old man sitting around the stove.

"I'll do better than that; I'll black your stove free of charge if you take our deluxe installation," said Jerry.

"What is a deluxe installation mean?" asked an old coffee drinker.

"It means we include your bathroom for the price of the kitchen. And for everyone in this room, I'll throw in a stove blacking free of charge," said Jerry.

Three of the old farmers raised their hands. Jerry and Robert got their address information and made an appointment to install the flooring.

All of the installations and stove blacking went well until they got to the last farmer. He wanted his kitchen, living room and bathroom done and both stoves blacked.

"It'll cost you a little more but we'll black both stoves for nothing," said Jerry.

They completed the job before sunset and were loading up the car. They were out of material and the stove black container was empty.

Just as they were getting in the car, they heard a loud explosion in the back of the house. They ran around the house and saw the entire back wall blown out. The old farmer was trying to help his wife up when Jerry rounded the corner.

"That stove you blacked just blew up and hurt my wife and 2 children!" said the farmer.

"Jerry, I told you not to put so much blacking on the stove!" said Robert.

"I didn't, but I poured what was left in the stove. I didn't know the old farmer was going to light it!" said Jerry.

"I'm a going to git my shotgun!" said the farmer as he ran back in the house.

"We'd better git before the farmer gits here!" they both said at once.

The car was just moving when the farmer cut loose with both barrels of an old 12 gauge. The 00 pellets hit the back of the car, shattering the window and blowing out the spare tire. Jerry gave it all he could as the farmer cut across the road and let go another blast. This one hit the right rear door and glass, blowing it all over Robert and Jerry and cutting there neck and face with glass bits. They could see the farmer loading again but they were out of range.

Neither Jerry nor Robert said any thing as they drove out of the farmer's road and turned toward Albany.

"That was a close one!" said Jerry.

"I know that old farmer by reputation and he'll come looking for us tomorrow with the sheriff," said Robert, looking over his shoulder. "Let's get home as quick as this old car can take us."

"I'm so scared I can hardly move enough to drive. I've been shot at before, but not by a shotgun. I'm bleeding down the back of my neck. It's either a shotgun pellet or a piece of glass. I'll get Ruth to look at it," said Jerry.

"Drop me off by my car. I'm going to take a few days off. I think I'll go visit my cousin in Atlanta until this thing cools off," said Robert.

Jerry's mind was racing about what to do. Marie was about well and Ruth wasn't needed any more. He had a few dollars in his pocket. He was confused but he would talk to Lyle and see the best way to go.

Jerry slid the car around the driveway. He finally stopped the old

Dodge and hurried in the house. Lyle was asleep in the old trailer but Ruth and Marie were up playing cards in the kitchen.

Ruth looked up and saw blood on Jerry and hurried to help him. She and Marie cleaned the small cuts on his back and neck. The glass cuts looked worse than they were. They cleaned up with no trouble and the bleeding quickly stopped, but Jerry was still very scared. He kept looking out the window to see if anyone had followed him.

"That was a close one. I don't ever want to do anything like that again. That stove blacking that Lyle gave us almost got us killed!"

Jerry explained what had happened. It was too dark to see the car but they would see it tomorrow. They all agreed it was a close call and they should leave as soon as he got the windows fixed.

"I think it would be better to leave and get the windows fixed up the road. I don't want to be around here when the sheriff comes looking for an old Dodge with Michigan plates, especially when it has bullet holes in the back and side," said Jerry in a frightened voice.

"That's a good idea," said Ruth. "We'll pack up early in the morning and leave. I guess dad will have to sleep in the house when we do."

At daybreak the next morning, Ruth and Jerry were getting their stuff together to leave as Lyle walked in the kitchen.

"What in the world happened to your car Jerry? It looks like it's been through a war!"

Jerry carefully explained what happened and how he poured the left over blacking in the stove because there was only about a cupful left and how the farmer or his wife lit the stove.

They all talked about what had happened and decided it was best if Ruth and Jerry left as early as they could. Lyle didn't want to be caught up in all the problems it would bring.

Lyle took his radio and Marie got the rest of her things out of the old trailer. Jerry backed his car and they hooked it up, then Ruth got in the car and they left without saying a word.

Ruth waved as they turned on the road and headed toward the main highway. Both of them were frightened and wanted to get out of there as quick as they could.

Hillbilly watched in wonder at the people running back and forth and doing a lot of busy things. She had missed her early morning meal and rubbed against Marie's leg in hopes she would be fed, but no such luck.

"Lyle, do you see what your hair brained schemes almost did. Jerry could have been killed and how would that make you feel? This has to stop and right now! I won't stand for any more of your shenanigans! Do you know what I mean, Lyle? I want Leone to grow up with a father!"

"I know Marie, it's time we do things that are above board. I know we can find some things to do that are not so close to the law," said Lyle. "Ruth and Jerry left so quick that he forgot his $100 and the bill of sale for the trailer. Well, I guess it's more for us. I'm glad to see them go. It has been a long 4 months building the trailer and you getting well."

Marie had all of their things packed in the new trailer. Lyle had his radio secured to a special shelf he built. The ice box was full of groceries and food for Leone. The lights on the car worked with the lights on the new trailer. Upon Marie's insistence, Lyle wrote a note and left it on the door for the doctor.

They walked around their new rig and talked about how nice it was. About that time, Hillbilly came running up for a pet. Marie opened the trailer door and she hopped in and settled down on the table looking out of the window.

"Marie, I'll do the best I can to make a living for us and stay out of trouble."

"I hope you keep your word," said Marie as she got in the car.

Leone was on the back seat playing with some toys Marie had made out of old spools of thread. He was a happy boy and was saying things to himself.

"I guess I am a vagabond. I missed the open road and all the fun we had," thought Marie as she looked first at the house and her tomato plants and then to the bare spot where the old trailer stood.

"Lyle, it really was the last tear drop, wasn't it?"

"Yes Marie, I guess it was. It's the end of our old way of life."

A last teardrop flowed down her right cheek as they turned on the hard road headed to who knew where. She thought about the old tear drop trailer and the house she almost had. She was finally at ease with her chosen vagabond way of life. Leone was in the back of the car and Hillbilly was in the trailer. She hoped Lyle would do as he said because it would be a long journey if he didn't. Marie was finally happy and content.

"Marie, this is a new start for us and everything is going to be hunky-dory and above the law," said Lyle as he fingered some "doctored" silver dollars in his vest pocket he had found in The Last Tear Drop. They turned and headed toward the open road.

EPILOGUE

Southern United States

Early Twenty First Century

If you listen carefully, you can hear the old Tear Drop trailers pull into their camp spot for the night. The odor of food cooking over a campfire fills you nostrils. Small children run and play and a few dogs bark. In the faint distance, you can hear the jingle of keys in an old Hudson. The crackling sound of Amos and Andy on an old radio can be heard in the distance.

The memories of the Lyles and Maries of the old vagabond society still roam the mists and dusts of the back roads of America. Their contribution to our way of life is with out equal.

Of course, there wouldn't have been modern 5th wheel trailers and state of the art motor homes without their contribution. The true essence of the open road was brought to light by the vagabond travelers of that era.

Our system of state and national parks has been greatly improved by the traveling wisdom of the old, wonderful vagabond society. It is no small wonder that people enjoy the majestic nature of America by following in the trodden pathways of the Lyles and Maries of yesteryear.

Even in today's modern words of travelers, there are still a few of the old style vagabonds who travel the back roads in the old ways. They are trying to keep the memories alive. They are a dying breed, but their memories and exploits will live on.

Lyle Parmeter finally caught the "East Bound" in Orlando, Florida in 1968, at the age of 80, from the same old heart problem that plagued him in the past.

Maria Evdokimoav Parmeter quietly passed from this earth in 1983 at the age of 75. Smoking three packs of unfiltered cigarettes a day finally got the best of her.

Both were cremated and their ashes scattered in the St. Johns River, near the old bridge on 17 & 92 west of Sanford, Florida.

Marie's ashes were scattered on one side of the river. Lyle's ashes were scattered on the other side of the river. Both in life and death, Marie and Lyle were always a river apart.

In the early morning mists on Lake Monroe, you may catch a glimpse of them getting into the old Tear Drop as they still wander the back roads in search of a resting place.

Contact L. Lee Parmeter

losone@cableone.net

or order more copies of this book at

TATE PUBLISHING, LLC

127 East Trade Center Terrace
Mustang, Oklahoma 73064

(888) 361 - 9473

Tate Publishing, LLC

www.tatepublishing.com